Power Play

CHELSEA CURTO

Proofreading by April Editorial

Copy editing by Britt Tayler at Paperback Proofreader

Cover by Chloe Friedlein

For the ones who thought they wouldn't find love again.
I promise it's worth the wait.

(And for the readers who love to see the six-foot-three NHL goalie get on his knees and search for his lost wedding ring—Liam Sullivan is for you)

AUTHOR'S NOTE

Doris Burke, a veteran NBA announcer, became the first woman to serve as a television game analyst for a championship final in one of the four major professional U.S. sports leagues.

In 2024.

She's been a broadcaster with ESPN since 1991, and in 2017, she became the first woman assigned to a regular-season role covering NBA basketball as a game analyst.

Do we see a trend here?

Power Play is about hockey, not basketball, but at its core, it's about women in sports and how much harder they have to work to reach the milestones men somehow accomplish at a much quicker rate.

When I started thinking about this story, I knew I wanted Piper's journey in broadcasting to show her commitment to hockey while also highlighting the very real, very degrading conversations men have about women who occupy spaces like professional sports.

If you pull up any post on ESPN about the WNBA, about the Kraken hiring Jessica Campbell, about *anything related to women in the sports world*, you'll find hundreds of derogatory comments. You'll see words like *not qualified.* You'll read sentences like *get back to the kitchen* and *no one cares.*

I've been a sports fan for years. I went to my first NBA game when I was four or five, and I haven't stopped going to games. It's disheartening to see the disdain some men have for our love of sports.

I know you're about to dive into a fictional world, but I can't write about women in sports without adding disappointing touches of reality to these pages.

That being said, some elements of the game of hockey have been altered to fit in a make believe world and be enjoyable for readers. Is the goalie really going to set the league record for most saves in a game? No. But in this book he is. Do athletes get drunk and married in Vegas after a win? No. But in this book they do.

A hockey season lasts eighty-two games, and in Power Play, the book takes place over the entire season. I can't include every game or every day because it would be TOO long, so you'll notice some slight time jumps from month to month to keep the story moving along! You'll also see some team names that resemble NHL teams. Because I don't want to get in trouble with anyone, I've switched locations around. I know the Lightning don't play in Vegas, but I don't want to get in trouble with ~trademark~ stuff.

Additionally, one of the main components of this book is Piper's sexual journey. It might seem silly that she was married for so many years and doesn't know how to give a blow job, but it happens. She's inexperienced, and while this book might contain the highest number of spicy scenes I've written, I hope I've laced them with emotion and feeling so you can see the growth and development of the two characters.

My DMs on Instagram are always open if you want to chat more, and I love hearing all of your unhinged thoughts as you read!

Enjoy!

Xoxo,
Chelsea

CONTENT WARNINGS

Power Play is a romantic comedy full of laughs, spice, and swoon, but I want to share a few content warnings that some readers might want to be aware of.

-explicit language
-multiple explicit sex scenes
-on page alcohol consumption
-on page physical violence (brief and not between the two main characters)
-sexist comments made by a side character (including a comment about non-consensual behavior)
-mention of infidelity
-mention of divorce
-mention of cancer (brief)
-mention of pregnancy (not the FMC)

As always, take care of yourselves and protect your heart. If you have any questions about any of the things listed below, please know my DMs are always open (@authorchelseacurto on IG).

DC Stars Roster

Maverick Miller - right winger
Finn Adams - left winger
Liam Sullivan - goalie
Hudson Hayes - defenseman
Riley Mitchell - defenseman
Ethan Richardson - center
Grant Everett - right winger
Connor McKenzie - center
Ryan Seymour - defenseman

Brody Saunders - head coach

CHARACTER CATCH UP

I write my books as standalone stories, but the characters from other books do overlap!

If this is your first book of mine, WELCOME! I'm so glad you're here.

Maverick Miller and **Emmy Hartwell** have their own book, **Face Off,** which is book one in the DC Stars series. It's a dislike to lovers, rivals with benefits, black cat x golden retriever story full of banter and spice. Maverick and Emmy might be my favorite couple ever, and they're in Power Play a bunch of times (spoiler alert: they're still happy!). Power Play takes place *after* the Face Off epilogue!

Maven Lansfield, one of Piper's friends, is also referenced throughout the book. She has her own story too. **Behind the Camera** is a single dad x nanny, roommates, NFL story. I love these two as well!

I'm not going to say anything else about characters and who they might end up with (there's a Coming Soon section that lists the other boys who are getting a book!), but I'm going to say this: I've left *lots* of bread crumbs for upcoming projects in these pages.

The DC Stars series is the first series I've written that was planned as a series, and I can't *not* leave Easter eggs throughout the book.

Want a hint? Not all the crumbs I left are for sports romance books. Some are, but some are very different genres.

Happy hunting!

ONE
PIPER

IF ONE MORE MAN TELLS ME I need to smile, I'm going to deck him square in the jaw and not give a damn about the repercussions.

I grumble about the audacity of the male species as I walk down the hallway of United Airlines Arena, home of the DC Stars hockey team, with a stride as determined as my five-foot-two frame can muster.

The team is deservedly off after a hard practice yesterday afternoon, and the building is quiet without their yelling and joking around. I savor the rare silence, knowing in thirty hours when we play against one of our biggest rivals, this place is going to be a madhouse.

The tension I've been holding onto all morning melts away when I push open the door to the athletic trainers' area and collapse in a chair.

"I hate men," I call out to Lexi Armstrong, one of my best friends and the head Stars trainer. "Can we eliminate them from the face of the earth? I'm thinking an aggressive strain of the man flu. That would knock them all out, and life would be infinitely better."

"Well," a deep voice says, and I jump a foot in the air. "This is awkward."

I glance across the room. Liam Sullivan, our goalie, is lying shirtless on a medical table.

A towel is draped over his lower half. The white scrap of terrycloth looks indecently small on his six-foot-three body, and my eyes can't help but drift to the tattoos I had no clue he had.

There are a pair of sparrows and intricate flowers on his ribcage. Fern leaves on his forearms. Artwork that's so unexpected, so hot, it's almost pornographic.

I squeak when I realize I've been staring and cover my eyes.

"Oh, my god. Sorry. I didn't know you'd be here, let alone be here and *naked*," I say.

"Hello, Piper."

"Hi. Yeah. I'm going to go. You're… there. And I'm not supposed to be here when your dick is almost on display. Totally unprofessional."

"I have a towel."

"That thing is like a sock."

"I appreciate the flattery."

I peek between my fingers and find him smirking at me. I huff and lower my hands, staring over his shoulder and not at his body laid out like some Greek god in waiting.

"I was here to see Lexi, but clearly she's busy."

"Ice," he says, pointing to the door to his left.

"Did she say how long she'd be gone?"

"No."

"Are you hurt?"

"Hamstring."

"Why are you shirtless?"

"Because my whole body hurts and I'm trying to make it feel better."

"Did the hamstring injury happen in the game on Monday?"

"I love the Twenty Questions game." He throws an arm over his face, and I can tell he's exasperated with me. Then again, he's always exasperated with everyone. "It's been acting up for a week. Shitty way to start the season."

I hum in agreement, like I know what it's like to be a hockey player with sore muscles. He lifts his leg and grips the back of his thigh, grunting out a noise that sounds like a tractor starting.

I take his momentary distraction as a chance to study him.

His jawline could be cut from glass, and his dark hair is longer than it was at the end of last season. There's a faint scar above his eyebrow, a mark from the blade of a skate he took to the face when he was a kid.

I only know about the injury because of a trade-off we made at Media Day my first year with the team. He refused to speak with the media—a trait that's still going strong—and I needed someone to fill the time before our newest draft pick jumped on the mic and answered questions from reporters.

Liam and I reached a compromise: one piece of information about his life as a hockey player, and he wouldn't have to talk to anyone else for the first half of the season.

He went with a graphic story involving stitches, but it worked like a charm.

Being the alternate in-game rinkside reporter and media coordinator for the team is a dream. A career opportunity I've been chasing for years, from working in the athletic box office when I was a student at Syracuse, to majoring in broadcast journalism with a specialization in sports, and then continuing on as an intern with New York's ECHL team. After, I moved up to the AHL team in Philly for four years before landing in DC with the Stars.

The position requires adaptability, though. I need to be

quick to switch gears and change the wording of prepared questions if a player gets busy postgame or doesn't want to cooperate.

Liam Sullivan is the definition of uncooperative.

I've spent the majority of my tenure here chasing him down the hall. Tugging on his jersey. Begging and pleading for him to give the cameras eight seconds of his time.

It hasn't happened yet, and I'm starting to think he enjoys being fined by the NHL for refusing to do any press.

That, or he likes to annoy me.

"You're staring," he mumbles without opening his eyes.

"No, I'm not," I lie.

"Twenty thousand people stare at me every night, Piper. I know when I'm being watched."

"In a different line of work, that would be creepy as hell." I smooth my hands over my skirt and change the subject. "If anyone can get you in peak playing condition, it's Lexi. She's the best in the league. Have you seen the little trophy behind her desk in her office? It says *World's Best Trainer*."

"Wow. I didn't even have to pay you to say that." Lexi laughs and walks into the room with a bag of ice. "You're the best hype woman ever."

"That's what I'm here for." I move out of the way so I can give her space to do her job. "Sorry for stopping by unannounced. I figured since the team is off, you'd have time to grab lunch."

"Sullivan was a last-minute addition to my schedule." She taps his shoulder. "On your stomach, please."

"So you can torture me?" Liam keeps the towel over his lower half and flips positions with a handful of expletives. "Happy?"

"Isn't he the cheeriest?" Lexi sets the ice on his left hamstring and grins when he curses again. "An absolute delight."

"I'm only going to be here a minute. Five, tops," he says.

"Yeah, right you are." She props a pillow under his leg. "At least twenty, grumpy ass. And if you try to get off that table, I'll tie you down."

"Wow." I lift an eyebrow, impressed. "You run a tight ship around here, Lex."

"I have to. These guys want a shot at the Cup, and the only way to do that is if they're in the best shape of their lives. Hobbling around with a weak hamstring isn't going to help Goalie here with his save percentage."

"My save percentage is fucking great," Liam says. "Third in the league last season."

"But not first. Are you doing the exercises I gave you?"

"Morning and night."

There's a reason Liam is in the goal: he's dedicated to the point of obsession. He lives and breathes hockey, and if Lexi gave him training to do on the side, I'm confident he's doing it religiously.

"Good boy." She pats his head, and I hold back a laugh at the flash of annoyance in his eyes. "Do you mind if Piper and I talk, or would you prefer to lie here and stew with your thoughts?"

"Don't mind. Gives me something to focus on besides how fucking cold this shit is."

"Eloquent as always." Lexi plops down in the chair I vacated and taps the spot next to her. "Is everything okay?"

"It's silly to talk about this when you're in the middle of your workday." I sit with her and sigh. "There are more important things going on. Liam's leg is probably worth eight million dollars. Shouldn't you be focused on stretching him?"

"Do you do this a lot?" Liam interjects.

"Do what?" I ask.

"Pretend like your shit isn't as important as other people's shit."

I blink, not sure how to answer his question.

Yes? No? I guess I do.

I guess I put other people first, preferring to help them solve their problems instead of agonizing over my own. There's always someone out there who has it worse, who would be envious of what I'm going through, and it feels wrong to complain about my stagnant professional life and dumpster fire of a personal life when the man in front of me is dealing with an injury that could affect his playing career and livelihood.

"Sometimes," I settle on, glancing back at Lexi. "It's personal stuff."

"What did Steven do now?" Lexi asks, referencing my ex-husband. "I swear to god I'm going to cut off his balls and dangle them from a stoplight."

"That's my cue to leave. I draw the line at castration. Yes, I'll keep icing. No, I'm not sticking around," Liam adds, then swings his legs over the edge of the table. He holds the towel at his waist, but it does little to cover the deep cut abdominal muscles stretching down his torso. "Lexi. Pipsqueak. See you tomorrow."

He disappears through the door to the locker room, and Lexi looks at me.

"Pipsqueak? That's new."

"That's only the second time he's called me that. It's not, like, a thing," I say, blushing.

"I've never heard that man say anything borderline friendly before. And a *nickname*?"

"That's not true. He wished Hudson happy birthday last week, and he didn't even roll his eyes."

Lexi reaches for my hand. "Are you okay?"

That's another question I don't know how to answer.

There's air in my lungs. Money in my bank account. I know where my next meal is coming from, and I have a warm bed to crawl into every night.

In the grand scheme of things, I'm *fine*.

Good, even, comparatively.

But I'm also sad.

Stuck in a rut and unsure how to break out of it. Overwhelmed, despite a lackluster life. Tired, even when I'm getting enough sleep. Lost, and I haven't strayed off the path I've been following: thirty-two, divorced, and attempting to start over.

"Steven keeps trying to renegotiate the assets we split in the divorce. He's suddenly interested in taking things he didn't want when he was busy sleeping with his secretary. And, on top of that, my boss made a comment during our monthly one-on-one meeting that was so slimy, I'm considering turning in my two-week notice." I wince. "Shit. Sorry. That was a lot to unload on you."

"Let's start from the beginning. Have I mentioned lately how much I *hate* your ex?" she asks.

She has. In great detail, multiple times a day. I wouldn't be surprised if she had a dartboard with his face on it somewhere in her office down the hall.

"No," I say sarcastically. "Can you remind me?"

"The guy is a damn millionaire. What does he want from you that he can't buy himself?"

"My apartment, which I got *after* the divorce. I had to spend the first hour of my morning listening to his lawyer talk to my lawyer about how the natural light fosters creativity and —" Lexi throws up her middle fingers, and I laugh. "He's not going to win that battle."

"I'm still mad you didn't let us key his car, but I guess that's the downside of being mature, classy women."

"It would've been for nothing. The Cybertruck he drives is hideous enough without you risking a criminal mischief charge."

"Don't worry about Steven. He'll probably fuck off soon and go back to the hole where he climbed out of. And if he doesn't, let me know. I'd love to have some words with that asshole."

"Thanks, Lex."

"Now to the other asshole. What did Charlie say?"

She knows my boss is one of my least favorite people in the world. Storming into her office and complaining about him has turned into a weekly standing date with us. One where we—and my other best friends, Maven Lansfield and Emerson Hartwell—quietly lament over the joys of being women in a testosterone-filled industry.

"It was a comment about my shirt." I gesture to the top I put on this morning, back before the day turned to shit. "He told me it would do me some good to pop open the top button. And then he added in a parting zinger of telling me I needed to smile more."

Lexi gags. "You need to go to HR. I doubt you'd be the first one to lodge a complaint against the dickwad. Promise me you'll go in next week."

"I promise," I say.

"Good. Moving to the good news portion of our day. Are we having dinner with the girls on Friday? A late starting game on Saturday calls for a night of delicious food."

"Yeah." I smile. "I made reservations at the new Italian restaurant downtown. It'll be nice to take my mind off the last couple of days."

"I hope you know we're here for you, Piper. The past few years have been shitty, but I have this feeling something good is going to come your way soon."

"Okay, you oracle. If you're so all-knowing, can you tell it to hurry up? I'm getting impatient."

"Course I can. I'll make some calls."

"You're the best, Lex. You are free for lunch, right? You don't have any other players who need your attention?"

"I'm free as a bird." She grins and stands. "Maybe we can TP Charlie's office on the way out. Or! We can send him a glitter bomb that explodes in his squirrelly face and give that prick a piece of our minds."

"Wow. Your quest for a takedown involves glitter bombs?"

"Why not?"

I link my arm through hers, grateful to have such a fierce woman in my corner. "Fine. But only because he's a grade A prick, and I could use a little fun."

TWO
LIAM

"HOW EASY IS it to have someone fired?"

Maverick Miller, the best right wing the NHL has ever seen, looks up from lacing his skates. "Shit, Liam. You want me out as captain?"

"Believe it or not, I think you're the best captain this team has ever had."

He beams and runs a hand through his dark brown hair. "Aw, shucks, Goalie Daddy. You're going to make me blush."

"Fucking hate that nickname."

I've seen the TikToks. The boys get a kick out of sending me the video compilations people make, laughing over the tags like *#thirsttrap* and *#daddymaterial* in the captions.

Unfortunately for me, the name stuck.

"Stop doing things the internet thinks are hot, and I won't use it."

"Biting my jersey isn't hot," I say.

"I don't see the appeal, personally. I'm not into your broody, grumpy fucker aura whose pregame rituals involve eating your clothing, but some people are."

"I don't *eat* my clothes."

"Hey, whatever you want to call it. I'm just glad there's

someone out there for everyone. Justice for the shirt eaters!" he says, and I scowl. "Who do you want to get fired?"

"Someone who doesn't deserve to be in a position of power."

"Is this a revenge tour of yours?" Maverick's eyes widen. "Oh, shit. Wait a second. Is this about the food and beverage people getting rid of the hot dog stand on the concourse? Because I'm pissed about it too."

"No, it's not, but we need to come back to that. Who gets rid of a hot dog stand?"

"Heathens," Grant Everett, Maverick's backup, yells. "Fucking heathens, that's who."

"We're picketing tomorrow," Ethan Richardson, our center, calls out. "Bring back the glizzys!"

"Look what you did, Miller," I say. "You've got Ethan using hot dog slang like it's cool."

"You know I have a flair for dramatics." Maverick grins. "Please don't tell me you want to sack Coach Saunders. I know we lost in the finals last year, but I think we found our groove in the offseason. We've been unstoppable in our first few games."

"It's not Coach. It's not anyone on the team. It's someone in a different department."

Eavesdropping on Piper and Lexi's conversation yesterday was accidental. I didn't mean to listen to them from the locker room while I was butt naked. I didn't mean to press my ear against the wall so I could hear better, but once I started, I couldn't stop.

When Piper mentioned the asshole things her boss said, I almost marched up to the broadcasting offices to give that douchebag a piece of my mind.

I'm already paying enough fines at the start of the season for refusing to talk to the media, though. Physically assaulting a guy who thinks he's important because he dictates who gets to hold a microphone at hockey games seemed like an easy way to land my ass on the bench.

I have to resort to other measures, and enlisting the help of Maverick Miller is the way to do it.

If he asks for something, it's generally taken care of in the snap of his fingers.

Poor shower pressure in the locker room? Fixed the next morning.

Shitty postgame food options in the family and friends lounge? Catering put together a new menu for the next home game.

Spearheading a project to design a women's locker room so Emerson Hartwell—his fiancée, our former teammate before she got traded, and the first woman to play in the NHL—wouldn't have to change in a cleaning closet? The space is nicer than ours.

There's a reason he's the team's golden boy: he's got a big heart, and he's a good guy.

"When did everyone get so vague around here?" Maverick pulls on his jersey and fixes it over his pads. "I don't understand what you all are talking about half the time."

"Because it doesn't concern you," Hudson Hayes, our starting defenseman, says. "Learn to stay in your lane, Cap."

"Because you're old," Grant chimes in.

"Because you'd rather stay in with your girl than come out with us like the old days," Ethan adds. "You're not fun anymore."

"Bunch of assholes," Maverick grumbles. "Everything good, GK?"

Goal Keeper.

A better nickname than *Goalie Daddy*.

"What would you do if you heard someone make an inappropriate comment to Emmy?" I ask, even though I already know the answer.

Maverick would burn their house down and ask questions later.

When we played against her ex, Maverick beat him to a pulp. Grinned when he was escorted off the ice after being ejected and tagged the fucker on Instagram with a picture of his bloody face and a middle finger, writing *fuck around and find out* under the photo.

Nothing he does is subtle.

"Who said something to her?" He stands and grabs his stick. "It was that new assistant coach of hers, wasn't it? I knew the guy was a dick when he—"

"Whipped," Riley Mitchell, the other defenseman, hollers, interrupting him.

"I am whipped, fuck you very much," Maverick says. "If you fuck with my girl, you fuck with me. Now shut up before I make you all skate laps." That quiets everyone down, and he turns his attention back to me. "Who said something about her?"

"No one said anything about Emmy, and thanks for the reminder to never piss you off. It's about someone else."

"Oh." He relaxes and grins. "Totally different story. I'd go to the source and confront them. Typically works best."

I yank my jersey off its hanger and tug it over my head. "Thanks for the advice."

Coach Saunders steps into the locker room. "Ten minutes," he yells, and everyone starts to grab their gear.

I stand, wanting to stretch and get loose before we take the ice. Halfway through my hip rotations, my phone buzzes in my locker. I pick it up and see my sister's name flashing across the screen.

If I don't answer, she'll keep calling back until I do.

Fuck if I have a game or not.

I prop the phone against my duffle bag, and the FaceTime call connects.

"I have forty seconds," I tell her.

"Are you in the locker room? Turn the camera around so I can see the cute hockey boys," Alana says.

"You're getting married in four months."

"It's window shopping. I'm not touching. Only looking."

"Disgusting. Half of them are fuckboys. The other half are in committed relationships—like *you*, last I checked. And none of them are good enough for my baby sister."

"Aw." She grins and puts her chin in her hand. "There's my favorite brother."

"I'm your only brother."

"I still love you the most, which is why I'm calling. RSVPs were due last week, and I didn't get yours in the mail." Alana levels me with a look. "What's the deal, Li? You don't want to spend four days in a luxurious hotel in Spain? I know you can afford it, you rich asshole."

"Says the woman who created a dating app worth so much money, your great-great-great-grandchildren are going to live comfortably."

"Don't try to compare our net worths. The contract you signed over the summer is obscene."

It is obscene.

Eight years, eighty-four million dollars. The highest for a goalie in NHL history, and I'm determined to prove I'm worth the investment after a shitty ending to the Stanley Cup finals a few months ago.

"I was waiting to see our practice schedule," I lie, biting down on the collar of my jersey.

Shit.

Maybe Miller is right.

"Bullshit," she says. "I talked to Coach Saunders, and that's when the 4 Nations Face-Off Tournament is happening. You're free those two weeks in February, which lines up perfectly with my nuptials."

"You talked to Coach Saunders?"

"We exchanged a couple emails. What's his deal? He's cute as hell."

"Single dad who might as well be a monk. Haven't seen him with a woman in years. Ever, I don't think."

"Maybe he's into men."

"Maybe." I sigh, irritated. "I was waiting to send my RSVP back."

"Waiting?" Alana repeats. "For, what? Pigs to fly?"

Everyone else on this planet might annoy the hell out of me, but I love my family.

My parents sacrificed years of time and energy when I was a kid learning to skate. Mom drove me to the rink six days a week. Dad never missed one of my games, even the ones on the road in Ottawa in the dead of winter.

The older I've gotten, the more there's been a different kind of pressure from them. The focus isn't on my athletic achievements. They don't care if I win the Stanley Cup or ride the bench for the rest of my career.

What's happening off the ice is more important to them: when I'm going to settle down. A wedding of my own. Retiring so I can have a family.

It's the subject of every get together. Christmas, birthdays. The one time I flew home for Mother's Day and got a two-hour earful about the lack of women in my life.

The only time I can block it all out is when I'm on the ice. When I'm in the goal and tracking the puck for sixty minutes a night. It's my safe space, but I also understand my job is always on the line.

One wrong move could cost me everything I've worked so hard for, so I don't let myself get distracted.

I hold myself to high standards during the season.

No sex.

No women.

One drink a week and in bed by ten o'clock.

I don't give a shit about the spotlight or attention or

partying at clubs. I like minding my business. Showing up to the arena, playing good hockey, then going home to my quiet apartment and my cat.

It's neurotic and obsessive. The guys call me boring. They tell me I'm missing out on things, but it works for me. My life is dedicated to the sport I've given so much of myself to, and it suits me just fine. So what if it hasn't included fucking around or meeting someone and falling in love?

I'm happy enough not to want to bother with all the extra stuff, but *fuck* if hearing another hundred questions about why I'm traveling alone isn't going to drive me insane.

"I'm coming," I say. "I wouldn't miss it."

"Are you bringing a plus-one?" she asks. "Perhaps some girl who wants a free trip with an athlete and has no clue your middle name is Fredrick? I need exact numbers for food."

Maybe I'm sick of the pity party people give me when they find out I'm single.

Maybe I'm so goddamn tired of answering the same question every day.

Maybe, subconsciously, I'm really fucking lonely. Terrified no one will ever love me because I'm too closed off. Too harsh. Too committed to my job. And I know dancing around that conversation is easier than giving it a name.

Whatever it is, it makes me blurt out a word I wish I could take back the second I say it.

"Yes."

"*Really*? I didn't know you were seeing anyone." Alana lights up. "Are you going to tell me about her? A name? An astrological sign so I can see if you're compatible?"

I shrug. "It's new."

"What the hell, Liam? How can I stalk her on the internet if you don't give me a name?"

"It's a woman." Being vague is good. Being vague gives me time to figure this shit out. To pretend I never said anything. "A nice woman."

"They'd have to be a saint to put up with your ass."

"I need to go. It's time to warm up."

"You better buy me a nice present!" Alana adds, and I hang up before she can say anything else.

I toss my phone under a spare jersey and grab my helmet.

Lying about a date was beyond stupid, but that's a problem for later. I have more important things to worry about than who I may or may not be dating, like winning this game.

Hockey is the priority.

It's always going to be the priority, and a girlfriend—real or imaginary—won't ever change that.

THREE
PIPER

"I HAVE something to tell you all," I say to my girlfriends once we settle into a booth at Mama Melrose's on Friday night. "And I could use some advice, because I'm woefully out of my comfort zone by admitting this."

"What is it?" Emerson—Emmy, as we all call her—rests her elbows on the table and stares at me with wide green eyes. It's the same look from when we met in high school, and even though we lost touch for a while after graduation, both busy with life and chasing our dreams, it's still wild to think about how long we've been friends. "Is it a sex thing? A fetish? I've seen some weird shit, Piper. Your secret is safe with us."

"No. *No*. It's tamer than that, and definitely more embarrassing." I pause, then let out a soft laugh. "But remind me to ask you about those stories after a few glasses of wine."

"Hey." Maven, the Stars' team photographer, nudges the bottle of Italian chardonnay we ordered out of the way. "You don't have to be embarrassed to tell us anything. This is a judgment-free zone."

"Remember when I was teaching Pilates and my pants split in two when I was demonstrating a pike on the

Reformer?" Lexi asks, and we all giggle. "Emmy brought me a new pair of leggings for my next class, and you two told me it was because I have an ass that won't quit."

"Still true," I say. "This is more personal, though."

"More personal than showing off my G-string to the shy single dad in the front row?" She sighs. "He never came back, which is such a bummer. He was cute."

"It's about my pathetic personal life. Everything seemed so scary after the divorce. Talking to men. Getting to know them. Putting myself out there and letting someone new see the parts of myself I'm still learning to love. So much of my adult life has been spent being part of a couple, and the idea of starting over again was nerve-racking." I drag a finger along the stem of my glass, building up my courage. "I took a step back to enjoy being single, to do the things I want to do when I want to do them, but lately I've been feeling lonely." I pause to take a sip of my wine. "Really lonely, if we're being honest. I see you all in love, and it makes me feel like I'm missing out on something important. Like I'm behind. I know I got my heart broken once, but I'd like to believe I can find love again."

"She's talking about you all being in love, ladies," Lexi tells Maven and Emmy. "Not my single ass."

I laugh and rub my arms, but I'm on edge.

I feel stripped bare telling the girls all of this. They'd never judge me; we've shared everything with each other over the course of our friendships, from horrible date stories to stuff we're dealing with at work, but there's something so raw, so *human* about sharing the things you're most afraid of. It's intimidating to put them out in the universe. To voice your fears and confront them head-on.

"It's normal to feel lonely," Maven says gently. "Society tells women we're supposed to hit these milestones by certain ages, or it's too late. Like, if we're not settled down by our twenties, we'll never find love or have time for children, and that's bullshit."

"I love when Mae's *fuck the patriarchy* side comes out." Emmy smiles. "For the record, it is bullshit. Look at me and Maverick. We're in our thirties. Sure, we're engaged, but we aren't married. If this were the 1940s, we'd be shunned."

"You're not behind, Piper. You're taking your time and waiting for the right guy to come along," Maven adds.

"How do I find the right guy when I can't even navigate this new world of modern love? Steven and I met my freshman year of college in the dining hall when phones weren't touchscreen." I stare at a photo of the Leaning Tower of Pisa hanging on the wall behind Maven's shoulder and tilt my head to the side. "I didn't have to go on any websites or list five places I want to travel to before I die in a dating app bio. He ran into me. I dropped my pancakes, and that was it. A love story that was wonderful until it wasn't, and now I have to learn how to start dating again. I spent five minutes on the apps last year and gave up."

"If you want to try them again, I'll vet the dudes to make sure they're worthy of your time. There will be *no* unsolicited dick pics," Lexi says.

"Thanks for fending off all the penises." I pat her thigh. "But what about sex? That's what I'm most worried about. Steven and I were barely intimate. The times we were, it wasn't very good. I mean, I'm assuming it was mediocre at best. I have nothing to base it off of, since he's the only guy I've been with. I didn't enjoy it very much though, and I don't think *I'm* very good. I can't launch myself back in the dating pool without knowing how to give a good blow job. How much tongue do I use? And what do I do with my hands?"

Our server picks that moment to appear. She sets the breadsticks on our table and looks at the four of us with a weak smile.

"Sorry to interrupt," she says. "Are you all ready to order?"

"Could you give us a few more minutes?" Maven flips over the menu. "I don't think we've decided."

"Sure." The server turns for the kitchen. Judging by her red cheeks, I'm afraid she's never coming back. "Take your time."

"Great." I groan. "I probably traumatized her. She didn't clock in thinking the people ordering thirty-dollar pasta dishes would be talking about blow jobs."

"Speaking of blow jobs: have you thought about a sex coach?" Lexi asks.

"What the *hell* is a sex coach?"

"Someone who helps you sort through hesitations you might have with intimacy or sexual-related things. My friend from college is a licensed one. She works with couples and individuals all the time."

"There's a job for that?" Emmy asks.

"There's a job for everything these days," Maven says.

"She comes up with a plan for you. Technique and home-work so you can practice," Lexi tells us.

"Homework?" I repeat. "I'm supposed to sleep with random men for, what? Science?"

"Isn't that what being single is about? Doing what you want with who you want?" Lexi tosses her dark brown hair over her shoulder and shrugs. "It's sexual freedom and exploration. Sounds fun to me."

"I appreciate the sex positivity and I'm glad there's someone out there who can help with that sort of thing, but it's way too intimidating to talk to a professional about my lack of experience. I don't know how I'm going to tell a man I'm seeing my ex-husband only made me orgasm five times throughout the course of our ten-plus year relationship. It would only prove how clueless I am in the bedroom, and who wants to sleep with someone who's clueless?"

"We're going to need some more alcohol." Lexi tops off my glass with fresh wine. "Taking some time to learn what you may or may not like in bed would be a good starting point. The internet can be helpful. There are articles out there so you don't have to talk to anyone if it makes you uncomfortable. And, if we're being honest, I've learned a lot about myself from romance books." She blushes at this, and I'm reminded how much I love my friends and their vulnerability. "I've realized I'm into things I thought I might not like by reading about them and learning through fictional characters. It sounds silly, but this is the happiest I've been sexually."

I laugh and take another sip of my drink. "I'm envious of your ability to go up to a man and get what you want. You walked up to that guy at the bar last weekend like it was nothing and ended up going home with him. I want to be able to do that."

Lexi's always been that way; confident in her sexuality. Able to voice what she wants and what she doesn't. She's slept with plenty of men, arguing that if they're allowed to go around and fuck anything that moves for their pleasure, she should be able to do the same.

"You have to work up to it, sweetie. You're not comfortable with it yet because you've never done it. It takes time and that's okay," she says.

"You can always ask us," Maven adds. "I'll tell you everything Dallas and I do in the bedroom so you can consider if you might like it too."

Dallas Lansfield is Maven's husband and the greatest kicker to ever play in the NFL.

They had a whirlwind romance and fell in love while she was a nanny for his—now their—daughter, June. It was impossible for them to stay away from each other, and they're still inseparable.

Sometimes when I watch the two of them together—and Maverick and Emmy—there's this aching sting of jealousy in my chest. Pressure behind my lungs, not because I'm attracted to their partners, but because my previous relationship never looked like theirs, even on our best days.

The further removed I get from my divorce, the more upset I am. I'm angry and resentful. For someone who's always been a lover, not a fighter, the person who gives third and fourth chances when she shouldn't have given a second, it's *exhausting* to despise someone like I despise Steven.

There's so much grief over wasted time. So much disappointment from years spent with a man who never looked at me the way my friends' partners look at them: like they hang the moon. Like they're grateful to even breathe the same air as them.

I wonder if I'm too late to ever have that again.

I wonder if there's still time for me to find my new happily ever after.

My entire previous relationship was spent being put in second place to his work. To his company and the investors who were helping him build a name for himself in a cutthroat tech industry. I was behind his money and his titles and his professional achievements.

And behind his twenty-three-year-old secretary, Julia, who he spent all his free time with and found far more interesting than me.

It must be nice to be someone's top priority. The object of all of their attention and everything they've ever dreamed about.

What would that be like?

"Sometimes I make Maverick fuck me while he wears my jersey so he knows who he belongs to," Emmy says, pulling me back to the present and shoving the past aside.

"As if the tattoo on his chest that says *Emmy's Pretty Boy* doesn't tell the whole world he's happily taken," Maven teases. "I've had to ask him to put his shirt on for official photos because he likes to walk around bare-chested and show it off."

Emmy sighs and twirls a strand of red hair around her finger. "I love that man."

"You all were friends with benefits first, right?" Lexi asks, and Emmy nods. "What if you tried something like that, Piper? A sexual relationship where you hook up and experiment with the same person."

"Where do I find him?" I ask. "Craigslist?"

"Only if you want to get murdered." She clicks her tongue and gives me a look like she's hoping I'm joking. "The dating apps are a great place to find a fuck buddy. If you put *not looking for anything serious* in your Tinder bio, men would flock to you."

"They would," Maven says. "And we can help make sure you get everything set up."

I smile and look around the table. My cheeks are warm. My heart is full, and, despite being single and going home to an empty apartment every night, I've never felt so loved.

"I appreciate all of you. You loved me when I didn't feel lovable. You showed me that the good kind of love—the kind that lifts you up and supports you when you're feeling low—is worth fighting for. Is worth waiting for, instead of settling for average." I wipe a tear away. "Sorry. I don't know why I'm crying. Just… thank you. Thank you for being here and believing in me when I didn't believe in myself."

"A toast." Maven lifts her glass, and we all follow suit. "To the women who get knocked down but come back stronger than before."

"To friendship that isn't competitive but collaborative." Emmy shows a rare display of emotion when she dips her chin and takes a deep breath. "Some people aren't lucky enough to have one friend like you girls in their lives, and I have three."

"You all said the mushy shit already, so I'm going with this: to better dicks going forward," Lexi jokes. "We're not settling for any man who only makes us come five times in ten years. We have new standards."

We cheers, and I laugh until my sides hurt. Until tears stream down my face not from sadness, but from joy. From being so damn happy. From feeling like I've finally found the path I want to walk down, and knowing I won't have to do it by myself.

FOUR
LIAM

PUCK KINGS

MAVERICK

The league really fucked us by making the majority of our games on Tuesday nights. Don't they know we have traditions?

HUDSON

It's almost like they don't care about your personal life.

MAVERICK

Last I checked, it wasn't just my personal life. Team dinner concerns all of you, and we're not stopping them this season. Not when our record has only improved since getting together once a week off the ice. Mondays will have to work.

RILEY

I hate Mondays.

MAVERICK

You won't hate them anymore because you get to spend them with me.

Aren't you lucky?

ME

Is there a way to permanently remove myself from a group chat?

EMMY

When you figure it out, let me know.

G-MONEY

Emmy is in here again? No shit!

Guess we need to change our name back to Professional Stick Handlers. That's inclusive, right?

EMMY

Don't change it because of me, Grant. I don't know why I keep getting added to these messages, and I'm going to leave. I hate it. I don't play with you all anymore. In fact, I'm the enemy now.

MAVERICK

Calm down there, Red. Your team has to win games before you can call yourself the enemy. How does your 1-6 start to the season feel?

EMMY

You're on the couch tonight.

G-MONEY

Oooh, Miller is in trouble.

RILEY

Get a room you two.

ME

For the love of god. Someone block me. Please.

EASY E

Wouldn't help, Goalie Daddy. We're always going to find you.

HUDSON

Do you talk to women that way, Ethan?

ME

No. He drools all over himself and uses his right hand.

G-MONEY

God damn. That's why you're never leaving the chat. Your one-liners are witty as shit.

MAVERICK

Don't be late tomorrow.

EASY E

I'm bringing hot dogs in memory of Dave's Dogs. RIP to a real one.

HUDSON

He didn't die.

EASY E

Might as well have. The hot dogs at the other places in the arena suck. Frank's Franks are fucking trash.

G-Money has changed the name of the chat to Professional Stick Handlers Because Puck Kings Isn't Inclusive RIP Dave's Dogs

G-MONEY

That's a mouthful, but we can make it work.

ME

I hate it here.

EMMY

Want to run away together, Liam?

ME

Yes

MAVERICK

You know what? I'm not even offended. I hope the two of you are very happy together. You have my blessing.

Emmy Hartwell has left the chat
You have left the chat

"I BROUGHT SALAD." I set the bowl on the island in Maverick and Emmy's penthouse apartment and lean against the counter. "And dressing."

Maverick beams and adjusts the buffet line to make space for the Caesar salad. "I'm glad you're here. What changed your mind?"

I shrug. "Don't know. Didn't feel like sitting at home, I guess."

"I knew you missed us when we weren't together." He pinches my cheek and I knock his hand away. "You doing okay? You looked stiff during morning skate."

"Hamstring. A lot on my mind. It's no big deal," I grumble, thinking about the call from my mom earlier this afternoon.

She chewed me out for not telling them about the date I'm bringing to Alana's wedding then grilled me for half an hour about a woman who doesn't exist. I've already started planning excuses for why I'm showing up alone. An expired passport seems like the most logical explanation, and I'm willing to pay someone to make me a fake document so I can cover my tracks.

"Shit. Your hamstring is still bothering you? I thought you were feeling better."

"I'm fine."

"Say it without grimacing."

"Fuck you."

"There he is." Maverick's grin is back as he opens the oven and pulls out a glass dish, setting it on the stove. "Glad you're not falling apart on me, Sullivan."

"Told you I'm fine." I grab a paper plate off the top of the stack and head for the lasagna Hudson's personal chef cooked. "Thanks for making me come tonight, by the way. I know I give you all shit, but if I'm forced to spend time with people, I'm glad it's you all."

"Wow." He wraps his arms around my waist and I roll my eyes. "*That* is the nicest thing you've ever said to me. You're on a roll lately, Goalie Daddy."

"Don't let it go to your inflated head." I pull out of his hold and move to the mashed potatoes Grant whipped up with his new mixer. He won't stop sending us photos of himself in an apron and chef's hat, and I'm going to be pissed if they taste like shit. "It's a one-time thing."

"A one-time thing I'm going to cherish forever. Dinner's ready," he yells, and there's a stampede of feet. "They aren't quiet, are they?"

"Nope." I add two pieces of grilled chicken and garlic bread to my plate then move it all to the side to make room for a slice of pizza. "Bunch of hooligans."

The noise in the kitchen amps up ten decibels as my teammates file in. Some of them brought their significant others. Some came solo. They're all here though, and it's pure fucking chaos.

There's pushing and shoving. A fork gets thrown and lands in the wall. Half a stack of napkins goes flying in the air. We got rid of real plates three years ago, shifting to paper products because shit always ends up broken when the Stars boys are around.

Especially when food is involved.

"Hi, Liam." I glance over my shoulder and find Piper smiling at me. Her grin is big and wide, and the blue sweater she's wearing brings out her eyes. "Glad to see you clothed and on two feet."

"Piper. Glad to see you not freaking out over my bare chest."

"You look better with clothes on."

"Figured as much. How did the castration go?"

"Whoa." Ethan looks between us. "Are you into castration, Little P?"

"No." She blushes and tucks a piece of blonde hair behind her ear. I feel like a jackass for making her uncomfortable. "It's a joke."

"Didn't know Goalie Daddy was capable of jokes, but I'm here for it." Ethan elbows my ribs. "Move over, you big lug. I want some marinara sauce and you're taking up too much space."

"Sorry," I grumble. "I'm out of here."

"Let me know how the chicken is," Piper says before I can make my way to the living room. She lifts her chin and offers me a shy smile. "It's my first time using the grill I've had for years, so it might not be edible."

I maneuver around the island and past my teammates. "If I get salmonella, I'll send you my hospital bill."

"I'm not sure I can afford it, to be honest. The best I can do is get you some water and saltines."

I rip off a piece of garlic bread with my teeth. "Fair trade."

"I'm sorry again for interrupting you and Lexi the other day. I hope you don't think I'm unprofessional."

"Pretty sure you're the most professional person in this room, Pipsqueak," I say at the same time Lexi drapes an arm over Piper's shoulder.

"So true," Lexi agrees, then glances at her friend. "Is that what you're wearing on your date later?"

"Yeah." Piper runs her hands over her jeans. A hint of cleavage appears when she moves up and fixes her necklace. It feels wrong to stare at her, so I glance away. "Do you think it's okay?"

"It's perfect," Lexi says, snapping her fingers. "Sullivan. You're a man."

"What gave it away?"

"First impressions of Piper's outfit?"

My fingers curl around the edge of my plate as I look her up and down.

Her blonde hair is long, slightly messy, and I wonder if she ran her fingers through it before she walked into the kitchen. There's a small smile on her mouth, like she has a secret she's keeping to herself. I move to the sweater that shows off the curve of her tits. Her jeans make her legs look long, and I find myself staring at the sliver of skin between her top and the denim for longer than I should.

Piper Mitchell is sunshine incarnate, and it must be fucking *exhausting* to always be so happy.

There's this presence about her that makes me think she's going to save the world or die trying. I've had a small, *stupid* crush on her since she introduced herself to me with that peppy attitude of hers, but I've always kept my distance.

She had a shiny ring on her finger.

I wasn't looking for a distraction.

There might not be a diamond on her hand anymore, but I'm still not looking for someone to take up my time.

I can't deny she's fucking gorgeous, though.

And I know I'm not the only one who thinks that way.

I've seen how my teammates stare at her when she's at practice or behind the glass at games. I know how they flirt with her and try to get her attention.

They'd never do anything to cross the line, but that doesn't mean they don't look.

"It's nice," I grit out. "Fine."

Lexi frowns. "*Fine*? We don't want her to look *nice*. We want her to look like a knockout."

"Don't listen to grumpy gills here," Ethan says. "You look hot as hell, Little P. If you feel like ditching whoever you're meeting later for some real fun, you have my number."

"Thanks, Ethan. Hockey guys aren't really my type, but I appreciate the offer," Piper laughs. "And thank you, Liam. Nice is still a compliment, and I love compliments."

"No problem," I say, turning a corner out of the kitchen and nearly running into Emmy.

"Whoa." She puts a hand on the center of my chest. "Easy there, Sullivan."

"Sorry. Distracted."

"By?"

I shrug. "Nothing."

She peeks around the corner to the conversation I left and hums. "Don't drop your food on my new rug."

"Wouldn't dare."

"But you can drop it on Maverick's new suit if you're feeling wild. It's hanging in the bedroom. He won't shut up about it, and if I have to hear another word about its *velvet interior*, I'm going to scream."

A laugh falls out of me. "It sucks not having you around anymore, Hartwell. I'd take you over your other half any day."

Emmy's laugh matches mine. She squeezes my arm, and I can't help but smile.

We got close when she was on the team, spending almost

an entire season together before an end-of-the-year trade sent her to Toronto. Not long after, the Baltimore Sea Crabs, our division rival, snatched her up with a lucrative contract.

I still see her plenty, but it's special when you get to play with someone you like. Someone who is like a part of your family. I'd run into a fire for Emerson Hartwell—all of the boys would—and I know she'd do the same for us.

"Insufferable, isn't he? But you can't help but love him."

"It's unfortunate for all of us." I ruffle her hair, and she gives my stomach a light punch. "Go get food."

She brushes past me. "I'm glad you're here, Liam."

I huff out a breath. "Me too, Red."

IT'S LESS chaotic out on the balcony than it is inside.

Thank fuck.

I need a break. A second to relax. A minute without the video games and yelling and my teammates annoying the shit out of one another.

I take a deep breath and savor the silence, the quiet lasting only a handful of seconds before the balcony door slides open behind me. I turn and see Piper standing in front of the large glass windows, her arms wrapped around herself. I frown at the sight of her.

"Oh." Her eyes meet mine and she blinks. "Sorry. I didn't think anyone was out here."

"You okay?"

"I didn't eat or drink enough today, and that usually triggers a migraine. I feel the makings of one starting, and I thought some fresh air might help. Gosh, it feels nice. It's too warm inside, and I love fall in the city."

I point at the lounge chair by the wall. "Sit."

Piper shuffles over to the chair and plops down. I sit next to her because it feels weird to be a mile apart. There's a long stretch of silence then she huffs out a soft laugh, the first to make conversation.

"The chicken was shit, wasn't it?" she asks.

I don't have the heart to tell her it was terrible. Undercooked and not edible. It's obvious she's never operated a grill, but I shrug instead and say, "I've had worse."

"You're being nice."

"Fine. It was shit, but I have also had worse."

"That helps." She closes her eyes, and a sigh escapes her. "What are you doing out here?"

"I got a phone call I've been dreading this afternoon, and I need to figure some things out," I say, and I have no idea why I'm telling her all of this. There's no way she cares, and it's not like she'll have a solution. "Can't think in there."

Piper's eyes fly open, and she stares at me. "Are you dying? Is your hamstring worse than you've been letting on? Is there such a thing as hamstring cancer?"

"Why the hell would you ask if I'm dying?"

"I don't know." She gestures up and down in my direction. "You're acting broodier than you normally do."

"I'm broody?"

"Figured it was a life-or-death situation on our hands. Why else would you be stomping around and sulking by yourself?"

"I'm not—I don't *stomp*."

"You don't move quietly."

"Is stomping the antonym for quietly?"

"I don't know. Should I get a thesaurus?"

My lips twitch up in a small smile. "It was my mom who called."

"Is *she* dying?"

"No."

"Is anyone dying?"

"Aren't we all dying?"

"Very existential of you, and a little deep for a conversation on a balcony, if you ask me. If no one is dying, why do you look like someone pissed in your Cheerios?"

"I thought I was broody. Isn't that reason enough?"

Piper laughs, and it's a light little sound. Something that sounds like the last days of summer and staying in bed. It's nice. Soothing. A noise I'd like to hear again.

"You look even broodier than normal," she adds.

"I told my mom I was bringing a date to my sister's wedding in February."

"That's not *that* terrible. Far easier to work with than dying. Why did you tell her you have a date?"

"Because I didn't feel like explaining why I'm traveling to Spain all by myself. I like to be alone. I prefer it, actually. But if one more person asks me when *I'm* going to get married, I might scream."

"Why don't you find someone to take with you?" Piper suggests.

"Everyone annoys me."

"Of course they do. Do you have any female friends? Someone who wouldn't mind playing the part for a few days?"

"Playing the part?" I frown again, not understanding. "Like an actor?"

"You should really join the romance book club with the other guys. It's called fake dating. You have someone pose as your girlfriend for the wedding, and when you get home, you stop pretending."

"You're telling me people go around asking other people to be their girlfriend to events? There's no way that happens in real life."

"*Fake* girlfriend. I've never done it, but I hear it happens."

"I'm not going to pretend to date someone. I'm going to be a shitty person and lie instead," I say.

"What lie are you going to use? It better be a good one."

"An expired passport. You can't argue with Border Patrol."

"Not bad, Sullivan. Probably better than the *Weekend at Bernie's* stint some of your teammates would try."

"That seems like too much work."

"So your sister's wedding, huh? I didn't know you had any siblings, and it's my job to know everything about you all. Is she older or younger?"

"Younger by four years. She was an absolute pain in my ass when we were growing up, but I love her. She met her fiancé when she moved to California to start a dating app, fell in love, proposed to *him*, then planned a wedding."

"You sound like total opposites."

"Completely different people. I'm sure this wedding is going to be over the top extravagant. She's always been outgoing and loves being the center of attention. Me? Not so much."

"Your job as one of the best goalies in the NHL makes perfect sense. You never have *any* attention on you."

"Shut up, Pipsqueak," I say without any bite behind it, and she laughs again. "When's your date?"

"Soon. I should probably get going." She swings her legs to the edge of the chair. Her thigh presses against mine as she stands. "Are you going to stay out here much longer with your broody thoughts?"

"Nah. I'm going to head home. I've seen the guys play enough *Grand Theft Auto* to last a lifetime, and I'm tired. How's your head?"

"Better. Amazing what some fresh air can do."

My gaze drags down to her jeans when she turns for the door. "Your outfit isn't fine, by the way. It's..." I trail off, hesitating. I try to find the word that would fit without sounding like a fucking creep. "Pretty. Really pretty."

"You think so?"

"Yeah."

"Thank you." Piper smiles at me, and it's the kind of grin that reaches every corner of her facc. Her nose wrinkles.

There are crinkles around her eyes and a half dimple on her cheek. I had no clue a compliment could make someone so happy, and I have a feeling she doesn't hear enough of them in her life. "Have a good night, Liam. I'll see you on the plane to Texas in a few days."

The balcony door clicks shut. I focus on the White House and Capitol Building in the distance instead of focusing on how for once, I really fucking hate being alone.

FIVE
PIPER

"OFF TO TEXAS." Lexi lifts her bag onto the charter plane and turns down the aisle. "Where everything is bigger."

"Why do I feel like a man came up with that slogan?" I toss my black leather backpack on an empty seat and stand on my toes, shoving my suitcase in an overhead bin. "It's probably compensation for what they lack in other departments."

"Without a doubt." She sits in the row across from me at the front of the plane. "I was thinking barbecue for dinner tonight. Want to join?"

"Maybe. Depends on how much work I can get done on this flight. I have the players' stats ready to go for tomorrow, but I'm behind on our next two games."

"Why doesn't anyone else in the broadcasting department help you? You're not the only reporter, and you're doing all this research for them."

"I don't mind it." I pull out my notebook from my bag and set it on my jeans, tapping the spiraled spine. "They're not thorough, and since I'm not permanently in front of the camera, it gives me something to do to stay busy."

"Not permanently in front of the camera *yet*," she emphasizes, and I smile at her optimism. "They could at least lift a finger every now and then. Did you go to HR about Small Dick Charlie?"

"Your nicknames kill me." I shake my head, grinning. "And, yeah. I did. They told me they're looking into it, and if anything else comes up to let them know."

"Good." Lexi sits up as the team starts to make their way onboard in their suits and ties. Coach requires business casual whenever they're in front of the media, but the second they get on the plane, their clothes start to come off. "Morning, boys. You all clean up well."

"Morning, ladies." Connor McKenzie, our backup center, tips his chin our direction. "Don't look at the shiner on my face. My eye is still purple from Monday's game."

"You probably deserved it," she says, and he flips her off. "Hey, Riley."

Riley looks up from his phone. His cheeks turn crimson and he waves, giving her a smile before nearly tripping over his bag. "Shit. Uh. Hey, Lexi. Piper."

"Morning, Riley," I say, chuckling as he walks away. "I swear every guy on this team is in love with you."

"I hope not. I think of them like my brothers."

"Please tell me you at least realize Riley has a crush on you."

"Riley? He's cute. A little young for me, but cute."

"Who's cute?" Maven plops in the seats in front of us, out of breath.

"Riley," I say. "Poor guy almost tore his Achilles tripping over his bag when Lexi said hi to him."

"*Stop*," Lexi groans. "We should be focusing on Piper and her attempt to get back in the dating game."

"No dating," I say, correcting her. "Sex. Casual. Fun. Big difference."

"Whoa. Who's having sex?" Maverick slides his sunglasses up into his hair and stops to look at the three of us. "Did one of the rookies do something stupid and get himself in trouble? Kids these fucking days. I never acted like that."

"Don't even try to lie to us, Miller. We know what you were like before Emmy came around." Maven sticks out her tongue. "You hit on *me*."

"I did not hit on you. I was testing your allegiance to my best friend." He smirks. "I saw the way you checked me out the first time you met me, though."

"Delusional." Maven sighs and plays with her wedding ring. "Your ego is definitely making up for something else."

"Hey, we can stand here and talk about my di—"

"Will you move?" The deep voice comes out of nowhere. I peer around Maverick's shoulder and find Liam taking up too much space in the aisle with his broad shoulders and thick thighs. "Some of us want to get to our seats and go to sleep. Hearing about your dick at seven in the morning sounds like a nightmare."

I hide my laugh with a cough, and Liam's eyes snap over to me. I wave and he tilts his head to the side, more of a greeting than I usually get from him.

I didn't mean to stumble into a conversation with him on the balcony at team dinner, but I'm glad I did. It's hard to get him to open up, to give away any part of himself, and hearing about his sister's wedding and seeing the way he lit up when he talked about her was the highlight of my night.

"I forget how grumpy he is before he's had his coffee." Maverick rolls his eyes and steps into Maven's row. "Morning, big guy."

Liam's attention moves from me back to the captain. He scowls and yanks his suitcase past our rows. "Don't fuck with me, Miller."

"Yes sir." Maverick salutes him, and I don't bother to hide my laugh this time. "He's just telling me he loves me."

Lexi snorts. "Sounds like he was plotting your murder."

"That's how Liam shows affection." Maverick hikes his

bag up his shoulder and starts toward the part of the plane where the players sit. "You ladies behave. I'm going where the real fun is. Try to keep it down."

When he leaves us alone, Lexi turns to me. "How did your date go?"

"Oh." I laugh and shrug, trying to play off the discomfort from thinking about two nights ago. The way I sat at the bar for thirty minutes, then forty-five, checking the door every time it swung open and coming up empty-handed. The later the evening went on, the more my heart sunk in my chest, mortified and exhausted from believing I could actually have a successful interaction with a man. "He, um, stood me up."

"You're joking." Maven spins around and glares at me over the top of the seats. "He didn't show? The *balls* on him."

"No text or anything. When I went to send him a message and make sure he was, you know, *alive* and not dead in a ditch somewhere, I found out he blocked me."

"This is why dating sucks. Men think they can pull this kind of shit without any repercussions," Lexi tells us. "Are you okay?"

"I'm fine." I add in a laugh to really sell it, and for half a second, I believe myself. "It's no big deal. I'm not going to lose any sleep over him."

Except last night when I was in bed, negativity raced through my head. It was an endless spiral, self-deprecating thought after self-deprecating thought until the sun came up and I could focus on the day, not my shortcomings.

I'm not pretty enough.

I'm not successful enough.

I'm too much of an inconvenience.

There's someone better out there.

I never used to have such shitty self-confidence, but when someone you love repeatedly tells you you're *good* but not *great*, over and over again, it wears you down. It burrows into every corner of your soul until you're left with nothing but fractured pieces of yourself. Nothing but attempts of trying to move on and giving up instead.

"It's okay. Really." I smile at the last guys climbing onto the plane, bleary-eyed, yawning, and five minutes late. "He wasn't for me. The next one probably won't be either, but I figured I'd have to go through some trials and tribulations before I found someone to have fun with."

I pull a pen out from behind my ear and open my notebook, trying to distract myself from the plane rumbling down the runway.

I've always hated flying, and focusing on anything other than the physics behind lifting in the air and *staying* in the air is the only way to keep from panicking.

"We'll find you a nice Texas boy at dinner. A man who can wear the hell out of his Levi's." Lexi glances at me. "You doing okay?"

"Yeah. You know I hate take off and landing." I squeeze my eyes shut and grip the armrests, attempting to take a deep breath. "I'll be okay."

"Think of the hot cowboys with boots and hats we'll see at dinner. And, hey, if we die, at least you'll go out with a vision of a sex god on your mind."

"Small victories." I laugh nervously as the wheels come up and we lift off the ground. I crack an eye open and breathe a sigh of relief. "That's freaking terrifying. I don't know how people do this every day. Forty-one times a season is more than enough for me."

"Get to work, love bug." She pats my thigh. "So we can have a rootin' tootin' good time tonight."

HOURS LATER, I yawn and stretch my arms above my head. My back is sore from the flight to Austin, and I'm tired from a busy day that shows no signs of slowing down.

I've barely had any time to catch my breath. As soon as the plane touched down, we were on the bus to the arena where the guys went through their full practice routine. Now it's off to the hotel to meet with the broadcast team to go over tomorrow's agenda.

As a chronic ten-minutes-early type of woman, I'm ahead of schedule, so I take a grateful breather outside the conference room. Voices travel through the door that's been left slightly ajar, and I hear a deep laugh. I pause, wondering what's so funny, and stop to listen.

"I swear to god, if I have to hear her ask one more stupid question about how their early skating years shaped their career in the NHL, I'm going to lose it," someone says, and I recognize the voice as Charlie's, my boss. "I wouldn't be surprised if she's slept with half the team already. Their mouths hang open when she walks around. Bunch of fucking teenage boys."

My fingers curl around the door handle. I grip the metal so tightly, my knuckles turn white. I put my ear to the door and press my body against the barrier so I can hear without making my presence known.

There's no way in hell I'm walking in there right now. Not until I know who they're talking about so inappropriately.

"You don't think she's hot? I bet she'd look nice bent over your desk," Doug, his co-announcer, adds.

"She's not horrible to look at. We could tag-team her. It'd probably loosen her up a bit."

"It's cute she thinks she's going to have a permanent spot on the crew. I almost feel bad for her. She does all that work, and no one is ever going to see it. At least she wears tight skirts. Gives us something to look at."

"She's so goddamn sensitive though," Charlie says. "She couldn't get through that interview with Miller talking about his childhood last season without crying. It was embarrassing."

"I've always said women should stick to the boring work: HR. Accounting. Leave the sports to the men."

"They can't even do HR right. I've had complaints against me for years and I'm still here. Good fucking luck getting rid of me. Who would they replace me with? *Her*? She'd sink us. I have almost as much power in this organization as the fucking CEO, and I know I'm not going anywhere."

"Hey." A throat clears, and a third voice joins the conversation. "Feels like we should be focusing on the schedule for tomorrow's game, not talking about someone who isn't here to defend themselves."

My hands shake as I take a step away from the door. Then another and another until I can't hear them anymore. Until I can't hear their laughter or the vile comments they're making.

Understanding dawns.

They're talking about *me*.

I'm the lone woman on our small team, and Maverick's interview? It was only possible because he said he wanted *me* to tell his story, not anyone else.

The men I've worked with for goddamn *years* don't see me as anything more than a dumb piece of ass.

Bile rises in my throat.

I taste acid on my tongue and my hands curl into fists at my sides as I rest my back against the wall and slide to the floor.

The urge to cry, to scream, to rage against the world pounds in my blood. It's close to slipping out, to breaking free, but I close my eyes and take a breath instead. I cradle my head in my hands and try to recite every positive affirmation I've ever learned. I try to focus on all the *good* I can grab on to, yet I can only think about how everything I've worked so hard for means absolutely *nothing*.

I've heard about women in the broadcasting industry experiencing misogyny, but I never thought I'd be subjected to something so blatant. Something so volatile and intentional, as if I'm not a coworker but a nameless body they could use until they got their fill.

There's no respect—I doubt there ever was—and every day I show up to work going forward, I'm going to have to live with the notion there's no room for advancement. No room for a promotion, because the people who could offer me that opportunity would rather keel over than watch me succeed.

A tear runs down my cheek, and I realize the job I love is tainted now. Holding a microphone won't ever be the same, and as I wallow in the hallway of a hotel in the heart of Texas, I know that's the saddest thing of all.

SIX
PIPER

WE LOST in Austin by a goal, and, after hearing my colleagues talk about me so lewdly, I couldn't bring myself to care.

The game came down to the final seconds. Maverick had a chance to tie it up, but his shot ricocheted off the left side of our opponents' goal as time expired.

I didn't arrange for any interviews after the loss. The guys prefer to decompress in the locker room following a defeat, not in front of the cameras where they're forced to say things they don't mean like *we gave it our all* and *we'll do better next time* to appease the media.

They're pissed as hell.

The plane ride back to DC last night was quieter than the trip over. Maverick hung his head the entire flight. Liam refused to look at anyone, and Grant, who's never in a bad mood, sat in his seat with his arms crossed over his chest.

Not a single dick joke was made.

I even avoided gossiping with my friends, popping on my headphones and pretending to sleep so I wouldn't have to explain why I didn't acknowledge my bosses when they walked on the plane and tried to joke with me.

Biting my tongue instead of lashing out was a Herculean task, and I have no idea what I'm going to do going forward.

Quit?

Uproot my entire life and work for a different team far away from DC?

Suck it up and pretend like I didn't hear what they said about me?

I can't bring myself to turn the other way, though.

It's uncomfortable to face the problem head-on, a confrontation I don't want to tackle and breathe life into, but if it happened to me, it's going to happen to the next woman.

And the woman after that.

A cycle that'll continue until *someone* brings those assholes down, and I refuse to be complicit while they waltz around with a badge of honor when they're no better than the scum of the earth.

Fuck if I ruin my reputation because of it.

To top it all off, Helen, the head of HR, asked to see me at the end of the day, and my mind automatically went to worst-case scenarios.

I'm probably going to be reprimanded for no-showing at the pre-game meeting. Scolded for missing out on a work commitment, something I've never done in my career, but I draw the line of fake smiles at sexual harassment.

"Hey." Maven lowers her camera and glances at me as the team wraps up practice. "Are you okay?"

"I'm fine." I snap my notebook closed and shove it in my bag. "Only having a mild panic attack about why the woman in charge of firing people wants me to visit her office."

"There's no way you're in trouble."

She wouldn't be so confident if she'd overheard the conversation between Charlie and Doug, which is exactly why I didn't tell her—or anyone else for that matter.

Those two have power, and I know I'm a piece in their game. They don't care if they take me down along the way.

"Never say never. Maybe one of the players complained about me."

"Please. The guys adore you. You're the only one half of them talk to."

"Wish I could get them all to talk to me." I gesture to Liam in the goal. He takes off his helmet and shakes out his hair, scowling at Ethan who tries to knock his skate with his stick. "That one over there still won't come close to a microphone. I swear he's allergic."

"Don't let one sour grape ruin the whole bunch."

"It would be nice if he were a little less sour. Like, neutral is all I'm asking." I stand from the bench where we've been spectating and sling my bag over my shoulder. "Are you heading out?"

"I was planning on it, but I can wait for you."

"I'll be fine. Probably easier this way. If I have to turn in my credentials, you won't see me escorted out by security."

Maven rolls her eyes. "You are *not* turning in your credentials."

"We'll see."

With a wave and a few deep breaths, I make it to the hallway where the administrative offices are located. I wipe my sweaty palms on my shirt then knock on Helen's door, waiting for her to answer.

"Come in," she calls out, and I swallow down a final gulp of air.

"Hi." I shut the door behind me, locking myself in the room with the woman who controls my future. "You wanted to see me?"

She gestures to the empty chair in front of her desk. I move toward it and notice Bradley, our rinkside reporter, in the other one. "Take a seat."

"Thank you."

I sit on the edge of the leather and bounce my thigh up and down. Nerves rack my body. It's nearly suffocating in here, the air thick and the tension high. I brace myself for what's coming, knowing there's no way this conversation ends well for me.

"This morning, I was informed of comments that were made about you by your colleagues over the weekend. I'm appalled by what I heard," Helen starts.

Oh my god. I whip my head to the left, my chest tight as I stare at the man beside me.

Did *Bradley* turn them in?

Charlie and Doug wouldn't have turned on each other, and Bradley is the only other person on our team. A quiet guy, he tends to shy away from confrontation. He shows up, does his job, and goes on his way.

We're friendly, but we're not *friends.* Definitely not close enough for him to feel like he has to protect me from the men he reports to, and I'm shocked he might be the one who took this situation to the people who could fix it.

I slump in my chair and turn my attention back to Helen. "I-I wish I could say it's the first time this has happened, but it's not. I, um, met with someone in HR recently to discuss a comment Charlie made to me during our weekly meeting; however, I didn't report what I overheard in Austin. I was planning on doing it today, but it's been chaotic with preparing for tomorrow's game. I'm sorry for waiting so long to come forward," I say, hanging my head.

Helen puts up her hand, stopping me. "You're not going to apologize to me, Piper. I'm the one who is going to apologize to you." I suck in a breath, letting myself sit a little taller as she continues. "What was said is inexcusable and has no place in our organization. I'm embarrassed by their behavior, and I'm sick to my stomach knowing it's persisted for years. Charlie and Doug have been fired effective immediately. Additionally, a team-wide memo went out about sexual harassment in the workplace, along with mandatory e-learning modules."

I falter at that.

Beneath all the bullshit Charlie said, there was truth to his words.

He's been with the team for two decades. Considered a god in every arena we visit, he was recently inducted into the Sports Broadcasting Hall of Fame. I doubt anyone's given a shit about how thick his HR file might be.

Until now, I guess.

"What does that mean for the broadcasting team?" I ask.

With Charlie and Doug gone, we're operating with bare bones. Down two people with a game in twenty-four hours and no one to replace them.

"Bradley is being promoted to head play-by-play announcer. He told me he's willing to handle it solo," Helen says. "I have the co-announcer position posted on the league's internal hiring board, and with how well the team performed last season, I expect applications from several interested parties."

"I announced for my college team," Bradley explains. "I might be a little rusty, but I can handle it."

"Piper, you'll be our lead rinkside reporter for the rest of the season," Helen tells me. "I've seen the work you put in. The dedication and time you spend on being knowledgeable about the players' strengths and weaknesses. You know them like you know the back of your hand, and it should've been your role from the moment we hired you."

"What?" I whisper.

"If you want the position, it's yours. You'll start on camera next week."

Shock rolls through me. I don't know if I want to laugh or cry. If I want to pinch myself to make sure this isn't a dream but *real life*. The room might be spinning, but it doesn't matter.

Lead reporter.

The only job I've ever wanted since I landed in DC, bright-eyed and ambitious with big dreams.

I've put in years of work with unpaid gigs and small

paychecks. Road trips across the country with teams who had losing records and interviewing players who didn't know my name. Having sweaty jerseys thrown at me and telling people —repeatedly—I'm a reporter, not a fan, when I hang out in the tunnel during intermission.

Spots like this are coveted in the league. Positions people inherit and don't retire from until late into their career. Some of my role models have fifty years of experience in the industry. It's rare to get promoted out of the gate, but I know I can do it.

I know I'm good in front of the camera. I stay cool under pressure and pivot when a wrench gets thrown in my plans. I spend hours researching, wanting to make sure what I'm asking is unique. Inquisitive, but not prying. A conversation, not a lecture.

I know there are going to be people out there who think I'm underqualified, and I can't wait to prove them wrong.

"Thank you so much," I finally say, finding my words and suppressing my emotions—the things that make me *sensitive* and *weak*. "It's an honor to represent the Stars organization, and I promise I won't let you down."

"I know you won't. You'll have a formal offer letter in your inbox tomorrow morning. Home and away games are included in the contract, with an extension possible after the playoffs." Helen folds her hands across her desk and drums her fingers on the wood. "What questions do you have for me?"

"I'm still catching up." My laugh is disbelieving as I try to process the last five minutes. "I'm sure I'll think of something."

"You know where I'll be if that changes. My door is always open," Helen says, and I spring to my feet.

When I'm safely in the hallway, a squeal escapes me. Before I can sink into the celebration of my first win in what feels like *years*, a hand rests on my shoulder. The touch is hesitant. I glance behind me and see Bradley frowning.

"You knew what they said." His jaw tenses. He pulls back his palm and shuffles backward. "You weren't surprised when Helen mentioned it."

"No. I wasn't." I give him a sad smile. "I was outside the door, and, after overhearing Doug and Charlie, I couldn't bring myself to go in there and face them. Maybe it was cowardly to run from it, but I—"

"It wasn't cowardly," Bradley says sharply, malice dripping from his tone. "I'm the coward. I tried to get them to stop, but I wasn't firm enough for them to listen. He was right to tell me to go to HR, and I'm glad I did."

"What? Who told you to go to HR?"

"Doesn't matter. What matters is I owe you an apology too. I'm sorry for what was said in Texas. About what happened more times than I'd care to admit. I should've spoken up sooner, and I'm just as guilty as they are."

Over a decade in the world of sports, and I've never had a man apologize for his behavior. It's always *she's too sensitive* and never *I fucked up*. *It was a joke* versus *what I said was wrong*.

Hearing Bradley own up to transgressions he wasn't directly responsible for gives me the tiniest glimmer of hope for the future of women in the league and beyond.

"Thank you, Bradley. You did the right thing, and it means so much to me you put your ass on the line."

"I'm really happy for you, Piper. You deserve the reporter spot. I'm much more comfortable on the mic calling the plays, not trying to wrangle players for interviews."

"I'll probably embarrass myself on television, but we'll see how it goes. I need to get going. I'll see you tomorrow."

I step around the corner for some privacy, fingers trembling as I type out a message in our group chat.

GIRLS JUST WANT TO HAVE FUN(DAMENTAL RIGHTS) AND GOOD SEX

ME

Guess who is the new rinkside reporter for the Stars?

LEXI

What the FUCK?

MAVEN

Are you serious??

EMMY

Oh my god, Piper. That's incredible.

MAVEN

How did that happen??? Details??

ME

It's been a wild few days. I have so much to catch you all up on. Doug and Charlie got fired. I got promoted. Bradley is a hero. This doesn't sound like real life.

LEXI

I'm crying for you.

MAVEN

It's so well deserved. A long time coming.

EMMY

Fuck Doug and Charlie.

LEXI

Seriously. Fuck them!

MAVEN

Let's celebrate!!!!

EMMY

Not tonight. I'm in LA for a game and am selfish enough to want to be included. You're not allowed to hang out without me.

ME

Wouldn't dream of it, Em. This weekend sounds perfect.

LEXI

Go buy a bottle of champagne or something, Piper!

EMMY

I just Venmoed you some money so you can splurge on something good.

MAVEN

Me too! Well, Dallas just Venmoed you some money. What good is marrying a professional athlete if you don't use his millions every now and then?

ME

I love you all so much <3.

I tuck my phone in my pocket, and pride nearly bursts out of me.

God, I hope my luck is changing.

I've had nothing to look forward to lately. No good news in a stagnant life of being *fine*, and it's nice to turn over a new leaf. It's nice to have a fresh start and a chance to make a name for myself.

I deserve this.

I've been *waiting* for this, *working* for this, dragging myself through the *trenches* for this, and I'm going to give it my all. I'm going to prove every last asshole who ever doubted me wrong.

SEVEN
PIPER

I CAN DO THIS.

I can do this.

I think I can do this.

Shit.

Can I really do this?

I fix the neck of the pink blazer I put on earlier this afternoon and stare at my reflection in the portable mirror I propped up on my desk in the Edmonton Bulls' media room.

The color is bold as hell, bright enough to be seen from across the rink, but it does little to calm my nerves.

My confidence is wavering. I glance at the clock and know I have five minutes before I need to head out to the ice, and my stomach somersaults.

"Hey." Lexi taps my knee. "You okay?"

"Yeah." I smooth out my high ponytail and add a touch of hairspray around the crown of my head to tame my flyaways. "I'm good."

"You've done this before."

"Not for real. I filled in for two seconds during a game when we had the worst record in the league a couple years ago. This is totally different. People are going to be watching.

The players actually care about what I have to say because they know me now. It sounds so cheesy, but this feels like the start of something new, and I don't want to mess up."

"What's the worst that happens if you do mess up?"

"I get fired? I become a meme for saying erection instead of election? I-I make a fool of myself in front of diehard fans who love to troll in the comments on social media posts?"

"You can *do* this, Piper."

"What if I only got promoted because they pitied me?" I whisper. "What if Charlie was right? That I'm only supposed to be on camera because of how I look, *not* because of my knowledge of the sport. I spent years of my life trying to be this woman who appealed to a man who, in the end, wanted nothing to do with me. This job is the most important thing to me, and I want this to go right."

"I want to show you something." Lexi laces our fingers together and squeezes my hand, helping me stand. She leads me out of the media room and down the visitors' tunnel. The roar of the crowd gets increasingly louder as we approach the ice. "They could've given this job to anyone, but they gave it to you. You know why? Because you work hard—harder than anyone else. Because you're smart and because you're capable. I know you're still learning to believe in yourself, and that's okay. But in the meantime, I don't want you to think you don't have a shit ton of other people ready to cheer you on. Look at this."

We walk to the end of the tunnel, right where the floor turns to ice. I blink and my vision adjusts to the bright spotlights above us. When I can see clearly, I nearly trip over my sneakers.

The whole team is lined up, organizing themselves in the same formation they take after they finish a game and interact with the opposing players.

Maverick is at the start of the line, followed by nineteen other guys in their bright blue away jerseys.

He skates in my direction, a wide grin on his face as he holds out his arm, motioning for a fist bump. My knuckles knock against his glove and he tugs on my ponytail with his free hand until a laugh slips out of me like popped champagne.

"Give them hell, Piper," he calls out as he skates away.

Each player repeats the motion until I get to the end of the line and Liam is the last one left. He slows to a stop in front of me with his larger gloves and his intimidating presence.

"*Piper*," he grunts.

"Liam," I say.

"Heard about the promotion. Congratulations."

"Thought you hated talking to the media."

"I don't see a microphone in your hand yet."

"Maybe I'm hiding one in my pocket."

"Your jacket is very pink."

"Some might say it's not pink enough."

"What shade is that? Pepto-Bismol?"

"Close. It's actually Mind Your Business," I say jokingly.

His snort is barely audible over the music blaring from the public address system, but I hear it loud and clear. He lifts his helmet until it sits on top of his head, the tiniest smile on his mouth.

We never spend this long talking at games.

He usually gives me a quick nod. A curt hello before grumbling toward the locker room, and I like the extra attention from him more than I should.

"Felt like I needed an extra boost of confidence tonight, and brightly colored clothing was a safer choice than downing some vodka," I explain. "Having access to a microphone while tipsy sounds like the recipe for an FCC violation."

"You're going to do great," he says, voice dropping impossibly low so I have to lean in close to hear him.

"And if I don't?"

I ask the question I know he'll answer honestly. Liam doesn't beat around the bush and there's never any hidden meaning in what he says; his bluntness is a blessing and a curse. He'll tell you exactly what he means, and somehow, I need to hear this from *him*.

"Then you dust yourself off and try again tomorrow. Or the next day. Or the next, until you fucking do it. But you don't have a damn thing to worry about."

"Wow. That's some surprising optimism from the guy who once told a reporter to piss off."

"I didn't like that reporter, and he can still piss off. You're a different story."

"A good different story?"

"Your fate is in your hands, Pipsqueak."

"That's not the sage advice I was looking for."

"You'll figure it out. And until then, you're going to be just fine."

Liam puts his helmet back in place and heads for the goal. He drops to the ice to stretch his groin. When he lifts his chin and gives me a slow thumbs-up, I take it as the biggest compliment in the world.

"WE'RE GOING LIVE to Piper in two," the voice in my earpiece says, and I wrap my fingers around my microphone. "First period interview with Hayes on deck."

"You good?" Bernie, my cameraman, asks.

"Yeah." I nod and turn my attention to the ice, watching Liam stop a goal with an outstretched arm. The clock on the big screen ticks down from fifteen seconds to ten, and the save solidifies a tied game at zero as we head into intermission. "I'm good."

The buzzer sounds and I get in position, waiting for the guys to finish their huddle before moving to the locker room for their break. Bernie holds up his finger in warning and I nod.

"Hudson," I call out. "Can I snag you for a second?"

"Shucks, Piper." He grins, skating up and stopping sharply enough to send ice shards flying at my feet. "I get to be your first interview? I'm flattered."

"You're the only person I trust to not get me in trouble eight seconds into this gig."

"You're right about that one." Hudson leans against his stick lazily. "You're going to do great, by the way."

"Elbow me if I forget what I'm supposed to say." I nod as my countdown cue goes from five to one, and I smile big and wide. "Thanks, Bradley. I'm here with Hudson Hayes, who had a solid first period on defense. Hudson, this time four years ago, the Stars boasted the worst record in the league and you were in the middle of an eleven-game losing streak. Tonight, you're keeping the defending Stanley Cup champions scoreless through the first twenty minutes. As the second most tenured player on the team, what growth have you seen in the four years that have passed?"

"We're all older than we were back then. Having experience—including losing—and leaders who went through those losses goes a long way. We've already been down in the dumps once and clawed our way out of it. We know we can do it again if we have to."

"Let's talk about the shot you had with three minutes to go in the first. It was a good look, but you came up short. You typically like to assist, not score. When you have an opportunity like that, what goes through your mind when deciding if you're going to pass or attack?"

"That was honestly supposed to be a pass." Hudson raises his voice over the announcement of a winning raffle ticket number, and I stand on my toes so I can hear him. "I thought Richardson had a better look than me, but the puck wanted to go to the goalkeeper instead. Almost lined up nicely. At the end of the day, I don't care who takes the shot, just that it goes in and we win."

"Last thing before I let you head to the locker room. This is the same match up we saw last season in the Stanley Cup Finals. It feels like there's some lingering tension between these two teams. I know we're nowhere near June, but what's it like playing against the opponent you hope to see later down the road?"

He rests his chin on his stick and looks down at me. "We know the regular season doesn't mean anything as far as bragging rights go. You could play well all year then falter in the playoffs when it matters the most. It is good to get a feel of the kind of gameplay we'll be experiencing come playoff time, though. The Bulls are a good team. They play hard, and this kind of matchup is exactly what we need to gauge how things are working for us."

"Thanks so much, Hudson. We're going to send it back to Bradley who's going to break down the stats from the first period."

Bernie gives me the all clear and my shoulders sag with relief. My grip on the microphone eases and I take a deep breath, my lungs filling with air for the first time in hours.

"I don't know why you were nervous. You knocked that out of the park, Piper," Hudson tells me. "You're a natural."

"It helps you're a good conversationalist. Far easier to talk to than someone like Liam."

"A wall would be better, I think. Would give you less attitude too."

I laugh. The nerves in the pit of my stomach dissipate, and there's a small part of me that thinks I can actually do this.

For real.

Every single day.

And be *good* at it.

"Thanks for taking the time to talk with me. I appreciate you being patient."

"You're going to go a long way." He knocks his knuckles against mine again and heads for the locker room. "And, hey. If Sullivan ever gives you a hard time about refusing to do an interview, send him my way. I'll put him in his place."

EIGHT
LIAM

"WHERE'S YOUR HEAD, GK?" Maverick clasps my shoulder in the locker room during intermission. "You're staring at the wall."

I shake my head. "I'm fine."

"You had a hell of a second period. Ten saves and not a single goal? Fucking impressive. We only have twenty minutes until we can get the fuck out of here and celebrate our hopeful victory against the reigning Stanley Cup champs somewhere fun. Can you *please* pull yourself together?"

"No problem."

"What's got you so distracted?"

Piper fucking Mitchell.

She looked goddamn sexy strutting up the tunnel with that microphone of hers. It was obvious her confidence wasn't there when we saw her before the game, but she seemed a hell of a lot more sure of herself after she finished talking with Hudson.

I've caught glimpses of her out of the corner of my eye all night.

That bright pink blazer keeps grabbing my attention.

So does her laugh.

I can practically hear it across the ice.

The more time that passes on the clock, the more relaxed she gets. Her shoulders move away from her ears. Her smile gets wider. More *real*, not some forced thing she's grimacing out.

It's obnoxious as hell.

Two seconds of seeing her in her element, and I can barely focus on the job I'm paid millions of dollars to excel at.

I need to get my head out of my ass before I cost us this game.

"Nothing," I say.

"Such a bad liar," he says under his breath, but he doesn't press me any further. "Just keep stopping those goals for the rest of the night and I won't give a shit what you're thinking about."

"Would be nice if you decided to score for once in your life. When did you get so selfless and start passing the puck?" I fire back, and he grins.

"There's my guy."

We skate onto the ice for the final period. Boos from the hometown crowd greet us, but I don't pay them any mind as I take my spot in the goal. I also don't pay the women sitting in the front row and wearing my jersey any mind.

They bang on the glass and try to get my attention. I ignore them, settling into the bliss of blacking out my surroundings. Of only focusing on the two hundred feet in front of me, not who might be in the crowd.

I've always been good at dulling the noise. At hearing what I want to hear and seeing what I want to see. I learned early on my brain doesn't work the way other people's do. I don't see colors or shapes. I see solutions to problems and every way a scenario can play out.

When I first started skating as a kid, I noticed how those differences translated to the ice. Every time someone has the puck, I anticipate the moves they could make. I analyze the outcome if they go left then right instead of right then left. Most of the time, I know what the opposing player is going to do before they do, and I'm one step ahead of them.

It's what's made me so good at my job.

Like right now.

The Edmonton Bulls' right wing likes to cross over center ice. Likes to accept a pass in the offensive zone, then fire off a backhand shot that I—

"Nice save, Sully," Hudson yells, whizzing past me when I catch the puck in the center of my glove.

"I gotta give you shit for not paying attention more often," Maverick adds. He knocks his stick against mine as the ref blows his whistle. "Gets your head out of your ass."

"Fuck off." I grab my drink bottle and squirt some water in my mouth. "And get out of my goal."

"Did you see the fan club behind you?" Maverick teases. "I thought they'd be here for Hudson, but that one girl has a shirt that says *Big, bad Sully can sully me up anytime.*"

"Better you than me." Hudson flashes me a sympathetic grin. "You know I hate that shit."

"You and me both," I grumble.

The attention makes my skin crawl.

I know it's part of the job.

I know it comes with playing in a high-contact sport that makes us seem tough and strong.

But, *fuck*, the fan obsession is weird.

Ethan had a stalker last year, a woman who showed up at every away game and stared at him from five rows behind our bench.

Grant gets messages on social media from fans asking how much they'd have to pay to spend a night with him.

Photos of Hudson walking his dogs shirtless in the middle of summer were used in an anonymous TikTok video, and he still hasn't figured out who took the pictures.

The sexualization is creepy as fuck, but the male fans are even worse.

After game five of the finals last year, my posts were swarmed with comments about how I should kill myself because I don't know how to do my job. There were mentions of letting my city down and being a disgrace.

And when they found Alana's account and said they were going to hurt her like I hurt the Stars fans' championship dreams?

I almost stopped playing altogether.

This sport is my lifeline though, and I don't want to give those asshats the satisfaction of having a hold over me.

They can all fuck off.

"Fifteen minutes to go," Riley says, huddling up with us. "Their offense looks gassed. Think if we keep playing them close and save our breakaways for the last few minutes, we'll be able to put this one in the bag."

Ethan snorts. "I'm tempted to lose the next face-off just to fuck with them."

"I kind of want to rile them up, land one of them in the sin bin and earn a power play where we can crush their spirits," Maverick says. "Fuck that they're champions."

"Grant said if we win, we're going to a country bar downtown."

"A country bar in Canada?" Hudson asks. "Sounds like something we'd find in those cowboy romances we've been reading at book club."

"I love the cowboy romances," Riley agrees.

I toss my bottle on the back of the goal and squat, ready for the next play. "Now I'm purposely going to let one past me so I don't have to get on a mechanical bull. And cowboy romances? What the fuck?"

"He fucks the nanny. It's hot," Ethan argues. "And don't get me started on the relationship she has with his kid."

"I'd pay good money to see Goalie Daddy on a bull."

Maverick looks at Hudson, Riley, Ethan and Finn Adams, our left wing. "We need to pull out this victory boys, so we can get Liam in a cowboy hat."

"I will murder you," I growl, and the ref blows his whistle again. "If you don't get your asses back on the line, I'm going to intentionally throw the puck out of the playing area to give them the delay of game advantage so I don't have to listen to you squawk. Get away from me and let me do my job, you fucking dogs."

Ethan salutes me and takes off toward our opponents for the face-off. "Yes, sir."

Maverick barks and skates away with more power than I've seen from him all game. Hudson and Riley hang back with me and get in their defensive stances.

"You know you probably encouraged him to get a hat trick, right?" Hudson laughs, and I roll my eyes.

"At least it would lock up this game," I say. "I'm tired."

"I wonder if the girls will go to the cowboy bar." Riley shifts to his left, knowing the Bulls players tend to play against the boards closest to their bench. "Lexi always makes the night more fun."

"If you shut up and stop these guys from getting close to the goal, I'll buy you a beer at this goddamn cowboy bar so you have a shit ton of fun," I say.

"Your wish is my command, GK," Riley yells, passing the puck to Finn over the red line and following after him.

I know I made a deal with the devil, but as Maverick rears his stick back and sinks a beautiful slap shot that will undoubtedly be on ESPN's Top Ten plays tomorrow morning, I don't give a shit about anything besides a win.

"UNBELIEVABLE SAVE, GK."

"Hell of a stop there with a minute to go on the clock, Sul."

"Play of the game goes to our Goalie Daddy." Maverick jumps on my back and wraps his arms around my neck. "I knew all it would take is some positive reinforcement from yours truly to make sure you had your best stat line of the season."

"It's October." I pull off my helmet and shake out my hair. I'm disgusting, and ten minutes under a blazing hot shower sounds like heaven. "No one cares about my stats in October."

"Great win, boys," a gentle voice says from my right, and I stop in my tracks. Turn my head slowly and spot Piper leaning against the wall. "Do you have a minute to talk about your performance, Mav?"

"Hey, Little P." Maverick slides down my back. "Anything for the best reporter on her first official night with a microphone."

Piper's eyes bounce to me. "Mind if I talk to you next, Liam? You really did have a fantastic game."

"Not doing an interview," I say. "Sorry."

"Come on, man. It's Piper," Maverick says.

"It's okay. Don't worry about it, Mav. He's not forced to talk to the media, and I don't want to push him." She smiles. "Have a good rest of your night, Liam."

"Oh, it's going to be good all right. He's coming with us to the western bar downtown. I hope you and the girls are going to tag along. We have a lot to celebrate," Maverick says. "A victory. Your reporter gig. It's going to be a blast."

"Wait a second. *You're* going to the western bar?" Piper asks me. "You? In a crowd of people? Where they line dance and play country music?"

It's my idea of hell.

The last place I'd ever want to be, but I bet it would be fun if she were there.

"Yeah." I shrug. "I said something stupid to Riley during the game and dug myself into a hole. I'm not happy about it."

"Please tell me I'm allowed to video you singing karaoke. It'll be the greatest night of my life."

"Dream on, Pipsqueak. I'm staying for one round, and if someone tries to get me on stage, they'll end up worse for wear."

"It was worth a try. Maybe you'll have a different perspective after a drink or two."

"Are you buying?"

Her lips split into a wide grin. "I could, if it'll keep you around for longer than eight seconds."

Maverick looks between us. "When did you two get so chummy?"

"We're not chummy," Piper rushes to say, her cheeks turning red.

She blushes a lot, I've learned.

When she saw me shirtless in the trainers' room.

When I complimented her at team dinner.

When she knows she's said something she shouldn't.

It's cute to see her panicking, and it kind of makes me want to push her buttons. Makes me want to see how close I can get to prodding her before she retaliates.

Maverick groans. "I have no clue what's going on, and I hate being out of the loop."

"You're not missing out on anything, Mav," she says, motioning for the cameraman to join them. "Let's talk about the game tonight. You had two goals, with one coming in the final thirty-five seconds of the third period. How do you feel about the team's momentum as we head into November?"

I trudge to the locker room, letting them talk shop and trying to ignore the way my mouth twitches up in a smile when I look over my shoulder and notice Piper watching me walk away.

NINE
PIPER

"I CAN'T WAIT to yee and haw all night." Lexi holds my hand as we maneuver to the bar through throngs of people. "I think I want to be a cowgirl."

"The fact that you had boots in your suitcase without knowing we were going to end up at a western bar in Edmonton is a sign you have a new calling in life," I say, narrowly avoiding a spilled drink. "Forget being an athletic trainer."

"Maybe I can be a trainer on a rodeo circuit. Emmy mentioned some distant cousin of hers has a ranch out west. That might be my next stop after hockey." She looks the boys up and down and grins. "It would only be for the jeans and boots, if we're being honest. I need to offer up some praise to the patron god of denim. You know I would never do anything with anyone on the team, but *damn* do the guys look good tonight in something other than their hockey gear."

I laugh and watch the team take up the entire floor space of Back Porch, the small and dimly lit dive bar we barged into ten minutes ago. Almost everyone came out tonight—even Coach Saunders—and they're decked out in everything from plaid shirts rolled to their elbows and frayed Levi's.

Grant has on a pair of boots and Ethan is wearing a cowboy hat he didn't have on when we left the hotel. There's a bandana tied around Maverick's neck, but he looks more like a sad bank robber who's never been in a heist in his life than someone who lives out west.

A for effort, though.

It's nice to see them all letting loose. They can be goofballs at practice, messing around and pranking each other with silly string and whoopee cushions like they're in middle school, but the second the puck drops and the clock starts for a game, they're professional. Men who know they have a job to do and are being watched by twenty thousand fans making sure they don't mess up.

The boys are definitely acting like they're off the clock now. From the way they're smiling for photos, signing shirts, and ordering trays of beer like they are cups of water, I think it's safe to say they're about to enter party mode.

"If we can get through the night without anyone getting arrested or lighting something on fire, it'll be a win." I lean my elbows on the counter and smile at the bartender. "Could I get a gin and tonic, please?"

"Make that two, please. Where's Maven?" Lexi yells over the growing noise. More people are piling into the already cramped building, and I'm willing to bet the Stars' whereabouts got shared to social media. We might be in enemy territory, but everyone loves NHL teams. "I thought she'd be here."

"She said she wasn't feeling well. Mentioned a headache and wanting to have an early night."

"I'll have to record the boys trying to ride the mechanical bull for her to watch on the flight home tomorrow. Ten bucks says one of them breaks an arm."

"Coach will kill them if that happens, but you know one of them is going to try."

The bartender sets a pair of glasses in front of us. When I pull out my wallet to pay, he shakes his head.

"Already taken care of." He hooks his thumb over his shoulder, and I lean to my left to see where he's pointing. "The guy in the blue shirt down there wanted to send them your way."

"Oh." I smile politely at the man. He's half the size of the hockey guys and dressed totally different with a tie, pens shoved in his shirt pocket, and a tweed jacket. He looks like he might be an accountant or engineer, and I lift the gifted glass in appreciation. "That was nice of him."

"Poor dude probably thinks his chances of getting lucky went downhill when the team got here, and now he's pulling out all the stops." Lexi knocks her glass against mine. "How will he ever survive?"

"Maybe his left hand will help."

"Piper Mitchell is *feisty*, folks, and she hasn't had a sip of alcohol yet." She grins and spins, surveying the scene in front of us. "Are you doing okay? You were phenomenal on the mic tonight, but it seems like you're holding something back. Like you don't want to celebrate this huge milestone of yours. One of the players didn't give you shit, did they? I'll put them through hell if they did."

I stir my drink and watch Riley pull out a roll of quarters from his pocket for the jukebox in the corner of the bar. The song changes from George Strait to Johnny Cash, the opening lines of "Walk the Line" blaring through the speakers, and I hesitate before answering.

I haven't told the girls about everything that's happened this last week. It's too powerful of a conversation to have over the phone, and to be honest, I'm still processing all the intense highs and lows I've gone through.

I *do* want to celebrate this huge milestone of mine because it should be celebrated, but I don't want it clouded by misogynistic assholes. The comments I still hear in my head and the way my confidence has taken a nosedive straight to hell.

Maybe I can start by enjoying tonight. Accepting drinks from men I don't know. Line dancing to loud music and riding a mechanical bull. There's not a better place in the world to welcome this new part of my life than with the team I love and one of my best friends.

I exhale. The weight I've been carrying around slowly slips out of my grasp as my smile turns from hesitant to bold, coming to life under the house lights and the smell of cheap beer.

"I'm okay. I needed some time to process some things, but I'm on the up now and excited to be here." I rest my head on Lexi's shoulder. "And please don't punish any of the guys. They've been nothing but nice to me. That lineup before the game? I had to hold back the tears so my mascara didn't run."

"We have a good group with them, don't we?"

"Yeah. We do."

I scan the rest of the crowded room, and that's when I see him.

Liam Sullivan.

Standing exactly where I thought he'd be—in a corner, drink in his hand, and the ghost of a scowl on his face. His white T-shirt hugs his chest and biceps, proudly showing off the tattoos on his arms. The jeans he's wearing are almost fitted to the curves of his legs I don't normally see.

My breath tangles in my chest when I move from his high-top Converse back to his face, because he's staring at me.

Looking my way with a dark and dangerous gaze that's tinted with a hint of trouble I'm not sure I should be getting myself into, but I can't look away. He tips his head to the side, an invitation there, and I've never been so curious about someone in my life.

"Will you give me a second?" I throw my drink back,

needing liquid courage, and set my empty glass on the bar. "I'm going to run to the restroom."

"Go." She waves me off and bites on her straw. "I'll be fine. The guy who sent the drinks over looks like he has experience in the accounting field, and I need advice about my 401k."

"I always thought the words *Roth* and *IRA* were sexy." I kiss her cheek and wipe my hands on my jeans. "I'll be back soon."

Pushing through the sea of bodies is difficult. I have to elbow my way past a group of women flirting with Grant and Ethan until I'm on the other side of the bar and free from the smell of sweat and stale beer.

"Piper," Liam says when I get close.

"Liam. Why are you standing all alone?"

"Prefer it that way." He brings his beer to his mouth, throat bobbing around a swallow while his eyes never leave mine. I pull my shirt away from my chest, the temperature suddenly stifling. "Having a good night?"

"Can't complain. What about you?"

He shrugs. Kicks a foot up on the wall behind him and crosses his arms over his chest, a vision of unbothered laziness. "I'm not exactly having the time of my life, but I could think of worse places to be."

"Ah. Guess that means you're not going to do that scene from *Dirty Dancing* then, are you?"

"Never."

"Have you seen it?"

"I have a sister, Pipsqueak. I've watched every romcom movie you can think of."

"What's your favorite?"

"*Four Weddings and a Funeral.* But you can't go wrong with anything featuring Meg Ryan and Tom Hanks."

"Wow. I never thought I'd be standing here talking about romcoms with you. Pretty shocking turn of events."

"It's after nine p.m. and I'm at a bar where they've played Dolly Parton six times in thirty minutes. Are you sure the movie thing is the most shocking part?"

"You make a fair point, Sullivan." I mirror his pose, resting up against the wall and dropping my head back. "I always wanted to reenact the part where Patrick Swayze lifts Jennifer Grey over his head. Among other things."

"Like?"

"Nothing from the movie. Dancing in the kitchen. Kissing in the rain. Getting matching tattoos with the person I'm in love with and being a total idiot." I sigh, the one drink making my tongue loose. My inhibitions lowered. "Stupid stuff."

"If it's important to you, it's not stupid."

"Very insightful."

"Call it bar wisdom." He sips his beer and holds the bottle by the neck with his large palm. "You didn't want to talk to the guy who sent you and Lexi that drink?"

"How did you know someone sent us a drink?"

"I'm paid millions of dollars to be aware of my surroundings. I see everything." He pauses before adding, "including the guy who was looking at you two like you were his last meal."

"Oh please." I laugh again. "Lexi, maybe. But not me. The attention was nice, though. I've never had someone hit on me before."

"That dude was staring at you, Piper. The drink for Lexi was him being polite so he'd seem like a nice guy and get her support when he tried to ask you out. You didn't recognize the game he was playing?"

"*Game* he was playing? Uh, *no*. There are so many attractive women in here. Why would he pay attention to me?"

Liam shakes his head. "Wow. Your ex did a real number on your confidence, which is a damn shame. He fucked you up, didn't he?"

I take a step away from him, mortified and ignoring what

might've been a compliment buried under his observation. "Will you excuse me?"

I move for the hallway to the right, wanting some space. Needing some air, even if it's hovering around forty-five degrees outside.

"Piper." Liam's voice follows me as I head for the bar's service door. "Hang on."

Before I can tell him I need a minute, his palm lands on my waist, heavy and warm. Fingers curl in the belt loop of my jeans and he tugs me toward him. I spin, my chest colliding with his, and I let out a startled gasp.

"I don't need your opinions about the poor decisions I've made in my love life," I say. "Yes, he did take away my confidence. Many times, by cheating on me. By diminishing my self-worth. By making me feel small and unimportant. I'm working on getting that confidence back, which is why I'm going to march over to the bar, tell that guy I'm interested, and see if he wants to sleep with me."

Liam's eyes widen. His grip falters slightly, fingers drifting to the small of my back. If anyone walked back here, they'd think they were interrupting an intimate moment. Something sensual between two lovers, and I can't help but drop my gaze to his mouth for the briefest of seconds.

"You want to sleep with Collar McCollarson? Khakis are that much of a turn on?" he asks.

"No. Yes. I don't know." I huff, irritated. Frustrated and confused. Humored by the nickname and obvious disdain for the guy he doesn't know. "Yes because I've only slept with one man in my life and want to have some fun. No because I don't know what I'm doing in the bedroom."

"You don't know what you're doing in the bedroom? What the fuck does that mean?"

"What do you think it means? My ex and I were barely intimate with each other, and I'm so inexperienced. As much as I want to be the woman who can do a one-night stand with a guy I don't know, I have no clue how to even approach the topic because I'm clueless about sex. I wish I could find someone who could… could teach me what to do without judging me. A no strings attached agreement that didn't mean anything, because I'm tired of being the only one in my friend group who isn't exploring her sexuality. I'm single, and I want to have fun. But I can't have it because I'm scared of ending up on Reddit in a *worst sex ever* thread."

My raised tone surprises me.

I run my tongue over my lips and snap my mouth shut. I want to crawl in a hole after admitting all that to the man that probably sleeps with everything that moves. The man that could have anyone he wants. One look at a woman and she's taking off her clothes.

Liam Sullivan doesn't need a sex coach.

"Define barely intimate," he says in a voice so low, I swear I might obliterate on the spot from the heat behind his words.

Each syllable is rough. Each vowel is sexy. It sounds like something he'd whisper in my ear when I'm on the precipice of an orgasm, and I'm not sure I can ever make eye contact with him again.

"Um." I clear my throat. My head is swimming, and I know it's not from the drink. "We rarely had sex. When we did, it was not good. Boring. I never—he didn't—" I drop my head back and stare at the ceiling instead of him. "I don't want to meet the man of my dreams and constantly wonder if we're not sexually compatible and he's too nice to say anything to me."

"Maybe you can find someone. Someone who could help. But you said hockey guys aren't your type, so it seems like everyone in the bar is out of the question."

I swear the earth stops moving at his implication.

I swear he steps closer to me, until the tips of his shoes knock against mine.

I swear his touch moves an inch lower, to the top of my

ass, and I shudder in anticipation of something that'll never happen.

It feels like it *could* happen, though.

Where else could he touch me? How good would it be? How would it feel to have those hands moving up my legs? Unzipping my jeans and pulling my underwear to the side?

I raise my chin a fraction of an inch and find him looking down at me. Impossibly close. Wickedly attractive. So goddamn good looking, my heart leaps to my throat and bangs like a drum.

I've always thought Liam was hot, but now I know he's the most beautiful man I've ever seen. Chiseled jaw. Sharp features. Eyes that track my every movement. I have his unwavering attention, and *holy hell* is that a shock to my system.

No one has *ever* looked at me like this.

"I could be into hockey players," I blurt out, desperate to play whatever game this is. It's mindless flirting, words that have no weight and meaning, but I want to keep it going. "If they knew what they were doing."

A loud cheer from down the hall snaps us out of the trance we've fallen into. Liam drops me from his hold as if he was burned, stepping back until there are a few feet of distance between us. He runs his hand through his hair and shakes his head once, clearing the cobweb of thoughts I'm aching to be privy to.

I selfishly hope they're of me.

"I should go before one of us does something that will get us in trouble," he says gruffly, still avoiding my eyes.

"What if I want a little bit of trouble?" I whisper, wondering if I'm reading this entire situation wrong.

I bet I am.

Liam probably likes confident women. Gorgeous bombshells who can walk into a bar and command the attention of everyone in the room. They're not nervous or shy or inexperienced.

There's no way someone like him would ever want someone like me.

"Then you know where to find me," he answers, and a jolt of electricity zips up my spine.

He walks away, the muscles in his back tense as his shoulders curl in and he drops his head low. He brushes past me, the graze of his shirt against my arm a phantom touch. I watch him slip out the exit, disappearing into the night and leaving me hopelessly curious and more turned on than I've been in goddamn years.

TEN
LIAM

I STRETCH out on my couch and groan.

It's been a long week and a half with road games. Sleeping in different time zones and thousands of miles of travel.

The loss in Texas sucked. I played well until the last two minutes when I let a slap shot get past me. It was a stupid play, one I've blocked hundreds of times. I don't know why I was caught off guard by the left wing coming at me, but I was.

Edmonton helped with the sting of defeat.

The victory was nice, but the icing on the cake was the few minutes I spent with Piper in the hallway at the bar away from the team. Touching her and feeling the warmth radiating from her skin has occupied every corner of my mind, and I'm glad for a night in. A chance to block out the outside world and do something other than think about *her*.

My phone is off so I won't get dragged into any annoying group messages. Pico de Gato, my rescue tabby cat, is curled up next to me, and there's jack shit on the agenda before I plan to head to bed.

It's nice to have an evening like this. I don't have to be laser focused. I don't have to be a professional athlete. I can let my guard down. I can take a second to *breathe* after finishing the first three weeks of the season.

I stroke Pico's fur and grab the remote, scrolling through the TV guide and trying to find something to watch. Before I can get too far, there's a knock on my front door.

Pico jerks awake and darts away at the noise, taking off for my bedroom and the spot in my closet where he likes to hide. I frown and wait, assuming it's someone at the wrong apartment. Someone who's stumbling home after having a few too many cocktails at happy hour, and I'm hoping if I ignore them, they'll go away.

Another knock comes, louder this time. I curse under my breath and turn on my phone, pulling up my doorbell camera.

I almost fall off the couch.

Piper is at my door.

She's standing in the hallway and studying her phone, her black heel tapping on the floor.

What the fuck?

How the hell did she get my address?

She's never been here before, and that shit isn't posted on the internet.

I stare at her in the camera, then close the app.

I could not answer.

I could lock myself in the bathroom so she can't hear me breathing on the other side of the door.

That would probably make me an asshole though, and as someone who's going to disappoint his family in the next few months with a string of lies about his personal life, I need all the good karma I can get.

Scrubbing a hand over my face and groaning, I stand and head for the door. Unlocking the deadbolt, I lean against the frame and stare at the short blonde.

She jumps back like she wasn't expecting me and lets out a soft laugh.

"Piper," I say.

"Liam." She blinks and smiles. Laughs again. "Hi."

"Hi. Please don't tell me this is an interview."

"No. I'm here on personal business." Piper tugs on her pencil skirt. My eyes bounce to her hips and linger there for a second—maybe it's two—before moving back to her face. "Can I come in?"

"Uh." I rub the back of my neck. I'm thrust back to when my fingers were in the belt loop of her jeans. Her gasp when our chests collided and how close I was to doing something really fucking stupid, like kissing her. "Sure."

Piper slides past me, and I close the door behind her. She walks down the hall, her heels clicking and clacking on the hardwood floor. There's a pep in her step and I follow behind her, still unsure of what the hell is going on.

"Wow." She looks around my living room. Walks to the floor-to-ceiling windows and presses her nose against the glass. "Look at this view."

"Nice, isn't it?"

"Do you mind if I sit?"

"Wherever you're comfortable. Want something to drink?"

Piper takes a spot on the couch, sitting on the edge of the cushions and running her palms down her thighs then back up. "Do you have any alcohol?"

"Beer? Wine? Something stronger? All three?"

"Whiskey, please. Neat."

I nod and open the liquor cabinet I keep stocked for the offseason. I grab a glass and pour her a finger of the amber liquid, handing it her way. "There you go."

"Thank you." Piper brings the glass to her mouth and finishes the drink in two gulps. "That's better."

I've seen her drink before.

At the western bar.

At a team fundraiser last season.

On a night when I reluctantly went to a club with the team during an away game. I hated every second of it, but the evening ended up better than it started: with Piper at a burger joint and ketchup on her nose.

She was drunk as hell.

Giggling uncontrollably and nearly falling off her stool. From anyone else, I would've been annoyed. With her, I thought it was cute. Endearing, almost, to see her let go for a while. She's normally so buttoned up. Professional and poised and someone who follows the rules. Watching her walls come down was the highlight of that road trip.

The whole damn season, probably.

I doubt she remembers it, but I do.

The dress she was wearing. The way she looped her arm through mine when we shuffled down the sidewalk and avoided piles of snow. How she stuck her tongue out when I said I didn't want anything to eat and the tipsy grin she tossed my way when I gave in and ordered a milkshake, just to make her happy.

It was the most I'd laughed in years.

When I tucked her into bed at the hotel and stayed an extra hour after she fell asleep to make sure she didn't throw up, I wondered what it would be like to laugh like that every damn day.

"So, Mitchell. Are you on the run?" I ask.

Her face softens. She drags her thumb over her bottom lip and sinks her teeth into the lipstick she's wearing. "Would you help me if I was?"

"Depends on the situation. Probably."

"You're sweet. I, um, wanted to talk to you about something." Piper sets down her glass and wrings her hands together. Gives me a nervous smile that's tight around the corners of her mouth, and I'm on edge. "But I think I'm going to need another drink first."

I fill her glass again and sit in the chair across from her. "Have you had anything to eat today?"

"A sandwich at lunch. Nothing for dinner, but the night is young."

"Young? It's eight o'clock and time for bed."

"Didn't know you were an old man."

"I didn't choose the lifestyle. The lifestyle chose me. No more alcohol until you get some food in your system."

"Fine." She downs the second drink faster than the first, and I'm wondering if I should get her some water. "Okay. I have, uh, a proposition for you."

"If it has anything to do with the media, the answer is no," I say sharply. "I'm not interested."

"It doesn't. It's about your sister's wedding."

That catches me off guard. "What about it?"

"I thought I could go as your date. Or your pretend date, like I explained the other night. We act like we're together so your family doesn't bust your balls about showing up alone. It's still technically a lie, but it'll be harmless."

"Why would you ever agree to come with me?"

"Because, in turn, you could help me with something."

"What kind of something?"

"It's about what I mentioned the other night at the bar. About, um, needing help in the bedroom?" Her voice squeaks, and blood rushes in my ears. "You probably forgot all about it, but I thought… you know what? I think I read the whole situation wrong. This was a terrible idea. Forget it."

She stands and heads for the door, practically running down the hall. I give her a head start before I stand and follow her. When I get close enough to touch her, I wrap my fingers around her wrist to stop her from leaving. I give her a gentle tug and she spins to face me.

Her cheeks are flushed. Her pupils are blown wide and she's staring at me. I take a step toward her and she moves backward, her shoulder blades pressing against the wall behind her.

"I didn't forget anything." I put a hand by her right ear,

almost caging her in. I can hear her breathing. Can see the freckles across her nose and catch a glimpse of the hint of green in her eyes mixed in with the blue. "Let's try that again."

"I wasn't kidding about wanting someone to... to teach me what to do in bed. It felt like you might be the *tiniest* bit interested in sleeping with me after that comment of yours, and I figured..." She trails off, looking at the floor. "I trust you. I know you have more experience than me, and we could both get something out of it, but now I'm realizing this is all silly. So incredibly stupid, and probably cause for me to get fired. Please forget I ever asked."

She pushes away from the wall and walks past me, heading back to the living room. I let her get some distance before I follow her again like a lost fucking dog.

My head is spinning. I have no clue if this is a joke. If this is for real or if she's fucking with me to prove a point about how men are trash.

With the things I'm thinking about—her on top of me. My name on her tongue. Twisted sheets and my hand running up the inside of her thigh until I found out how wet she could get—I'd tell her she's right.

I'm an animal, and I hate myself for it.

I also hate myself because I'm more than a *tiny* bit interested.

I'm really fucking interested.

I've been interested for years.

When she said all that stuff at the bar, my brain almost short-circuited. All I could hear were words like *barely intimate. Not good. No strings attached.*

I can't believe she was with someone for an entire fucking decade and he never took care of her. Never worshiped her and never made her feel like she was important.

Her ex-husband is a piece of shit.

When I get to the living room, she's pacing. Doing laps around the couch and tapping her fingers on her forearms.

"Hey," I say, and she looks up. "Want to order a pizza?"

"A pizza?"

"If we're going to talk about fucking each other, you need to eat some food so you're level-headed. Especially after those drinks."

A blush creeps up her neck. The crimson color settles on her cheeks. "Did I really ask you to fuck me?"

"A little more eloquently than that, but, yeah. You did."

"And you're not kicking me out?"

"I'm not."

"Does that mean you're… you're open to the idea?"

"What kind of pizza do you like?" I grab my phone off the coffee table. "Pepperoni? Veggie? Supreme?"

"Um." Piper sits on the couch again and covers her face with a pillow. Her voice comes out muffled when she says, "Pepperoni with veggies, please."

"Get comfortable, Piper. You're going to be here a while, and you're not going to hide from me again."

ELEVEN
LIAM

I TOSS the empty pizza box in the trash.

We went through almost a full pie while we watched some shitty reality television show Piper said she liked, and I put the last two slices in the fridge so she can take them home when she leaves.

I wash my hands and grab the bottle of whiskey, pouring a glass for myself. I never drink the night before a game, but this situation calls for it.

"We're going to talk about this like adults," I say, sitting next to her on the couch. "Why did you come here, Piper?"

She takes a minute to answer. If I had to guess, it's because she's afraid she's going to get rejected. The second she puts this idea in the world, it gives me a chance to shoot her down. And, judging by the way she's still not looking at me, I'm willing to bet she's been shot down a hundred times in her life.

"I word vomited at the bar," she starts. "I didn't mean for all of that information about my personal life to come out, but it did."

"That's the unfortunate thing about vomit. You can't take it back."

Piper's laugh is soft. "Please know I would never be here if

I didn't get the impression you might be interested in hearing what I had to say."

"I told you you knew where to find me."

"I didn't, actually. I had to coerce your address out of Maverick and make up a lie about delivering a box of sponsorship materials."

"You found me, though."

"I did. And if he asks how you like the new brand of protein shakes I brought you, just roll with it."

It's my turn to laugh. "Noted."

"After the bar, I went back to my room and did some reflecting about how I made a fool of myself. The more I thought about it, the more I thought an… arrangement between us could work. I want to explore my sexuality. You're a single guy." Piper sits up and her mouth drops open in horror. "Oh, no. You are single, right?"

"I am."

"Thank god."

"I'm flattered you want me so badly, Mitchell." She lifts the pillow sitting on her lap and throws it at my head. I smile and catch it out of the air. "Goalie, remember?"

"Okay, show off." She smiles too and picks up where she left off. "Add in the bonus of you not having a date to your sister's wedding, and I figured we could both benefit from it. Taking me would be easier than finding someone on a dating app."

"A dating app? Please. I'd use forged documents instead."

"Really? You don't think showing off a photo where you're holding up a fish you caught is cool?"

"I'd rather bury my head in the sand."

"I would've been shocked if you felt otherwise. Is being here a complete invasion of your privacy?"

"No. An invasion of my privacy would be taking a picture of my dick and posting it online."

Her eyes bounce to the front of my shorts and linger

there. A blush crawls up her neck, and now I'm thinking about her on her knees. What my cock would look like in her mouth and how deep she could take me down her throat.

This is all her fucking fault.

I wasn't thinking like this before.

"I'd never do that."

"I know you wouldn't. Why are you asking me? You're an attractive woman. You could find a guy on Tinder, or down the street at any restaurant who would be willing to sleep with you. It wouldn't be very difficult."

"I meant what I said earlier: I trust you, and I know—well, I assume—a big part of intimacy is rooted in trust. I don't want to be with someone who might laugh at me, and I *really* don't want to wind up on the internet. I read a whole thread about the worst blow jobs guys have ever received, and I'm afraid to ever put something in my mouth again."

I did not have Piper Mitchell sitting on my couch and saying things like *blow jobs* or *putting things in my mouth* on my bingo card for the night, but I still snort out a laugh.

"What makes you think you can trust me?" I ask.

She's so nice. The kind of woman who finds the good in everyone, even if they aren't deserving of it. I want to make sure she's not holding me up on some pedestal.

"The night at the club when I got drunk, I woke up safe in my hotel room the next morning. I know that was because of you." Her eyes meet mine, and she smiles. "It wouldn't have ended that way with every man."

Christ.

I did *not* expect her to remember that.

She could barely walk straight, for fuck's sake, and she knows I tucked her into bed?

My cheeks heat. I don't know the last time I blushed, but right now, my skin is on fire.

"Let's start from the beginning," I mumble, switching

gears. Trying to get away from whatever the hell I'm feeling right now.

"I figured we could—"

"The very beginning. Tell me about your ex."

"Steven?" Piper deflates. "We met in college and dated while he worked at a tech startup. He proposed to me when we were in our early twenties, and we got married really young. He made a lot of money very quickly when his business took off, thanks to his dad's connections, and he kept making more of it. There was this obsession with being successful. Being the best. All of his time, energy, and attention went into work, and I got pushed to the side."

"Then you got divorced."

"I, um, saw a text I wasn't supposed to see. He played it off like I was imagining things. Like I was crazy. Then—" She groans. "This next part never gets any less embarrassing."

"You don't have to tell me if you don't want to."

"It's important to the story. We hadn't slept together in almost a year. I wanted to convince myself it was all in my head and decided to surprise him during his lunch break. He landed a big investor the day before, and things like that always put him in a good mood. When I walked into his office, he was going down on his secretary."

"What a fucking prick."

I've played with guys like her ex. The ones who mess around and don't think they'll ever get caught because they consider themselves invincible. Maybe their wives or girlfriends know what they're doing behind their backs and don't give a shit, but I can't imagine having the life everyone else wants and still wanting *more*. Like being at the top of the pyramid isn't enough.

They want to get their dicks wet. Want to walk around like they're gods because of their name or their job or how much money is in their bank account. There's no humility, just ego. Everything is about having the attention on them.

I fucked around a little my first few seasons in the league. I slept with a woman or two and got caught up in the fun of being an athlete who never had to work hard to get laid, but it lost its appeal pretty quickly. That's not who I am.

And I've always thought guys who cheat are the bottom of the fucking barrel.

"It's almost like he wanted me to find him. Turns out, he'd been sleeping with her for months," she says. "He blamed me for not fulfilling his needs, filed for divorce, and here I am: a woman in her thirties who's only been with one man. It's sad, isn't it?"

"It's only sad if you make it sad. Seems more like you're free from a selfish idiot who probably couldn't find your clit even if it had a big flashing sign pointing to it."

Piper tries to bite back a laugh but fails. "That's strangely comforting."

"I can be considerate occasionally. Excuse the vulgarity, but why not watch porn? There's plenty of stuff out there. It's all fake as shit, but you'd get the idea."

"I have." Her cheeks turn even pinker and my mind—my fucking traitorous mind—wanders to Piper with a computer on the bed next to her. Her fingers slipping under her shorts and her head against the pillows. I knock back all of my drink and wipe my mouth with the back of my hand. "I know it's not the real thing, and I don't want to have a visual learning experience. I want to be hands-on. I want to figure out how things are supposed to feel and how things are supposed to sound. I want to know if what I'm doing is good."

"What—" I glance at my empty glass and consider pouring myself another shot. Maybe two. Fuck the headache I'll have tomorrow. "I need you to explain this all to me very carefully, Piper, so I understand exactly what you're proposing."

She gnaws on her bottom lip. Twists her hands together and takes a deep breath. "I would like us to be intimate with each other. I want you to be my guide in the bedroom. My coach, to put it in sports terms. Sex is a big component of it, yes, but I also want to learn the other things that make up a physical relationship. I know how cheesy this sounds, but I really think my happily ever after—my *real* happily ever after, because I refuse to believe the first one counts—is out there. I don't want to miss out on my soulmate because I don't feel confident in the bedroom and hide myself away. And, even if I don't hide and end up meeting someone, a guy has barely ever made me orgasm. I've just… I've been made to feel embarrassed while being intimate too many times, and it makes me never want to try again."

"Guys who care about you won't give a shit if you can orgasm or not," I say. "They also won't stop trying after one failed attempt."

"This is about me too though, and my journey. I lost so much of myself when I was with Steven, and I want to find it again. I don't want to be a pushover who always puts others first. I don't want to be quiet and timid and… and told I'm supposed to act a certain way. For once in my life, I want to be selfish. I want to have fun and I want to have sex and I want to be the woman who takes whatever the hell she wants. I want to not give two shits about what anyone thinks of me, Liam, and for some reason, I think you can be the one to help me with that. I mean, the other night at the bar was the most I've been turned on in *years* and you barely touched me. That has to mean something, right?"

I stare at her, and pride ripples through me.

Her cheeks are a rosy red and there's a glint in her eye that wasn't there when she knocked on my door. I've seen Piper Mitchell a dozen different ways over the years, but this right here might be my favorite one.

Determined.

Blunt.

Sexy as hell.

"If I were to say yes, we'd need rules. Strict fucking rules and an iron-clad plan for the next few months."

"What did you have in mind?"

"If I'm going to help you in the bedroom, you're going to help me at my sister's wedding. We're going to have to get to know each other well enough for you to answer questions my family might have without it being obvious we're bullshitting them."

"Easy enough. Research is my job. Besides, I've been curious about you for a while now. The more I get to know you, the better."

That makes me nervous. Makes me want to reinforce the walls I normally put in place to keep people out when they try to get close, because my business is *my* business, not theirs. But then Piper smiles at me. Reaches out and puts her hand on my arm. Her thumb strokes over my tattoos, and I melt a little bit.

I'm weak as shit.

"Right. Okay. Yeah."

"What are your other rules?" she asks.

I have no fucking clue what my other rules might be because I didn't expect to spend my night casually discussing sex with the woman I've had a crush on for fucking years.

Do I even know how to speak?

Can I form a coherent thought?

"Communication," I say, pulling something out of my ass. It sounds important, though. Like a rule I *would* suggest if I was thinking clearly. "You can't hide from me when we're talking about something in the bedroom. I need you to be upfront about the things you like. The things you don't like. If you assumed you'd like something and end up hating it, you can't keep that to yourself."

"Wow." Piper laughs. "You sound like you've done this before. Are you a secret sex coach on the side?"

"I haven't had sex in four years. But no. I've never been someone's sex coach before."

"*What?*"

"What?"

"You haven't—but you—I thought—"

"I don't sleep with women during the season."

"And the offseason?"

"Haven't been interested in anyone."

She shifts on the couch and straightens out her legs before crossing them at her ankles. "Have you slept with a lot of women?"

"Depends on your definition of a lot. I wasn't a fuck boy like some of my teammates, but I've had sex."

"Were you—did they think you were good?"

"Yes," I say, and her face turns red. "I know what I'm doing."

"Do you have an exit survey? A rating scale from one to five? Maybe I could make one up for us if you agree to… to fuck me."

"I'm not a boy, Piper. I don't need surveys or ratings. I'm a man, and I know how to listen. Listening goes a long way, and it's not difficult to do."

She nods and wets her lips with her tongue. I try not to stare at her mouth. "What other rules were you thinking?"

"If we're going to do this, we're going to be exclusive. No one else is going to fuck you if I'm fucking you," I say. "I'm not someone who likes to share. What's mine is mine."

"That won't be a problem." Piper looks at me, her gaze heated and heavy. "I could barely ask you to sleep with me. I don't think I could do it again."

"Good." I rub my jaw. I agreed to join No Shave November with the rest of the guys, and the stubble on my cheeks scratches my palm. "I need to think about this for a few days. My priority is hockey. It's what I'm paid to do. I'm not going to sacrifice the thing I love more than anything in this world for sex."

Piper bobs her head. "There's no rush. Thank you for

even entertaining this idea. I know it's farfetched, and I won't be upset if you say no. I figured, why not? I'm doing all these other new things in my life. Might as well add good sex to the list too."

"If I say no, will you ask someone else?"

"Um." She taps her fingers on her thigh and shrugs. "Maybe? I haven't gotten that far yet. I guess I will. I have nothing to lose. It's not like my personal life can get more pathetic."

I grind my teeth together and nod. I really fucking hate the idea of someone else—like one of my goddamn teammates—touching her and gloating about it.

It tempts me to say yes on the spot, but I need to think with my head, not my dick. I need to consider the pros and cons about agreeing to her plan before I get too deep into a mess I can't claw my way out of.

"I'll text you what I decide."

"Perfect." Piper offers me a tentative smile and stands. "Have a good rest of your night, Liam. Thanks for the pizza."

"Take the slices in the fridge for your lunch tomorrow."

Her smile stretches wider. "I will. Thank you."

She walks away, and when I hear the front door close behind her, I drop my head in my hands and groan.

Letting Piper sit on my couch for almost two hours might be the biggest mistake of my life, because I already know my answer is going to be *fuck yes*.

TWELVE
PIPER

"DOES ANYONE NEED MORE WINE? What about cheese and crackers?"

"Will you sit down, Maven? You've been running around nonstop for the last hour, and that doesn't include the fabulous dinner you made us." Lexi tugs on her arm and pulls her onto the couch. "We can pour our own drinks."

"Sorry." Maven laughs and sips her water. "You all know I love hosting, and it's my first time having people over at the new house."

"I would love to host too if I lived here." I glance around the living room and admire the decor and furniture. The freshly painted walls and the windows that look out to three acres of land without a neighbor in sight. "I can't believe you all built this from the ground up."

"I love it so much. I've always lived in apartments, and I'm so excited to have a yard. To have a porch and a tree-lined street." Maven sighs, blissfully content. "This is a dream come true."

"It's so beautiful. Definitely worth making the drive." Emmy pulls her legs to her chest and rests her chin on her knees. "I'd love to live outside the city in a place like this. With enough land to have a garden full of fruits and vegetables and space to build an ice rink in the backyard."

"Aren't you and Maverick looking to buy?" Maven asks. "I thought you went to an open house last month."

"We did, but when we're both home for longer than a night and not exhausted from our games, the last thing we want to do is talk about neighborhoods or HOAs. It's like everything else we're doing: it'll happen when it happens, and until then, life is good," Emmy says.

"I love your love." Lexi sighs. "It makes me so happy."

"It took sifting through a dumpster of trash ex-boyfriends to find Maverick, but it was worth it. After my last breakup, I told myself I was content with being alone. That it's what I wanted, and I'd be happier without a man. When I'm with him though, I realize how much I don't want to be alone. It scares me how much I love him sometimes, because what if he decides one day he doesn't want me anymore? It's terrifying to put so much trust in someone not to break your heart." Emmy realizes what she's said a second too late, and her mouth opens in horror. "*Shit.* I'm sorry, Piper. I didn't mean—"

"I know you didn't." I wrap my arm around her and rest my head on her shoulder. "Maverick is *not* Steven. Just because I was sad doesn't mean you're not allowed to be happy."

"We can talk about something else."

"Like Piper's sex life? Any luck on finding someone on Craigslist?" Lexi teases.

"What?" I squeak. "Nope. Nothing. Not a single thing to report."

"You're such a bad liar." Maven narrows her eyes. "You're hiding something."

"Ugh. Fine." I groan, knowing they're going to wear me down eventually. "I, um, have a development on the whole *getting better at sex* thing."

"Finally." Lexi grabs the bottle of chardonnay and fills up

her glass. "*This* is what we should've been talking about all night."

"Before I start, you all have to swear what I say doesn't leave this room. You can't ask me about it when we're not behind closed doors. You can't tell anyone on the team. It's very private and very personal."

It's been almost a week since I proposed my idea to Liam.

We've had three games—two away and one at home—so I know he's been busy, but he hasn't given me an answer one way or another about where he stands and I'm going out of my mind.

Putting myself out there was *hard*, but I have to be prepared for a possible rejection.

He said it himself: he doesn't date during the season. And while I know we're not falling in love or anything profound like that, this will be a time commitment. For someone so dedicated to his craft, asking him to give up precious hours away from the thing he's passionate about might not go over well.

"Whoa." Maven scoots to the edge of the couch opposite me. "This is serious, isn't it?"

"Very," I say. "I need you all to swear on girl code."

"Swear," Lexi says, and Maven and Emmy echo the agreement.

I take a deep breath and a sip of my wine. "Something happened at the bar when we were in Edmonton."

"I *hate* being on a different team. I miss out on all the exciting stuff," Emmy grumbles. "Please tell me you had a wild night of sex with some nice Canadian. Isn't there a position where you do it on a mechanical bull?"

"Okay, if those are your expectations for this story, you're going to be very disappointed. There was no kinky bull riding, but I did step *way* out of my comfort zone by telling someone how uninspired I felt in the bedroom and asking them for help," I confess.

"What do you mean *someone*?" Lexi presses. "Who the hell did you ask? Is it someone famous? Is that why you're being so secretive?"

"It's Liam," I blurt out, and all three girls gape at me. "I told him about Steven and the lack of intimacy and—*oh my god*. I said I'm not sure a guy can make me orgasm. I can't believe I did that."

"We need to back *way* the fuck up. How the hell did you end up telling him all of that? What did he say? Is he agreeing to it?" Emmy asks, and there are so many questions I don't have the answer to.

"It all just happened. One minute I'm telling him I could be into hockey players and the next he's saying I know where to find him. So, I found him. Proposed the idea. Asked if he would be my coach, and now I'm in limbo while I wait for him to decide if this is a good idea or not."

"And by coach you mean—"

"Sex and everything that comes with it."

"Did he say *yes*?" Maven asks.

"Not yet, and I'm mortified. It's been a week. He hasn't paid any attention to me. He won't even look my way, and I know the answer is going to be no. Why else would he drag it out for so long?"

"Can we pretend he says yes for a minute? Let's imagine there's a world where he agrees to help you." Lexi grins. "You're going to sleep with *Liam*."

"This is a safe space, so I know there won't be any judgment. I love my husband very much." Maven sets her water down. She cracks her knuckles and laughs. "But I can't help but be curious about Liam. I've always thought he'd be the best on the team in bed. A little freaky, maybe. The perfect amount of roughness without hurting you. He'd be big on consent, which is so fucking sexy, and he doesn't strike me as someone who would be very selfish, if you know what I mean."

"Honey, we all know what you mean," Lexi says.

"I think that's why I went to him," I admit quietly. "He's a little rough around the edges and nearly impossible to read, but I know he'd take care of me. I know I'd be safe with him. I wouldn't be a conquest or a notch in his belt. He wouldn't brag to the team. He's always been determined; he wouldn't stop until he had a hundred percent success rate with me."

I don't want to tell the girls I've been thinking about him since I stopped by his apartment, but I have.

I still remember when he caged me in against the wall and his voice turned rough.

I still remember the flash of heat behind his eyes when I originally told him about my idea.

Liam Sullivan has been on my mind, and there's a part of me that's desperate to feel his hands on my body. To know what he tastes like, what he sounds like. How meticulous and careful he'd be in the bedroom and if he's as good as he claims he is.

I already know the answer, and it makes me want him even more.

"This is a big deal, Piper. Are you two going to date? Are you going to tell the team?" Maven asks, the voice of reason I need in my biased thoughts.

"No. We're going to pretend to date for his sister's wedding, but there wouldn't be a romantic relationship—only a physical one. And I wouldn't tell the team. I don't want them to think differently of me because of who I may or may not be sleeping with. I've worked so damn hard to get where I am, and I don't want to throw that away."

"They wouldn't treat you differently," Emmy assures me. "Look at me and Mav. We were together when I was on the team, and no one cared. They were happy for us, and the boys bug me on a daily basis asking when they're going to have a niece or nephew. If Liam starts walking around with a smile on his face, they're going to have questions."

"That's a good point. And is he going to sleep with other people?" Maven asks. "Are you?"

"No. It would be exclusive."

"You have to tell us when you hear from him," Lexi says.

"I'm not going to get my hopes up. I've actually already written the idea off. It'll be fine. I'm not in head over heels for the guy. Maybe—" My phone buzzes on the table, cutting me off. I grab it and find a text from Liam. "Oh, shit. It's him."

I slide my thumb across the screen, bracing myself.

LIAM

My apartment. Friday at 6 pm.

ME

Is this a yes to what I asked?

LIAM

Yes.

ME

Cool. See you then!

My hands shake as I stare at my phone. It's silent on the other end, and I don't know why I expect another message to come through. This is *Liam* we're talking about, a man of few words and even fewer emotions.

Who just agreed to be my *sex coach.*

Holy *shit.*

"He said yes," I say. "Oh, my god. I'm going to sleep with Liam."

"Hell yes!" Lexi cheers. "Our girl is going to get laid."

"Are we allowed to get a full report?" Maven asks. "I will sell my left kidney to know what he's like in bed."

"He's a private person. It wouldn't feel right to give away details of his personal life," I say.

"*Fine.* We don't need details, but you're going to have to give us *something,*" Lexi says.

"We'll use that Schmidt clip from *New Girl* to figure out his size," Emmy says. "That's fair, right?"

"I'll give you the *New Girl* clip," I agree, and they cheer.

I read his message again, then a third time. It's curt. Straight to the point and not beating around the bush, and I can't help but smile at how *Liam* it is.

I've never been one to be a double texter, but just this once I decide to give in and tell him what I'm thinking.

ME

I'm excited, by the way.

Three dots appear then disappear. It takes a full two minutes before his response comes in, and when it does, my smile stretches into a wide grin.

I can't help it.

LIAM

Me too.

THIRTEEN
LIAM

PIPER KNOCKS on the door to my apartment ten seconds before six.

There's a moment of hesitation before I wrap my fingers around the knob and throw the door open.

"Hi," she says breathlessly with bright red cheeks. The dress she's wearing is a pretty, flowy thing that fans out at her hips and stops at the top of her knees, and I thank the weather gods for the unseasonably warm temperatures we've been having this week. Her hair is down, her smile is hesitant but beautiful, and it feels like I got punched in the gut. "How are you?"

"Good." I take a step back, motioning her inside. "Come on in."

I get a whiff of her perfume when she brushes past me. I wonder if my whole apartment is going to start to smell like flowers if she keeps coming around, and I guess there could be worse things in life.

"Thanks. How's your night?"

"Can't complain." I follow behind her, assuming my role as a lost dog again. "Want a drink?"

"No. Alcohol will lower my inhibitions, and I want to be

present tonight." Her laugh is light as she sits on the leather couch and sets her purse at her feet. "But don't let me stop you from having a good time."

"Nah. Don't need it."

Silence settles between us, and I know I'm going to have to be the one to break it.

I'm the one who told her to come over. She's going to have certain expectations. Things she wants me to do and things she wants to learn. Plus, with her lack of experience, there's no way in *hell* she's going to be the one to make the first move.

"I'm going to ask the question I don't want to ask, but I have to ask before we start any of this. When was the last time you were tested? You mentioned your husband was a fucking ass—sorry. Unfaithful to you, and I want to make sure there's no—"

"Ex-husband," she says, interrupting me, and her lips twitch. "He is an asshole, though."

"My bad. I don't know how that insult got in there."

"Must've been a casual slip of the tongue. As for the unfaithful part, I took a test after I found out about his affair. Everything came back negative, and I haven't been with anyone since."

"I don't have anything to report on my end either."

"Being celibate for years will do that to you, I guess."

I huff out a laugh. "When we get to the sex portion of this arrangement, I'd like it if we used a condom."

"That's fine by me. Safety first, right?"

"Right. Do you have a preference on what type? Latex? Synthetic? Glow in the dark?"

"Glow in the dark?" Piper bursts out laughing, and it eases the tension I've been carrying around all afternoon. "That's not a real thing, is it?"

"According to Grant it is. The picture on the box is of outer space. I guess you use them when you want your dick to be out of this world."

"Oh my god." She clutches her side and wheezes. "It's not a dick. It's a rocket ship."

"I mean, you can ride both. They both make you see the stars. I'm not an astronaut, but I think they both involve thrusting."

"You're making me get a cramp." When she finally settles down, she wipes her thumb under her eye. "I feel like I should be taking notes, because I am downright *clueless* about aesthetically pleasing condoms that transport you to different galaxies. What else do you have for me, teach?"

"Okay, smart-ass. This next part might make me sound like a prick, but it needs to be said. I like you as a person."

"Shucks, Liam. I like you as a person too."

I bristle at that, glazing over her compliment before I can think about it for too long. "That being said, we're not dating. This arrangement between us is only physical. I'm not your boyfriend. My priority is hockey. When the two of us are intimate with each other, I'll treat you right. I'll show you what you want to learn. In the real world, though, I'm not going to hold your hand."

"Wow," she deadpans. "I'm falling in love with you already. Please stop being so irresistible. You're making it impossible to stay away."

"Sarcasm isn't a cute look on you, Mitchell."

"You're smiling."

"I'm not smiling. I'm grimacing."

"Sorry. My mistake. You're right about the physical component. I'm finally doing my dream job, and work is my focus. I want to stay in DC long term, and the way to do that is to perform above and beyond the expectations in place for me. That won't happen if I'm distracted. We'll have plenty of fun, but it's confined to the bedroom until we head to your sister's wedding. After that, we can break this off and get on with our lives."

Piper is eager to get the ball rolling. She's moved to the

edge of the couch and is watching me in the way I've seen other women watch me: like she's going to stake a claim on me. Like I'm something she wants very, very badly.

And, *fuck*, I want her too.

Now that I can have her, now that I can touch her, I'm fucking *desperate* for it.

The guys tell me I need to relax, and this is me relaxing. Finally letting go and enjoying what's around me.

I walk toward her. She tracks my movements until I stop right in front of her. I reach down and curl my fingers under her chin, lifting her head so our gazes collide.

"I wasn't kidding about communication, Piper. You need to tell me what you're thinking and how you're feeling. If there's something you don't like, we stop."

"I promise I will. Are we going to go to your bedroom?"

"No. We're staying out here tonight."

"Why?"

"We have plenty of time. If you're doing it right, sex isn't just about sex. It's about the build-up. Foreplay. The things that happen *before* the main event. I can't fuck you how you like if I don't know what makes you wet, can I?"

Her throat bobs around a swallow. "No. I guess you can't."

"This is going to be a long process. I'm going to ask you questions during it, and I want you to answer them honestly so I can get to know you better."

All this shit is rigid and formal. So unsexy and far from the encounters I've had in my past, but she's counting on me.

I've never liked letting anyone down.

"What kind of questions?"

"Do you like to be teased?" I ask. "Do you like things fast?"

"Um." She drops her head back and stares at the ceiling. "I think I might like to be teased. It's… that's what I do when I'm touching myself. I try to prolong it. When my ex and I were together, he always just kind of… put it in."

"Fucking hell." I pinch the bridge of my nose and groan. That dude is an absolute moron. "Okay. Tonight we're starting with kissing and some touching. That's it. I'm never just going to *put it in*, Piper. When we get there, I'm going to get you off at least twice before I fuck you."

"Now I really feel like I should be taking notes. Do all guys act like this?"

"The smart ones do."

"Why?"

"Some of us can get off just from watching you get off. Eating pussy is one of my favorite things in the world."

Her wide eyes drop to the front of my gym shorts like they did the other night. This time, she doesn't look away. She studies the outline of my half-hard cock and bites her bottom lip.

"You really like it that much?"

"Yes."

"Why?"

"I like knowing what I'm doing is working, and when you're going down on a woman, you can tell." I touch her cheek and trail my fingers down her neck. "I can feel it. Hear it. Taste it."

"That's sexy," she whispers. "That you like it."

"Can I kiss you, Piper?"

"Oh. Um. I might not be very good at kissing either. Steven was never very affectionate with me, and I haven't kissed anyone in the years that have passed. I probably use too much tongue. Too much—"

"That doesn't answer my question. Can I kiss you, Piper?"

It's her chance to back out of this. To run away before we start something we can't take back. I don't want her to have any regrets, and I want her to be really fucking sure this is what she wants.

And that she wants it with *me*.

"Yes," she whispers, voice so quiet, I'm not sure she actually said it.

"Yes what?"

"Yes," she repeats, louder this time. "You can kiss me, Liam."

I don't know how many first kisses I've had in my lifetime. A couple dozen, maybe? I've never been nervous about any of them until right now, because she's trusting me to get this right. She's counting on me to give her the fun she's never had, to make sure she learns so the next guy she's with won't be disappointed, and I've never liked being a failure.

"Close your eyes," I say. "Tilt your head to the side."

She listens to every direction I give her, eyelashes fluttering closed and neck bending at a slight angle. Her hands sit in her lap, nervously tapping on her thigh, and I thread my fingers through hers to give her a quick squeeze so she knows it's okay to touch me.

I move my other hand to her face, cupping her cheek. There's a hitch in her breathing and she's practically shaking. I dip my head, kissing her neck, and I almost groan.

She tastes like fucking sunshine.

Her skin is warm and soft, and a quiet moan escapes her as I move my lips up the line of her throat, not stopping until I get to the corner of her mouth.

"You sure?" I ask one last time.

Piper turns her cheek, her lips less than an inch away from mine. "Positive."

That's all I need to hear.

I close the distance between us. My mouth lands on hers and I swallow down her soft exhale. She wraps her arms around my neck and tugs me close, and I can't help but smile at her enthusiasm.

"Is it—am I allowed to make sounds?" she whispers, pulling away from me slightly. "Or should I stay quiet?"

"Do what feels right. I like knowing what I'm doing is working, so I prefer hearing you. But I'm not every guy."

"Okay." Piper nods, determination sparking behind her eyes. "Then I'm going to keep making noises."

I run my hand up her leg, wanting to touch her. Wanting to *feel* her and figure out if she loves or hates what I'm doing. Her fingers move to my hair and tug on the longer strands near my ears, and I take that as a sign I can give her more.

My tongue swipes across her lips, coaxing her mouth open. I hum when she opens right away, welcoming me in, and I can't help but wonder what her tongue would feel like running up the length of my cock.

Like nirvana, I bet.

"Okay?"

"Perfect," she murmurs, and the praise lights me up. Makes me kiss her a little rougher, a little harder, and she groans again when I gently bite her bottom lip. "I-I like this. Am I doing okay?"

"You're doing great, Piper."

My thumb brushes up her thigh, under the hem of her dress. I want to go even higher, up to the seam of her underwear so I can see if she's wet. So I can see if she's being honest and not just trying to stroke my ego, but I hold myself back.

I can be patient.

"I didn't realize making out with someone could be so hot."

"Lie back," I tell her. "Get comfortable."

She pulls away from me, and when I look at her, I can't help feeling smug. Proud of the way her lipstick is smeared and how her eyes are glazed over. The content smile on her mouth and how much brighter she seems, even after two minutes of affection.

Piper Mitchell's love language is physical touch, and I'd be willing to bet she's a fan of words of affirmation too.

Fuck the guy who never gave her what she needed to help her shine.

"Like this?" she asks, her back on the couch and her head on the pillows behind her.

"Yeah." My eyes rake over her body—the strap slipping down her arm. The way her dress hugs her tits. The freckles on her knee when she props her leg up and the hint of lace on her hips. I stare at her greedily because I fucking *can*. "That's great."

I've been restricting myself for so many years. I've been disciplined and followed diets and exercise regimens and strict sleep schedules.

But now? Now I'm going to allow myself to have a lot of fucking fun.

"Liam?"

"Yeah?"

"Can you kiss me again? Please?"

I hold myself above her, my chest almost pressing against hers. I bring my mouth to her ear and whisper, "I think I'm going to like it when you beg."

FOURTEEN
PIPER

IT'S no surprise Liam kisses me like he does everything else in life: meticulously. Purposefully. Obsessively, almost, to the point I wonder if he lied to me about not having sex in four years, because he's *that* good.

I never thought I'd have the best kiss of my life with Liam Sullivan, but here we are.

I'm consumed by him. He's touching me, encouraging me, coaxing sounds out of me I didn't know I could make, and somehow, I want *more*.

I adjust our positions, nudging him backward until he's sitting upright on the couch. I push up onto my knees and straddle his lap, doing what feels right. His palm slides up my thigh and stops on my waist. When his thumb strokes across my bare skin, I'm electrified.

Is it supposed to feel this good?

I know it's only his hand, but I've never been so turned on.

It's like I'm aware of every inch of my body. Hypersensitive to the press of his fingers and the shapes he's drawing on my skin.

I wonder if the sensations take getting used to.

I wonder if I'll stop feeling fluttery after we've moved on to lesson number ten or twelve.

I wonder if it's him or if it's me, the slow and sensual display of affection more than I've received in years.

"Slow down," Liam mumbles when I try to roll my hips. He moves his mouth to my neck, sucking the skin there in a way that makes my eyes roll to the back of my head. Makes my breathing stutter and my fingers dig into his muscles because it feels like I'm about to float away. His tongue licks at my collarbone, and I don't know if I hate him or love him. "We're only kissing tonight."

"Do you not want me?" I ask.

Stronger women wouldn't consider a question like that at time like this, but that's not me.

Not yet.

I've been the girl in a new piece of lingerie, posing on the bed and *begging* to be touched, only to be told no.

I don't want this to go any further if it's one-sided.

It's supposed to be casual and fun, and I'm not looking for romance or candles or rose petals on the bed. That doesn't mean I want to learn with someone who's only placating me, though. With someone who's doing this as a pity favor because they feel *sorry* for me.

My ego can't take it.

Liam doesn't answer. He lifts me off his lap like I weigh nothing more than a sack of feathers. With painstaking care, he puts me on my back again. Nudges his way between my legs and glances down at me.

His eyes are blazing. His face is red. He carefully touches my throat, a juxtaposition to his swollen lips and the rough and hungry way he kissed me a few seconds ago.

"I'm hard as a rock, Piper." He wraps his fingers around my wrist. Guides my hand down his stomach so I can feel his cock straining against his shorts, and I inhale sharply. "Don't think for a goddamn second I don't want you. That I'm not enjoying this."

When he pulls away, I blink up at him, a silent question hanging there. He gives me a single nod, encouraging me, and I run my fingers across his clothes.

"Wow," I whisper. I trace down his length and back up, only pulling my hand away when he rocks his hips forward. "That's because of me? Just from kissing?"

I know how dicks work, but I had no idea something so *innocent* could elicit this kind of response from a man.

When I kissed Steven, it was bland. Quiet with quick pecks on my mouth that missed half the time.

And he *never* got hard.

"Yeah." Liam's voice is raw and hoarse. Tinged with desire, and I imagine his words against my neck or the curve of my knee. Between my breasts and thighs. "When a guy is in the moment, anything can make him hard."

"Then why aren't we doing more?"

"You deserve to be fucked right, Piper, and that means taking our time. Going slow and working you up to it. I'd hurt you if I tried to push inside you right now, and that's the last damn thing I'm ever going to do, okay?" I nod, biting my lip to keep from smiling as he continues. "You're going to listen to me so this can be good for you, and I'm telling you we're not doing anything else tonight. Okay?"

Hell.

I love bossy Liam.

I've heard him shout out calls and bark out orders on the ice. I've watched him pinpoint where his teammates were weak on a play, but being on the receiving end unlocks a different side of me.

I want to listen to his every word. I also want to know what would happen if I disobey. I squirm, a distant thought of his hand on the curve of my ass invades my mind, and I think I might be ruined.

"Okay," I whisper, the word heavy on my tongue.

His thumb grazes over my nipple and I stifle a groan. It's too much. It's not enough. "Good."

"Do I get to touch you? I want to see what you look like."

"Not tonight. This is about you, remember?" Liam lowers his mouth to my breast. He blows a hot puff of air against my dress and I whine. "I wonder if I could make you come like this. By teasing you. Riling you up. Would you beg for it?"

I would.

I'd get on my knees and promise everything I have if it meant I could find the release I'm so desperately craving.

A warm, aching feeling starts low in my belly. It's like a fire; dull at first, then turning into an inferno the longer he touches me. The longer he keeps his mouth inches away from my nipple, another puff of air ghosting over my chest.

I've experienced it before when I've been in bed and lifting my hips, trying to find the best kind of friction.

It's never been like this, though.

Powerful.

Addictive.

A whole-body experience.

"He never did," I admit. "It usually took some work to make me finish. Sometimes I can't even make myself finish."

"That's the wrong thing to tell me, Piper." He pulls the straps of my dress down. The cool apartment air bites at my skin and his gaze never leaves mine. "I've always liked a challenge."

"Are you always this confident?"

"When it's something I know I'm going to win I am."

"Then maybe you should hurry up."

Liam lifts his eyebrow, a grin curling on his mouth, and I'm worried I said the wrong thing.

Was that sexy? Obnoxious? Too forward? Not enough?

I'm used to keeping my mouth shut in the bedroom.

Smiling instead of speaking. Nodding instead of moaning, and I have no clue if I'm doing this right.

"I see the wheels turning in your head," he says.

"You're talking to me and I thought I should talk to you. I don't know if you even like to be talked to, but I—"

"I like to be talked to. I like to be told what to do too." His grin melts into a smirk. "Can I look at you, Piper?"

"Look at me?" He lifts his chin my way and understanding dawns. "*Oh.* Yes. You can."

His eyes drag down my body from my neck to my collarbone. A string of expletives tumble from his mouth when he gets to my chest, and I know my skin is bright red.

"*Fuck.* Perfect fucking tits. I knew you'd be pretty underneath your clothes."

He cups my breast and pinches my nipple between his thumb and pointer finger. I don't bother to hide my moan, and when he lowers his mouth and *sucks*, I almost levitate off the couch.

"Shit," I whisper, a new and unexplored sensation clutching me tight. "I like that."

He moves his mouth to my other nipple, and I think I might die. I think my tombstone is going to have to read *perished from the grumpy goalie's mouth on his living room couch*, because he swirls his tongue in a pattern I've never felt before, then bites—*hard*—and I can't remember my name.

I slip into a trance, reveling in his hands on my body and their exploratory path. When he strokes the underside of my breast, my toes curl. When he pinches my nipple again, adding more pressure than before, I loop my arms around his neck so my hips don't leave the couch. And when his free hand brushes against the front of my underwear in the cruelest teasing touch, I know I'm going to fall apart.

"I think I need more," I pant. "I think I'm close. I don't know. It's never felt like this before. I'm—" I suck in a sharp breath, not knowing what I need or how to voice it, only that I want him to never, *ever* stop. "*Please*, Liam."

"There's that word again." He moves his hand away from between my legs, and I whimper at the loss. "Tell me what you're feeling."

"My skin is on fire. There's this… this *energy* in my stomach. Like I'm close to something but I can't reach it yet. I've come before but it's not… this is totally different. It's never been so intense."

"Because it hasn't been done *right* before. If I keep touching you, do you think you could come?"

"Would it be okay if I did? I-I like what you're doing."

I don't know the proper protocol here, and I just want to be *good*.

My foreplay knowledge is limited, and I've never tipped over the edge to an orgasm without some form of penetration.

To think Liam could do it with only his mouth has me angry about all the pleasure I've ever missed out on.

"Fuck, yeah it would be okay if you did. *God*, I want to see it. I want to hear it. You don't have to last long for me, Piper, and when you're close, I want you to let go. Don't think about anything else besides how *good* you feel, okay?"

I nod and take a deep breath, exhaling when he puts his mouth on me again. I moan when he strokes up my thigh, his long fingers bunching the skirt of my dress like he wants to see more of me.

When I think he's going to move to my other breast, Liam surprises me by kissing me again. It's heavy, passionate, and he nearly folds himself on top of me to get close. I'm not sure where I end and he begins, only that this feels unbelievably *right*.

I lift my hips, a frantic need pulsing through me and clawing at my spine. He presses his thumb against the front of my underwear, finding my clit without ever breaking our kiss, and I detonate.

My body trembles as I ride the high, the sensation simultaneously unfamiliar and welcome. Liam sends another orgasm racing through me when he rubs his thumb in a slow, torturous circle and whispers, "Take it all, Piper. You're so good, you deserve it."

I don't know how long it takes for me to calm down. Five minutes? Five years? When my legs finally stop shaking and my breathing evens out, I open one eye and find him staring at me.

"Hi," I whisper shyly, watching with blissed out wonder as his mouth hooks up on the right side in the start of a smile. "I'm afraid I'm dead."

He runs his hand down my leg and kisses my knee. "You gonna haunt me from the afterlife, Mitchell?"

"I think I might. It's your fault I feel like this."

"And how do you feel?"

"I'm not sure I can form coherent sentences and you want to know how I feel?"

"It's the perfect chance for your exit survey. It's fresh in your mind."

A laugh bubbles out of me. "Do you really want an exit survey?"

"Seems like I was promised one."

"It's pretty clear how you did. I came on your couch."

Liam hums. "Yes, you did. What did you like about it?"

My cheeks heat at his blunt question. "Is there going to be a debrief after each lesson?"

"If it'll help you figure out what worked and what didn't, we might as well. You're not going to hurt my feelings."

"I wouldn't hurt your feelings if I didn't come?"

"No. We'd take a break and try again. And if you didn't finish, that's fine too."

"Should I come every time? I've had sex more times than I've orgasmed. Seems like the math is off there."

"It's not a requirement, but a guy should always try. It's

fucking easy for us to get off, and we should be the last priority."

"Oh." My smile falls. "So when we're together, I'm always going to come first?"

"Always." He looks down at me and frowns. "Are you okay?"

"Yeah. I'm learning how much I've missed out on, and it's humiliating. I'm thirty-two. I've been *married*, for god's sake, and I don't know the rules of orgasming. He made me come five times, Liam, in ten years. That's it. I made excuses for it, and now I'm thinking it's because he didn't find me attractive. It's because he didn't want to spend the time making sure I understood. It's because I was bad in bed. He had experience before he met me, so I know it's not him."

"Don't do that," Liam says fiercely. "Don't blame yourself for his shitty intimacy. It took me ten minutes to figure out you like when I suck on your tits. You don't need a degree in anatomy to know what turns a woman on, and that tells me he was lazy. Selfish and a giant fucking prick."

"That's because you're a sex god." I take a deep breath, winded from the conversation and the sweet bursts of pleasure. "You're an anomaly."

He barks out a laugh and touches my knee. "That's the orgasm talking. Give it to me straight, Mitchell."

"The kissing was nice. I like that thing you did with your tongue."

"Nice," Liam repeats. He drags his thumb across his bottom lip and a line of wrinkles form across his forehead like he's angry at the world. "Weather is nice. A hot shower is nice. I don't want the way I touch you to be *nice*. I want it to be fucking mind-blowing."

"It was good," I blurt out. "Really, really good. The best kiss I've ever had."

"What about where I touched you? Was it too much?"

"I liked that a lot." My voice turns quieter as I try to

gather my courage. As I try to come to terms with the fact the man in front of me is fixing my dress. Smoothing his hands over the fabric and watching me with a hopeful gaze that makes my heart do a somersault. "I liked when you—" I swallow and rest my hand on my chest. "Touched me here."

He nods and sits back on his heels. "Good. I'll do that again next time. Is there anything you didn't like?"

How you didn't slip your fingers inside me. How I didn't get to touch you. How I can't stop picturing your cock and wondering if I'd even know what to do with it.

"I liked it all."

"You're really giving me some confidence here."

"Four years off and you haven't lost your touch. You deserve an award. Maybe some gold stars."

"Watching you come is enough of an award for me, but I've always been motivated by positive reinforcement. What did you learn tonight?"

"I didn't realize I was going to be put on the spot." I laugh nervously. "Um, I guess that my chest is more sensitive than I thought. I never pictured enjoying your mouth on me, but I did."

"Does the idea of my mouth gross you out, Pipsqueak? Be honest."

"*No*! It's not that. I know how anatomy works, but I always figured Steven never touched me anywhere because it wouldn't feel good for me."

"Do you touch your tits when you get off by yourself?"

"No, but I'm going to have to start." My cheeks flame and I clear my throat. "Do you want me to..." I trail off and glance at him. His hard length is obvious through the thin material of his shorts, and I can't stop staring. Can't stop daydreaming about touching him and making *him* fall apart. "Give you a hand?"

"I can't tell you how badly I want to say yes to that offer." Liam tips his head back. The tendons in his neck stretch as he stares at the ceiling, and his hand flexes at his side. "But we'll save it for next time."

"There's going to be a next time?"

I feel drunk on the aftermath of his careful and considerate touch. High on how *powerful* I feel. Disoriented from the recognition of learning what it's like to be with someone who wants to be with you too.

More importantly, I feel *alive*, awakened from a slumber of sorrow and grief. For the first time in forever, I'm catching glimmers of myself, the me that disappeared far too long ago, and I like what I see.

"That was the preseason, Piper. The season is long, with lots of games. Lots of practices." Liam grazes his fingers down my cheek, and I sigh under his touch. One time, and I crave him. I'm a plant and he's the sun, and I'm a maniac for his warmth. He curls his hand around my chin and my palm rests on his arm, drawn to him like a magnet. "You and I are going to have a lot of fun."

"I've always liked having fun, and it feels like I've been missing out on so much for so long," I breathe out, a wild exhale rattling my lungs. "Am I allowed to ask for a kiss before I leave, or is that too… relationship-y? I don't want to cross a line."

"Not crossing a line at all." His eyes light up and he leans forward, mouth inches away from mine. His lips press against mine in something soft and slow. "Text me when you're home?"

"Worried about my wellbeing? That might go outside the scope of the bedroom, Sullivan."

"It might, but I'm still going to do it. I told you I'm going to treat you right, and this is lesson number one. You should always send your orgasm provider a text when you get home so they know you're safe. And maybe a picture of your tits too."

I laugh, light and free. "I'm taking notes right now."

"Good. There's going to be a quiz next week."

"Is there? Maybe you can bring the glow in the dark condoms and I can bring the glow in the dark lingerie. We can see who lights up the best."

"That'll be a fun game." He drops another kiss to my forehead, and I untangle our limbs. I stand and stretch my arms above my head, a happy sensation settling in my bones. "I'm serious, Piper. Let me know when you're home."

Is this what it's like to be cared for?

If Liam can show me this much affection after only one night together, how is the man of my dreams going to treat me?

Will he show me off in public? Dip me low in front of a crowd of people and kiss me like there's no tomorrow?

He's proving to me there are good men out there, and for the first time in a long time, I have hope.

"I will. I promise." With a salute, I check to make sure I'm not going to flash anyone in the hallway then head to the door. "Good night, Liam."

Liam doesn't say anything else as I hurry away, but I can feel his attention follow me long after I've slipped into the night.

FIFTEEN
PIPER

ME

What's your favorite color?

LIAM

Haven't really thought about it. Why?

ME

Curious minds who will be playing your fake girlfriend want to know.

It's probably something boring like gray.

LIAM

I'm going to guess yours is pink.

ME

What gave it away?

LIAM

Definitely not that blazer you wore again last night. Think you burnt my retinas, Mitchell.

ME

I can give you a reference for an ophthalmologist if you need one.

LIAM

Attachment: 1 image

ME

Glow in the dark condoms DO exist!!!!

LIAM

I stopped in for milk but made a detour for the latex. Now you can say your life is complete.

ME

This made my whole day!

LIAM

Is the bar that low?

ME

No. I'm just really fascinated by this whole phenomenon and the reasoning behind it.

Are you going to Friends and Family night?

LIAM

Don't really have a choice.

ME

Are you bringing people?

LIAM

Back to the Twenty Questions game, I see.

I'm coming alone.

ME

Oh. That's sad. Nobody should go alone.

LIAM

When you think about it, we're all alone.

ME

Back to your existentialism I see.

Well, I'll be there. I'm your friend, so you won't be totally alone.

Physically at least. I can't speak on a metaphysical level.

LIAM

Never thought I'd read glow in the dark condoms and metaphysical in the same text thread.

ME

You're a goalie, Sullivan. I need to keep you on your toes.

LIAM

Considerate as always, Pipsqueak.

FRIENDS AND FAMILY night is one of my favorite parts about working for the Stars.

The organization opens up the arena for players to bring their loved ones down to the rink for a couple hours. It's a low stress night, an evening with games and prizes and watching the guys live a normal life away from screaming fans.

The tradition has been going on for years, implemented by Brody Saunders in his first season as head coach. He likes to talk about how camaraderie isn't built during practice but outside it. Events like this give the team a chance to kick back on their day off, enjoying time with their families during a stretch of home games.

"Why aren't you on the ice?" Maven leans over the boards and stares at me. "You look very sad sitting alone."

"If by sad you mean content, then, yes. I'm wonderfully sad." I laugh and drop my elbows to my knees. "Can't a girl watch safely from the stands without being heckled?"

"She can, but you always do things with the team. Last season, you participated in a hot dog eating contest and nearly choked to death. Please don't tell me you prefer processed meat over ice skating."

"I don't know how to skate. I never learned."

"*What*? You've worked for hockey teams for years. You're around the ice almost every day."

"The key word there is *around*, not on. My job keeps me firmly on dry ground, and I have no complaints."

"How have you never learned?"

There's a moment of hesitation before I answer her.

I could tell her about the time Steven tried to teach me. How frustrated he got when I didn't understand the physics behind the movements. The yelling when he said he couldn't be around someone who didn't give their best effort and the disappointment on his face when I fell and couldn't get up.

It might have happened a decade ago, but I haven't stepped foot on a rink since.

I smile and shrug instead, feigning nonchalance.

"When I interview the guys, it's always in the tunnel. Being proficient on skates isn't part of the job description," I say.

"Let me teach you! It's so easy when you get the hang of it and—"

"I'm fine, Mae. You don't need a liability trying to pull you to the ground. I'm having fun watching you all."

"Are you sure? You can hold my waist. We can start a skating train. You know the team will join in."

"I'm positive. Do a couple more laps and we can grab a drink in the lounge when you need a break."

She blows me a kiss and I scan the rink, smiling at everyone having a good time.

Grant and his youngest sister, a figure skater, are doing laps around everyone else. Ethan is chatting with a woman who doesn't look very interested in what he has to say. Hudson is laughing with his dogs as they slide across the ice and Maverick and Emmy are involved in some sort of game of tag.

I can't figure out the rules, but I think Emmy is kicking his ass. Judging from the grin on his face, though, he's damn happy to lose.

"Allergic to the ice?" a deep voice draws out, and I smile when I notice Liam standing in front of me.

"Something like that," I say. "Taking a break?"

"Yeah. Playing keep away with Riley's nieces is kicking my ass. Those girls are ruthless."

"They should meet Emmy."

"I'm going to tap her in and let her do a few rounds with them." He rests his stick against the boards and lifts the hem of his practice jersey, wiping the sweat from his forehead with the shirt that boasts his number. 32. "She's probably faster than me."

"She's definitely faster than you."

His smirk tells me he knows I'm right. "Why aren't you socializing with everyone? This whole thing seems like your kind of scene. People. Talking. Loud noises."

I thought our first time talking one-on-one after he kissed me into oblivion the other night would be awkward, but it's so natural. Like we're two best friends shooting the shit, and I don't feel uncomfortable at all.

Nothing's changed, and it makes me so happy he's not going to treat me any differently after I orgasmed on his couch.

"You're having the time of your life, aren't you?" I tease.

"What gave it away?"

"Your scowl tells me you think this is a *blast*. I'm not socializing with everyone because I don't know how to skate."

"You don't? Have you been on the ice before?"

"Once. It didn't end well."

Liam hums and doesn't ask for more details. "Do you want to learn?"

"That's okay. I'm perfectly content up here."

"I'll do a couple laps with you. It'll be a nice breather from having my ass handed to me by seven-year-olds."

"That's not the compliment you think it is, Sullivan."

"Wasn't meant to be a compliment, Mitchell." His mouth twists into a small smile. "Come on, Pipsqueak."

"It could be hazardous. You could fall. What if I dislocate your shoulder and you can't play? I'd feel so guilty."

"I leg press double your bodyweight at practice, Piper. Unless you're planning to turn into the Hulk, you're going to have to work very hard to pull me down."

Reporters for rival teams call him a brick wall for good reason. His broad shoulders, cut biceps and supposedly legs of steel tell me he'd be nearly impossible to throw off kilter.

My brain comes up with an image of Liam lifting me up. Throwing me over his shoulder and carrying me down a never-ending hallway without exerting an ounce of energy.

A hand on my thigh that slips under my clothes.

The other on my ass, squeezing.

The fantasy is hot.

Sensual enough for me to press my thighs together and swallow down the lump in my throat in an attempt to get the thought out of my head.

"Promise you won't make fun of me?" I ask.

"No. But I won't laugh loud enough for you to hear."

"Asshole," I say, but I stand and move toward him. "I don't have any gear."

"What size shoe are you?"

"A seven."

Liam holds up a finger and crosses the ice. I'm always so focused on game play and he's always stuck in the goal, immobile unless the puck comes close to him that I forget how *beautiful* he is when he skates.

It's effortless.

Like he's gliding on air or walking on water.

I could watch him move for hours.

He comes back a minute later and holds up a pair of white skates that are scuffed up around the toes. "No excuses now."

"Are you a magician? Where did you get those?"

"We ask people to bring an extra pair so we can donate equipment to our community outreach organization. See if they fit."

I reluctantly kick off my sneakers and exchange them with the skates. I lace them up and stand, unbalanced and close to tipping over.

"They fit, unfortunately. Should I put on a helmet? What about some pads? Last time I tried to get out there, I fell about eighteen times."

"That's it? Should've made it to twenty."

"Twenty would've probably ruined my love for the sport."

He offers me his hand and I make a split second decision to say *fuck it* and try, because what good is my life if I'm constantly watching from the sidelines? Missing out on all the good things happening around me because I'm scared of failing?

I know this is a safe space. A chance to learn without any repercussions, and I take his hand in mine.

A line of calluses sits at the base of his fingers. His palm is warm even in the cool temperature of the arena and his hold on me is sturdy and soft. Like I could tumble headfirst toward the ice and he'd catch me before I hit the ground.

His arm bands around my waist, his other hand settling on the small of my back to guide me. I can feel the heat of him through the wool of my sweater, and his closeness gives me an assuredness I didn't have the first time I was wearing skates.

"There you go," he murmurs as we make our way down the straightaway. I stumble on the first corner, but his grip never wavers. "You're doing great."

"I look like a baby deer, don't I?"

"More like a baby giraffe. You're carrying all your weight in your upper body and that's throwing off your balance. Evenly distribute it. Relax and glide through each step, like you're pushing the ice away from you."

I listen to his patient instructions. Focusing less on flailing and more on using the ground as a point of power helps, and the change makes everything marginally easier.

The first lap is atrocious. It takes us almost ten minutes to make it around the rink. Kids pass us, and one even points at me and laughs. Liam's scowl scares him off, and I can't hold back my smile despite how terribly this is going.

"Hudson's dog is moving faster than me." I glance at the golden retriever sliding on his belly and burst out laughing. "He has far more poise than me too."

"Four legs are an unfair advantage."

"Could you put some blades on your hands and level the playing field, please?"

"Compare yourself to Seymour's kid. She can't stand up straight."

"She's also a one-year-old who can't wipe her own ass, Liam. It's cruel to be better than her."

He chuckles and we start another lap. "Someone suggested we do a baby crawl race during intermission one day. Can you imagine the chaos?"

"Sounds like it could be both the most dangerous and the most entertaining thing to ever happen in this arena." I wave at Maven and she gives me a thumbs up, her head resting on Dallas's shoulder. "How old were you when you learned to skate?"

"Four. I grew up in Chicago. My dad signed me up for a Blackhawks kids' camp one summer, and I never looked back."

"You were always destined for greatness. Meanwhile I'm over here looking like an idiot and being shown up by kids twenty years younger than me."

"You don't look like an idiot. You're learning. There's a difference." Liam lifts under my arms when I start to lose my footing again. I squeak as we make a sharp turn and almost run into the boards. "We all suck at something the first time."

"I would be a lot better if my first experience on the ice was like this. It would've made me want to take some lessons, not hide from the rink."

A muscle in his jaw ticks. "Bad teacher?"

"Bad everything. Thank you for being patient with me."

"You don't need to thank someone for doing the right thing."

"Old habits, I guess." He starts to pull away, and I panic. "Whoa. Stop. Come back. Where are you going?"

"I want you to try on your own. I'm going to skate ahead and you're going to aim for me."

"Did you not miss the part where *children* are lapping me? What if I fall?"

"Who cares if you do?" Liam stops sixty feet ahead. "You can do it, Piper."

There's magic in his gentle encouragement. Affirmations I've never heard before, and, for half a second in a world of pretend and make believe, in a reality where I'm lifted up instead of brought down, I know I *can* do it.

So, I move.

I shuffle forward, each stride becoming more confident the longer I stay on my feet. Maverick and Emmy skate by, grinning and cheering me on. Grant pulls out his phone and starts recording me, chanting my name and lifting his fist in the air in celebration.

Even Liam has a grin on his face.

The faintest hint of one tugs on his mouth, and he's never been more beautiful than right now with his quiet joy. The subtle way he inches backward so I have to skate farther and farther, proving to myself I'm capable and strong.

"How do I stop?" I ask, barreling toward him.

"Bend your knees and turn your skates sideways," he says.

I try to listen to his instructions, but I lose my center of gravity instead. I careen forward, seconds away from falling, and I swear my life flashes before my eyes.

Before I can do anything remotely close to stopping, I run straight into Liam's chest, sending him flying onto the ice while I go down with him.

"Shit. Fuck. Oh no." My legs buckle out from under me and I land on his stomach. "Are you okay? Are you alive? Am *I* alive? Is my hand going to get sliced off?"

"You're okay," Liam says, and I open my eyes. He's spread out on the ice like a starfish, arms out straight and legs wide. "My ass, on the other hand, isn't."

"Will it make you feel better if I pretend like the crash is payback for making fun of my blazer, not because the definition of *sideways* flew out of my head when you yelled it at me?"

"It's deserved then. I wasn't prepared for you to actually go Hulk on me, Mitchell." He groans and pushes up on his elbows. "You might have a future in the NHL with defensive moves like that."

"Did you hit your head? Why aren't you wearing a helmet? This is a lawsuit waiting to happen."

"I'm fine. No damage besides my left ass cheek. Good thing I'm going to be on my knees during the game tomorrow, not my butt."

I can't help it.

I burst out laughing at the absurdity of it all.

Our positions.

The way he lifts his hips and touches his backside, like he's checking to make sure it's intact.

My pathetic skating skills and how I'll never, *ever* do this again.

"This was a travesty." I blink down at him. He looks up at me, still wearing that grin and not in any hurry to move me off of him. "What do we do now?"

"We forge on and try again."

"That's a pretty positive outlook for a guy who scowls more than anyone I know."

"Maybe I'm turning over a new leaf. I'm inspired by your fearlessness and your inability to stop."

"Look who's funny with the sarcasm." I put my hands on his chest and push onto my knees. "Rinkside is where I belong. It's safest over there."

"One more lap, then we can get a drink." Liam's thumb strokes along the hem of my sweater and brushes against my bare skin, leaving a trail of heat in his wake. "Consider it part of your lessons."

"Okay," I whisper, incapable of saying anything else. I don't know what lesson he could be talking about, but I'm ready to be the most dutiful student in the world. "Only if you're buying."

He drops his hand away, and I miss his touch already. "Your first teacher might have been shitty, Piper, but you have me now. I know how to take care of a woman."

One more lap turns into two then three. It becomes painfully obvious with every circle we make how different he is from the man of my past.

And, judging by the cocky smirk he's tossing my way, he knows it too.

SIXTEEN
PIPER

ME

Hello! Are you busy tonight?

LIAM

Depends who's asking.

ME

I am! Does that change how you're going to answer?

LIAM

Possibly. If it involves other people, I have plans.

ME

And if it doesn't involve other people?

LIAM

I'm listening.

ME

I figured we should get to know each other before your sister's wedding, and I was going to invite you over.

It's not like a date or anything!

It's two friends casually talking about things you like and things you don't like.

LIAM

You're doodling my name in a journal, aren't you?

ME

Guilty.

Do you drink coffee? What's your favorite food? Which is better, breakfast or dinner?

LIAM

Yes. Meatball sub. Breakfast.

ME

Great! Now I know everything about you! Should be easy to convince people we're in a relationship when I have no clue how you take your coffee.

With eight sugars and extra pumps of vanilla, probably.

LIAM

Black.

ME

Darn. So close.

LIAM

Point taken. Send me your address. I'll come by after weight training.

ME

Could we maybe add in another lesson? One that doesn't involve ice skating but you on your knees?

LIAM

One orgasm and you're learning to speak your mind?

Glad my fingers can give you some confidence.

ME

I'm going to hide now.

See you later!

GIRLS JUST WANT TO HAVE FUN(DAMENTAL) RIGHTS AND GOOD SEX

MAVEN

Dinner tonight? June is at a friend's house and Dallas is out of town for an away game. I'm bored.

EMMY

I'm in Pittsburgh with a bowl of room service pasta.

LEXI

I'm sorry to hear that.

EMMY

You don't like Pittsburgh?

LEXI

I don't like room service pasta. I'll spare you the details.

EMMY

Lovely.

ME

I'm busy tonight. Sorry!

LEXI

Okay, casually dropping that on us? What are you busy with?!

MAVEN

Or WHO are you busy with?

ME

32.

EMMY

That's either Liam's number or thirty-two men.

LEXI

I kind of hope it's thirty-two men. Talk about a plot twist.

ME

Sorry to disappoint, ladies. Just the one man.

LEXI

And is he disappointing you?

ME

... no comment.

But he's definitely NOT disappointing me.

LEXI

Damn. Goalie Daddy can get it.

LIAM, I've learned, is always early.

I look out the peephole and find him outside my apartment at seven on the dot, standing in the hallway with his hands shoved in the pockets of his sweatpants like he's been waiting for an hour.

"Hi," I say when I open the door. I look him up and down and frown at his wet and wavy hair. A rogue lock curls on his forehead, and I want to brush it away. "Aren't you cold?"

"I'm almost two hundred pounds. If I had a coat on, I'd be sweating."

"I apologize for the temperature you're about to experience. You're going to think it's a sauna." I step back so he can slip inside. "You can put your shoes wherever."

"Jesus, Mitchell. It's like a fucking terrarium in here. Are you a lizard?" He scowls, hands drifting to the quarter zip he's wearing. He yanks at the hem, pulling the cotton over his head, then tosses it on the floor. "I'm going to melt."

"Open a window and stick your head outside. You'll be fine." I grin when he scowls again. "How was the weight room?"

"Hell. Much like the temperature in this apartment."

"And how is your ass from our fall on Wednesday?"

"Bruised beyond fucking belief. Playing last night was painful. How about your knee?"

"Fine. My ego is more damaged. Lexi caught the whole thing on camera, and it's humiliating." I shut the door behind him and turn the deadbolt. "Did you eat dinner?"

"I grabbed a sandwich on my way over. I can't go too long after a workout without putting fuel in my body."

"Want a tour?"

"Sure. If we can make a pitstop in Antarctica along the way, I'd be fucking grateful."

I nudge him with my elbow and lead him down the hall to the living room. "This is where I spend most of my time. I don't have a home office, so I do a lot of my work on the couch."

"It's bright, which comes as no surprise based on your wardrobe." Liam peers at the bookshelf in the corner and the potted plant with leaves that crawl down two shelves. He touches the stack of coasters I bought on a solo trip to Italy the second the divorce papers were signed, then glances at the pile of blankets on the ottoman. "Very you."

This is the first time I've had a man in my apartment, and I wonder what it looks like through his eyes.

I moved in after my separation, using the money from our prenup to create a home that's totally mine. To create a place that doesn't hold any ghosts from the past.

There are fresh coats of paint—yellow, blue, fuchsia, and green—on the walls. New finishes on the cabinets and kitchen drawers. Backsplash in the shower and a funky lamp on my bedside table.

It's my safe haven. A place full of all the love I missed out on for so many years, brought to life with photographs of me with my friends. Postcards that are displayed on the fridge from all my travel destinations. Tabs in my books that mark the scenes I hope to live out one day.

Like me, it's a work in progress. Something that's only getting better as time goes on, but it's *mine*.

"My last place was modern. Monochromatic and full of sharp lines. It felt so sterile in there. I hated it," I say.

Liam turns his attention to the bookshelf. "You like to read?"

"Yeah." I smile and run my finger down one of the spines. "I love to escape in a good book. Gives me hope in the world, you know? It's a shame you're not part of the boys' book club. I'd love to hear your opinions on dark romance."

"I'm dyslexic." His shoulders curl in as he says it, his tall frame nearly shrinking in half. "It takes me a while to read something, and I have a hard time imagining things creatively. I'd never survive in a book club."

"I had no idea."

"I like to think I hide it well."

"What about audiobooks? You could try the content in a different form."

"Does that count as reading? The guys would probably say I'm cheating."

"They absolutely would not. Audiobooks *are* reading, Liam, and they're a way to make stories accessible to everyone."

"Oh. Maybe I'll check one out then."

"Is your dyslexia why you don't like to talk to the media?" I sit on my couch and gesture for him to get comfortable wherever he wants. "You never do interviews."

He picks the chair by the fireplace and perches on the edge of it. "I don't like to talk to the media because I had a bad experience my rookie year in Minnesota."

"What happened?"

"This dickbag journalist started going in on my family. He asked if my mom's breast cancer showed any signs of coming back. Brought up my sister and her old party habits. Mentioned my dad and his job as a postal worker, as if it was beneath him. It's like I was a punching bag. I've never trusted anyone with a microphone since."

My heart almost shatters in two.

I knew there had to be a reason for his disdain.

Liam isn't an asshole.

He's blunt and closed off. Far from being a people person, but not malicious. Learning someone was purposely condescending to him in the name of journalism makes my blood boil. Makes me want to get the name of this jerk and make sure he never works in this league again.

"I'm so sorry that happened to you, Liam. I'm not excusing their behavior, because what they did was so shitty, but we're not all like that. I'd never talk about something so invasive."

"Doesn't change that it happened." A muscle in his jaw works, and I want to hug him. I want to tell him it's okay. I want him to know that for as long as he's with the team, I vow to *never* air out any of the personal details he wants to keep safe. "So, there you go. The reason why I'll never stand in front of a microphone again."

"Is your mom okay now?" I ask gently.

"Yeah. Been in remission six years."

Relief floods through me like a dam. "I'm so glad to hear that, and I'm really sorry for bringing up something so personal."

"Not your fault." He lifts his chin, eyes meeting mine. "You said you wanted to spend tonight getting to know each other?"

"We don't have to. I'm sure I can figure it out as we go and—"

"It's a good idea. Being around my family for four days is going to be tough if I don't know how you take *your* coffee. Let me guess: milk, six sugars, and some sort of hazelnut twist."

"I don't drink coffee. Caffeine can be an instigator for my migraines, so I stick to chamomile and hibiscus tea instead."

"How often do you get migraines?"

"Depends. Sometimes I go two or three months without having one. Other times I get one once a week. There's no rhyme or reason to it."

"Do you take medicine for them?" Liam asks.

"Over the counter stuff. The prescription drugs are too expensive to take regularly even with my insurance. I try to do acupuncture and visit the chiropractor, but every appointment adds up."

He rolls his lips together and stares at me, assessing me in a way that makes me feel on display. "I have a sensitive question to ask."

I draw my knees to my chest and wrap my arms around my legs. "Let's hear it."

"You have money, don't you? Your ex is a millionaire."

"How do you know he's a millionaire?"

"Casual internet information anyone could find if they wanted to." Liam pauses, and a stormy look clouds his dark eyes. "His nose is crooked."

"It *is* crooked, isn't it? He's so self conscious about it."

"Would be a shame if someone decked him in the face to even it out."

I tip my head back and laugh. "Please save the physical violence for the ice. As for the money, our prenup was iron clad. I was young and naïve and thought we would be together forever. I didn't bother to push for more ways to protect myself if the marriage dissolved. I ended up with enough to afford a place of my own, pay off some debt, put away savings, and that's about it. I can barely keep up with healthcare on my salary, but I *refuse* to ask him for more spousal support. He'd find a way to hang it over my head."

Liam stands. He walks to the couch and sits next to me. His touch is soft on the curve of my elbow, fingers pressing gently into my skin, and I glance over at him. "Do me a favor, Mitchell. The next guy you fall for, make sure he's not a tool with a punchable face."

"I like that that's the bare minimum for men now. You've got yourself a deal, Sullivan." I smile at him. "Is Alana your only sibling?"

"Yeah. I wouldn't have survived if there were two of her. She's a firecracker. I think you'll like her."

"I can't wait to meet her, even if it is under false pretenses."

"What about you? Siblings? Pets?"

"Nope. I'm an only child. God, is this what people do on first dates? It's so *boring*."

He shrugs. "Don't know. Haven't been on a first date in years."

"I never thought the bedroom might be the easy part. This is excruciating. Do you have pets?"

"I have a cat."

"*What*? Where was he when I came over?"

"Hiding. He hates people. Takes after me with that." Liam smiles and scratches at his beard. "His name is Pico de Gato, and I found him when I went on a school trip to Costa Rica. He wouldn't stop following me around, so I flew back after the trip and brought him home with me. Only understands Spanish, but we make do."

"Do you speak Spanish?"

"I'm fluent in it."

"Wow. I've learned more about you in five minutes than I have the whole time I've been with the Stars."

"I'm a boring person. I go to practice. I come home. I eat and sleep, and I repeat the cycle over and over again. There's hardly anything worth knowing in there. Do you speak any other languages?"

"I know sign language. I have a cousin who is Deaf, so I learned ASL when I was younger."

"Alana knows sign language too. You all can shit-talk without me knowing."

Silence settles between us, and I sigh. I reach out and play with the fringed edge of the blanket draped over the couch.

"I'm not sure what other questions I have," I admit. "There's probably a website out there that has a list, but I'm afraid to look at it. It's probably overwhelming."

"You have my number. You can text me if you think of something you're curious about."

"I figure you care about what your family thinks about your personal life, which is why you agreed to this fake dating thing in the first place. Being comfortable and familiar with each other would make things easier."

Liam hums, and I think I might have hit the nail on the head. "I'm not embarrassed that I'm single. It's more that I'm sick of all the questions. When am I going to have kids? Why haven't I settled down? Who am I dating?" It's his turn to sigh, but it doesn't sound like it holds any real frustration. "I'm twenty-nine. Hockey is the love of my life right now. It's not always going to be that way, but I want to enjoy *this* for as long as I can."

"There's nothing wrong with wanting to live in the moment. You have plenty of time to figure out what you want down the road."

"Appreciate the pep talk." He reaches over and wraps his fingers around my ankle. His thumb strokes up my calf, and I blow out a breath. "Do you want to keep talking, Piper? Or do you want to do something else?"

"Something else," I say, gathering the courage to tell him what I want and wondering how he's going to react.

Liam's eyes roam down my body, a hungry, greedy blaze behind his gaze. "Ready for another lesson?"

"What did you have in mind?"

"We're going to stick with what we did last time. Sex, even if it's only being used for pleasure, can be emotional, and I don't want to do too much too soon. We're going to ease into it to make sure you're comfortable."

"We can go slow," I hear myself say, but I think I might be out of my body. Craving his mouth on my skin and dreaming about how he'll make me come tonight. "Patience is a virtue, right?"

He tugs on my leg, hard enough to move me, and I suck in a ragged breath. My back presses against the seat of the couch as Liam runs his hand up my thigh and toys with the stitching of my lounge shorts.

"These are fucking distracting," he murmurs, his voice a husky rasp.

"Then take them off. I'd hate for you to be off your game, teach."

SEVENTEEN
LIAM

PIPER IS JUST as soft as I remember her being.

I savor her as I inch my hand higher, dipping under her shorts to the top of her hip. I graze over the waistband of her underwear, desperate to know if they're another lacy pair like she had on the other day.

Blue, maybe. Or bright pink.

I snap the elastic against her waist and hum when she hisses at the sting of pain. I smooth over the mark I left behind with my thumb, half tempted to rip the silk shorts in half so I can see how fucking perfect she is without any clothes.

"Did that hurt?" I ask, wanting to figure out more about her. Wanting her to figure out more about her. "Was it too much?"

"No." She shakes her head, blonde hair going everywhere. Her palms slide up the back of my shirt and she presses against my skin with warm hands. "It wasn't too much."

"Good." I nudge her knees apart and she wraps her legs around my waist. "We're going to do things a little differently tonight."

"Are we adding fingers this time?" Piper lights up, excitement in her eyes. "Or are you going to be a tease again?"

"I'm a tease because this is figuring out what you like. What gets you to the edge and makes you feel good. What fun would it be if we skipped the parts that can be just as nice as the real thing?"

I pull my hand out of her shorts and rest my palm on her stomach. She exhales, a ragged breath that has me buzzing with energy.

Fuck, the things I want to do to her.

I wanted to fuck her against the wall at the bar a few weeks ago. Wanted to put her on her knees and tie her hands behind her back. Wanted to drag her into the bathroom and set her on the counter so I could go down on her, tasting her pussy that I bet is sweet as hell until she moaned my name for everyone to hear.

And when I got to see her in skates?

Eyes wide and trusting as she followed my every instruction?

I liked that the most.

My restraint is growing thin.

I'm trying to do this right.

I'm trying to go slow so she's not anxious or self-conscious when she meets the next dude she wants to sleep with, but seeing her like this isn't doing a goddamn thing to help.

"You don't have to go easy on me. I'm not going to break, Liam. Why are you being such a nice guy?"

"You know what they say: nice guys finish last. And it's true." I move up her body to her chest. I pluck at her nipple, fucking delighted to find she's not wearing a bra. "I'm too busy watching you come first to care about winning."

She huffs out what I think is a laugh. I bring my mouth to hers and she lifts her chin, meeting me halfway.

"Are you going to finish tonight?" she murmurs, and the question is fucking wicked. "And if you are, can I watch?"

"Do you want to watch?'

"Yeah." She touches my cheek. Drags her thumb across

my beard and tugs on my bottom lip. "I want to see what you look like when you come. I want to see how big you are and how hard you can get. I want to see how you like to touch yourself so I can touch you like that too. I want to see if you make a mess."

I grab her jaw, and there's a shift in her breathing. Her lips curl into a smile that matches mine, like she's egging me on. Daring me to play a game with her, but she doesn't know she doesn't stand a chance with me.

"The only place I'm going to make a mess is down your throat or on your tits," I say.

Piper's eyes get even wider, and I worry I'm overdoing this.

I might hate talking to people in real life, but I've always been a talker in the bedroom. The guy who will walk you through it, step by step, and tell you exactly what I see. Exactly what I taste and hear.

For someone who, based on what she's told me, is probably used to silence in the sheets, this might be too vulgar. Way too forward. I say the word *pussy* and she blushes.

When she pushes up on her elbows and kisses me like we're going to fucking die tomorrow, though, I know this girl isn't as sweet as she thinks she is.

She has fantasies. Desires. Things she wants to try but is afraid to voice, and fuck if I'm not going to get them out of her.

"Bedroom," she says against my mouth, and I nod.

I stand without breaking our kiss and scoop her into my arms. I carry her down the hall, narrowly avoiding hitting her head on a picture frame.

"Which room?

"Left. No—" She dips her chin and kisses my neck. Runs her tongue up the line of my throat, and I almost lose my footing. "Your other left."

"This one?"

"No. The next one."

"There are three more doors, Piper. Is it the middle one or the one on the end?"

"Does it really matter? Pick a room, Liam. Any room. We can work with whatever real estate we find. Take us to the shower, for all I care."

"You don't think I'm going to fuck you in every room and against every wall?"

"Against the wall? What are the logistics behind that?"

"I'll take care of the logistics. You just have to hold on."

Piper exhales against my neck, her breath warm and her laugh sweet. "I don't like that you're doing all the work. I know I'm the student, but there seems to be an imbalance happening here. Share some of the load, Sullivan."

"You want to do some of the work?" I finally find what I think is her room and almost break the door in. I walk to her bed and set her on the mattress, taking a step back. "Show me how you touch yourself."

"*What?*" Piper blinks. "How does that help me learn what to do with a guy?"

"Because I'm going to watch you and tell you the things you like. You might not realize you like them because you haven't experienced them yet. I'm going to help read your body."

"I'm starting to think you're some woman whisperer," she mumbles, eyes looking everywhere but at me. I wait, letting her decide if this is something she wants to do. "Okay. But you can't make fun of me."

"I'd never make fun of you."

Her face softens and she nods. "Are we keeping our clothes on or off tonight?"

My dick throbs at the thought of her naked and spread out for me. It's tempting to give in and say *fuck it.* To be reckless and carefree, but I want to do this right.

She deserves it.

"On." My voice is hoarse. I'm so hard I have to adjust

myself over the front of my sweatpants. Her smirk is taunting, and I'd do just about goddamn *anything* to see her choke on my cock. "They'll come off next time."

Piper lies flat on her back and lifts her arms above her head. Her shirt moves up her stomach, and I get a glimpse of the underside of her tits. "How do I—should—where—"

"Touch yourself like you do when you're alone. Pretend like I'm not here." I pause and take off my shirt, throwing it to the side. She whines when she sees my bare chest, eyes roaming over my body unabashedly. I don't give a shit she's ogling me; I flex my muscles, showing off. "But I'll give you some inspiration."

"You're also inspiring me to go to the gym tomorrow." She laughs again and relaxes against the stack of pillows behind her. She bends her knees and spreads her legs, giving me a view of her covered pussy. "Will you come be close to me while I do it?"

I move before she can finish the question.

The last thing I want is for her to feel unwanted. Like she's doing this for me instead of herself. I crawl on the mattress and take up the space between her thighs again.

"What do you want, Piper?"

"You."

What a dangerous fucking word.

"Me?"

"Yeah. Kiss me, Liam."

I might be tough on the ice, but when she's under me, saying my name like I'm important, like I'm so much more than a hockey player who stops a couple goals every night, I'm goddamn *weak.*

I don't think there's anything she could ask for that I wouldn't give her.

So, I kiss her.

Softer this time, until she's making breathy little moans from the back of her throat. Until the fingers on one of her hands press into the muscles at my neck, urging me closer, and the others dip inside her shorts.

"It's been a while since I've done this," she whispers. I pull away and glance down at her, finding her eyes closed and her mouth parted slightly. "I've watched videos to figure out what I might like, but I haven't found the answer yet."

"Have you tried toys?" I rub my thumb over the curve of her knee. "Those sometimes work wonders."

"No. Maybe I should." Her back arches, nipples pointed and hard against her shirt. I can't see it, but I can *hear* it: the wet glide of her finger. The rhythm she settles into and her quiet groan. "I've never come from sex."

"Because you need more stimulation. You like to be touched somewhere more sensitive." I wrap my fingers around her wrist, guiding her hand out of her shorts. The hand in my hair drops away and rests on her stomach. I put my thumb over hers, leading her to her clit, and I press down on the spot she liked the other night. Her moan is louder this time, her legs snapping tight against my hips, and I grin. "There you go, Piper. That feels better, doesn't it?"

"*Fuck.* It doesn't feel better. It feels like heaven. How—" Her eyes squeeze shut and she gasps. Drops her head back and bites her bottom lip. "*Liam.* Can you—I need—" She grasps the sheets. "I want my fingers inside me again, but I can't get a good angle."

"Hang on." I pull my thumb off her and she groans, lifting her hips at the loss of contact. I tug on her shorts and work them down her thighs until they're hooked around her ankles. I slip them off and toss them to the pile with my shirt. "*Christ.*"

"What?" Her eyes fly open and she looks at me. "What did I do wrong?"

I shake my head, every ounce of self-control telling myself to not jerk off. To keep my hands on her, not my throbbing dick, because this isn't about me.

But seeing her in that white thong makes it *really fucking difficult* to behave.

Hunger like I've never experienced before rolls through me when I find a wet spot on the front of the cotton, her arousal clear and evident.

I want to wrap her underwear around my fist. I want to keep them in my pocket and find out what she tastes like. I want to rub them up and down my cock until I stain them with my cum.

"You didn't do a goddamn thing wrong. You're perfect, Piper."

She melts at the praise and tips her legs open wider. Her fingers disappear inside her underwear, and I never should've taken off her shorts.

Now I can see too much. Can hear too much. Can imagine it's my cock fucking her, not her pointer finger, and I watch with wonder as she angles her wrist to get deeper.

"Can you—" Piper pauses for a breath. "Could you touch my clit while I'm—"

"Fucking yourself?" I finish for her, and her face turns crimson.

"I think that will help me finish."

I crowd her space and hold myself over her. I bend forward, one hand resting on the mattress next to her head, the other teasing up her thigh. Circling her hip bone and dropping low on her stomach.

"Remember what we talked about last time?" I say low in her ear. "Don't think about it. I'm not here. Just take it, okay?"

She nods, exploring. The hand not in her underwear moves to her chest, and I watch her touch her tits. I watch her pinch her nipple through her shirt then hum in appreciation.

"Good," she whispers. "That feels so good."

I keep my mouth shut and let her sink into the moment without any distraction. I'm mesmerized by the way she tries a speed then changes her tempo, a few seconds faster, a few seconds slower.

She takes her time, drawing her pleasure out. When her breathing shifts, I push my thumb against her clit again.

"*Oh.*" Piper writhes on the sheets. "I like them both at the same time."

"Yeah?" I grunt and circle over her underwear. She cries out my name and it goes straight to my dick, a shot of adrenaline that makes me impossibly harder. "Are you close, Piper?"

"I think I am," she whispers, bobbing her head. "It feels like last time."

"You're doing so well, baby, and I can't wait to watch you fall apart for me."

That sends her over the edge.

Her legs convulse and her body trembles. A bead of sweat rolls down her cheek and her hips jerk up, the aftermath of the orgasm taking every bit of her energy.

I keep touching her, only slowing my thumb when she begs me to stop. After she calms down from the high, she groans. Cracks an eye open and looks up at me.

"How're you doing?" I ask, popping my thumb in my mouth and groaning at the faint taste of her.

"I'm so happy." Piper giggles and pulls her hand out of her underwear. Her fingers are wet from her pussy, and I stare at them like they're my last meal. "Why the hell has it never been that good when I've been by myself?"

I climb off her, standing so I can work out the cramp in my legs. "You like penetration, but you really like your clit being touched. My suggestion? You get a small vibrator you can use during sex. You can have a guy buried inside you and still get off."

She blinks at me, a dazed look in her eyes. "Do guys like when women use toys? It's not cheating or anything?"

I shrug. "Granted it's been a while, but I like when they

do. Why not? I want you to get off. Who cares if it's my fingers or something that vibrates?"

"Too bad your dick doesn't vibrate."

"The only special feature it has is glowing in the dark."

Piper bursts out laughing and rolls onto her side, smiling at me. "Should every orgasm feel that good?"

"Can't say I've been on the receiving end of an orgasm like that, believe it or not, so I can't give you the whole answer, but I imagine they can be. If you're doing them right."

"You're definitely doing something right, smart-ass." She stretches out her legs. There's a glint in her eye that wasn't there before. "You got to watch me, Liam. Do I get to watch you?"

EIGHTEEN
PIPER

LIAM'S BODY is a study in masculine beauty, and it's making my post-orgasm boldness waver because I'm so distracted.

Sharp features. Dark chest hair. Chiseled muscles from his shoulders to his abdomen. Everything about him is jaw-dropping, and I could stare for hours.

"Come here," he says roughly. I practically race across the bed to the edge of the mattress to be near him. "Do you want to see?"

"Nah. I think I'm all set," I tease, the joke falling short when he tugs his briefs down his thighs.

His cock springs free, and my tongue almost falls out of my mouth.

He's thick and big, inches longer than Steven and any of the men I've seen on the other side of my laptop screen. The crown glistens with pre-cum, and a fresh wave of assuredness rolls into me as I study him, not wanting to miss a thing.

I did that.

He's turned on because of *me*.

Of all the women in the world, *I'm* the one making him rock hard.

Maybe I'm not as bad in bed as I think I am.

I sit up on my knees. This close, I can see the tension in his jaw. The heat of his gaze and the soft breath he lets out when he wraps his fist around his shaft. He runs his thumb through the pre-cum and uses the moisture to coat his length, stroking up and down.

"You look like you have a question," he says with a strained voice. "What's on your mind?"

A lot of damn things.

I wasn't kidding when I told him Steven used to just put his dick in me. I've never watched a guy touch himself, and I wonder if there's a certain rhythm to it. A tempo they prefer and a pace they like best.

"How long does it take you to come?" I ask.

"Depends if I'm doing math in my head to keep from blowing a load." His throat bobs around a swallow. "Watching you touch yourself did a number on me, and I'm not too proud to admit it turned me the fuck on. I'm not going to last long."

"You like watching?"

"Yeah. More than touching sometimes." Liam's eyes lock on mine. He stares at me as he jerks himself off, and I don't know where to look. I want to see how heavy he is in my palm and how many tugs it would take for him to finish in my hand. Would he like it if I used my mouth? "Think it might just be you I like watching, though."

His soft admission, whether true or not, encourages me. I grasp the hem of my shirt, pull it over my head, and throw it with the rest of our clothes in the corner of the room. Liam whines when he sees my bare chest.

"*Piper*." My name comes out like a moan. A plea and barely above a gasp. His Adam's apple works as he drops his head back and grunts. "You don't have to."

"Look at me, Liam." His neck jerks forward and his eyes snap open. His attention moves to my chest when I press my breasts together, kneading the soft flesh. "I *want* to."

"Oh, *fuck*."

"Do you like what you see?" I ask.

"I thought about you in the shower the other night," he rasps, and it comes out slurred. Like he's a little tipsy and drunk on the sight of me. "The real thing is so much better."

I've thought about him too.

More than I should, probably, because we're *friends*, but I can't help it.

I've thought about big hands looping under my thighs and dragging me to the end of the bed. Fingers that push inside me, stretching me, followed by his thick cock. Both of us tumbling toward nirvana together, a mess of exhausted breaths.

"What can I do to help you? Do you want me to talk you through it? Stay quiet? Should I touch myself somewhere else?"

He shakes his head. The vein in his forearm pops under the tattoo of a a fern leaf. Sweat rolls down his neck and lands in the hollow of his throat. I have the urge to lick it away. "This is enough."

"It is?"

"Yeah. This is perfect. I'm serious when I say I'm not going to last long."

I've never been perfect or enough a day in my life. I smile, dizzy from his attention and the intimacy shrouding the room.

"That's the biggest compliment I've ever gotten. Almost as big as you. *God*. Look at you. You're going to fuck me with that thing? I'm going straight to the stars."

His laugh is muffled by a ragged groan. His strokes turn rough and uncoordinated as his control slips out of reach. Liam stares at me the whole time, his gaze full of want and desire, and I'm learning *this* is how I should be looked at in the bedroom. Not like I'm asking for too much or being a bother.

"I'm close," he grits out, and I watch his hand.

"You like to grip it tight?" I ask, and he nods. "You go all the way down and twist at the top. What about the head?"

"It all feels fucking good." He squeezes his eyes shut. His shoulders tense and his hand moves faster and faster, desperate for his own pleasure. "*Fuck*, Piper. I'm going to come."

"My chest," I tell him. "You can use me."

"Sit on your ass."

I hurry to get in position, not wanting to miss a goddamn thing.

Seconds later, his warm release lands on my breasts. He groans, loud and low. His movements slowly cease until he has nothing left inside of him. When he finishes, he takes a deep breath and almost falls over.

"Wow." I drag my fingers through his cum. I've felt the substance before, obviously, but never like *this*. Never in a spot so visible, like I'm being marked. "That was the hottest thing I've ever seen."

"Was it?" Liam uses his thumb to spread his cum across my chest. He circles my nipples and paints my skin a shade it's never been before. "Goddamn. I did make a mess of you. You look perfect."

"Really?"

"Yeah. Now I'm imagining you with cum on your face. Down your throat and on your ass."

My heart races in my chest imagining those things too. "Where do you usually finish?"

"On my stomach in my bed with a washcloth beside me."

"That doesn't sound sexy at all."

"Trust me, it's not."

"What about when you're with a woman?"

"C'mon, Pipsqueak. My memory isn't that good." He winces as he tugs on his softening cock one more time. "In a condom, I guess. Finishing on someone's tits definitely warrants a conversation prior to doing it. Imagine if I didn't give you any warning about what was about to happen."

"I probably would've dropkicked you."

"And it would've been deserved."

"You can clean up first." I gesture to the door on his right. "The bathroom is through there."

I watch Liam waddle away, pants shoved past his knees and his sculpted ass gloriously on display. When the door shuts, I lie on my back and stare at the ceiling. My heart races, and I grin at how the night has gone.

Heat rises on my skin when I touch my chest again, the reminder of him still on my breasts.

I never thought the male orgasm could be attractive. Steven would lie there. Make a noise or two, jerk a few times, and finish.

But Liam?

Liam is a work of art.

I'm committing the ways he moved his hands to memory, wanting to try them myself the next time we're together. I'm trying to remember the grunts he made so I can know if what I'm doing to him is working.

The door to my bathroom opens and snaps me out of my trance. Liam's pants are back in place, and he looks more put together than he did a few minutes ago.

"Your faucet leaks," he says.

"It does. I've been meaning to get maintenance in here to fix it, but I keep forgetting."

"I'll bring some tools next time I'm over."

"You know how to fix a faucet?"

"No, but YouTube does."

I laugh. "Sounds like I might end up with a flooded bathroom."

He holds up a washcloth. "Brought you something to clean up."

"Thank you." I reach out to take the damp rag, but he doesn't hand it over. "I can—"

The mattress dips under his weight. He wrings out the cloth and water rolls over my breasts. "I like this part. The caretaking."

"You do?"

"Yeah. I've always liked making sure people are okay."

"You hate people."

"Not everyone." He looks at me. "I tolerate some."

"Ah." I giggle when he gets close to under my arms. "Guess I'm one of the lucky ones."

"Ticklish?"

"Very. My feet too. Touch them and I'll scream."

"Noted." Liam moves the rag away and bends down to grab my shirt. "I think you're all set."

"Thank you." I slip the clothing over my head. "Are you heading out?"

"Do you want me to head out?"

I glance at my bed with longing.

I'm aching to be hugged. To be shown nonsexual physical affection after doing deeply intimate things.

It sounds silly and cheesy and—god forbid—romantic—but I've always been happiest when I'm holding someone's hand. When their arms are around me. The touches ground me. They calm the worries I have about asking for too much.

"Sure. Whatever you want."

"Piper. What did we talk about with communication?"

"That I need to do it." I sigh. "Do you think you could stay for a few minutes? Maybe lie with me?"

"That wasn't hard, was it?"

"Debatable. My palms are sweating."

Liam lifts my hands and wipes them with the clean corner of the washcloth. "All better."

Emotions hit me all at once, and I have the urge to cry.

Between the outstanding orgasms and feeling sated in a

way I've never experienced, the adrenaline of watching Liam, and the anticipation about what's going to happen the next time we're together...

Everything is swirling in my head, and I need a second.

I wipe under my eyes. "Sorry. I'm making this weird."

"I told you sex is emotional." He lifts his chin toward the pillows. "Get comfortable."

I lay on my side and stare at the wall. The duvet cover rustles behind me and then Liam is wrapping his arms around my waist. Pulling me close to his chest and breathing warm air against my neck.

"Is it normal to ask someone to hang out after you hook up with them?"

"Personal preference. Some people can't wait to leave. Others need a little more time. There's no right or wrong answer."

"Good to know." I sigh and relax into him. "Are you doing anything fun this weekend?"

"No. We have four games over the next seven days, so any chance I can sit around and relax, I will."

"Any plans for Thanksgiving?"

"Hoping the DC Titans can keep their perfect season—and my fantasy football team—alive. I'll watch the game. That's about it."

I spin in his hold, wanting to see him while we talk. "Are all professional athletes friends with each other? Is there some cool club you're a part of where you need a password to enter? Something like, *douche canoe*? Or *big bucks millionaires*?"

His laugh shakes my chest. "Shockingly, no. Some of us share the same agent. A lot of people run in the same circles. I try to be cordial enough with everyone I meet, but I'm not buddies with them. I did go to college with Colton Clark who plays basketball in Orlando."

"That guy is a phenom."

"No kidding. He's younger than me, but we've done a few promo things for the school."

"Who's the most famous person you have in your phone?"

"You think very highly of me. I told you I'm boring."

"Come on. There has to be someone impressive."

"I might have Ella Wright's number. Or, her publicist's number, at least. Maybe I deleted it."

"You've talked to the world's *biggest* pop star? *How*?"

"Charity event a couple years ago. Nice woman. Catchy music, too."

"And here I was thinking I was cool because you and I have texted a few times. Then you go and one-up me with the biggest flex of all time." I huff. "Let me go back into my hole of being a nobody."

"You're very cool, Blondie. And definitely a somebody."

"You changed nicknames on me." I touch his chest and trace the outline of his muscles. "What happened to Pipsqueak?"

"Dunno." Liam shrugs and tucks a lock of hair behind my ear. "I don't want you to think I'm insulting your size or calling you meek. Figured I could switch it up."

"If you were five-foot-six with a small dick, I'd probably be offended. Given you're a giant with a massive cock, I'll allow it."

He bursts out laughing, and it's the most beautiful sound I've ever heard. I want to bottle it up so I can listen to it again. I want to tell him all the jokes in the world so I can see his mouth split into a wide grin.

"Wow. That made my whole day."

"More than the orgasm?"

"It's pretty close."

"I didn't know complimenting your dick would be a game changer, but I'm glad I could help."

"It's not about complimenting my dick. Which, thank you, by the way." He pulls back a bit and takes my chin between his fingers. "It's because you're getting more sure of yourself. Two weeks ago, you wouldn't have said that to me. Now look at you: you're a dick stroker."

"If only. Someone won't let me stroke anything yet."

"What was that saying about patience being a virtue you mentioned earlier?"

"Yeah, yeah, yeah. Am I taking up too much of your time? Pico must miss you."

"Doubt it. I bet he's grateful to get rid of me."

"No way. You're probably the best cat dad out there."

"The highest accolade I could have, to be honest. Fuck the Stanley Cup."

A yawn escapes me. "I'm going to close my eyes. You wore me out."

Liam rests his hand on my hip and squeezes. "Sweet dreams, Piper."

My muscles relax and my limbs get heavy. Sleep threatens to overtake me, and just as I'm slipping into unconsciousness, I dream Liam kisses my forehead.

NINETEEN
PIPER

STEVEN

I've sent you a dozen emails, Piper. Are you going to respond to any of them?

I really don't want to have to get my lawyer involved, but I will.

Can you take five minutes out of your very not busy day to look at them?

ME

Are you going to Maverick and Emmy's tomorrow for Thanksgiving?

LIAM

Yeah. Beats cooking dinner for one.

ME

Do you like to cook?

LIAM

I do. Just not a whole turkey. Pico and I can't eat that much.

ME

I heard some of the guys say they have personal chefs. Hudson was complaining that his quit the other day. Do you have one?

LIAM

Nah. Being in the kitchen is a nice way to shut off my brain after a long day on the ice.

ME

You like to stab things with knives, don't you?

LIAM

It's a good anger management lesson. Better onions than someone who pisses me off.

ME

Uh oh. Who pisses you off?

LIAM

Everyone.

Tonight? Ethan fucking Richardson. Kid has too much energy for his own good. We had to skate twenty extra laps after practice because he and Grant wouldn't stop goofing off.

ME

You're twenty-nine and calling your teammates kid? Okay, boomer.

LIAM

I feel one hundred.

ME

When is your birthday?

LIAM

June 27th. You?

ME

August 19th.

LIAM

Alana is going to try and chart our astrological compatibility. Tell her it's a load of shit and she'll stop.

ME

I'd never insult an astrology girl. We're going to be best friends!

"SORRY I'M LATE!" I announce in the foyer of Maverick and Emmy's place. I slip off my shoes and shake out of my coat without dropping the dessert I brought. "And I have pie!"

"Little P!" Ethan scoops me up in a hug and spins me around. "There you are."

"I know you're only greeting me because you want food."

"Guilty." He sets me down. "We're growing boys. You know we can't go ten minutes without eating."

"You aren't kidding, are you?"

"Dead serious. I'm glad you're here. It's not the same without the whole gang around, and I was starting to worry something happened to you."

"I'm alive and well." I pat his shoulder and follow him down the hall. "I was feeling under the weather this morning. The road trip kicked my ass."

"You mean North Dakota kicked your ass. Place was fucking freezing." He tosses a grin over his shoulder. "Better than Florida. That place is a nightmare."

"At least it'll be warm when we're down there next week."

We round the corner into the kitchen, and I wave hello to everyone. The team is already here, drinks in hand as they enjoy the spread of appetizers on the island. A TV blares from the living room, coverage for the Titans game underway, and I'm instantly warmer being surrounded by my favorite people in the world.

"Hi, babe." Lexi kisses my cheek and passes me a water. "Happy Thanksgiving, my little Piper Pumpkin."

"Happy Thanksgiving, Lex." I set the pie on the counter and hug her tight. "God, you look good. How many days a week are you doing Pilates?"

"Six. It's put me in a really good headspace these last couple of months. I'm tired as hell going from the arena to teaching in the evenings, but I'm feeling very positive and centered lately. It must be working."

"I'm so happy for you. We need to get the team to another class. Watching them suffer on the Reformer was worth the week of sore muscles."

"That was hysterical. There's nothing like watching grown men almost cry. Especially when you have a hand in their demise." She grins at me. "You look particularly glowy today."

I touch my cheeks, my skin windburned from the walk over in the cold. "Thanks. It's borderline hypothermia."

"I mean you look happy. What's your secret?"

"Being divorced and free from a shitty relationship?" I joke with a laugh. "I don't have a secret. Not really. Work is going well. The team is playing well. I got hit on at the grocery store last night, so I'd say things are looking up."

"*Oh?* Was he cute?"

"Yeah. He's not my usual type, but seeing how poorly things with the last guy I thought was my type turned out, that's not a turn off. I've seen him in the spice aisle before."

"And you haven't said hi to him?"

"Given I feel unloveable half the time, I'm not sure I have

the courage to interact with him. But maybe I should try. That's what my therapist says."

"That's my girl." She slings her arm around me and kisses my cheek. "Any word from douche bag extraordinaire lately?"

"Yeah, unfortunately." I sigh and rest my head on her shoulder. "A text yesterday morning. I ignored it. No use dredging up old stuff, you know?"

"If you want him gone, just say the word. I have people who can take care of it."

"*Take care of it*? What, is this a hitman thing?"

"I mean, kind of? A friend of a friend is friends with the President's daughter, and her bodyguard is a trained sniper. He could make it look like an accident and no one would ask questions."

"Thank you for looking out for me, but I think I'm going to keep my homicide count at zero for now." I scour the kitchen, smiling at Connor tossing grapes in Riley's mouth. "I know Maven is at the Titans game out west, but where the heck is Emmy?"

"Trying to stop Maverick from wearing an inflatable turkey costume. She's losing that battle."

"That's got to be a sight." I laugh and squeeze her waist. "I'm going to do a lap. I'll be back."

The boys all greet me with bright smiles and kisses on the top of my head. Grant pulls me into a video he's making for social media. Hudson distracts me with a conversation about romance novels that lasts fifteen minutes. I listen to Ethan complain about a hot dog stand in the arena, trying to look interested but ending up really confused.

When I finally break free from all the mayhem, I wind up in the empty dining room and take a breath. I massage my temples, the phantom ache of pain throbbing across my forehead. When I look up, I gasp at the sight.

"Wow," I whisper.

A long table arranged with lit candles extends from each

end of the room. The white tablecloth is neatly pressed, and a bouquet of beautiful marigolds sits in the middle of the setup.

I'm used to this space being empty, used for mini hockey games at team dinner. There are marks on the walls from the soft pucks the guys fire at each other. A whiteboard next to the door has a score table going, and I see poor Hudson is at the bottom of the leaderboard.

"I was on napkin folding duty," Liam says from behind me.

I laugh and spin around. He's leaning against the wall and looking *good*. "You were not."

"I was. Do you think any of those other knuckleheads could sit still long enough to do this?"

"No. Just you, Liam."

"Happy Thanksgiving, Piper."

"Happy Thanksgiving." I give him a once-over and quirk a brow. "What the hell is on your socks? Is that an alien?"

"Wow. That's fucking rude. It's Pico."

"*Aw.*" I move closer and see the socks have the cat's face printed on them. "Did he get those for you himself?"

"Why do you think I'm so rich? It's not because I'm a good goalie. It's because my cat has opposable thumbs."

"Damn. I'm in the wrong industry."

"It's a lucrative market." Liam stands up straight and towers over me. "You good? You were holding your head a second ago."

"I'm fine." I smile brightly at him. "I've been under the weather all morning. Worn out, you know? I have a little bit of a headache, but I'm persevering."

"Do you need—"

"*There* you are." Emmy walks into the dining room, interrupting him. She hugs me tight. "I was worried you got roped into playing video games, and I know how terrible you are at *Call of Duty*."

"Not my strong suit."

She moves her attention to Liam. "We're going to start doling out the food in a few minutes. I know you don't like the pushing and shoving, so feel free to get a move on."

"I appreciate the head start."

Emmy's eyes flick between us. "Are you two behaving yourselves?"

"If by behaving ourselves you mean admiring the napkins Liam folded, then, yes, we are," I say. "Though you know how scandalous setting a table can get."

"Mhm." A loud crash comes from the kitchen and she groans. "Fucking hell. I knew we shouldn't have used the nice plates. Maverick and I made a bet on how many would get broken tonight."

"Let me know the spread and I'll knock a few off if it works in your favor." Liam puts his hands in the pockets of his jeans and looks past her shoulder. "You want some help with that?"

"I've got it. Thank you, though. Glad you both are here."

When Emmy disappears, I give Liam a sheepish smile. "I might have told the girls about our arrangement. I blame the wine I'd been drinking." I hide my *Please don't hate me* expression behind my hands. "Hence her not-so-subtle innuendo."

"Lovely. Now Maverick is going to give me shit and I'll never hear the end of it."

I wince. "Sorry. I'm not giving them any details, only that I propositioned you."

"It's fine. I figured you'd tell them eventually. They're your best friends, and keeping a secret from them would be shitty. If Maverick says anything, I'll kick his ass."

"I'd like to see that. They know I wanted to explore in the bedroom, and it would've been impossible to hide why I'm walking funny when you eventually fuck me. What would I say? My ass is sore from riding a bike?"

He snorts. "I'm not going to rearrange your insides, Piper."

"Are you sure about that? As for my friends, I swore them to secrecy. None of us would ever violate girl code."

"Girl code?" Liam wrinkles his nose. "The fuck is that?"

"Unspoken rules of womanhood like not dating a friend's ex. Holding her hair back if she's sick. Talking her out of bangs when she's intoxicated and thinks she can pull off a new hairstyle. Keeping your girlfriend's secret from your partner because she asked you to." I bite back a laugh at his confused expression. "Those kinds of things."

"Women," he mumbles. "So fucking complicated."

"No more complicated than *you*, Scowly McScowlerson."

"Look who's coming up with the witty nicknames now."

"Is that why you don't date during the season? Because we're complicated?"

"I don't date during the season because it's distracting and bleeds too much into hockey. It's why I haven't invited you to my hotel room at an away game. This part of my life is first during the season. I don't need an orgasm to survive."

"Huh." I tap my cheek. He *hasn't* asked me to come to his room when we've been on the road. I figured it was because he was tired from practice or jet lag, and his reasoning makes sense. "Interesting."

"Any other questions about my personal life before we start on the sweet potatoes, Pipsqueak?"

"About a million. I won't be able to get to them all, and that's disappointing."

"I'll give you a freebie during the green bean casserole course," he says, turning for the kitchen. "Only because I really fucking hate green beans."

I SIT BACK in my chair, stuffed from a delicious meal. Half the food was catered by the most popular restaurants in town, and I don't think I can eat another bite.

"This was so good." Lexi sets her napkin on her plate and groans. "Someone is going to have to roll me out of here."

"Give me ten minutes and I'll be ready for round two," Ethan says.

"We have a game tomorrow," Hudson draws out. "If you puke, I'm not going to be happy."

"Okay, Dad." Ethan rolls his eyes. "Some of us are young and have a faster metabolism than you."

"I'm going to shove you into the boards if we have to skate more laps because of you." Riley glares at Ethan across the table. "Do you ever shut up?"

"Settle down, children." Maverick taps his wineglass with a knife and stands. He ditched the inflatable turkey costume halfway through the meal, and he looks downright *pissed* to be in normal clothes. "I'd like to say a few words."

"Uh oh. It's never good when Cap wants to say a few words," Grant whispers, and everyone bursts out laughing. "We're going to be here for an hour."

"You get to do ten extra laps before the game tomorrow for that comment, Everett. You all know I'm not one to be serious, but I want to be for a few minutes. First, thank you for being here. When I think about the word thankful, a couple things come to mind. At the top of that list is my Emmy girl. The life we share and the careers we get to do side by side. There's no one else I'd rather have kick my ass in a game, baby." He glances down at her, a wide beam on his face. "Then I think about you all. I couldn't pick a better group of players to go through the grind of practice and games with. Day in and day out, you all are there cheering me on. Calling me out on my bullshit. Making me a better leader and a better player. I know we haven't won the Cup yet, but we're close. I can feel it, and I wouldn't want to do it with anyone else."

"Shit, man." Grant grabs his napkin and blows his nose. "You didn't tell us we were getting into the deep stuff today."

"We were supposed to eat turkey and play video games,

not cut our hearts open. Fucker." Ethan wipes his eyes. "Not cool, Miller."

"You'll get over it." Maverick looks down at Emmy again. I'm not sure I've ever seen someone so happy. "I know we fuck around and have a good time, but for a second, I want us to be serious. I want us to share something we're thankful for. It doesn't have to be anything big, but I swear to god, Ethan, if you say someone's boobs, I'm going to strangle you."

"You're putting us on the spot here, Cap. That means you have to go first," Riley says, and everyone murmurs in agreement.

"That's easy. I'm thankful for the love of my life. The family we're going to start trying to have soon and the chance to be a dad. I never had that growing up, and getting to be a parent with my favorite person in the world makes me a real lucky bastard."

Everyone tells us what they're thankful for.

Hudson goes the deep route with self-reflection.

Ethan doesn't mention anyone's chest, but he does mention his three motorcycles.

Grant surprises me when he talks about the nonprofit he's working with to give young women a foot in the door to the world of sports.

When it gets to be my turn, I hesitate.

"I have a lot to be thankful for over the last few years, but if I had to narrow it down to a few things, it would be new opportunities, growth and confidence. I have a long way to go, but as someone who wasn't sure what was waiting for her on the other side of a broken relationship and my whole life getting uprooted, I'm proud of how far I'm come." I laugh and wipe my hands on my skirt. "Okay, wow. That got very personal, very fast, and I'm sorry for over sharing. Ethan, please talk about someone's chest and save me."

"Oh, Little P. Now you're speaking my—"

"Knock it off." Maverick rolls his eyes. "I'm going to tell

you the same thing we told Emmy. You're part of us, Piper. If someone hurts you, they have to deal with us. And I like our odds."

"You're the last one, Goalie Daddy," Riley says. "Are you gonna tell us what you're thankful for?"

"Patience," Liam says.

"Wow. That was *so* insightful." Ethan smirks. "Probably the wisest thing I've ever heard. Care to elaborate there, Sullivan?"

"Nope."

"C'mon. You know GK is a man of almost zero words."

Conversation picks up around me about the game tomorrow, but I'm not listening.

I'm too busy watching Liam and trying to understand what, exactly, he's being patient for.

TWENTY
PIPER

"I CAN'T BELIEVE it's already December." Lexi sits next to me on her living room couch and groans. "This year is going by way too fast."

"I miss the days when I was a photographer for the NFL, not the NHL. It was so nice to be done with the season in February." Maven sighs and sips her water. "We're only two months into the season with *weeks* to go. I'm exhausted."

"I'm bruised in places I didn't know I could bruise." Emmy rubs her forearm, a purple mark sitting above her wrist. "Damn pads are doing little to keep me from getting injured."

"Meanwhile I'm over here wishing the season would slow down. I love my job." I rest my chin in my hand and smile. "I've had fun every year I've covered hockey, but this one is by far the best."

"A toast to our superstar rinkside reporter." Lexi lifts her glass, and we all follow her lead. "To knocking down sexist pigs and taking the job that's rightfully yours."

I sip my wine and laugh. "You all are the best cheerleaders. Thanks for being my support squad."

When I filled the girls in on the whole story involving my promotion, they were, as expected, livid.

There was crying.

Anger.

Lots of yelling and plans to ruin my former boss's life.

It was hard to go through that situation, but having them by my side has made it easier.

"Speaking of December, how's it going with Liam?" Lexi asks. "Have you two banged yet?"

I almost spit out my drink. "*Jesus*, Lex. Could I get some warning next time? A segue before we dive into my sex life would be nice."

"When have I *ever* been discreet? That's not my style."

Liam told me I can talk to the girls about our arrangement, but I'm not sure I want to.

I'm hesitant to tell them about the low rasp of his voice. How his teeth bite my bottom lip and the look on his face right before he comes, half full of wonder and half full of insane lust.

It feels wrong to share parts of his private life with other people, especially after he told me about his bad experience with a reporter.

He's my friend, and I don't like thinking I'm betraying him if I give away specifics so freely.

"No," I finally say. "We're going slow."

"Wow." Emmy smirks. "I'm not sure I've ever met a guy who thinks with his head instead of his dick when it comes to sex."

"Sometimes waiting is more fun," Maven tells us with a sly grin. "It makes you *really* want it."

"I didn't think I'd like having to wait, but I'm learning so much about myself."

"Like what?"

"Well, I found out I like foreplay, when that was something I never used to consider. I'm not going to run off and have a one-night stand tomorrow, but it's empowering to finally be almost sure of myself. I'm getting back the pieces that belonged to someone else, and now they're finally my own."

"Goddamn. I love women," Lexi says. "We're so strong, aren't we?"

"It amazes me how you've stayed so positive the last few years," Emmy adds. "I know I'm not all sunshine and rainbows, but you've been through hell, Piper. You find out the man you love is having an affair—that alone would've led me to do something that would get me sent to jail. You get divorced. Your boss absolutely *sucked* and said horrible shit about you. But look at you. You're practically fucking glowing. When you could've given up, you didn't. How the hell do you do it?"

"When my world was falling apart, it was like my brain knew it wasn't the end of my story. It was the end of a chapter. Would I do it again if I had the choice? God, no. Divorcing an egocentric workaholic who refuses to take responsibility for his actions is draining. But Steven cheating on me was the best thing that could've ever happened. Imagine if I spent forty years in a soul-sucking marriage where I never got the things I needed? Where I never heard I was doing a good job or that he was proud of me? I can live without sex, but I can't live without being hugged, and he *never* wanted to hug me." I pause for a breath. "I'm so glad I only wasted ten years of my life, not half a century."

"Me too. And this next part of your story is going to be even better," Maven says.

"It already is." I laugh, desperate to tell them something *good* in my life for once. "I've orgasmed more with Liam in a month than I did my entire relationship with Steven."

"Shut the fuck up," Lexi squeals. "*Hell yeah.* That's our girl."

"I never thought I could be happy about my friend's

orgasm count, but here I am, *ecstatic*." Maven claps. "You deserve a hundred more."

"Okay. That's enough about me. Someone else tell us something fun. Did you all get your gala dresses yet? It's a week away," I say.

"I got mine," Maven says. "But I might not go. I've been so tired lately, and a party where I'll have to be on my feet all night sounds miserable."

"You love parties." Emmy frowns. "Are you sick?"

"Sick? No." She pauses and rests her hand on her stomach. "I'm pregnant."

One second, I can hear out of my right ear. The next, I can't.

We all scream.

Lexi almost tackles Maven and I burst into tears. Emmy wraps her arms around her, creating a dogpile, before I yell at them to not hurt the baby.

When the dust settles, we're one big blubbering mess. I'm not sure who is crying more: the hormonal mother-to-be, or her three best friends.

"Details," I say. "We need the full story."

"Dallas and I have been trying for a while. Nothing was happening, so we decided to go in for testing. The doctor said everything came back normal and to be patient. Well, after seven months of being patient, thinking it wasn't going to happen for us and looking into adoption agencies, I took a test. It was positive."

A fresh wave of tears hits me. "I'm so happy for you."

I know how much Maven loves being a mom.

She's always excited about her career and supporting Dallas, but she was *made* to be a mother. Her adoration for June is out of this world, and there's no doubt in my mind that Lansfield Kid #2 will be any different.

"We're so happy too. Dallas is at Mav's tonight with some of the guys, and he's planning on telling them while he's there.

We wanted to do a big announcement at team dinner next week, but I couldn't wait. I wanted you all to know. You're my sisters, and I hope you'll love me when I'm in bed by eight and can't go out because I'm so damn tired. I don't want to know what it's going to be like come April and May. I'll probably fall asleep standing up."

"We can do a *Weekend at Bernie's* bit when we go out to dinner," Lexi says. "We'll scare so many people. It's going to be great."

Emmy's phone dings with a notification, and she laughs. "I think Dallas must have told the guys. Maverick just sent me a photo, and his eyes look red and swollen from crying." She holds up the screen, and we all giggle at the picture. "That man is the biggest fucking softie."

"What does it say under the photo?" Lexi squints at Emmy's phone. "*Come home. Going to fuck you six ways to Sunday until I put a baby inside you too. Don't care if the guys are still here.* Wow. And they say chivalry is dead."

"Whoops." Emmy's cheeks turn as red as her hair and she shoves the phone under her thigh. "Ignore that."

"Six ways to Sunday? Is that a new move?" Maven teases. "I haven't tried that one yet."

"You've tried *something* that works."

Before I can join in on the ribbing, my own phone buzzes on the end table. I pick it up, surprised to see Liam's name.

We text occasionally. He'll send me a message now and then. A check in after practice. Asking how my day is going and if I've had enough to eat. A few days ago, when I told him I hadn't had lunch yet, he marched up to the broadcasting offices in his pads and a sweaty jersey, put a sandwich on my desk and left without saying a word.

Sometimes he'll send me pictures. A photo of Pico, blurry from the tabby cat running out of the frame. A view of the night sky when he said to go outside and look at the full moon.

They're all short. Barely more than four or five words. From someone else, I might consider it an afterthought. A throwaway conversation to pass the time or ask when we're going to hook up.

With Liam, they mean something, and I'm lucky to have a friend like him.

LIAM

I'm assuming you heard the news too?

ME

Wait a second. You're at Maverick's? Spending time with people? Are you ill??

LIAM

I'm a social butterfly now, Mitchell.

ME

Oh, this is like one of those kidnapper things where someone else has your phone, isn't it? There's no way this is the Liam Sullivan I know.

Blink twice for help.

LIAM

Attachment: 1 image

ME

Sorry. Can't say I'm too familiar with your middle finger.

LIAM

Might as well learn to be. I'm going to fuck you with it soon.

Two at first. We'll work up to three.

I know I'm bigger than the prick you were with before so it'll take some getting used to.

I let out a squeak and drop my phone. Maven looks over at me, concerned.

"Are you okay?" she asks.

"Fine," I almost yell. "Work things. Thing. A thing at work. Maybe it's food poisoning? I'm not sure. I'm going to use the bathroom."

I launch up to my feet and almost sprint down the hall. Locking the door behind me and leaning against the wall, I read his message again.

I'm going to fuck you with it soon.

It's the next step in our lessons, and I've been anticipating it since he got me off using only his thumb.

What the *hell* is it going to be like when he actually pushes inside me?

ME

Are you sexting me around your teammates?

LIAM

No. I'm in the elevator heading to my car with my kidnapper.

A laugh races out of me.

ME

Tell your kidnapper to look the other way. I don't want him reading this next part.

LIAM

He's staring at the ceiling and not paying attention. Seems like a nice guy.

ME

Do you really think I can take three of your fingers?

LIAM

You can take everything I give you, Piper.

I fan my face. My skin is an inferno, and I think I'm

burning alive.

ME

And when is this happening?

LIAM

Eager?

ME

No. Just want to check the calendar and make sure I'm free.

LIAM

Busy next few weeks. Charity gala. Christmas.

How about before our road trip to Vegas?

ME

You're making me wait until the end of December?

You're cruel.

LIAM

Patience, virtue, etc.

ME

Hate you, etc.

LIAM

No, you don't.

No, I decide, holding my phone to my chest, a giddy smile on my face and my heart thumping under my hand. *I don't.*

TWENTY-ONE
LIAM

I'VE ALWAYS HATED the holiday charity gala the Stars put on.

Every year, two weeks before Christmas, I'm stuck standing at the bar in a fancy hotel, miserable as I sip a seltzer with lime because I have a game the next day.

There are too many people. Too many handshakes and conversations about what I could've done better in the last game, as if Joe Robertson, the season ticket holder with the beer belly who has never stepped foot on the ice, is someone I should take advice from.

It's also loud as fuck in here.

"Hey." Hudson nudges my side and I blink at him. "Are you ready for the auction?"

"No."

"Same. I really hate this part of the night."

"So do I," I grumble under my breath. "Can't I write a fucking check instead? I don't need soccer moms fighting over me."

"At least they revamped it. Remember when the prize was an outing at a place of the highest bidder's choosing? Now it's a night in the arena with all the players, a nice dinner, and no opportunity for any extracurricular activities."

"Still can't believe that guy pinned Riley to the wall, licked his ear, asked if he could pee on him, then took his dick out before Riley could answer. I'm not one to kink-shame, but that kind of shit is vile without consent."

"Almost as bad as the fan clubs at away games." Hudson laughs. "Did you bring anyone tonight?"

"You know the answer to that."

"Right. Single Sullivan. Just the way you like it."

"Did you?"

"Yeah. Her name is Alyssa. I started seeing her a couple months ago, and things are going well. I like her a lot, man."

Hudson is different from any other athlete I've met. He's rarely aggressive on the ice, and that tenderheartedness you see when you interact with him is genuine.

He's a nice fucking guy. A total empath, he loves things deeply: his dogs. His friends. His family back home in Georgia.

He's also a hopeless romantic.

Has been from the day he first introduced himself to me. He believes in fairytales and happily ever afters. Love at first sight and all that other bullshit. A serious relationship-ist, he's someone who dates with the purpose of having a future with a woman and has never had a one-night stand.

I think he'd pass out if someone slept with him and snuck out without contacting him again.

"Happy for you, Hud."

"Thanks." He points through the crowd. "There she is."

I look in the general direction of where he's gesturing. Before I can figure out if he's talking about the brunette or the redheaded woman, a flash of blonde catches my eye. I turn my head half a degree to the right and there, directly across the ballroom, is Piper, looking right at me.

It's the first time I'm seeing her tonight, and it's a punch to the gut.

Her silver dress hugs her curves and her hair flows down her back like ribbons of sunshine. When she reaches to set her glass down on a server's tray, my heart nearly skips a beat.

The back of the dress is even better than the front, complete with a low dip in the material that shows off so much fucking skin.

She's beautiful.

Show-stopping, and I'm practically gawking.

My throat goes dry. When she smiles at me, big and bright and fucking devastatingly, I shove my straw in my mouth and take a long sip of my drink, wishing it were something stronger.

I'm not looking at her like she's my friend.

I'm not looking at her as a man who has his priorities sorted out and isn't interested in anything serious.

I'm looking at her like my heart is about to flatline. Like I'm close to meeting my end, and this is the first time in my life I've ever regretted being a professional athlete.

If I was a doctor or a teacher or fucking *anything* besides a star goalie paid millions of dollars to be damn good at my job, I'd take her out on a date. I'd woo her and show her how a man should treat her inside and outside a bedroom.

But I'm not.

So I lift my hand in a pathetic wave instead. Her eyes bounce to the empty spot to my left and I nod, inviting her over.

"Hey." Hudson nudges my side. I blink and snap out of my trance. "You okay?"

"*Great*," I grunt. "I'm great."

"I'm going to steal my date back. I'll catch up with you later?"

"Yup. Sounds good."

I have no clue what I'm agreeing to. I'm too distracted by

the sway of Piper's hips. The plunging neckline of her dress and the necklace resting between her cleavage. Heels that give her added height and the bright red lipstick painted on her mouth.

I want to smear it with my thumb.

I want it on my cock, a souvenir from fucking her throat and making her swallow.

My fingers grip my glass so tightly, I don't know how it doesn't shatter.

The whole outfit is sinful.

Goddamn indecent, honestly, and knowing what's underneath those thin straps and silky material is a hazard to my health.

Every man in the room watches her as she moves toward me like some sort of goddess. Even my teammates do a double take. I want to break Grant's neck for how long he stares at her, but I'm no better.

"Hey," she says when she gets close, and I wish she had stayed away.

I wish I hadn't spotted her, because now that I have, I smell her perfume. I see the dark blue makeup on her eyelids. I feel the heat radiating from her, and I don't fucking know why I want to curl up beside her in my bed and keep her there.

My crush on her has only gotten worse now that I know what she sounds like when she comes. The moans she lets out when I touch her clit and the way her toes curl when I pinch her nipples nice and hard.

Piper Mitchell is under my skin, and the next time I touch her, I won't be so nice.

"Pipsqueak," I say, clawing for any sort of normalcy.

"How's your night?"

"How do you think it is?"

She tilts her head to the side and assesses me. "Miserable, by the looks of it. Could you just—" Her fingers touch the edge of my mouth, lifting it up in a fake smile, and she grins. "There we go. Much better."

"Don't make me look too approachable. I can't stand another thirty-minute lecture from a guy who played in a beer league twenty years ago and thinks he's qualified to give out unsolicited advice about my technique."

"Come on, Liam. Surely you know his years playing Sunday rec games far outweigh your experience in the NHL. You should definitely listen to him."

I snort. "I'd rather listen to the pointers Grant tries to give me. At least he knows the rules about high-sticking."

"I almost feel bad for the person who bids on Grant at the auction and wins. They're going to have to deal with his restless energy for hours."

"Don't remind me about the auction."

"Oh, no. Have you had a bad experience? I think the whole idea is ridiculous, to be honest. If we were doing this with women, people would be outraged. But with hot guys who play hockey, it's okay? Talk about a double standard."

"Wow." My lips twitch. "You think I'm hot?"

"How is that the only thing you heard out of that whole speech?" She puts her hands on her hips, and I wonder if she's wearing underwear. There's no way she could be with how tight her dress is on her skin. "Are you even listening to me?"

"Course I am. You're talking about hockey, right?"

"You're not funny."

"Then why are you smiling?"

Piper huffs and leans against the bar next to me. "I'm not smiling."

"Kind of looks like you are."

"Guess my pink blazer did more damage to your eyes than I thought. Why don't the guys bid on each other? Seems like the logical way to make sure no one ends up with a creep."

"Management doesn't allow it. Someone else has to make

the bid: a season ticket holder. A kid with their parents' credit card. Figured next year I could come down with the stomach bug and avoid the whole thing altogether."

"That's a good plan to have." Her laugh is light, and she waves at someone across the ballroom. "I should mingle. I'll see you after the auction?"

"If I don't poke out my eyeballs first."

"Good." She heads to a group of people hanging out near the bar on the left side of the ballroom. "Hang in there, Liam."

I do my best to not watch her ass as she walks away, and I fail fucking miserably.

MY HANDS ARE SWEATY.

The lights are so goddamn bright, and I wish I'd ditched my jacket before climbing up on stage.

"Next up is Liam Sullivan," the emcee announces. My name echoes out to the crowd, and everyone cheers. I give them a grimace and a wave. It's far from the flashy charisma my teammates showed up here, but I'm doing my fucking best. They're lucky I didn't bolt when Emmy forked over forty thousand dollars to win the bid on Ethan to piss off Maverick. "The opening bid is going to start at five thousand dollars."

"Five thousand," a man in the audience calls out, and I play with my cufflinks.

"Six thousand?"

"Six," another deep voice says.

"Seven thousand?"

"Seven," someone chimes in, and I shade my eyes with my hand, trying to spot the woman who entered the bid.

I find her in the front row with a group of girls. When she holds up her champagne glass, I can't control the way my lips twist in an unfriendly way.

"Seven," the emcee repeats. "It's time to make this interesting. Ten thousand dollars?"

"Ten," the first man says.

"Eleven," the woman adds, and I wipe my hands on my slacks.

"Twelve," a new voice adds.

It's one I recognize, and I whip my head to the right, surprised to see Piper holding a paddle, her arms crossed over her chest.

A slow grin forms on my mouth. There's determination in her gaze. Razor sharpness to her posture and a steel tint in her tone I've never heard from her before.

You have to be assertive to work in her industry. Piper's shown her scrappiness when she's trying to wrangle someone into the media room. The change in her voice when she's talking to a man who considers himself superior to her just because she's a woman.

I've never seen her like this, though.

Ruthless. Like she's waiting to attack, and I fucking like it.

"Thirteen," the first woman says, flipping her hair over her shoulder like this is a walk in the park.

Piper scowls. "Twenty thousand."

The audience whoops and hollers, getting into it. The two women go back and forth, and it's like I'm watching a tennis match. When the bid reaches thirty-five thousand, I have no clue who's going to give up first.

"Thirty-six?" the emcee asks the woman in the front row.

She consults her friends, having a hushed conversation before shaking her head.

"Sold to the feisty blonde on stage left," the emcee announces, and relief floods through me.

I practically run off the stage, eager to get out of the spotlight. I push through the hordes of people and ignore some of the guys trying to get my attention. When I finally reach Piper, I'm almost out of breath.

"What the hell was that?" I ask.

"I overheard that woman talking to her friends in the bathroom, and I didn't like what she said about you." Piper swirls her drink and scowls. "I'm all for women supporting women, but not when they're being bitches and describing how they'd use you for the night."

"Sticking up for me, Mitchell?"

"Yeah. I am." She lifts her head defiantly. "You're my friend, and I'm not going to let people have their way with you."

"I wouldn't have given her any attention if she won."

"Why not?"

"I don't think my fake girlfriend would've liked that very much, and it doesn't feel right to smile at someone else when I'm too busy thinking about what you sound like when you come."

Piper's inhale is sharp. "You know exactly what I sound like when I come."

"Trust me, Piper. I listen to it on repeat."

"Yeah, well, I think about you jerking off on repeat."

"Fuck waiting until the end of the month. Come home with me tonight. I owe you a lesson."

"Are you sure? You have a game tomorrow." The tension between us magnifies when she takes a step toward me. To anyone passing, we're two people in deep conversation, but we both know the last thing we're going to do when we leave is talk. "I don't want to mess up your routine."

"Turns out, I've been playing some pretty fantastic hockey since I kissed you the first time."

"I guess we shouldn't mess with fate then, should we? Shucks, looks like I'll have to go home with you and get off on your couch again."

A laugh whooshes out of me. "Sorry for your trouble. You ready to head out?"

"I was ready the minute you sent me that text message a

damn week ago. Are *you* ready to head out? I'd hate for you to miss all the excitement here."

I level her with a look. "I've wanted to bend you over the bathroom sink since I saw you tonight. The only excitement I want is your tight cunt. Let's go." I head for the exit then stop to look over my shoulder. "Do you have thirty-five thousand dollars?"

"No." Piper grins and saunters toward me. She's a vision of pure fucking sex and a test of my patience. "But you do."

"Using my money, Mitchell?"

"Protecting you, Sullivan. There's a difference. And look. Now you get to see me naked. I'd say it paid off in the end."

I match her grin. "Protect me all you want, Pipsqueak. I like it when you defend my honor, but I'm going to like it even more when you say my name when you come."

TWENTY-TWO
LIAM

PUCK KINGS

MAVERICK

Goalie Daddddyyyyyyy. Where did you gooooo?

G-MONEY

Liammmmmmm. Come backkkkkkk.

EASY E:

We're going to do karaoke lol

HUDSON

Stay where you are. It's not safe here.

EASY E:

Everyone loves karoke!!!!!

RILEY

Look who is a spelling bee champ!!!!!!

EASY E:

Guck u

G-MONEY

Liam is probably missing us as much as I miss him.

You have left the chat
Easy E has added you to the chat

EASY E:

U can run but u cnt hde, mthrfkr

HUDSON

A for effort, Richardson.

"WHAT KIND of music do you like?" Piper rests her head against the seat and turns her chin to look at me on the drive to my place. "Heavy metal? Gongs? Monks chanting?"

"Gongs? That's not a thing, is it?"

"I don't know." She shrugs. "It could be."

"Gongs are not on the list, believe it or not. I don't listen to a ton of music. When I'm heading to the arena, I like to blast classical music. It mellows me out. Any other time, I'll listen to anything except country. I fucking hate country."

"You looked like you were having a blast at the western bar. I saw you smiling."

"Now you're imagining things. That was hell on earth."

"Rude of you to insult Dolly Parton like that, but okay."

I drum my fingers on the steering wheel. The roads are quiet for a Friday night, and I know we don't have long until we get to my place.

"How much have you had to drink?" I ask.

"Enough where I had the balls to bid on you for over thirty thousand dollars knowing you were going to be the one to pay for it." She laughs and closes her eyes. "Not enough to not know where I am. I'm mildly buzzed at most. Why?"

"We're going to go a step further tonight, and I want to make sure you still want to do this."

"I'm a big girl, Liam. I'm of sound mind and can make my own decisions, and I want you."

I turn into my parking garage and shift my Range Rover to park. I glance over at her and rest my hand on her knee, squeezing once.

"Ready?" I ask, giving her one more chance to back out.

We both know the second we walk into my apartment I'm going to have my way with her.

"Ready," she says. I climb out of the car and hustle to her side, opening the door. Holding out my hand, she swings her legs to the side and jumps to the ground. "So chivalrous."

"Probably the last chivalrous thing I'm going to do for you tonight."

"That's not true. Some would argue your quest for my orgasms is as chivalrous as it gets." Piper grins at me, and I snort. "What did you mean by a step further?"

"You used your fingers last time, but tonight I'm going to finger you. I'm going to touch you everywhere I haven't touched, and you're going to suck me off."

She nearly stumbles when we get into the elevator. "I forget how blunt you are sometimes. Okay. Yes. I-I want all of those things. Will you help me through them, though? And make sure I understand? You're going to have to guide me."

"That's why I'm your coach, Piper. So we can do it together."

When we reach the top floor, we walk down the hall and stop in front of my door.

"Nice wreath." She points at decoration I put up earlier this week. The evergreen branches are adorned with LED lights and candy canes, and you can see it from a mile away. "I figured you might be more of a Grinch type, but I'm glad I was wrong."

"The owner's granddaughter was selling them for a school fundraiser, and I couldn't say no. Kind of looks like Christmas threw up on it, doesn't it?"

"That's putting it mildly."

"I like it."

"You do have a heart after all."

"I'm full of surprises."

I tap my keyfob against the door and push it open. As she slips past me into my apartment, I take a final breath for my sanity before closing the door and locking it behind us.

Piper walks backwards. Her heels click across the floor and her eyes stay on me. She takes off her coat and throws it to the side, not bothering to care where it ends up. The strap of her dress falls down her left shoulder, and she doesn't put it back in place.

"You're awfully far away," she says, voice rough around the edges but soft in the middle. Like she's afraid I'm going to leave when the only place I want to be is here with her.

I move toward her, not needing to be told twice. I lift her off the ground in a swift motion and press her against the wall. Her breath stutters and she grips my hair, giving the ends a hard little tug that has me daydreaming about what that hand is going to feel like wrapped around my cock. Jerking nice and slow until I come in her palm.

"All night I've been wondering if you're wearing underwear." I hike her dress up her leg until the silver fabric pools at her waist. I run my hand from her calf up over her knee, not stopping until I reach the curve of her thigh and inch higher. "*Christ*. You aren't, are you?"

"Underwear would ruin the whole outfit." Her head tips back, hair spilling over her shoulders. The other strap of her dress falls down, hooking around her elbow and showing off the tops of her tits. The flush on her skin and how hard she's breathing. I've barely touched her, and she's already worked up. "Are we going to do this here?"

"No." I peel her off the wall and she wraps her legs around my middle. "My bed. Want to spread you out so I can see every inch of you."

She cups my cheek and strokes the beard I haven't bothered to shave. It's pathetic how I melt into her, like I've been starved for human contact. Years without being touched has me close to begging. Shaking when her nose bumps against mine before she kisses me, soft and slow.

The way she brushes her tongue over my mouth is teasing. The way she moans when I yank her dress all the way down and take her breast in my hand is dizzying. I lose my footing when she gets more assertive, teeth biting at my lip, hands scratching at my back, and nearly trip on the rug in the hallway before righting myself at the last possible second.

Her laugh is wicked, and it fuels some savage part of me to treat her in a way no one else has. To make sure she's blissed out and thoroughly wrecked, all because of me.

I shove the door to my bedroom open. Walk to the bed, drop her on the mattress and bend forward to click on a lamp. Piper looks up at me, and with the moon shining in through the window, it looks like there are stars in her eyes that match the ones outside. Bright flecks of silver and gray cloud her vision, and she reaches for me wordlessly.

I untie my shoes and shuck off my tuxedo jacket, kicking them out of the way. My fingers work to undo the knot of my tie, and there's a moment where I consider asking her to let me tie her hands up. To tease her until she's on the cusp of screaming my name, and only then would I let her come.

Piper watches me raptly, her gaze moving from my feet to my throat to my hands as I ball the tie up and toss it with the rest of the growing pile. Her attention lingers on my chest when I unbutton my shirt, and when I pull it off, she hums her approval.

"Sit on the edge of the bed," I murmur, and she's quick to comply. Quick to scoot. Quick to rest her feet on the rug and wait for the next instructions. "Such a good listener."

A smile works its way onto her mouth. She rolls her lips together and lifts her chin in my direction. "Are *you* wearing underwear?"

"Someone told me I had a massive cock recently." I unfasten my slacks and work the zipper down. "Felt like it was a crime to freeball it at such a classy event."

Her laughter bounces off the corners of the room. Dissolves the last remaining sliver of hesitation hanging between us and sparks a fire up my spine.

Fuck, I want to make her come.

I want to make her come more than I've wanted to do anything else in my life.

But I also want to make her laugh again. It's been so long since I've heard a sound like that—sweet. Calm. Pure fucking joy, and I want a slice of her happiness.

"Forget 'Jingle Bells'. How about 'Jingle Balls'?" Her grin splits her cheeks, proud of her joke. "So, what's the verdict?"

I step out of my pants and nudge them away with my toes, leaving me in a pair of black briefs. Her eyes flash in recognition when she realizes how hard I am.

"Underwear. Sorry to disappoint."

"Wow." She licks her lips, and I want that tongue on my shaft. Swirling over my head and licking me from the base to the tip. "Feels like I'm overdressed. Should I—do you want me to—"

"Ditch your clothes and lie on the bed." I reach for the drawer of my bedside table and yank it open, searching for a marker. "Get comfortable."

She stands and takes off her dress. When the material gathers at her waist, she shimmies it down her thighs until it pools at her feet, leaving her totally fucking naked.

Thank god I've made her keep her clothes on up to this

point. I'm not sure I would've been able to get through the first times we were together if she showed off her whole body.

She's too mesmerizing, from her full tits to her belly button. Smooth skin everywhere and hips I can't wait to grab when I fuck her from behind.

"I'm self-conscious." Her hands cover her chest and her stomach. "I guess I'm self-conscious about everything these days. I know I shouldn't hide from a guy, but I've never loved how I look without my clothes on. Probably because no one else ever has. I think my boobs could be bigger. My stomach could be smaller and my thighs touch."

"Hey." I hook my fingers around her chin and tilt her head back so she's looking at me. "I have a mini lesson for you. Want to hear it?"

Her throat bobs around a swallow and she nods. "Yeah."

"If you take your clothes off in front of a man and he doesn't drop to his knees to worship you, get the hell out of there. I don't care if you're naked. *Run.*"

"And risk public indecency?" she whispers, and I laugh. "This must be a very serious mini lesson."

"Might be the most important one I teach you. His jaw better be on the goddamn *floor* when he sees you naked. If not? He's not worth it. You're too damn nice to waste your time with more pieces of shit," I say, meaning every syllable. Every word and every goddamn letter.

She sits on the edge of the bed and wiggles back until she can stretch out. Until she can bend her knees and spread her legs, giving me a direct view of her pussy. She's wet and pink and so fucking pretty. "Is your jaw on the floor?"

It is, and it feels like my heart might be too.

Somewhere down by my feet, and I'm never going to be able to pick it up.

"I don't know my name right now," I manage to get out. I climb on the bed and sit next to her, kissing her forehead. "I'm losing my mind."

"Is that why you're holding a marker?"

"No. I'm going to figure out the spots where you love to be touched the most. Going to mark them so I don't forget. So *you* don't forget, if you want to touch yourself when I'm not around." I draw a circle around her left breast, pinching her nipple as I go. "I'm going to learn everything you like, Piper. And once I do, I'm going to fuck you better than he ever did."

TWENTY-THREE
PIPER

TIME OF DEATH: 10:37 p.m.

Cause of death: Liam telling me *I'm going to fuck you better than he ever did.*

It makes me feel so *wanted.* So *desirable,* I could explode from the heat of his words.

His touch is torture, teasing me as he moves the marker to the other side of my chest. He draws a circle around my right breast and my back arches off the bed. Liam's chuckle is sexy, a wicked noise that tells me he's just getting started.

And when he closes his mouth around my nipple, I turn into a writhing mess.

"You're the most beautiful woman I've ever seen." He takes my nipple between his teeth, and I swear my vision goes blurry. Fades to black when he sucks the pointed peak. "And to think you've been hiding all of this under your outfits at work. Fantastic tits. Pretty cunt. I can't wait to memorize every fucking inch of you."

I hold the sheets with a death-like grip, needing to stabilize myself. It's already too much but somehow not enough.

"I like that," I whisper, doing my best to be more vocal about the things I enjoy so a man will do them again. So I can get comfortable asking for it because it's what makes me feel good. "When you put your mouth on me."

"Yeah?" Liam mimics the sensation on my other breast. He bites and sucks harder, drawing a whine out of me.

"Can you go lower? Down to my stomach?"

"Asking for what she wants." His mouth moves over the underside of my breast. Across my ribcage and down my body. "That's an A plus from me."

"Even lower." My fingers thread in his hair, and I give his head a gentle shove. A prompting to tell him exactly where I want him to touch me next. "Please."

He kisses my belly button and sucks on the skin above my hip bone. "I'm so proud of you, Piper."

I'm so proud of me too.

My knees open and Liam drags the marker down my left leg. He makes a mark on my inner thigh and moves away, his weight settling between my legs as he lies on his stomach.

"I want to get off, Liam, and I want you to be the one to do it."

"Baby, I'm going to be the only one to do it." He tosses the marker away and strokes up my calf, over my knee, until he's using both thumbs to spread me open. To explore me meticulously until I *burst*. "Make sure you say my name nice and loud when you come."

This is my first time being so exposed to someone. I feel vulnerable as he looks at me up close, the most intimate parts of myself on display without a care in the world, and I quickly learn I love it.

My self-consciousness melts away when Liam mumbles *perfect* and *amazing*. Bliss sparks behind my eyes when his right thumb moves to my clit and rubs in a slow and methodical circle. My toes scrunch and my breath catches in my throat. His left hand grips the inside of my thigh before moving up to my stomach and pushing down.

"God," I breathe out.

"No god here, Piper. Just me, and I'm not going to save you. I'm going to wreck you."

I lift my hips, shamelessly asking for more. Wanting to be wrecked. "Keep doing that. A little harder."

"Like that?" he asks, adding more pressure.

"Perfect. That's perfect."

"Do you want to come like this first? Or do you want me to fuck you with my fingers until you come on my hand?"

"Both?" I sputter at the blunt question. At not knowing which option sounds best. "Can I have both?"

"Greedy little thing." Liam kisses my knee and increases the speed of his fingers as they circle me. He's not inside me, not yet, and I can't think of anything else except for how *good* he'll feel when he finally is. "But you know I'll give you whatever you want."

I do know that.

If I asked him to stop, he would.

If I asked to touch him instead, he'd let me.

He might be the one with the size and the strength, but I'm the one with the power.

Liam pinches my nipple with his free hand at the same moment he gives my clit a light slap and I gasp, electricity running through my veins. The orgasm rips through me, delirious pleasure catapulting me to the sky. It's the most intense one I've ever had, a full-body experience that has my eyes pricking with tears and my legs shaking.

It takes me a minute to come down. The ecstasy subsides as his fingers still. As he leans forward, body over mine, and kisses me. I groan, aching for him, and he sucks on my bottom lip before pulling away.

"Where are you going?" I ask.

"You don't think I'm done, do you?" Liam lifts me gently off the sheets until I'm sitting up. He scoots behind me and leans against the pillows. When he's settled, he pulls me toward him, my back against his chest. "We're getting you comfortable for this next part."

"Is it going to hurt?"

"It might hurt at first, but we'll go slow."

"Okay." I swallow and relax into him. My muscles are heavy, and he coaxes my legs open again with gentle hands. "I trust you."

Liam wraps a hand around my chin, turning my neck so he can kiss me. As I sink into it, he drags a finger over my entrance. He pushes inside me, slow at first, and I squeeze my eyes shut.

"Breathe for me, Piper," he says, against my mouth. "There you go."

There are only a few seconds of pain before it gives way to something else. Something aching and filling and new. It's so different from when I touched myself in front of him, and it hurts far less than I thought it would.

It's exquisite.

"Fuck," I whisper, the fullness almost overwhelming. "And this is just one finger?"

He brushes his nose against mine, and then there is more of a stretch. A sensation deeper inside me in a spot that's never been touched before. Not with sex. Only him. "Just one."

"Christ," I gasp. "And I asked you to fuck me? I'm going to die. I hope heaven is nice, because my time on earth is almost up."

Liam buries his laugh in my neck, kissing along my collarbone and up my throat. "I'm not fucking you tonight, sweetheart. But when I do, you'll be ready. You're going to take all of me, and you're going to look so good doing it."

I'm not sure about that, but that's future Piper's problem. Something to worry about later when the time comes, because right now, I want to enjoy *this*.

The way he slides his finger out of me then presses back

in. How his other hand moves back to my clit, a rhythm of pushing and circling that makes my entire body warm. Makes awareness bloom low in my belly, knowing he's going to make me come again.

It makes me cry out. Makes me reach an arm behind me and wrap it around his neck, searching for his mouth so he can kiss me again.

"You said two fingers," I pant. "Can we try?"

"You sure?"

"Please," I beg.

"You'll tell me if you want to stop? If it hurts?"

"I'm going to hurt *you* if you stop."

He laughs again, pulls out of me, and kisses my cheek. "I'm not going to stop. But only if you open your eyes and watch while I fuck you."

My eyes fly open, and I turn my attention between my legs. His hand is big, fingers thick, and he grips the inside of my thigh. There are a few seconds of teasing. Of him acting like he's going to do it before he does, and it's the most wonderful thing of my life.

My arousal coats him. His pointer finger is wet, covered in me, and I wonder what it would look like on his cock. On his mouth and on his tongue, and *god* do I want those things too.

Liam presses against my entrance with two fingers. I moan as he gently works them both in, a steady slide until his first knuckles disappear, then his second. Soon, I can't see them at all, and he kisses my ear.

"You're so fucking tight, Piper. Fucking clenching around me," he whispers. "Goddamn. Makes me feel like I'm the only one who's ever touched you like this."

He *is* the only one who's ever touched me like this.

My hand instinctively rests on my thigh, and his wrist bumps against mine. I move my touch to my stomach, fingers drifting to my clit.

I want to help him get me there. I want to be a part of it,

and when I touch myself at the same time he curls his fingers inside me, relief like I've never experienced before starts at the base of my spine.

"Liam. *Liam*. I—I'm going to come," I say frantically, and he tucks a strand of hair behind my ear.

"So come," he says nice and low. "I can't wait to watch."

I try to hold out, but I'm not able to hang on. My second orgasm ebbs toward me. It takes over, a wave crashing over, and I moan his name as I combust into a thousand different pieces.

Liam surprises me, maneuvering out from behind me so my back is against the pillows. I'm breathless and weightless as the mattress dips and his hands are back on my legs, but this time, he's between them.

"What are you doing?" I pant, disoriented.

"Haven't tasted you yet." His thumb presses down on my clit and my hips lift on their own. "Need to taste you."

His tongue licks a hot swipe over me, and *fuck*. I like this more than I like his fingers. My entire body is sensitive, alight with nerves and stimulation, but there's no way in hell I can do a third.

"I'm not sure I—"

"Don't care. Could eat you out even if you don't come. You're my new favorite meal."

I try to get there again, try to chase after it, but I come up empty-handed. I'm frustrated and disappointed, mad that this feels *so good* yet I can't do anything about it.

"I'm sorry." I touch his cheek and he looks up at me, his lips wet and his eyes hooded. "I'm not going to be able to. It's not you, it's—"

He kisses my knee. "There's nothing you need to apologize for."

"I don't want you to do the work and—"

"Nothing about that is *work*, Piper. I do it because I like to do it, not because I have to do it. If you want to take a break, we can take a break. I got to taste you on my tongue. I'm set for the rest of the night."

"I want to do the same for you, but I'm not going to be very good."

"Let's move to where we have more room. Can you get on the floor for me?"

"Yeah." I swallow and slide to the end of the bed. My legs are shaky when I stand, and I wobble to the middle of his room. "Do you want me to sit?"

"On your knees would be perfect." He follows behind me, and I drop to the ground. "Have you given a hand job before?"

"I don't think I'd call it a hand job. It was a few quick jerks and that was it."

Liam's fingers hook in the waistband of his briefs and he slides them down his legs, stepping out. His cock bobs free, and I lick my lips at the sight of him. "We'll start there."

I nod and inch forward. My knees rub against the rug as I get closer to him. I rest my hands on his thighs, studying his cock, then look up at him. "What do I do?"

"Spit in your hand, then wrap your fingers around me."

I hesitate for half a second before I spit in my palm and slowly wrap my fingers around his length. There's pre-cum leaking from the slit, and I use my thumb to rub it over his head. "Like this?"

"Perfect," he rasps. "That's perfect. Stroke up and down. You can—*fuck*, Piper."

I'm slow at first, wanting to get used to the feel of him in my hand. How heavy and warm he is and the vein that runs from his tip to his base. The saliva gives me friction, aiding me in my movements as I get comfortable with the mechanics behind it.

When I find a rhythm, I add a twist of my hand like he did when I watched him, and he hisses.

"Too much?" I ask, and his fingers grip the back of my head.

"Fucking incredible," he says, and I beam at the praise. "Squeeze a little harder."

I grip him tighter. His hips buck forward and the muscles in his thighs tense. I glance up, marveling at his half-open mouth. The pinch of his eyebrows and the way he's stroking my hair.

I kiss the side of his shaft, running my tongue up to his head. "I want to taste you too, Liam."

"Christ. Okay. Put your mouth on it, but don't bite. It's like sucking a popsicle or a lollipop. Like you're slurping, kind of. *Fuck*, that's the worst analogy I can give. Just… anything will be perfect."

I appreciate the visual description and I open my mouth, resting him on the tip of my tongue. He's salty with a hint of sweetness. I'm not sure I love the taste, but I love the *feel* of him. I take a deep breath and close my lips, hollowing out my cheeks like I have a popsicle in my mouth, not his nine-inch monster dick.

I gag. Tears burn my eyes and he pulls out of me, taking a string of spit with him.

"Good. *Good*, Piper." His thumb wipes away the tears from my cheeks. "Let's try again. This time, breathe through your nose. Relax your jaw."

I lean forward, taking him back in my mouth. I suck and lick, careful to not use my teeth. My tongue swirls over his head, and his grip on the back of my head turns rough.

"Oh, *fuck*," he groans. "Shit. Use a little more of your tongue and—*goddamn*. You're doing so well. Try using your hand too."

I wrap my hand around the base of his shaft. I surprise myself by taking him another inch deeper down my throat, turning my hand in a clockwise motion at the same time.

"Do guys like it this way?" I pop him out of my mouth and lick all the way up. "Does it feel good?"

"I don't give a fuck what other guys like. This is what *I* like, Piper, and it's *my* cock in your mouth, right? No one else is going to have you like this. Not until I've gotten my fill of you."

Oh.

I like this side of Liam.

The side not afraid to be crass. To be possessive and rough and say exactly what's on his mind. I know he's been careful with me up to this point. I appreciate his willingness to teach me, to make sure I'm comfortable, but I'm also a woman with needs.

"Then don't be careful with me," I challenge. "Fuck my mouth like you want to, Liam. Show me how you like it, because I know it's not going this slow."

My demand unlocks something in him. A part of him he's kept tucked away, and when I say it, I see the moment a switch flips. The second he hears me handing over control, and he jumps at the chance to act on it.

"Hold still." He twists my hair around his wrist. His eyes meet mine, and I give him a nod, letting him know I'm okay. That I *want* this. That I don't want to be treated like a nice girl, but a woman who can get a little messy. "Don't stop until I come down your throat."

I'm enthusiastic this time, licking and sucking him with vigor. Letting the tears fall down my cheeks and my breath catch in my chest.

I'm encouraged, motivated by his low groans and the snap of his hips. And when I get him the deepest yet, almost to the back of my throat, he holds my head there.

"Going to come," he grumbles, and he does.

His release is warm, and I wait until he lets out a loud moan. Until his movements slow and his fingers let go of my hair.

I pop him out of my mouth, making sure I get every drop. I swallow and look up at him, warmth settling in the spot behind my ribs when I find him already looking at me.

"How did I do?" I ask softly. "Was that okay?"

"It was perfect. Unbelievable." Liam touches my cheek. "How the hell did you wind up in my bed?"

"Technically, I'm on the floor. And I guess it was desperation," I tease. "A pathetic attempt where I threw myself at you, remember?"

"There's nothing pathetic about the way you're embracing your sexuality."

"Would you sleep with me again based on that performance?"

"Without a doubt," he says. "That was great for your first time. And, hey. Bonus points for not biting off my dick."

"Now I'm terrified to give you another blow job." I laugh and wipe my mouth with the back of my hand. "Do you mind if I clean up? I'll head out after."

"Want to stay the night?" He loops an arm around my waist and helps me to my feet. "It's late."

"Would I be invading your space?"

"No."

"Are you sure?"

"Yes."

"Why did you have a marker in your end table?"

"Because I do the Sunday crossword puzzle in bed."

"And you use a marker? Are you a serial killer?"

"Last I checked I wasn't."

"Those answers are very enthusiastic."

"Do you want me to scream them?"

"I wouldn't hate it."

Liam laughs and tugs me toward the bathroom. When he looks at me over his shoulder, I feel a shift in the universe. Like something is changing, but I can't figure out what.

And when he smiles at me, I feel it in my heart too.

TWENTY-FOUR
LIAM

I WAKE up to an empty bed.

Judging by the moon shining through my window, it's still nighttime. I reach over to the side where Piper fell asleep a few hours ago. She was curled around me, her hand on my chest and a leg thrown over mine, snoring softly.

And I… just kind of stared at her.

Like a certified creep.

Which, in hindsight, is super fucking weird, and I'd rather die than tell her I know how many freckles she has across her nose.

There are twenty-fucking-three.

Her hair was wet and her face was makeup-free from our shower. She was warm. Soft. Really fucking nice to have in my arms, and… I don't know.

I haven't had a woman in my bed in years. I haven't held anyone in years, and it was nice not to be alone for once. To not fall asleep thinking about my job or the games we have this week or if I hit my protein goal for the day.

I wanted to enjoy the simplicity of it all for a minute because I *never* get to enjoy stuff like this.

The sheets are still warm, and I wonder if she snuck out because she was afraid of things being awkward.

I don't blame her.

Going from no interaction with men to giving him a blow job and sleeping over is a big jump.

I sit up, glancing around the room and searching for a trace of her. My eyes snag on her dress in a ball on the floor, and it gives me hope she's still here. Kicking the sheets off, I stand and fumble with a pair of boxers from my dresser before I start down the hall, looking for her.

"Piper?" I call out.

The kitchen is empty, and so is the guest room. The living room is also deserted, but a flash of color outside the windows catches my attention. I look at the balcony door and notice it's half open.

I walk over, and that's when I see her. She's leaning over the railing, a blanket draped around her as she looks up at the night sky. Her hair is a wild, tangled mess and the socks on her feet are three sizes too big.

I push the door open and step outside. The December air bites at my skin, making me wish I threw on a sweatshirt before I left my room.

"Hey," I say.

"Did I wake you?" She turns to look at me, her chin resting on her shoulder and a smile tugging on her mouth. "I thought I was quiet."

"No. I woke up and saw you were gone. Figured you might've run."

"From all the kicking you do in your sleep?"

"I don't kick."

"The bruise on my shin would say otherwise." I roll my eyes, and her grin stretches wider. "Want to join me?"

I move across the deck and lean my arms on the railing. "Are you wearing any clothes under that big blanket of yours?"

"One of your shirts. Felt like it was more appropriate than my formal dress or going naked."

"My building manager might've complained about the nudity." I lift my chin in her direction. "Which shirt?"

"I don't know. One from a stack that smelled fairly clean and not like the sweaty jersey I normally see you in." She opens the blanket, showing off what she picked. It's an old shirt from college that hangs down to her knees. It has my last name on the back, and I bet I'd really like seeing *Sullivan* stretched across her shoulders. "It's comfy."

"That's one of the lucky ones."

"Well. Hopefully it helps you win tomorrow. Or, today, I guess. God, I'm messing up your sleep schedule, aren't I?"

"Game isn't until eight. Don't need to be at the arena until four. I can take a nap in the morning." I yawn and tap on her wrist. "Move over, Sunshine. I'm fucking freezing."

"Sunshine?" She holds open the blanket and I slide in beside her. Our sides press together, and it's like an inferno in here. "I get another nickname?"

"Figured it fit. You're bright. Warm. You make people happy."

"When skies are gray? Do I make you happy, Liam?"

"Yeah, you do. And not many people make me happy."

"Feels like I should make that a plaque or something. *I make Liam Sullivan happy*. And under it, I'll add *I also swallowed his cum. Maybe that's the key to happiness*."

A laugh rushes out of me. I can't help it. Not when she grins up at me with mischievous eyes. Not when I can literally *see* her gaining confidence every time we're together.

I have the time of my life when I'm on the ice. Being in the middle of an intense hockey game is thrilling with adrenaline and high-stakes and nonstop action.

This is a different kind of thrill.

The kind I could get addicted to if I'm not careful.

And for once in my life, *careful* is the last thing I want to be.

"Someone's got jokes. Two orgasms—sorry, three, forgot about the one in the shower—later and you're a stand-up comedian, Mitchell?"

"Made you laugh, didn't I?"

"I swallowed a bug. That was me choking. Kind of like you did on my cock earlier."

Her laugh echoes mine, and she nudges my ribs with her elbow. "Tit for tat, huh?"

"Tit for something. And you have nice ones."

"That was so cheesy. Want to sit? I was really enjoying looking at the stars before *someone* came out here and interrupted me. That lounger you have in the corner is calling my name."

"I come out here sometimes. Not when it's thirty-eight degrees and I'm freezing my balls off." I lead her to the cushioned chair and sit down first. I spread my legs so she can fit between them and she leans back, resting against me. Taking the blanket from her, I drape it around us haphazardly, creating a cocoon. "I like to look at the night sky. Helps quiet my mind."

"How do you think the season is going so far?"

"Is this on the record or off?"

Piper pinches my knee. "The only time I'm in interview mode is at the arena. This is me being curious."

"I think there's a real chance we go far in the playoffs. We're good enough to win the whole damn thing. Just need to stay focused the next few months."

"I think so too. Boston is going to be tough to get through, but I think you all can do it. Do you have any pregame rituals? I only see you in the tunnel. What happens behind closed locker room doors?"

"I eat a candy bar and listen to classical music before every game."

"A candy bar? What kind?"

"Something with chocolate, but I'm not picky."

"Wow. I'm not going to lie, I'm surprised by that. I thought you'd eat oranges or something."

"I'll eat those too. They aren't part of tradition, though."

She pauses for a beat. "Thanks for the cuddling lesson, by the way. Now I know where I'm supposed to put my hands when a man has his arms around me."

"You didn't have to ask for this one."

"No, I didn't. Should we do some more get-to-know-yous? How else do you kill time in the middle of the night?"

"Give me your questions. I know there's something churning in that head of yours."

"Why do you rarely post on social media?"

"Ah. You've been stalking me."

"Don't flatter yourself."

"I don't care about social media, and I don't think fans should have access to my life outside of the arena. They get me for eighty-two games a season, and that's plenty. If a fan wants to take a photo with me when I'm out in public, I will. But to think I owe you constant updates about my day-to-day activities because you cheer for my team is fucking bizarre."

"You're so right. I stopped posting as frequently on social media after my divorce because I didn't want people to know what I was up to and judge me for it. I know Steven keeps tabs on me, and it's like he's waiting for me to do something wrong so he can latch onto it and make it a big deal."

"Why the hell did you ever marry that guy?"

"He wasn't always like that. He used to be much kinder, but money changed him. When he was at work, he had to act like an asshole to get ahead, and that persona bled into his personal life. As time went on, I realized we weren't compatible anymore. I would've ended it if he hadn't cheated on me, and some days I'm mad I didn't attack first."

"Prick," I mumble under my breath, and she hums in agreement.

"What do you want to do after you retire?"

"Coach, maybe. I'm not sure I'd be any good at it. My teaching style is probably yelling at people when they're doing something wrong, but I'd like to have a hand in the next generation of players."

"I could see that. You probably blow a whistle very aggressively."

"Is there another way to blow it?" I pause and wonder what I should ask her. "What's your biggest fear?"

"Wow." Her laughter dies in her throat and she tips her head back until our eyes meet. "Heavy hitting stuff there, Sullivan."

I shrug. "Way more interesting than what kind of potato you like best."

"I've never thought about it. Huh. I guess I'd say tater tots, with curly fries as a very close second. As for my biggest fear..." She trails off and blows out an exhale. I see her breath in the cold air, and I hug her closer to me. "Being alone. All I want is to be loved. Romantically, I mean. I have friends who love me. Parents who love me. Colleagues who love me. But I want that... that consuming obsession that comes with someone else being your lifeline. The kind of love where, if they died, you'd be heartbroken. Bedridden for weeks because you're not sure how you'd go on. It's funny that I thought I had it before. I wasn't anywhere close."

"Would you get married again?" I ask, and she nods.

"I don't want the whole production like I had last time—*god,* it was atrocious. The ceremony was in a church in the middle of summer when it was ninety-six degrees outside without any air conditioning. There were three hundred guests, and I knew about thirty of them. I hated it. But, yeah, I'd get married again. If I met the right guy."

"I don't think you're going to end up alone."

"It could happen. I've never been someone's favorite person. I've never been someone's top priority. I was married to a man for *years* and always came in second place. Maybe that's what I'm destined for: being almost perfect, but never quite good enough," she says softly.

"You're my favorite person."

"You don't have favorites. In fact, you dislike almost everyone."

"I tolerate some, remember? I have a favorite now, and no one else comes fucking close."

"Really?"

"You win by a mile."

"Well." She dips her chin and shivers under the blanket. "You're one of my favorites too."

"One of? Guess I need to step my game up."

"You're doing just—" She screams, cutting herself off. "What the hell is that?!"

I look to where she's pointing and snort when I see Pico stalking our way. "That's Pico."

"He looks like a goddamn lion in the dark!"

"He'll be very glad to know you think so highly of him." Pico jumps onto the chair and stares at us. "*Te di de comer. No puedes seguir teniendo hambre.*" He flicks his tail, and I roll my eyes. "*Está bien. Una porción más y ya! Tus ojos suplicantes no siempre van a funcionar.*"

"Whoa," Piper whispers. "That was really hot."

"What? The Spanish?"

"Yeah. What did you say to him?"

"I told him he's already eaten today, but I'm going to give him a little more food. Then I said his begging eyes are getting old. Look at him. He acts like he's being starved. Asshole."

Pico turns his nose up at us and slinks back to the balcony door and the warm apartment.

"What a cute guy."

"Great. I don't need you two teaming up against me."

"I'm going to bring him a basket of treats next time I come over. He's going to love me." She yawns and closes her eyes. "I think I might go back to bed. It's cold and I'm getting tired. Guess talking to you bores me to sleep."

"Finally. I can't feel my left ass cheek." I slip out from behind her and stand. When I'm on two feet, I bend down and pick her up, carrying her in my arms. "Might spend all my time on the ice, but it doesn't mean I enjoy being cold."

"I can walk, you know." Piper buries her face in my chest and yawns again. "I got out here on my own."

"Yeah, but I wasn't around. I am now, and this is how you're getting back inside."

"Bossy. Hey. You're going to let me spill my guts without telling me what your biggest fear is? Doesn't seem fair to me."

"I don't like heights," I say, stepping into the living room.

"You looked over the edge of the balcony."

"Because I'm familiar with the space."

"We've been out on Maverick and Emmy's patio."

"I don't look down. Just out."

"Ah, I see. Tricking your mind into thinking it's not up high." She taps the side of my head and smiles. "Smart, Sully."

I like her using a nickname with me. It might be the same one half the guys use, but still. It makes me think she's comfortable enough around me to call me something stupid. And that feels important.

I drop her on my bed and take the spot next to her. Piper flips onto her side and tugs on my arm, asking me to hold her. I kiss the top of her head and rest my chin in the crook of her neck, terrified to tell her my biggest fear isn't heights.

It's how much fun I'm having. How relaxed I feel when she's around, and how the more time I spend with her, the more I don't want this thing between us to end.

TWENTY-FIVE
LIAM

ALANA

Still waiting on your date's name!

ME

So you can stalk her?

ALANA

Am I a bad person for wanting to make sure my big brother is being treated right?

What if she breaks your heart?

ME

You don't need to worry about that.

Going through a tunnel and losing service.

ALANA

I'm watching your pregame coverage on TV right now, asshole!!!!

PIPER

I was wondering...

ME

About?

PIPER

I know hotel room hookups aren't part of our lessons, and I respect the space you want on the road.

But do you want to hang out tonight?

As friends!! Not a date!!

I really don't want to be sucked into the New Year's Eve shitshow of the Vegas Strip and figured we could get a burger after the game?

ME

I'm down for burgers.

PIPER

Hooray! Maybe I can convince you to get another milkshake.

ME

You were quick to tell me it's not a date, Pipsqueak.

PIPER

I don't want you to think I'm using you outside our bedroom parameters or anything. Behind closed doors, remember?

ME

I didn't get that impression.

PIPER

Okay, good!

ME

Going to take a nap. We'll talk after the game.

PIPER

You're going to play great, Sully! See you out there!

THE CROWD in Vegas is relentless.

They always are, but with the added buzz of the holiday and pregaming that's probably lasted all day, they're even more fired up.

They've been screaming nonstop the whole night. Pounding on the glass and trying to break my focus with heckling and boos.

Unfortunately for them, I'm playing my ass off and don't hear shit. I've stopped every shot through two and a half periods, and I'm on track to break the NHL record for most saves in a game.

"You're on fire tonight," Maverick says during a media timeout. "Think you can break it?"

"Already told you I don't care about the record." I squeeze my water bottle and wipe the sweat from my forehead. My heart rate has never been this high, and if it weren't for the adrenaline pounding in my ears, I'd be worried. "Just want the win."

And a hot shower.

And Piper in my bed.

She's come over a few times since the charity gala. Sometimes it's only for a few minutes while she's out running errands, and it's just enough time for me to press her against the wall and slip three fingers inside of her.

Occasionally she'll stop by for longer, her knees red from dropping to the ground and sucking me off, not stopping until

I finish in her mouth and she swallows me down with a wide smile.

She slept over earlier this week.

It was accidental. We fell asleep during a movie, and I woke her up in the middle of the night to move her to my bed.

I wasn't going to be a dick and kick her out.

"He's twelve away," Riley says, snapping my daydreams in half as he glances at the statistics notebook open on the bench. Coach is an old school guy, preferring to keep track of stats by hand instead of digitally. "Thirteen will make history."

"Cut it out," Coach says. "Let him do his job and you all do yours. We're up by one, but we know how quickly these games can change. Someone can get hot, and that's all it takes. I need you to lock in. Focus on your man. Richardson, you were late on the last face-off. You gotta move the stick quicker. React. Don't anticipate."

"Yes, sir," Ethan says, showing Coach the respect he deserves.

"Hayes. Number thirty-eight almost slipped past you with a breakaway. Watch your left side."

Hudson nods, and I know the wheels are turning in his head.

"Miller," Coach continues. "Where the hell is your aggression tonight? It's like your mind is somewhere else, and that's not you."

"Sorry, Coach." Maverick dries his face with a towel. "I'm distracted."

"You better have a good reason. That wrist shot on our last possession was weak."

"Agreed. Emmy is in the crowd tonight, and I always play a little sloppy when she's around. Can't stop looking at her." He gives us all a sheepish grin. "We also decided to say fuck it and elope tonight, and I really don't want to have a bloody nose for the pictures. She'd kill me."

"Shut the fuck up." Grant jumps to his feet. "Are you serious?"

"Yeah." Maverick reaches into his skate and pulls out a small bag with two rings inside. "Been carrying these around all game. Wanted to keep her next to me before I put this on her finger later."

The guys all go wild. Someone squirts a water bottle in Maverick's face and another jumps on his back. The timeout goes from play making to celebrating real quick, but not one of my teammates seems to care.

"Christ." Coach rolls his eyes, but he grins and pulls Maverick into a hug. "You're a sneaky fucker."

"I'm here for the next ten minutes, Coach. I promise. Let's get the win so I can marry my girl."

I yank off my glove so I can shake his hand. "Congratulations, man."

"Thanks, dude. You're coming, by the way. I don't want to hear any bullshit about being tired or wanting to spend the rest of the night in your room. You're my friend, and I want you there."

"I wouldn't miss it," I say. "And I won't even complain."

"Fucking right you won't." Maverick grins and kisses my cheek. "Now go get that fucking record."

The Lightning's offense has been more aggressive coming out of the timeout. Like they know it's sink or swim and they're struggling to stay alive. They start firing off shots like madmen, each one a little sloppier than the last. Fatigue is setting in for all of us—I see it in our boys too—and I know if I can hang on a little longer, if I can stay focused for a few more minutes, I have this one in the bag.

I take advantage of the stoppage in play to grab a drink of water. I stretch my back and see Piper behind me. She's right against the glass in her usual spot, a notebook in her hand and scribbling furiously. After a few seconds of staring, she looks up and spots me.

She waves and gives me a thumbs up. I nod her way, not wanting to fall too far down the rabbit hole that can happen when I look at her for too long.

Especially when she's in her element.

Piper comes alive at the rink, all fierce determination and excitement about the game. I can tell she genuinely loves her job, exuding a confidence she's still trying to find in other parts of her life when she has a microphone in her hand.

The whistle blows, and I'm pulled back to reality. I shove the thoughts of her naked body spread out on my sheets from my mind. I forget the smell of her perfume and the bite of her nails digging into my skin and focus on the job ahead of me.

Now that this record is close—I'm only four saves away—I *really* fucking want it.

I've clawed my way to being one of the best goalies in the league after getting drafted in the sixth round eight years ago. I've worked hard, stayed in my lane, and never been boastful about my achievements as a player.

But being able to say *I'm* the one in the history books would be fucking cool.

The next five minutes pass in a blur. My muscles ache. Sweat stings my eyes, but I don't dare move my attention away from the puck for a single second.

I stop a backhand shot. A slap shot that almost sneaks under my left knee. A gnarly wrist shot that has me squeezing my legs together in a butterfly position, my whole body tumbling forward, snatching the puck out of the crease before any of the Lightning players can go in for a second chance at a goal.

The announcer tells the crowd there's one minute left, and I start to mumble the alphabet to myself, just like I always do, saying the letters and counting each tick of time as we get closer and closer to the end of regulation.

When I catch another save—lucky number seventy-one—just as the horn sounds, I drop my stick and collapse on the ice. It's cool on my overheated skin, and before I can breathe, my teammates are piling on top of me.

"Let's fucking GO," Riley yells.

"Hell of a game, Sully," Hudson says from somewhere close to my ear.

"Think Richardson just broke my ribs." I laugh, feeling really fucking proud.

"Best goalie in the league." Maverick shoves my shoulder and rolls away from me. "Wouldn't want anyone else protecting our team."

"Thanks, guys." I groan when I finally stand on two feet. My legs almost give out on me again, but Grant loops an arm around my left side. Hudson loops an arm around my right, steadying me just like I steadied them for the last sixty grueling minutes. "I'm going to need at least twenty minutes in the shower. Might need someone to wash my ass. My legs are shot."

"I love the fuck out of you, GK, but I draw the line at ass washing." Grant wrinkles his nose. "Maybe in seventy years."

"God, I hope I'm dead by then."

We slowly skate over to the bench where the rest of my teammates greet me. I exchange handshakes with all of them, sheepishly waving to the crowd after the PA announcer lets the arena know I just broke the all-time save record. The referee hands me the puck that sealed the deal, and I'm overcome with a wave of emotion I so rarely experience.

I skate off the ice as fast as my exhausted legs will allow, not wanting anyone to see me like this: vulnerable. Worn out. On the verge of crying because I've been playing hockey for goddamn *years* and I've never had my name on anything.

I dip my head and walk down the tunnel toward the visitors' locker room, hoping to escape before the media starts to hound me. I know Coach is going to ask me to talk to reporters and I'm going to write another check and pay the fucking fine, wanting to keep this moment untainted from whatever they might try to ask.

Before I can make it too far, Piper falls in step next to me.

"I'm not going to hound you for an interview," she says, her short legs working double time to keep up with me. "Maverick has that covered."

"Good."

"Hey." She touches my elbow, and I stop. "Are you okay?"

"I'm fine." I pull off my helmet and scrub a hand over my face. "I'm just—" I gesture vaguely around me, trying to find the right words—"I don't know."

"Oh, Liam. I'm so proud of you." She launches herself at me in a hug, holding me tight. I rest my chin on her head and exhale, cradling the back of her neck awkwardly with my glove. She feels so nice in my arms. "It's okay to be emotional. You did something incredible."

"Thanks." I clear my throat. "I'm proud of me too."

"You don't owe anyone a conversation." Piper pulls away and touches my cheek. She doesn't show any sign of being bothered that her outfit is now covered in my sweat and stench, and that almost makes me emotional too. "Forget the media. Forget reporters. You take this moment however you want. It's *yours*, not anyone else's. The day you do decide to talk about it though, I better be first in line for an interview."

"I promise you will be, Pipsqueak." I chuckle. "I know we said we were going to have a low-key night, but I think this changes things. The guys aren't going to let me hide. Add in the whole Maverick and Emmy thing, and I'll be shocked if I can sneak back to my room before sunrise."

"What do you mean the whole Maverick and Emmy thing?"

"You didn't hear? They're eloping."

"*What?*" she almost screeches. "Are you serious?"

"Maverick's been playing with the rings in his skate all night."

"Of course he has. He's such a romantic." Piper huffs and puts her hands on her hips. "That woman has some explaining to do." She turns back to the ice but stops halfway up the tunnel. "We'll see each other tonight, right?"

"Why? You need something from me, Piper?"

Her eyes rake over my jersey and pads. Color invades her cheeks, and I wonder what she's thinking.

"A couple somethings. Think you can lend a hand?" she asks.

"Always willing to help." The guys start to make their way into the tunnel, and the noise amplifies. Someone has a bottle of champagne, and I have no fucking clue where they got it. "See you soon, Pipsqueak."

"I really am proud of you, Liam," she says.

From her, it means more than the damn record itself.

TWENTY-SIX
PIPER

I CAN'T MAKE it to the stands to question my best friend about her surprise wedding because the rest of the team comes barreling down the tunnel holding a cooler of Gatorade and a bottle of champagne. I know what's going to happen before poor Liam does, and as he turns around, the bucket of orange liquid gets dumped on his head.

I wait, wondering how he's going to react. I'm surprised when he wipes his eyes and lets out a loud laugh. That spurs the guys on, and they erupt in cheers.

"Holy *shit*!" Maverick yells. "That was un-fucking-believable, Sully, you fantastic fucking goalie." He kisses Liam's cheek, and I giggle when Liam rolls his eyes. "A shutout performance. The most saves in NHL history. A win that puts us at the top of the Eastern Conference standings. I'm fired the fuck up, baby!"

"Four minutes until we're on, Miller," I call out, and he salutes me.

"Stop manhandling me." Liam shoves Maverick off of him, but I see the smile he's trying—and failing—to hide. "I did my job. That's it."

God, I love watching him like this.

Unbridled happiness. Joy oozing out of him when he's surrounded by people who lift him up. Love for the game and the guys who helped get him here.

Liam puts his whole heart into everything he does, and being witness to that work paying off fills me with immense pride.

I love being happy for my friends, and right now, I'm so happy for him and all he's accomplished.

"You did more than that." Riley throws an arm over Liam's shoulder. "One of the greatest of all time."

"Time to celebrate." Grant rips off his helmet and chucks it at the wall. I make a note to scoop it off the floor after my interview with Maverick so I can give it to one of the fans waiting outside the tunnel. A group is gathered, hoping to snag some gear from the guys, and I love making someone's night. "We're pregaming this wedding at a club. Watching a couple sick in love exchange vows. Then we're headed to the Strip and burning this place down! An afternoon flight tomorrow means we can rage all night."

"Coach will chew your ass out if you show up to the plane drunk," Ryan warns.

"YOLO, Seymour. I don't give a fuck."

"The Strip? Really? I thought it would be a wedding chapel and beers after," Liam says. "Not some EDM club."

"Dude." Hudson puts his hand on Liam's chest. "You know I'm never one to encourage us to get shit-faced, but you have to participate in *all* the activities. We have a ton to celebrate."

"Fine." Liam pulls off his jersey, makes eye contact with me, and tosses it my way. "But only if Everett is buying. He's off his rookie salary and can finally afford the good shit."

"Fuck yes!" Grant lifts his fists in the air. "I'll buy you a bottle at the VIP section we end up in."

Liam shoves his way to the locker room. "I regret everything."

"Ready, Cap?" I ask, and Maverick marches toward me. I motion our cameraman, Bernie, over. He holds up a finger letting me know we have one minute until we're live, and I nod. "I can't believe you're getting *married*," I say softly, and Maverick beams.

"Me either. I'm still waiting for the day Emmy wakes up and realizes she can do a hell of a lot better than me." He laughs and a dreamy look settles on his face. "I love her so much. I saw her six minutes ago, but I miss her. I can't imagine not spending the rest of my life with her. When we were walking around before we had to head to the arena, I looked at her and told her I wanted to marry her today. She thought I was kidding, so I went in and bought two shitty rings from a gift shop on the corner, took her to the marriage license bureau, picked one up, and now here we are. Hours away from tying the knot."

It's hard not to be emotional when you hear the infatuation infused in his words. The deep joy she brings him and how without her, he'd be incomplete. I've never been a big believer in soulmates, but these two were destined for each other.

This is what I was talking about to Liam the other night.

In every lifetime, in every reality, in every version of their story, Maverick is going to pick Emmy.

She's it.

His top priority.

His only focus.

The owner of his heart.

If she disappeared tomorrow, he'd burn the world down to find her.

And if he couldn't?

He'd leave this world before living without her.

It hurts my soul to be so *happy* for them but so envious too. To desperately want what they have while simultaneously being terrified to try again and fail… again.

Could I learn to trust? Could I learn to believe? Could I feel lovable and like I'm enough?

"You don't want a wedding?" I ask, retreating from my inner turmoil. "You love being the center of attention."

"I love her. And I want to marry her. Tonight. I don't give a fuck about a wedding, and neither does she."

My eyes well with tears and I brush them away. "I'm so happy for you two. Thank you for loving my best friend the way she deserves."

"Ten seconds," Bernie says, and I fan my face.

"Pull it together, P," Maverick teases, ruffling my hair. "We have to show a little bit of professionalism."

I laugh when we go live, holding up my microphone. "Thank you so much, Bradley. I'm here with Maverick Miller after a thrilling win in regulation against the Las Vegas Lightning that showed Liam Sullivan setting the NHL's record for most saves in game. Mav, what kind of growth is the team going through right now, and how is that growth helping the team long-term?"

"We're hungry. Obviously we all wanted to win the Cup last year and came up short. That loss might have been the best thing to happen to us, though. We've had to grow up. We've had to stop taking defeats so personally and figure out how we can get better because of them. This isn't the same team as last season, and if we can keep that kind of momentum going, I think we'll be sitting real pretty come June."

"We can't talk about tonight without mentioning Liam's performance. You two have played together for years. What was it like watching him snag that seventy-first save?"

"God." Maverick runs his hand through his damp hair and grins. "Sully's a beast. He's who I want defending my goal when the game is on the line. He just puts his heart in it, man. Doesn't gloat. Doesn't make it about him. He's a good fu— freaking guy, and to be able to witness him make history is pretty incredible."

"Last thing, Maverick. You're heading into the new year with the best record in the East and the second-best record in the league. What kind of confidence does that give you with a four-game road trip coming up at the start of January?"

"Job's not finished," he says. "Records don't mean anything right now. We're feeling good about the chemistry we have with each other, but until we're lifting the Cup over our heads, we've got work to do."

"Thanks, Mav. Enjoy your night," I say, and Bernie cuts the camera. "You know I hate asking questions like that, but it's what the fans want to hear."

"That's okay, Little P. Your questions are some of my favorites." He pulls his jersey over his head and hands it to me. "You're coming out with us, right?"

"Wouldn't miss it for the world."

"Good." He grins and heads for the locker room. "Gotta get cleaned up before I see my girl. Catch you on the bus!"

I wave and start grabbing all the gear the guys dropped. Gloves and jerseys get added to my pile, as well as Grant's helmet. It weighs me down, and I know I'm about to make some kids very happy.

"This is my favorite part of the night," Lexi says, taking some of the load from me. "One of these days we need to make the guys come back out and sign everything when they finish their debrief with Coach. I could do without the smell, though. It's fucking horrible."

"Maverick and Hudson sign stuff from time to time. They sneak out and when they get on the bus, they claim they were using the bathroom." I spot a boy waiting against the railings. He's leaning into the tunnel, his hand outstretched and a hopeful look on his face. I walk up to him and put a pair of gloves in his palm. "There you go, buddy."

"Thank you." His eyes widen. "I love the Stars. I want to be a goalie like Sully when I grow up."

"I bet you'd be very good at it. Do you live in Las Vegas?"

"No. Maryland. My mom is here for work and brought me with her. I saw the Stars were playing and I begged to come. We always go to games in DC."

"We do a kids' camp in the summer, and Liam will be there. You should sign up." I struggle to reach in my pocket and pull out one of my business cards. "Give this to your mom and tell her to email me if she has any questions, okay?"

"Okay." The boy nods and I think he might be about to cry. "Thank you so much."

"You're welcome so much."

I move closer to the ice and spot a little girl wearing a pink Stars jersey. I recognize it as Emmy's from when she was on the team, a special edition the people in merchandise did for Valentine's Day, and I beeline to her.

"Hi," I say, squatting down so I'm eye level with her. "What's your name?"

The woman next to her lifts the girl in her arms and strokes her hair. "You'll have to speak slowly so she can read your lips. She's Deaf."

"Oh." I stand and drop the gear so my hands are free. "*Hi,*" I sign. "*What's your name?*"

The girl looks at her mom who smiles and nods. She slowly uses her hands and spells, "*Lucy.*"

"*Hi, Lucy.*" I wave. "*My name is Piper. Do you like hockey?*"

"*She wants to play in the NHL one day like Emerson Hartwell,*" her mom explains, speaking and signing at the same time.

"*Emmy is one of my best friends. That's a very good dream to have. Here.*" I reach down and rifle through the jerseys, finding the one I'm looking for. "*That belongs to Maverick Miller. He and Emmy are close, and he'd want you to have it.*"

Lucy clutches the jersey to her chest and smiles.

"When did you learn ASL? Not many people know it," the woman says.

"My cousin is Deaf. I grew up signing."

"Thank you so much for stopping and giving us some of your time. You made her whole year."

"Of course." I grin at Lucy. "*If you're ever in DC, you have to come to a game, okay? I can see if Emmy can be there too.*"

"*Okay.*" Lucy grins back. "*Thank you.*"

"I'm Madeline," the woman says.

"Piper. It's nice to meet you."

"We'd love to visit, but I'm not sure we'll ever make it to DC. I'm a chef at a restaurant here in Vegas, and being a single parent doesn't give us a lot of time to travel. Thank you for the invitation, though."

"It doesn't have an expiration date. You're welcome anytime." I smile and press one of my last business cards into her palm. "*Bye, Lucy. It was nice to meet you.*"

I distribute the rest of the players' gear to the waiting fans, and when I make it back to the tunnel, I'm exhausted.

"I need a shower," Lexi says. "I smell like sweaty boys."

"It's disgusting." I stick my hands under a sanitizer dispenser and rub them together, trying to get some of the stench off me. "You're going out tonight, right?"

"Hell yeah, I'm going out tonight. I brought the cutest outfit. What are you going to wear?"

"I put a few dresses and skirts in my bag. Nothing that's appropriate for a wedding, but I'll see if I can pull something together."

"That's the point of a Vegas wedding. You don't have to be pulled together." Lexi laughs. "Oh, hey, Liam. Nice game tonight. You were incredible."

He nods at her and a bead of water rolls down his forehead from his post-shower hair. "Thanks."

Lexi looks between us and gives me a sly grin. "I'll give you two a minute."

When she disappears, I smile at Liam. "What's up?"

"You're good with kids."

"I am?"

"Yeah. I was watching you hand out gear. Your signing..." He tips his head to the side. "It's beautiful."

"Oh. Thank you. I'm rusty these days, but I try to watch YouTube videos so I can stay somewhat fresh. You never know when you'll need it, like you just saw with Lucy over there." I shrug. "If that makes someone feel included and comfortable, I want to offer that to them."

"Do you want to have kids?"

I roll my lips and hum. "I'm not sure, to be honest. I like kids, but I'm undecided on if I want my own. I'm still learning to trust people, and that would require a lot of trust."

"That's fair."

"Do *you* want kids?"

"Yeah. I think so. I could see myself being a dad." He shoves his hands in the pockets of his slacks. "But that's a ways off."

"Did you come out here to ask me about my future as a mother?"

"No." Liam snorts. "It was to form an escape plan for tonight so we can sneak out without staying at a club until four in the morning. I might die if I'm still awake when the sun comes up."

"No one's going to notice if we leave. We'll just say I'm hungry and disappear."

"I like how your brain works."

"Thanks." I grin. "Lexi and I are going to get ready together, so we'll probably meet you all at the club. I *still* need to track Emmy down and give her an earful. I'll see you later tonight?"

"Sounds good."

"Save me a dance, Sullivan," I say, brushing past him and heading for the team bus. "I'm going to be very disappointed if I don't get a few minutes alone with you in a dark corner somewhere."

"You want another lesson, Sunshine? In exhibitionism this time?"

"Maybe." I tap his chest and saunter away. "You'll have to find out."

TWENTY-SEVEN
LIAM

I CAN'T STOP STARING at Piper from across the club.

Haven't been able to take my eyes off her since she walked in here with her short skirt and high boots. I swear the music stopped when she came through that door with her hair down her back and glitter on her chest and cheeks. The makeup catches in the strobe lights every few minutes and pulls my attention away from the conversations I'm trying to have.

"You good?" Hudson snaps his fingers in my face and I blink. I cut my gaze away from watching her on the dance floor, her arms above her head and her hips swaying to the music next to Lexi. "You're staring off into space."

"Sorry. Thought I recognized someone." I sip my beer and wipe my mouth. "You're not drinking?"

"Someone needs to get us to the wedding chapel and back to the hotel safely later," he says over the thumping music, and I nod in agreement. "Sure as shit not going to rely on Everett or Richardson to find the way."

"Would be a fun game, though. How's it going with that girl from the gala? Alisha? Eliza?"

"Alyssa, but close. We broke up. She said I was being too clingy. When I backed off and gave her some space, she stopped returning my calls. Stopped wanting to hang out." He shrugs, but I can tell he's bummed and trying not to show it. "Wasn't meant to be, I guess."

I lean in close so he can hear me when I say, "You'll find her."

"Thanks, man. I'm going to grab a water. You need anything?"

"Nah. I'm going to finish this then make a round."

Hudson nods and turns for the bar, stopping briefly to apologize to a woman with long brown hair for running into her before disappearing in the throng of bodies. I don't even get a second of reprieve, because Grant replaces him at my side.

"GK," he slurs, way drunker than anyone else here. "Take a shot with meeee."

"Can you even stand on two feet?"

"Pshhhhh. Who needs to stand when someone can carry me?" Grant holds up the handle of vodka he's carrying and taps my chin. "Open up, big guy."

I know the only way to get rid of him is to appease him, so I squat down. I pop open my mouth and swallow the absurdly generous pour Grant tips in my mouth. "This isn't even the good stuff."

"Maverick bought all the good stuff," he yells before moving away to annoy another teammate. "Find him."

I roll my eyes and scan the crowd, trying to locate my captain. I spot him at a table in the VIP section, Emmy and Piper flanking him on either side. She must be worn out from dancing. Finishing off my beer, I leave it on the end of the bar with a stack of other empties and head for them.

"There he is." Maverick crawls over Emmy so he can hug me. "Get your ass over here. We're doing a shot flight."

"The fuck is a shot flight?"

"Shots of different kinds of alcohol." Emmy lines up five

glasses in a line. "You can't say no. I'm the bride, and I want you to join."

"Damn you, Emerson Hartwell." I glance down at Piper. "Want to share the bench, Pipsqueak?"

"Sure." She pats the spot next to her and I sit. My thigh presses against hers, but she doesn't pull away. "Been wondering where you were."

"Looking for me?" I ask in her ear over the noise, and she shrugs.

"Maybe." Her eyes sparkle and she grabs two glasses, handing one to me. "To Liam. The NHL's record holder for most saves in a game."

I grumble at the toast and attention but knock the drink back with ease. "That's the good shit."

"Fantastic, right? Top of the line tequila. Smooth going down." Maverick gestures for us to pick up the next drink like some alcohol-pushing salesman. "Now the vodka."

"This one is for Maverick and Emmy," Piper toasts. "To a lifetime of happiness."

We go through the flight until I've had more shots in ten minutes than I've had in the last five years. I set the last glass down and lean back, the alcohol already settling in. I feel it in my blood. In the back of my head. At the edges of my vision where things just start to turn fuzzy.

It's been ages since I've been drunk.

When I drink, I know when to stop. I know my limits and when I'm getting close to pushing past them. I can tell I'm already teetering into buzzed territory. Moving slowly to intoxicated, but tonight, I think I'm going to enjoy it.

"Didn't know you were a lightweight." Piper taps my knee. "Your cheeks are red."

"You want to have a drinking contest, Mitchell?"

"What does the winner get?"

"What do you want?"

"You." She flips her hair over her shoulder and grins. "How can we make that happen?"

I'm tempted to kiss her right here, right now.

Emmy and Maverick are in their own world. I could tell them I was on fire and they wouldn't even look at me, but Piper is.

I like having her attention on me.

I like knowing she's watching.

I like that she scoots closer to me and drums her fingers on my thigh.

Fuck. She's so pretty.

Has she always been this pretty?

I think she has. It's why I've been looking at her for four years.

Because she's so pretty.

Hell.

I'm drunker than I thought.

"Do you want to dance?"

"Do you know how to dance?" she asks.

I glance at the dance floor. There are hundreds of people, all moving in their own way. Some are jumping up and down. Some have their arms in the air. Some are swaying their hips.

Off the ice, I'm uncoordinated as hell. Can't find a rhythm to save my life, but I'm not going to let that be the reason I don't get to put my hands on her tonight.

"I'm sure I can figure it out," I say, and I grab the bottle of tequila sitting in the middle of the table. "Want something else to drink before we head out there and I embarrass the shit out of us?"

"Probably for the best." She takes the bottle from me and unscrews the cap. "But I don't want to waste a glass."

I lift an eyebrow. "What's your plan here?"

"Open your mouth," Piper says in some husky voice I haven't heard from her before, and my mouth pops open. My dick twitches in my jeans. She stands and I rest my hand on her hip, steadying her. "Such a good boy, Liam."

My skin burns as she drags her fingers down my jaw and across my beard. I'm not sure I've ever been this turned on outside the bedroom before, and I never knew I was into receiving praise.

I'm so hard, so on edge with wondering what she's going to do, I can't do anything but watch her with hungry eyes.

"You're smart." She rests the bottle against my lips and tips it up, filling my mouth with tequila. "How can you get the alcohol from your mouth into mine?"

I tug her toward me until she's sitting in my lap. Until her skirt hikes up her thighs and I can touch bare skin. Keeping my eyes on her, I cup her chin and tilt her head back. She squirms and lets out a soft moan when I lean forward and tug on her bottom lip.

Her lips part and I grip the back of her head as I spit the tequila straight into her mouth.

"Swallow it," I murmur when I can talk again. "Just like you did my cum." Piper's eyes flare with heat, staying on mine as her throat bobs and she sticks out her tongue, showing me an empty mouth. "Thatta girl."

She slides off my lap and stands. I'm slow with my perusal of her. I look her up and down and notice her hard nipples and the flush on her cheeks. The way her skirt is slightly off center.

So pretty.

Piper holds out her hand and I take it, threading our fingers together and letting her tug me out of the booth. I was right—Maverick and Emmy don't even look up as we walk away, the ground a little wobbly underneath me.

I expect her to lead me to the dance floor, but instead she heads for a secluded section of the club, away from my teammates and the loud bass. There, she leans against the wall, wraps her arms around my neck, and yanks me toward her.

"What were you saying about a lesson in exhibitionism?" she whispers, and I glance around, checking out our surroundings.

We're hardly noticeable in the dark lighting, but something tells me she wishes we were front and center, and I'm going to play this out to give her what she wants.

"You still want that?" I run my fingers down her arms and lift them above her head, pinning them in place with one of my hands. "Or is that the alcohol talking?"

"You're drunker than me," she says, and I know she's right.

I feel my inhibitions slipping away. My decision-making skills are going out the window, and I want to do this before I forget. Before I get to the point of no return.

I bend down and kiss her, taking her mouth with mine, and I feel her smile against my lips. She hums when I use my tongue, my teeth, when I run my free hand up her waist and stop on her ribs.

Maybe I've been too uptight in the past.

Maybe I should've let go a little bit more, but I'm glad I didn't.

Otherwise I wouldn't be able to have this, right here, right now, with her.

I don't want anyone else.

"Touch me, Liam," she whispers, turning her head so I can kiss her neck. So I can run my tongue down her throat and get a view of her cleavage. "Please."

I move my hand to the waistband of her skirt. Lower until I'm on her thigh then working up toward her hips. My fingers dip under the fabric, and when I get an inch higher, I find her bare, wet, and fucking ready for me.

"No underwear? Making out with me in the corner of a club where anyone can see me slip my fingers inside you? I'm starting to think you're needy for me, Piper." I nip at her ear and press two fingers inside her. "You are, aren't you?"

"I am." She groans and drops her head back. "Why has it never been like this before?"

"Because you weren't with me. Because you were with someone who didn't know jack shit about what you liked. How to get you off. I bet he didn't know that when I do this —" I curl my fingers, smirking when she bites down on her lower lip to keep from yelling out my name. "It makes you want to beg. And when I do *this*—" I drop her wrists from my hold and move my other fingers to her clit, rubbing in the circle she likes. "You're going to come all over my hand."

"Liam," she whines, eyes closing and chest heaving.

"Come on, Sunshine. You know you want to," I say, and my words are slurred. I don't know if it's from the alcohol or her, but I don't give a shit. "For me?"

Piper clenches around my fingers. The orgasm races through her so quickly, I barely have time to react. To pull out of her and hold her up so she doesn't fall to the ground. I tuck her close to my chest, stroking her until a choked sound leaves her throat and tickles my ear.

"You…" she pants. "Are too good at that."

"What would your exit survey say?" I kiss her forehead and brush the hair out of her face. She lifts her chin and looks at me with bloodshot eyes but a pleased smile. "Decent? Average?"

"Fine. It would say fine."

"Guess I'll have to take you to the bathroom and try again." I fix her skirt. There might be two of her. Maybe I have two sets of eyes. "You okay?"

"I think I'm flying."

"I think you're drunk."

"I think you're pretty." She touches my nose. "And I think I need another drink."

"Who needs another drink?" Grant appears out of nowhere with a fresh handle of alcohol. "Don't you worry,

Little P. I have the hookup. But drink fast. It's almost wedding time!"

I groan and shove him away. "Fucking menace."

Piper giggles and sways in place. "This is fun. Let's go have some more fun, Sully. Do you want to have fun with me?"

Fuck being responsible.

It's hard to want to do anything smart when she's looking at me like *that.*

Satisfied. Happy. Really fucking beautiful.

My chest aches and I rub my hand over it.

"Lead the way," I say, not knowing how the fuck the night can get any better.

TWENTY-EIGHT
LIAM

PUCK KINGS

HUDSON

Good morning, everyone! Bus for the airport leaves at noon!

MAVERICK

f32ytf8hdhjgfds

HUDSON

What was that?

G-MONEY

h3 said hez deadd

HUDSON

Still don't understand.

EASY E

way 2 fuckng cheery. Tf is wrong wit u?

HUDSON

You call it cheery, I call it sober and feeling great. Went on a run at sunrise and it sure was nice.

G-MONEY

ur sick in the head

I'M GOING to kill whoever left the curtains open in my hotel room.

I groan and try to sit up, but my head is throbbing like someone whacked it with a baseball bat.

Repeatedly.

My throat is dry as shit, and when I try to open my eyes and get my bearings, everything hurts too fucking much.

"Christ." I press my fingers into my forehead to get rid of the pain in my skull. "This is a new level of hell."

"I'm dying," a voice next to me says around a whimper, and I shoot straight up.

I roll to the right and fall off the bed, landing face-first on the carpet that smells like utter shit. There's another noise and I slowly look over the edge of the mattress to find Piper curled up on the bed.

Her hair is a mess. There's glitter on her cheeks and arms and a little pink mark below her ear. One foot has a sock on it, the other doesn't, and she's clutching a pillow to her chest.

She looks how I feel: like I've been through the fucking ringer.

"You're in my bed," I say.

"No." She rolls on her back and drapes an arm over her face. "You're in my bed."

I scan the room.

There's a pink suitcase against the wall. A pair of heels

under a chair. A bra slung over a lamp and four notebooks on the desk.

No gear. No skates. No sticks.

Definitely not my room.

"Why did I come back here last night?"

"Don't know," she groans. "I can't remember anything after Maverick and Emmy's wedding."

That's like a bucket of cold water on my head. "Maverick and Emmy got *married*?"

Piper reaches for the bedside table and fumbles around. She grabs her phone and taps the screen before turning it my way.

There's a photo of Maverick and Emmy kissing under an arch. Another of the team clapping and cheering. One of me, my arm around Piper and her head on my chest. A final picture of Emmy on Maverick's back, a *Just Married* sign hanging from between his teeth.

"Holy shit."

"How drunk were you?" she asks.

Pretty fucking drunk.

I remember bits and pieces.

Loud music and flashing lights.

Leather seats inside a limo.

There was laughing and dancing… I think?

After that, everything is blurry. Disjointed flashes of memories I can't put together.

"Heavily inebriated, apparently." I scratch my jaw and pause when something cool rubs against my cheek. I pull my palm away and stare at my left hand. There's a silver band around my ring finger, and my blood turns to ice. "What the *fuck* is on my hand?"

"Your fingers, probably."

"What's on my fucking finger?"

"I don't know. Skin? A nail? Do you really need an anatomy lesson when it feels like I'm dying?"

She sits up, and that's when I see it.

A silver ring on *her* finger, and I almost stop breathing.

"Piper," I say slowly. "You told me Maverick and Emmy got married."

"We *just* went through the pictures, Liam. Grant sang an Adele song. Ethan bought us all hot dogs. It was beautiful, honestly. Well, as beautiful as a Vegas wedding can be."

"Then why the hell do you have a ring on *your* finger? And why the hell do I have one on *mine*?"

She lifts her hand and stares at the piece of jewelry with wrinkled eyebrows and a half-open mouth. Understanding dawns, and she gasps.

"Did we—there's no way I—you don't—" Piper shakes her head. "Oh, no. No, no, no, no, *no*. We didn't—how did we —I can't—what the *fuck*? I'm not supposed to be married again. That means I'll be divorced again, and… *shit*. I'm Ross fucking Geller."

I pinch the bridge of my nose. I need water. Ten aspirin and to sleep for days. There's no way this is happening. "What's the last thing you remember about last night?"

"The hot dogs Ethan handed out when we got out of the chapel with Maverick and Emmy. He mentioned something about a Dave? After that, I can't tell you a thing. What the *hell*? I can't believe they let drunk people get married. It's unethical. Illegal, probably, and I'm going to sue the *shit* out of them."

"It's their entire fucking business model. Who was the most sober last night? Definitely wasn't me."

"Um. I'm not sure. Lexi disappeared at some point. God, I hope she's not murdered in a ditch somewhere." Piper takes a second to think. "Okay. Wait. *Wait*. We all tried to do a human pyramid, but none of us could balance because we were too intoxicated."

"How the hell does that help us figure out who was sober?"

"It tells you who wasn't sober."

I curse under my breath and grab my phone, hoping something sparks my recollection of last night. I find my lock screen has been changed, the team photo from the start of the season replaced with a picture of Piper squatting in the middle of a sidewalk, her arms looped around my calves as she tries to lift me up.

My arms are out at my side. My hair is a mess. The top two buttons on my shirt are unfastened. My shoelaces are untied, and that's when I see it: the grin on my face.

I almost don't recognize myself.

Fuck.

I look like a happy idiot, and I don't know the last time I smiled that big.

"Are you okay?" Piper asks, and I blink up at her.

"Huh?"

"You look like you saw a ghost."

"I'm fine." I run my hand through my hair and pull up the team group chat, reading through the messages from the last twelve hours. "Hudson is sober. Fucker went for a run this morning."

"Oh *yeah.* He was giving everyone water! When I tried to dump it on his head, he tossed me over his shoulder and walked me to a very nice chair."

I don't like the thought of my teammate putting his hands on her. I know it's because he was helping take care of her, but still.

It stirs up something inside me that I don't like, and I grind my teeth together to get rid of the feeling.

"What room are we in?" I ask.

"Um." Piper rolls over and looks at the hotel phone. "636."

I find Hudson's name in my cell and hit call, waiting for him to pick up.

"What's up, man?" he answers after two rings.

"Room 636. Now," I grit out before tossing the phone on the sheets. The reality of the situation starts to unfold in front of me, and I stand. "Fuck. *Fuck.*"

"What's wrong?"

"What do you mean what's wrong? I can't be *married.* I don't date. I don't do relationships, and I sure as fuck don't get *married. Fuck.* I must've been plastered out of my mind. And without a prenup in place? No PR statement planned? My agent is going to fucking kill me." I pace to the window then back across the room. "God only knows how much of an idiot I looked like last night and what kind of videos are on social media. I don't have time for immature shit like this. We're less than four months out from the playoffs and now I'll have *a marriage* looming over my head? Unbelievable. Did you know what was going on before we allegedly exchanged vows?" I scrub my hand over my mouth, wincing at the reminder of metal on my skin. "Is this some sort of prank? All part of your plan and why you came to me to fuck you?"

"Are you saying I *planned* this?"

"I don't know what I'm saying, Piper, only that I'm trying to figure out how we went from making out in a club to being husband and fucking wife. I didn't have a say in it, so someone must've."

Piper's face falls. Her bottom lip trembles, and the second the words leave my mouth, I know I've said the wrong thing. I've been too mean, too aggressive, too much like her piece of shit ex, and I instantly want to take back the last two minutes.

I want to crawl into a hole and hang my head because she doesn't deserve to be on the receiving end of my attitude, and she really doesn't deserve to be blamed for something I know is a surprise to her too.

Fuck.

"If you think I came to you for sex lessons because my long term goal was to marry you, you're the most conceited man in the world. I came to you because I trusted you. Because we're friends, and now, I'm not so sure about that."

"Piper."

"I'm going to take a shower." She throws off the sheets and swings her legs to the end of the bed. She stands and shuffles to the bathroom, turning her back to me, and that's when I realize she's wearing my jersey.

The extra one I pack in my carry-on in case my checked suitcase gets left on a tarmac somewhere.

I stare at the letters stitched across her back. My number below her shoulder blades. The way it hits her thighs and shows off the rest of her legs.

She looks perfect.

It's dangerous for her to walk around in that.

It might make me think this whole marriage thing is a good fucking idea.

"I'm sorry. I didn't—"

"I was starting to think I might be ready to try dating again, but after hearing what you just said, I'd rather stay single. I know my self-worth, and it's not being called manipulative."

When she shuts the bathroom door with the softest *click* instead of slamming it in my face, I want to grab a pillow and scream. I want to get on my knees and apologize for what I said.

The only two things I've been sure about the last few years are hockey and her.

And now, since I'm a miserable asshole, I've fucked up one of them.

A knock throws me off-balance and I charge for the hotel room door, yanking it open.

"Coffee?" Hudson grins and holds out a tray of Styrofoam cups. "Thought you might need some caffeine to revive yourself."

"Get in here." I grab the drinks from him and storm to the seating area. "And sit."

"I don't know how Piper takes her coffee so I—"

"She doesn't drink coffee," I grumble, glaring at him. "Triggers headaches."

He lifts an eyebrow. "That's an interesting thing to know about her."

"Shut up. How do you know Piper is here?"

"I walked you two back."

"You did?"

"Yeah." Hudson picks a spot on the couch and unwraps a croissant. He takes a bite, groaning as he swallows. "God, that's good."

"Hayes," I snap. "I need you to focus on me, not the goddamn pastry."

"Sorry. You know food is my kryptonite. Okay. Yeah. You couldn't find the elevator, so I led the way."

"Did you drink at all?"

"One beer."

"I need you to tell me exactly what happened last night," I say, even though I don't want to hear it.

"You want the whole story?"

"Every fucking detail."

"We were at the first club until about one. After, we left to go to the wedding chapel where Maverick and Emmy got married. Really nice ceremony." He rips off another chunk of his pastry and waves it around. "Then… let's see. We hung around for a while before going to another club. At that point, it was almost three. We stayed there until about five, then we came back to the hotel."

"I said every detail. Where in there is *me* getting married?" I hold up my hand, and Hudson doesn't act surprised by the ring on my finger. "Because I sure as shit don't recall this happening."

He frowns. "You don't remember?"

"If I remembered, I wouldn't be eight seconds away from a panic attack, would I?"

"You brought that on yourself, man."

"Excuse me?"

"After Maverick and Emmy got hitched, you and Piper agreed to a drinking game. I don't remember the rules, but whoever won got to pick the other's punishment. Well, you won, and when she said 'Just pick something stupid,' you responded with 'Let's get married too. Look at all the love around us.' I was very confused because you were *very* excited. You kept going up to couples heading into the wedding chapel and telling them congratulations. Giving them hugs and talking about how love is the best. You might be a little bit of a dick when you're sober, but turns out you're a friendly drunk, Sully. Who would've thought?"

I cradle my head in my hands.

I'm not impulsive.

I'm not spontaneous.

I like knowing the plan well ahead of time and sticking to it.

This is so not like me, and I make a silent vow in my aching head to never, *ever* fucking drink again.

Especially because I blamed Piper for something that's entirely my goddamn fault.

"Is there a chance it's not legitimate?" I ask. "Did we actually go through with a ceremony? Or was I all talk?"

"I mean, I was a witness. There was an officiant. Papers were signed. It seemed pretty real to me."

"Why would you let us go through with something so stupid? You know I don't date. You know I'm not interested in having a relationship, *especially* during the season. And, *Jesus Christ*. You know Piper went through hell and back with her dickbag of an ex-husband."

"You're an adult. You can make your own choices. I asked you multiple times if this is what you wanted to do and you said yes. Repeatedly. When I changed the wording of the question so you couldn't just bob your drunk head to show signs of agreement, you still answered yes. This is *not* my fault."

"You could've stepped in and done something," I challenge. "Taken me back here. Walked us away from the wedding chapel. *Anything*."

"It's not my responsibility to keep you in line, Liam."

I blow out a breath and press the heels of my palms in my eyes. "How many people know about this?"

"From the team? Only me. Everyone else was plastered. There's no way they remember."

"Okay, okay. How do I fix it?"

"That's a loaded question." I lift my chin and find Hudson eyeing me hesitantly. "You sure you want the answer?"

"Obviously."

"You either stay married, or you get a lawyer and start the process for an annulment."

That makes me burst out laughing. "Why the fuck would I stay married?"

"I don't know. Maybe deep down you wanted to get married? What's the saying? Drunk actions are sober thoughts?"

I lift my chin and glare at him. "I'm playing the best season of my career. I don't have time to play house with someone."

"Piper," he says. "Not someone."

"Hi, Hudson," she says softly, right on cue.

I tell myself not to look at her, but I have to see her. I have to know she doesn't hate me for what I said, because I really fucking hate myself.

I glance over my shoulder and she's standing there with wet hair. Wearing jeans and a Stars T-shirt that doesn't look nearly as good on her as my jersey did.

She offers Hudson a small smile and ignores me completely.

That hurts more than the hangover.

"Hey, Little P." He stands and hugs her, and it pisses me off when she wraps her arms around him. When she takes a deep breath and rests her cheek on his chest. "How ya feeling?"

"Like I got hit by a truck. My head is pounding, and I don't know if it's a migraine or the alcohol."

"Both, probably." He laughs and squeezes her, releasing her after a beat. "I didn't know you don't drink coffee. I could've brought you something else."

"How do you know I don't drink coffee?"

"Liam just told me."

"Oh. He's right. No coffee for me." She takes a seat on the couch. "Last night was a shitshow, wasn't it?"

"Shitshow is putting it mildly. Corralling hockey players around Vegas without anyone getting lost, robbed or in a fight is a blast." He sits next to her and grins. "Speaking of last night, I was talking to Liam about your situation."

Her spine stiffens and she rests her hands on her thighs. "I know Liam is eager to get out of this predicament, and so am I. I'm going to call my lawyer when we land in DC and get the ball rolling on paperwork. Instead of being thirty-two and divorced, I'll be thirty-two and divorced twice. That'll be fun to put on the Christmas cards this year."

Piper is trying to act like she's tough and brave with her sarcasm, but there's sadness in her eyes. Defeat in her self-deprecating smile. That fear she told me about—of being alone—radiates off of her, and now another person is trying to leave her.

"Hayes suggested an alternative," I blurt out, and her eyes finally snap over to me. "He said we could stay married."

I've never been a fixer, but this situation is making me want to be the ultimate problem solver. She shouldn't look so upset. She shouldn't look so mad at the world. She's sunshine and happiness and everything good in the world.

Not… not whatever the fuck this is.

"Stay. Married." Piper says each word slowly and frowns. "Why would we stay married when you just yelled at me because—"

"You *yelled* at her?" Hudson asks. He rises to his feet and towers over me. "I know you're pissed about this but that doesn't give you the right to—"

"I didn't *yell*," I grind out, standing and matching his stance. "I'd never yell at her. I was frustrated and raised my voice. I didn't fucking *yell*. I would never do anything that made her—"

"Both of you are yelling right now and you need to stop. Sit *down*," Piper snaps, and we drop to our seats. "Liam, there's no logical reason for us to stay married. I know we're pretending to date for Alana's wedding, but that doesn't mean we have to—"

"Hang on," Hudson interrupts. "You two are going to pretend to date for a wedding? What the hell is that about?"

Piper finally looks at me. She subtly shakes her head, and I understand what she's saying.

"It's a long story," I grumble. "And you're never going to hear it."

"You're allowed to have your secrets. I won't pry. As for this whole wedding debacle, there are two options here. You call your lawyers and they'll get the annulment going. It's very clear neither one of you was of sound mind, so it shouldn't be hard to justify the dissolution of the marriage. The other option, like I said, is staying married."

"And what would be the benefit of that?" Piper asks.

"My health insurance," I say slowly, and for the first time since I woke up, I finally feel like I can think straight. "Our insurance is lightyears better than yours."

She blinks. "Why would I want to be on your insurance? That's not logical enough of a reason to stay married."

"Migraine medication. Access to doctors who can help you diagnose and treat. Chiropractors. Acupuncturists. Massages. It's all covered under our plan. And if it's not, I can pay out of pocket for it."

"Absolutely not. I'm not going to be indebted to someone because they want to pay for some of my medical work."

"Helping someone because you're able to doesn't mean they'll be indebted to you. It's the right fucking thing to do," I say, furious she's lived a life where she's had to repay someone because they were nice. "And think about it, Piper. We're already keeping up this charade for my family. It's not like it's going to be a major inconvenience."

"So, what, I'll live with you? Introduce you as my husband?" She bursts out laughing and touches the ring on her finger, sobering just as quick. "I don't want my next marriage to be a sham, Liam. I want it to be because I love the person. Because they love me. Because we want to spend the rest of our lives together, not because we were intoxicated. That's not us. You've said you don't want a relationship. Why burden yourself with something so unnecessary?"

"I'm going to side with Liam on this," Hudson says gently. "You've been through a tough legal battle, Piper, but this seems like something you could benefit from. You set an end date—the end of this season, the end of next season, whatever you decide. After you get what you can out of it, you go your own way."

"I need to think about it." Piper gnaws on her bottom lip. She wrings her hands together and stares at the floor. "This is a lot to digest when I feel like crap."

The look Hudson shoots me from across the living room says to keep my mouth shut and not protest.

So I don't.

"Thinking it over is a good idea," he agrees, looking

between us one more time. "If you two are good, I need to make sure the rest of the team is alive."

"Yeah, go." Piper tucks her chin. "Thank you for coming by and explaining everything to us. I think it goes without saying we're going to keep this between the three of us for the time being, right?"

"My lips are sealed," Hudson promises.

"I'm, uh, going to go too. I'll give you some space," I say. I don't want to leave like this, but I know it's for the best. She needs to think and so do I. "I'm really sorry for what I said, Piper."

"Thank you," she mumbles.

Hudson waits for me to grab my stuff. When we're out in the hall, I groan.

"This is the worst day of my life."

"You'll figure out a solution."

"Happy fucking New Year, right?"

"I don't know." He smiles and clasps my shoulder. "I think there's a chance this might be the best year yet."

"You're way too optimistic," I grumble.

"Nah. I just see things you don't."

TWENTY-NINE
PIPER

I'M SO glad to be home.

The plane ride back from Vegas was miserable.

When Lexi and Maven asked what was wrong, I put on my headphones, said I didn't feel well, and pretended to take a nap.

I lied to my friends, all while my wedding ring sat tucked under my shirt, looped around my necklace chain.

I don't know why I kept it. I'm not delusional enough to think there was any emotion behind the drunken decision to get hitched. It was all alcohol, no heart, and it's not the start of some epic love story.

It might've been a mistake, but I'm considering his offer to stay married.

Liam made good points about his insurance. When I asked Emmy about the coverage she has, she let me know the NHL is generous with the things included in their plans.

I could see all the specialists I needed to.

I could get a prescription for medicine that manages the pain in my head.

I could splurge on services I never let myself indulge in because of how expensive they are.

There are far worse people to be married to than Liam Sullivan, even after his outburst the other morning.

I've spent all afternoon on the couch writing out the pros and cons. The list is long, and after hours of debating back and forth, I've come to realize it would be silly to not take advantage of the situation we've found ourselves in.

A knock on my front door pulls me from my internal debate. I frown and check the time.

It's too late for the girls to be stopping by. Maven fell asleep hours ago. Emmy is in Calgary for an away game and Lexi is grabbing a drink with some minor league baseball player.

There's a half second of fear Steven might be on the other side, and relief is a swift current when I check the peephole and find Liam standing there, his hands behind his back.

We didn't talk on the flight to the East Coast. When we landed in DC, I caught an Uber home before he could bring up what happened.

I'm still so mad at him.

I'm mad at what he said.

I'm mad at his reaction.

I'm mad because I couldn't hate him if I tried.

Heaving a deep breath, I open the door and stare at my husband.

"Hey." He lifts his chin and rakes his eyes over me. They linger on the shorts I slipped on after my twenty-minute shower, and a muscle in his jaw works. "Can I come in?"

"Are you going to blame me for forcing you into a marriage again?"

Liam blows out a heavy sigh and shakes his head. "No."

My fingers wrap around the door frame, and it's my turn to look at him.

His shoulders are hunched and his shirt is wrinkled. I'm pretty sure his coat is on inside out, and his beanie is halfway off his head.

He looks like shit, and my heart almost breaks in two.

"You can come in."

He nods and walks into my foyer, taking up too much space. When I close the door behind him, he hands me a bouquet. "I brought you tulips. Wasn't sure how you felt about roses, so I went with something a little more neutral."

"Roses are on the bottom of my list. Peonies are my favorites. But I do like tulips. What are these for?"

"An apology."

My breath tangles in my chest. "No one's ever bought me flowers before."

"I'm sorry the first time you're getting them is under these circumstances. I took my shit out on you. How I reacted in Vegas was uncalled for."

"It was uncalled for."

"I'm not going to lie: finding out we got married really pissed me off. You know what my priorities are. You know where I put my attention and what my focus is."

"You've made it very clear the only relationship you're interested in having, Liam, is with hockey. Did you make me feel like the thought of being married to me was your worst nightmare? Yeah, you did. But I'm pretending it was the thought of marriage as a whole, not me specifically you have a problem with."

"I don't like many people, Piper, but I like you." Liam lifts his chin. His heated gaze snags on mine, and pressure builds behind my ribs. "I think you've become one of my best friends, and treating you that way was out of line. I hate myself for it. This thing between us is going to be meaningless when you find the guy you're going to settle down with, but until then, I don't want you to walk around believing I think you're a mistake. You're not."

"Forty-eight hours ago you were furious at the idea of being married. What changed?" I challenge.

"Do you really want to know?"

"Yes."

"We didn't have practice this morning, so I went for a run to clear my head. I got turned around and ended up in front of the Capital Area Food Bank. There was a big sign in the window that said VOLUNTEERS NEEDED. I went in. Don't know why I went in, but I did. I spent a few hours sorting food donations for people who wonder where their next meal is coming from. For high school students who are working part time jobs while also going to classes. It hit me how fucking *selfish* I was being about all of this." His shoulders curl in and he hangs his head. "I have millions of dollars. I could break my leg tomorrow, never play again, and I won't worry about money for the rest of my life. I'm mad about the pressure a drunken wedding might put on me while someone four blocks over is going to bed hungry and trying to figure out how they're going to put breakfast on the table for their kids. *That* is fucking pressure. My reaction to this whole thing with us was totally out of line."

I don't know what to say. I don't know what part of that story I'm hanging onto the most. The fact he considers me one of his best friends? His selfless heart? His ability to admit when he was wrong?

All of the above?

"That sounds like an emotional day," I finally whisper, and he rubs the back of his neck. "And it was very kind of you to spend your morning there."

"It was needed. Helped me get my head out of my ass."

I bring the bouquet to my nose, and a smile sneaks out of me. "Put your coat on the rack and come to the living room. I'm going to put these in some water, and I'll meet you there."

I head to the kitchen, and Liam's footsteps follow me. I busy myself with unwrapping the flowers, cutting the stems and arranging them in a vase. It's probably petty to stall for time, but I want to make him sweat a bit.

Satisfied with how the arrangement looks, I set it on the

kitchen island and head for the living room. Liam is on the couch, staring at the framed photo on the coffee table.

"Your parents?" he asks, pointing to the picture from when I was a kid.

"Yeah." I join him on the sofa and pull my feet under me. I set a blanket over my lap and lean back. "Judy and Elijah Mitchell."

"Where do they live?"

"They're down in Florida. They retired a couple years ago and headed south for the warmer weather. Do your parents still live in Chicago?"

"Yeah. In the house I grew up in. I've tried to move them out of the city onto a piece of property that has a lot of land, but they don't want to leave. They're stubborn."

"Sounds familiar." I rest my elbow on the cushion and look at him. "Thank you for the flowers. They're beautiful."

"They don't fix the problem," he grumbles. The gears switch to the situation we've found ourselves in rather than small talk. "I'm not putting a Band-Aid on it."

"I've been thinking about the problem." I reach for the notepad I've been scribbling on all day and hold it up so he can see. "I made a very extensive pros and cons list."

"You've been busy. What's number one on the con side?"

My lips twitch. "How grumpy you are. Followed closely by how much you kick in your sleep."

"Valid."

"Before I tell you my opinions, I want to know what you think we should do."

"I've gone back and forth. An annulment makes everything go away. No one will ever know—besides Hudson, that fucker—and we can pretend it never happened. Staying married means it'll end in divorce when we're ready to move on, which is a lot harder to hide. The flip side of that, though, is you'll have access to my bank account. My insurance and, as much as I hate to say it, my name."

"What do you mean?"

"Everyone in this city knows who I am. You mention you're Liam Sullivan's wife, and you're going to get things you didn't have before. It's a shitty privilege because I'm no better than anyone out there doing their job, but it exists."

There's a flutter in my chest when he says that word.

Wife.

"What would that mean for our personal lives? We're not going to cohabitate, are we? It's strictly a legal obligation for medical benefits."

"Correct. You live your life. I live mine. If you want to keep doing our sex lessons, we can, but I'm not sure if that would complicate things more. There's no obligation to me. Well, besides Spain for the wedding," he adds, almost like an afterthought. "But I can understand if you want to back out of that too."

It's my turn to be selfish, because I can't imagine stopping our lessons now.

We're nearing the finish line, and I've been dreaming about what sex would be like with Liam.

Everything up to this point has been earth-shattering.

He's set the bar high for future relationships because he's thorough. Persistent. A giver who isn't happy until *I'm* happy, and it's disarming to be taken care of physically and emotionally.

There are the orgasms that rattle my world.

But there are other smaller, more important things.

The way he holds me after we've cleaned up. The kiss to my forehead and his arms, heavy and steady, as my feet come back to the ground.

I know people look at Liam Sullivan and see a professional athlete, but with me, he's so much more.

Kind and considerate.

Soft and tender.

A man with a heart so big, I never have to worry about where I stand.

He's my best friend too.

And I'm certain down deep in my soul, no matter which way this goes, there won't be any resentment or anger at the end of it all. It won't be like the last time I was married. I won't be wishing I could take days or weeks or months back.

He'll make me as happy as he does right now, and what a gift that is.

I glance down at my list, and I know it doesn't matter what might be on the con side. I've made my decision.

"I don't want an annulment," I say slowly. His chin jerks up and he looks at me. "We're sleeping together. We're going to pretend to date. How hard can a marriage-with-benefits be?"

Liam's grin is slow and beautiful. He reaches across the cushions and wraps his fingers around my wrist, giving me a little tug. I tumble toward him, our chests almost pressing together and our mouths inches apart.

"I want you to be sure," he murmurs. "Don't say yes because you think it's what I want to hear. Don't say yes because you think it's going to make you cursed down the road. Don't say yes because you think men are going to care how many times you've been divorced. Say yes *only* because you really and truly want to be legally bound to me, Piper. Because you want to be my wife and benefit from what I have to give you for now."

"I know you have access to things I don't, but that's not the only reason I want you to be my husband, Liam." I lick my lips, and he follows the path of my tongue. "The time I've spent with you is the most fun I've ever had. I feel free. Like when I go back into the dating world, I won't be afraid. We don't have much time left before we've fulfilled all the parts of our agreement with the lessons and your sister's wedding, and

I want to be greedy. I want to have fun for a little while longer."

"We keep this between us." He brushes his nose against mine, and I close my eyes. "We don't tell anyone else. Not your friends. Not the team."

"I think we're supposed to kiss to make this official." I dig my fingernails into his thigh. "Man and wife and all of that."

"Looks like you're going to have to be in charge of this lesson. What else can you teach me, Piper?"

Before I can say anything else, Liam's mouth is on mine.

His kiss is lazy. Slow and sensual until I'm kicking the blanket off the couch and straddling his lap. His hand rests on my lower back then drifts down to cup my ass. I feel him hard under me, the length of his cock pressing against me in a torturous way, and then cool metal brushes against my skin.

Holy shit.

He's still wearing his wedding ring.

"How's that, *wife*?" he asks, his lips moving to my jaw. "Official enough for you?"

My words catch in my throat. I can't speak, too enthralled by the path of his palms and where his mouth might go next.

I can only nod, sinking into the pleasure of knowing I might have made the best decision of my life.

Getting married a second time is a hell of a lot more fun than the first.

THIRTY
LIAM

I'VE WORKED HARD to be in the position I am as starting goalie, but it's nice to have a night off now and then. It's nice to take a breather during back-to-back games. It's nice to sit on the bench and watch my teammates play instead of tracking the puck for sixty minutes. They're way more fun than vulcanized rubber.

And having the night off while we play the worst team in the league is a treat.

I'm exhausted from the last week and a half.

Vegas.

Piper.

Getting married.

Three games, two wins and a loss.

Piper.

One accidental sleepover turned into another one two nights ago. We stayed up late talking about nothing and everything. Stupid shit. Deep shit. Funny shit. I told her about my early days as a college player. She shared the stories about her first exposure to hockey and how quickly she fell in love with the sport.

The other times she comes over and we hang out, Pico will

curl up between us. She'll stroke his fur as she hooks an ankle over my calf, a smile on her mouth while I tell her about the hoops I had to jump through to get the stubborn cat back to the States with me.

It feels so fucking *easy*, but everything with Piper is easy.

The buzzer sounds at the end of the second period, and I stand with the rest of the guys. I take my time skating to the tunnel, grateful not to have to spend intermission on a trainer's table because my legs are sore as shit.

"Lucky bastard," Maverick grumbles as he passes me. "I wish I could have the night off."

"Seems like you do with how terribly you're playing," Hudson says, and I smirk.

"Fuck you, Hayes," Maverick tosses back, but there's no bite behind it. Those two are best friends and calling each other on their shit is practically a love language. "Maybe you could try for an assist in the third period instead of hanging back and fixing your hair while the rest of us are in the offensive zone."

"Says the guy who looks in the mirror more than anyone I know," I throw in, and Hudson grins my way.

"Knew you were on my side, Sully."

I hop off the ice and glance around the tunnel, looking for Piper. I couldn't find her during the first intermission and figured she was interviewing Coach, but I still don't see her.

Another quick scan leaves me empty-handed. I frown and glance around again.

"Have you seen Piper?" I ask Hudson, and he shakes his head.

"No. Haven't seen her since the game the day before yesterday."

"Excuse me." A microphone gets thrust in my face and I whip my head to the left. A guy who can't be over twenty is blinking up at me. The polo shirt he's wearing has a stain on the collar, and he doesn't have a badge, just a name tag that says *Dusty* on it. "Can I ask you a few questions?"

"Oh, no." Hudson sighs. "Wrong move, kid. Never ask Liam Sullivan if you can ask him a few questions. You're not going to like the answer."

"Who the fuck are you?" I practically growl.

"I'm, uh, the fill-in reporter for tonight's game."

"What the fuck is a fill in reporter?"

"Maybe I should talk to someone else," Dusty sputters.

"No, you're talking to me. Where's Piper?"

"I-I don't know. I'm usually the sound guy, but I got a text an hour ago from my boss saying I needed to cover the rink-side reporter spot tonight."

I sidestep past him and hightail it to the locker room. I ignore my teammates and shove the door open, making my way to my locker. Using my teeth, I pull off my gloves and grab my phone. My notifications show I don't have any missed calls or texts or communication at all from her, and that really fucking worries me.

I stopped by her place last night, dropping off dinner on my way home from weight training. She seemed fine when I left, teasing me and calling me a bench warmer ahead of tonight's game.

Hitting her contact info, I press my phone to my ear, waiting for her to answer.

"Pick up," I mumble. "Come on, Sunshine. Pick up."

When she doesn't, I almost break the phone in two. I storm to the athletic trainers' room and barge inside.

"Liam?" Lexi looks up from the whiteboard on her lap. "Are you having hamstring tightness?"

"Where's Piper?" I ask.

"She said she had a migraine and wouldn't make it tonight. That was a couple hours ago, and I haven't heard from her since."

I curse under my breath and make my way back to the

locker room. I sit on the bench in front of my cubby and stare at the floor, wondering what the fuck I'm supposed to do.

"Hey." Hudson clasps my shoulder and I look up at him. "You good?"

"Piper isn't here. Lexi said she had a migraine. She never misses work, so if she's sick, it must be bad."

"Okay." He sits next to me. "Did you try to call her?"

"Yeah. No answer."

"Try again. We have a few minutes before we need to be back on the ice. If she doesn't answer this time, text her."

I know his advice is good, so I listen to him. She doesn't answer the second time, and it's hard to not let panic claw at my throat.

"What should I say?" I ask.

"See where she is and if she needs anything. Hopefully you get a response by the end of the game."

My thumbs fly across the screen, typing out a message.

ME

Hey. Can't find you at the game. Lexi said you have a migraine.

Do you need anything? I can stop by after.

I lock my phone and tuck it under a jersey. If Coach catches me with it, he'll make me skate laps until I collapse. "Done."

"Nothing you can do but wait, man."

"How are you so good at all of this?"

"What, communicating with people?" Hudson teases. "Thank my parents. My mom and dad had a great relationship. They talked about everything. I grew up learning to share what I'm feeling instead of letting it fester into something toxic and unfixable because two people don't want to be honest with each other."

"Sounds horrible," I say.

"It kind of is. The truth hurts sometimes."

I've never missed a day of practice.

I've never not dressed because of sickness or fatigue.

I've never left a game early, but I'm considering it tonight.

This sport is my fucking *life*, but what good is that life if someone I care about needs me and I can't be there?

I drop my head back and groan.

I told Piper she's my best friend, and I wasn't lying. I'm happier when she's around. Everything is more tolerable when she's there, too, and her absence is noticeable.

So is my attraction to her.

I've been trying to fight it.

Even more so now that we're fucking *married*, but it's getting harder to deny and hide.

My head is screaming at me to go check on her. To say *fuck hockey* and make sure she's okay, because suddenly waiting twenty more minutes seems like too long to find out.

"What if I left early?" I say under my breath. "I wouldn't sit the third period."

"You'd be fined," Hudson says.

"Don't give a shit about that."

"Do you want to leave early?"

The only thing I want is to know she's okay.

I'm sure she is.

She probably turned off her phone and fell asleep. She probably wouldn't want me to bother her.

"No." I stand and grab my gloves. "We still have work to do on the ice."

He glances up at me with a slow smile. "You like her."

"Everyone likes Piper."

"You *like* her. You care about her. You also care about your job, and you're not sure how to balance the two."

I grind my teeth together. "You're an observant motherfucker. Doesn't matter if I like her. We're never going to be anything except friends."

"Right." He stands too and smirks. "Sure you aren't."

THE THIRD PERIOD drags on forever. I keep checking the clock, finding only seconds have passed. I tap my skate, now wishing I was in the goal instead of on the bench and stewing in my thoughts.

When the final buzzer sounds, I'm the first one on my feet. Skating to the locker room like a bat out of hell. I ditch my gear and stand there shirtless, checking my phone, and not finding a response from her.

I scrub my hand over my face and sigh.

She's fine.

Perfectly fine.

But when Hudson's eyes meet mine from across the room and he tips his head to the side, mouthing the word *go*, I know where I need to be.

Where I *want* to be.

I'll make up an excuse for my departure later.

I change out of my jersey and pads, reluctantly putting my suit back on and heading for the garage. The drive to her apartment feels like it stretches for hours. When I finally park and make it up to her floor, I gently knock on her door.

"Piper?" I call out, trying to keep my voice from being too loud. "It's me. Are you in there?"

What if she passed out and hit her head?

What if she threw up on herself?

What if she's hurting so badly she can't walk?

The door clicks unlocked and opens. Piper stands in front of me with a blanket draped over her head and body, and my heart nearly stops at the sight of her.

She looks exhausted.

Physically worn out and sleep deprived.

"Liam?" She squints at me. "What are you doing here?"

"Lexi told me you weren't feeling well. I wanted to come by and see how you were doing."

"I'm okay." Piper winces and steps back, feebly motioning me inside the dark foyer. "Headache turned into a migraine, and I knew I wouldn't be able to be around the bright lights at the game."

"Did you take your medicine?"

She yawns and wraps the blanket tighter around her. "I haven't filled it yet this month. I forgot."

"What good is this marriage if you're not going to use it for things you need?"

Her cheeks flush and she shrugs. "I was going to do it this week. I've been pain-free so much lately, I got cocky."

"You'll fill it tomorrow and use my name so you can get it rush delivered?"

"Yeah. I'll fill it tomorrow. Did you come from the game? Did we win?"

"Four to one. Petersen did well in the goal."

"Better than you?"

"You know the answer to that." I step into her apartment and shut the door softly behind me. I cup her face in my hands and stroke my thumbs over her cheeks. She's burning up, her skin hot to the touch. "I was worried about you. What can I do to help?"

"You don't have to help. I know how to deal with it by myself. I've been doing it for years."

"Just because you know how to do things by yourself doesn't mean you should have to. Where were you before I got here?"

"My room."

Piper walks down the hall, and I follow behind her. I'm practically vibrating with nervous energy. I want to make sure she has water. I want to make sure she has enough blankets. I want to do whatever I can to take the pain away from her, because I don't like seeing her so small and hurting.

She slips under the covers. Her eyes flutter closed and her nose scrunches up, a cute line of wrinkles forming between her eyebrows.

"Did you text me?" she asks.

"Yeah. When you didn't answer, I wanted to come by and check in."

"The light from the screen hurts my head, so I turned my phone off."

"I figured as much. Also thought you might've fallen and hit your head."

"Not this time." She fumbles with the items on her bedside table and lets out a strangled groan. "Dammit."

"What's wrong?"

"I left my headache hat in the freezer. It helps with the—"

I'm heading for the kitchen before she can finish that sentence. I pull open her freezer and find a sealed bag in the front of the drawer with some sort of black Velcro contraption inside. I pick it up, cursing at how cold it is, and turn for her room.

"This shit is freezing," I say, and her laugh is quiet. "You put this on your head?"

"It helps with the pain. The numbness is nice." Piper sets a washcloth on her forehead and holds out her hand. I unzip the bag and set the headache hat in her palm, watching her slide it over her hair until it covers her eyes. "Oh, that's much better."

"Do you need anything else?"

"More sleep. I'm so tired. I'm going to rest my eyes for a while."

"I'll be here when you wake up."

"Good." Her smile is warm. A sight that makes me tingly and confused and elated all at once. "That makes me really happy."

THIRTY-ONE
PIPER

I DON'T KNOW how long I sleep, only that it's the best sleep of my life.

I sink into deep dreams of floating on clouds. I bury myself under the covers and savor the stillness of my room. Every now and then I'll wake, restless for only a second or two before I'm unconscious again.

The pressure in my temples starts to cease. The pain in my head slowly retreats until I'm blinking my eyes open. Until I'm warm and rested and on the verge of feeling like myself again. I stretch my arms over my head and pull the headache hat away from my face.

I blink into the dark, getting my bearings. Soft light filters under my door, and I swing my legs to the edge of the bed. Tapping my phone screen, I see that it's just past three in the morning, the rest of the world asleep while I'm firmly awake.

Wrapping a blanket around my shoulders, I open the door and glance down the hall. The hum of the heater is the only noise in my quiet apartment, and I make my way to the kitchen for a glass of water.

A figure on the couch in the living room nearly causes me

to scream until I realize it's *Liam*, his tie half unknotted and his shirt rolled to his elbows. His neck is bent at an awkward angle and one of his shoes is off, the polka dot sock on his left foot proudly displayed.

He's beautiful in the flicker of the lamplight. It's such a different sight from who he is when he's in the goal or when his head is between my legs—the dominant, possessive archetype of a man.

This is him stripped down.

Achingly tender.

Unbelievably kind.

My breath is a knot in my chest as I stare at him.

He stayed this entire time.

He's folded himself onto the couch, in clothes that look far from comfortable, so he can wait around and check on me.

I know I told him I'd be happy if he was here when I woke up, but actually *doing* it is something I wasn't prepared for.

I move toward him until he's close enough for me to reach. I touch his shoulder gently, not wanting to startle him, but he jolts awake. Sits up straight and jerks his head to the left then the right until his eyes settle on me.

"What's wrong?" He rests his hands on my shoulders, touching me as if he thought I was a part of his dreams. "Are you okay?"

"I'm fine." I brush my fingers over his jaw and the beard he hasn't shaved in months. "I can't sleep anymore."

"What do you need? Water? Food? A shower?"

"I was on my way to get water then discovered the giant ogre sitting in my living room."

"C'mere." Liam heaves a deep breath, strong arms banding around my waist until I fall into his lap. I snuggle into his chest, welcomed by the scent of cologne and laundry detergent and the faint trace of sweat clinging to his button-up shirt. "How did you sleep?"

"Really well. I didn't realize how exhausted I was."

"How's your head?"

"Are you only a fan of Twenty Questions when it concerns someone else?"

"When it concerns your health, yes."

"My head is better. I'm still sensitive to light and sound, but I—"

Liam clicks off the lamp on the table next to us, plunging the room in shadows without a second thought. "How's that?"

I bite back a smile at his thoughtfulness and rest my hand right above his heart. It's racing a mile a minute, a ferocious beat that has me curious what he's thinking about.

"Perfect," I say, because it is.

"I have water for you. And your medicine, which, according to the emergency nurse hotline, you need to be taking if you want to prevent future migraines. It's only fifty-six percent effective, but that's a hell of a lot better than taking nothing, believe it or not. Doris gave me a fucking earful for not being on your ass about your pills."

"You called the emergency nurse hotline?"

"Yeah. Asked them what I'm supposed to do and how I can take care of you. I took a lot of notes. I'll show you when the light isn't triggering. My handwriting is chicken scratch, but you'll get the idea. I also got your prescription refilled and delivered so you're covered for the next few months. Didn't like the thought of you needing it and not having it."

It feels like someone wraps a hand around my heart and squeezes unbearably tight, not letting go. I'm glad the lights are off, because otherwise he'd see the tears in my eyes and think I'm hurting when, really, I'm so ridiculously happy.

No one's taken care of me when I've been sick before.

It's always been an inconvenience, as if I *planned* to be in pain at a certain time.

I've had to fend for myself, wallowing in bed for twenty-four to forty-eight hours not because I'm stubborn and helpless, but because I'm too exhausted to make myself something to eat. Too worn out and lacking the energy I need to be a fully functioning human.

But Liam is here.

Holding me after leaving the arena, and that feels like it *means* something.

It has weight and importance, a significance I'm going to stew over when he leaves.

"Guess I should listen to Doris," I say hoarsely.

"You better. She wasn't happy with me."

"Wouldn't want that to happen again. What were some of the ways she said you can take care of me?"

"Well, I got a whole lecture on photophobia. Then I got scolded for not tracking your medication, but when I told her I got your headache hat for you, she told me I was doing a good job. Made me feel like a million bucks."

"Who knew you were so into praise?"

"Only from seventy-five-year-old nurses and you, apparently. Everyone else can fuck off."

I laugh and bury my face in his shirt. "I think I need a shower. I haven't rinsed off since yesterday morning, and I feel disgusting."

"What about food? When's the last time you ate?"

"Um, breakfast yesterday? I think? I haven't been hungry, but I should try to eat something."

"All right, Pipsqueak." He stands and lifts me in his arms. "Let's get the ball rolling."

"Liam. It's the middle of the night. You have practice tomorrow and need to get some sleep."

"No practice. Coach canceled morning skate. I don't have anywhere to be until the weight room in the afternoon."

"Okay, forget practice. It's still the middle of the night, and I can fend for myself. Really. You don't have to do all of this."

I catch a glimmer of heat in his eyes as we walk down the

hall. His jaw is tense and the frown on his mouth makes it feel like there's a pit in my stomach.

"You're doing it again," he murmurs, and I lift my chin to stare at him.

"Doing what?"

"Pretending your shit isn't as important as my shit. It is, Piper, and it really pisses me off when you think I'm doing this for any reason other than because I *want* to. I get that you think you're being a pain or too demanding—that people have made you think like that before— but I'm fucking *begging* you to ask for help from someone who wants to be here with you. When you do, you're going to learn there are a lot of people out there who would drop everything. Including me."

His words consume me. They wash over me, a tidal wave I have no idea how to respond to.

I'm not sure I can.

It's too raw. Too real. Too much outside the labels we've curated for ourselves, and thinking of him as anything other than the grumpy goalie who is my friend and bedroom coach terrifies the *hell* out of me, because I've seen what I could lose. I've seen the man Liam is and the ways he measures up to Steven, far outweighing him in every single category.

He *wants* to be here.

He *wants* to help, and this is all so new.

I want him here too.

"Okay," I whisper, gripped by the fear of rejection but shoving it aside because I trust Liam. I trust him so much it hurts. "Would you stay and help me?"

"There's nowhere else I'd rather be." He makes his way to my bathroom, only setting me down when the water is running and steam billows out of the shower. "Take off your clothes."

"You take yours off first."

His fingers deftly unknot the tie around his neck. Pull it free from his collar and toss it on the marble floor. The buttons of his shirt come undone next, one by one until he's bare-chested and staring at me.

My hands shake as I tug my sweatshirt over my head. I've been naked in front of him a dozen times now. I've had his fingers inside me and my mouth on his cock, but there's something startling about this moment that makes it feel *different*.

Monumental, almost.

He's seen me when I've been at my most vulnerable. When I'm hurting and weak and small, he stuck around.

I know I'm taking off my clothes, but I think I might be letting down my walls too. Crashing through that fear and leaning into him because he's sturdy and strong and unwavering.

His eyes never stray from mine as I step out of my sweatpants. They stay on my face, a softness I've gotten used to seeing behind the dark brown whenever he looks at me. I climb into the shower and water streams down my body. Liam joins me a second later, his presence welcome.

"Sit," he murmurs, pointing to the ledge attached to the wall. I can barely fit on it, my ass taking up too much space, but I listen, dropping to the cool stone and watching him wondrously. "Want to wash your hair."

Liam unhooks the shower head and wets the blonde strands. I sigh at the way his fingers massage my scalp, the pressure he adds where I'm holding onto lingering pain.

"Doris also told me massaging might help." He sets the shower head aside and uses both hands to press at my temples. A groan slips out of me, my limbs going pliant and relaxed. "But you tell me if it's too much."

"Perfect," I whisper, and I don't know if I'm talking about the massage. About him. About all of this. "It's perfect."

I think I fall asleep when he lathers the shampoo in my hair. I think my brain turns to mush when he drops to his knees and washes my feet and legs. Across my stomach and up to my shoulders until I'm covered in soap suds. He kisses me, and a lightbulb goes off in my head.

It's bright and it's blinding and the only thing I can see.

Holy *shit.*

I have a crush on my husband, and that was *not* part of the plan.

THIRTY-TWO
PIPER

LIAM

How are you feeling, Pipsqueak?

ME

Like a new woman. Thank you for all your help!

LIAM

Glad to hear it. See you bright and early.

LIAM

Attachment: 1 image

Pico likes you more than he likes me.

ME

Well, obviously. I'm a delight!

LIAM

Are you?

ME

Watch it, Sullivan. You called me your best friend.

LIAM

I have no recollection of those events.

ME

Attachment: 1 image

Now you have a photo of my middle finger.

LIAM

Want another lesson tonight?

ME

I have dinner plans with the girls. I bailed on them last week and don't want to bail again. Sorry!

Tomorrow?

LIAM

Early game on Sunday. Rain check?

ME

Definitely.

ME

About our next lesson…

LIAM

I'm listening…

ME

Are you free this afternoon?

LIAM

No. Volunteering with some of the team at the animal shelter.

ME

Bring Pico home a friend!!

LIAM

He might claw my eyes out if I tried.

LIAM

No game tonight or tomorrow. What are you doing?

ME

Shopping with Lexi and trying to find some outfits for our trip.

Why the hell did you just send me five thousand dollars?

LIAM

Because I can.

Buy yourself something nice, wife.

ME

Hi.

LIAM

Sunshine. What are you up to?

ME

Is it silly to say I miss you?

AS A FRIEND.

LIAM

Still doodling in your journal, aren't you?

ME

Yup. Your name is in hearts everywhere.

Maybe I'll get it tattooed on my wrist.

LIAM

You're obsessed with me. I knew it.

ME

Wait. What's your middle name?

LIAM

Starts with an F.

ME

Fucker?

LIAM

Original.

ME

Fed Up?

LIAM

Now you're on the right track.

ME

We've been playing tag the last few weeks.

LIAM

I know. Now you're it.

Get your ass over here.

AS A FRIEND.

"THIS WAS DELICIOUS." I scrape my fork across my plate, wanting to get the last of the marinara sauce from the chicken parmesan he made. "How did you learn to cook so well?"

"My mom." Liam puts a dirty pan in the sink and smiles. "She's always in the kitchen. I remember the first time she let me cut up the carrots for chicken noodle soup one winter. There's something cathartic about it to me. Maybe because it's like hockey; it's precise. Exact. You can't skip ahead. That's always been how my brain works."

"If you were forced to cook only one meal the rest of your life, what would it be?"

"Pancakes. Breakfast for dinner is severely underrated."

"I love pancakes."

"Next time you're over, I'll make you some."

"Talk about five star services. Orgasms. Food. Access to good healthcare." I laugh and spin on the barstool. "I'm all set up with a new doctor. You were right about using your name, by the way. I felt a little slimy saying I was Liam Sullivan's wife, but it's too late to take it back now."

"You're using it for a good cause, not to get into a club or something." He tosses a dirty napkin in the trash. "I made dessert too."

"Wow. This is a full-fledged meal." I jump off my seat at his kitchen island and slide up next to him. "What did you make?"

"Chocolate chip cookies. You always sneak a couple extra at team dinner… I thought they might be your favorite."

"They are my favorite." I grin and look up at him. "I'm wondering if you're the one obsessed with me, Sullivan."

"Consider this a mini lesson."

"Oh, I like when you get into teacher mode. You should buy a pair of glasses."

"Is roleplaying on your list of things to try?"

"I mean, maybe? I wouldn't be opposed to it."

"Then be quiet, Ms. Mitchell, so you can learn something," he says sternly, and I practically melt. "A guy should be doing nice things for you in and out of the bedroom. They should be noticing things you enjoy. Places you like to be touched. Food you like to eat. It's simple stuff, honestly."

"And if they're *not* noticing these things?"

"Means they're only in it for the sex and don't see enough of a future with you to want to learn your likes and dislikes."

"Wow. Okay. That's important. What other lessons do you have for me?"

"You know what we're doing tonight."

His eyes turn dark and he threads his hand through mine. With a gentle tug, he leads me down the hall. I follow behind him, my breath sharp and shallow.

I knew this moment was coming.

I've been waiting for it.

Dreaming about it.

Counting down the seconds until we got *here*, but I'm still nervous as hell. Trembling when he opens the door to his bedroom and guides me inside.

He was right when he told me there are emotions associated with sex, and I'm *scared*.

Scared that I won't be good enough for him.

Scared he'll compare me to the other women he's been with and not want anything to do with me anymore.

Scared we'll do this and he won't be interested anymore.

I can make jokes. I can play it off with sarcasm or quick wit, but under all these games of pretend, I'm starting to think I have feelings for him—*real* feelings—and I'm terrified how this next step might change things between us.

I'm still working on myself.

He doesn't want anything serious.

I *know* that, but it doesn't dull my attraction to him.

At first, I thought my pull to Liam was because he was the first man in years to show me any attention. The first man to listen and seem interested in what I had to say.

Over time, though, I'm learning it's *him* I'm drawn to.

The guy at the supermarket doesn't do anything for me.

The guy at the western bar didn't do anything for me.

Liam does something for me, and tonight I get to have him exactly how I've wanted him from the very beginning.

"Hey." He rubs the inside of my wrist. My eyes shoot to his, and he's watching me. Studying me. Clawing past the layers and finding the most intimate parts of me, and *god* that makes my chest ache. "What's wrong?"

"Nothing." I shake my head and smile. "I'm fine. Let's do this."

"Piper. Don't hide from me."

"It's silly. I'm supposed to get on my knees and blow you. You're supposed to fuck me. That's how this arrangement works, right?"

"We're not *supposed* to do anything. I need you to be honest with me, and right now, you're not being honest."

Damn him and his ability to read people.

I walk to his bed. The mattress sags under my weight and I sigh. "I'm nervous. Not for the physical aspect of it, but for the emotional aspect. You've been so nice to me these last few months. Teaching me. Being patient with me. I want this to be good for you. I want you to get off and enjoy what you're doing. I don't want this to be a one-way thing. I've always felt so rejected after sex, and it makes me think I'm the problem. Like I'm not going to be able to satisfy you."

He moves toward me and drops to his haunches, right between my legs. He cups my face in his palms and runs his thumbs over my cheeks. "I am never going to reject you," he says so softly, I think I might be dreaming this all up. "Ever. And I want you to know I enjoy everything I do with you, Piper. Eating dinner. Holding your hand. Watching you get off and not getting off myself. It's going to be good because it's you and me, but I need you to know just fucking existing with you in my orbit is enough. I don't need the other shit. Forget sex. Forget blow jobs. Forget every lesson we've had. We can go to bed right now and I'll still think the same way about you tomorrow."

His words carve a spot on my heart—the lonely, sad, forgotten part I thought might never get attention. They tattoo themselves over every inch of the organ, erasing the old. Getting rid of the bad and making me believe them too.

"Thank you," I whisper, but the two words feel inadequate. Hardly worthy of the way he's building me up. Laying a brick each and every time we're together until soon I'll stand on a pedestal high above my former self. "Thank you for being patient with me. I want to do this, Liam, and I want to do this with you."

There's a tremor in his hand that wasn't there before as he reaches up and pulls my hair free from its ponytail. As he brushes his nose against mine and kisses me softly, gently, like I'm the most precious thing in the world.

I expect him to jump right into it, but he doesn't.

He keeps kissing me, his lips bruising mine, until I can't take it anymore.

I reach for his shirt and pull it over his head, tossing it aside and urging him along. I run my hands down his bare back and smile against his mouth when he hisses at the bite of my nails along the line of his spine.

Liam eases me onto my back so I'm flat on the mattress. His palms run up my thighs to the waistband of my jeans, fingers toying with the button.

"Good?" he asks, unfastening the silver clasp and dragging the zipper down.

"Perfect," I murmur, lifting my hips so he can yank the pants off my legs.

When I'm free, I sit up, discarding my shirt until I'm in nothing but the lingerie set I bought the other night with Lexi.

The purchase was an impulse buy because I wanted to make tonight special, but from the way Liam stares at me, from the hollow of my throat to the small mole next to my belly button, I know I could've shown up in a sack and he'd be looking at me the same way.

"What—" His throat bobs. He glares at the blue lace like it's offended him. Like he wants to rip it to shreds. "What are you wearing?"

"I wanted something sexy and—"

Liam crawls on top of me, his body weight heavy over mine. I can tell he's hard through the fabric of his joggers, his cock straining against the cotton.

"You are the hottest woman I've ever seen. You don't need lace to look fucking incredible, but goddamn Piper, does it make you irresistible." His fingers move to the strap of the bra, snapping it against my skin then sucking on the mark he left behind. "I'm going to fucking ruin you tonight, baby."

I whimper and wrap my legs around his waist, drawing him nearer to me. I arch my back so I can reach his mouth, kissing him again as he cups my breast and drags his thumb over my hard nipple.

"I didn't know your favorite color," I say, turning my head so he can kiss my neck. So he can move down my body. His mouth closes around my breast and sucks over the lace.

"Favorite color is whatever you're wearing." He pulls both cups down, exposing my chest to the cool air of the room. "Black. Pink. Red. *Blue*. Want them all." His large hands push my breasts together, and he groans. "Want to fuck your tits."

"Fuck me first," I challenge, my arm snaking between us so I can cup him through his sweatpants. "Then you can fuck my tits."

He nudges my hand out of the way so he can settle his fingers between my legs. His knuckles brush over the front of my underwear and he groans again. "*Fuck.* You're already wet, aren't you?"

I grab his wrist and guide him, helping him tug my underwear to the side. "Have been since dinner."

He touches my clit with his thumb then slides a single finger in me, nice and slow. "Should've put you on my kitchen counter and fucked you right there."

I relish the careful way he goes from one finger to two to three. It's easier than when we first started all of this, my body adjusting to him and craving him. I'm already on the brink of an orgasm, the high creeping up on me suddenly and stealthily as I hold onto his hair, bliss just within reach.

"*Liam*. Please. Can you—"

He curls his fingers in me. Dips his chin, sharp teeth sinking into the flesh of my breast, and I explode.

The room spins around me. Bursts of light take over my vision and I grind into him, wanting—*needing*—a little more.

"You can give me two, can't you?" he says into my neck, thumb pressing on my clit as a cry sneaks out of me. "There she is. So fucking pretty."

The second one isn't nearly as aggressive but it feels just as good, a satisfied ache settling low in my stomach as Liam's movements slow.

"Fuck," I pant. A bead of sweat rolls down my forehead and I brush it away. "I think I'm on top of the world."

He hooks his fingers in the waistband of my underwear and pulls them off, shoving them in his pocket. "Take off your bra."

"What are you doing with those?"

"Saving them for later."

That sends my mind racing. I fumble with the clasp of my bra until my breasts spill free and I'm naked on his sheets, looking up at him. "Take off your pants."

He climbs off me and stands, yanking his sweatpants and briefs off. "Bossy."

"Condoms?"

"Have a whole box. And, yes. They glow in the dark."

I burst out laughing. "Are you serious?"

"Yup." Liam turns to his bedside table and opens a drawer. "You said you're already on top of the world, Piper. I'm sending you to the stars next."

"Another first. Speciality condoms." I watch him pull out a box and a plastic tube. "Lube?"

"Yeah. I know this isn't your first time, but I wanted to have it on hand. Just in case."

"What are you talking about? I'm a professional. So much sex with so many people."

He rolls the condom down his length. I prop up on my elbows, wanting to see each step. Wanting to learn how he likes to do things so I can help next time.

Liam climbs back on the bed. He nudges his way between my thighs and grips my knee. "What positions have you tried?"

"Missionary."

"Did you like it?"

"It was fine."

"Okay, so you're not a fan. Noted. We're going to do something similar that's more enjoyable, but if it doesn't feel good for you, tell me and we'll do something different. Put your leg on my hip. There you go."

I blow out a breath. My eyes shut and my hands clutch the sheets around me. "I'm ready."

I know it's not my first time but it *feels* like my first time with the anticipation. The waiting and wondering of how it'll feel and how much I'm going to like it with him.

I do my best to stay relaxed. To sink into the bed as the head of his cock teases over my entrance. I hiss when he pushes inside me, the sensation on the edge of painful while also being deliriously, unfathomably perfect.

We groan in unison when he rocks his hips forward, the first few inches of his length burying in me. Stars cloud my vision, but it only lasts for so long because Liam takes hold of my chin.

"Piper," he almost growls. "Open your eyes and look at me when I fuck you."

THIRTY-THREE
LIAM

I'VE FOUND HEAVEN on earth, and it's being inside Piper Mitchell.

Fuck.

She's so tight. So warm.

So fucking *perfect* I never want to fucking leave.

Her eyes fly open. Her lips part and she inhales a deep breath, chest rising and falling rapidly.

"Put your other leg on my waist," I tell her, but I'm not sure I'm even speaking coherent words. My brain is a jumbled mess, everything confusing and distracting as she lifts her leg and I get another inch deeper.

"Oh, *fuck.*" Her eyes stay locked on mine, big and wide, and her back arches. "That's—"

"Better?"

"So much better. *Liam.* I need you to—this is—*move.* Please."

"Give me a second. If I move, I'm going to come."

"So *come.*"

"Not yet," I grit out. "Need to enjoy your perfect cunt first."

I grip her leg so tightly I'm sure I'm going to leave behind a bruise. It's taking everything in me not to thrust all the way into her so I can see how well she takes every inch of me. To see what she looks like when she comes on my cock.

I hold the base of my shaft and push forward another inch, going impossibly slow. It's the only way I'll hold onto my self-control. The only way I'll get through this with a scrap of dignity left, because I am seconds away from begging her to move into my apartment. To let me take care of her every night and every goddamn morning, because I can't think of anything else.

I'll feed her. I'll fuck her. I'll treat her right. I'll give her whatever she wants so she knows she won't find anyone better than me.

"Liam," she groans, and I love the way she says my name. How it tumbles from her mouth like a fucking prayer. "I can take more."

Goddammit.

That's probably the worst thing she could've said to me, because now I don't want to be gentle.

I don't want to take my time.

I want to see my cock buried in her.

I want to see how deep I can get. How fast I could make her come and how tight she'll clench around me.

I'd let her suffocate me and I'd say thank you from the afterlife.

"Hang on." I bring her knees to her chest, using them as leverage. I'm almost halfway inside her now, and *Christ*, it's so good. "Okay?"

"*Yes.*" Her nails dig into my back. They scratch down my skin and settle on my hips, urging me forward. "Is that all of it?"

I bark out a laugh. "We've got a ways to go, baby. Deep breath for me. I'm going to add a little more pressure."

Piper nods, and I thrust forward as gently as I can. I groan, the years of loneliness catching up to me way too fucking quickly. I know I only have a couple minutes before I finish, before I fall headfirst over the ledge because her pussy is too *goddamn perfect* to want to try to last longer.

I've thought about this moment long before she ever asked me to fuck her.

Back when she was still married, that ring on her finger taunting me.

When the ring disappeared and I heard she was single.

When I started going out of my way in the arena to see her, to make sure she was okay, to have her smile at me because it made my whole fucking day.

When we had that night in Canada.

When she's been in my bed the last few months, possessiveness gripping me at the sight of her in my shirt with a hickey on her neck.

I've been wanting Piper for *years*, and now that I have her, I'm going out of my fucking mind.

"I think I might come from this," she whimpers. "And I've never—"

"I'm a greedy bastard, Piper. You know I like having all your firsts," I say, snapping my hips to the music of her moans. "Almost there. God, I can't wait to see what my wife looks like when she takes all of my cock."

With one final push I'm seated all the way inside her, my cock fully buried and my mental capacity dwindling. It's a dizzying feeling, one I know I wouldn't be experiencing if this were any other woman.

It's because it's *her*.

She rests her chin on her chest, glancing down at where we're joined. "Holy shit."

"Mini lesson time. Want to make this even better for you?"

"How the *hell* is that possible?"

"Touch yourself. Your tits. Your pussy. Wherever you want. It's going to help you get off. It lets me watch you, and you know I'm a fan of that."

She reaches out, fingers landing on her clit and moaning when her hand bumps against my shaft. "There's—your—I'm so *full*."

I rock forward and snap my hips. My eyes roll to the back of my head when she tightens around me. When she whispers my name and grabs my hand, her fingers intertwine with mine as she rests them on her heart.

"Fucking perfect. Perfect pussy. Perfect mouth. God, you're incredible."

"Are you going to come?" Piper asks, blinking up at me with pink cheeks and the faintest smile on her pretty little mouth. "Are you going to finish inside me, Liam?"

I've never hated a condom more.

I know wearing one is the smart thing to do.

I know I'd regret it if I went without it, but *goddamn* if I don't want to paint her with my cum. Want to watch it leak down her leg then shove it back in her so she knows who makes her feel so fucking good.

"Where else do you think I'm going to finish? Going to make you mine, Piper."

Mine for the time being, my brain challenges, and I shove the thought away.

"Could you—maybe a little—*oh*. Right there, Liam. Just—"

I pinch her nipple at the same time I slam into her forcefully. Purposefully. Letting her know I'll give her anything she fucking wants, and I feel the second her orgasm grabs her. She cries out, nice and loud, chanting my name again and again until her throat goes hoarse. Until her eyes close and a tear rolls down her cheek.

I don't last a second longer, thrusting one more time and wanting nothing more than to join her on the other side. I collapse forward. I gasp through a choked inhale, the muscles in my legs convulsing until I've spilled everything I have into the latex and nearly killing myself in the process.

"God"—I groan—"fucking damn."

"Are you okay?" Piper touches my forehead and I nod, not knowing my name or where I am, only that everything is fucking magical.

"More than okay," I pant. Her hand moves to my hips, tracing along the base of my cock, and I groan again. "*Shit*, Piper. It's really—I'm—"

"I want to see," she whispers.

I nod, somehow controlling my limbs enough to pull out of her. I wince at the loss of contact, and she moans. She lifts her hips like she's asking for more. There's blood on the condom. The latex is stained red, and I rub my thumb across her stomach.

"Did I hurt you?"

"No." She shakes her head and lifts up on her elbows, seeing the blood. She glances down at the sheets, at the small stain on the navy blue, and she winces. "I'm sorry. I thought that might happen. I'll help you change the sheets. I—"

"Fuck no you won't." I kiss her, needing to taste her. Needing her to know this is *fine*. "You think I give a shit about some blood? You haven't had sex in years, and we both know I'm bigger than your ex is."

Piper huffs. "That wasn't subtle at all."

"It wasn't meant to be. The blood was bound to happen, and it's not a big deal. If you weren't so exhausted, I'd fuck you again. I'd see if I could get you to make an even bigger mess. Maybe even on my hand. I'll tell you something, Piper. Men aren't bothered by things like that. If a guy cares about a little blood, you need to kick him to the fucking curb. You know why?"

"Why?" she asks, blinking up at me.

"Because it shows you did such a good job, sweetheart. Look what you did to me." I carefully ease the condom off my length and tie it off. I hold it up to her so she can see it full of my release, and her eyes go wide. "I'm so fucking proud of you."

I know this is casual between us, but for a woman who's never been shown any sort of intimate affection, who's never had *her* pleasure made a top priority, this is going to make her emotional.

I anticipate it. Before she can react, before she has a chance to get in her head and overanalyze what happened, I toss the condom in the trash. I gather her in my arms, my fingers working out the knots in her hair.

"That was so liberating," Piper whispers. "It felt amazing, but *my god* I liked watching you come undone." Her thumb rubs along my collarbone. "And knowing I was the one making you fall apart makes me really proud."

She fucking wrecked me.

Rocked my whole world, and I'm not sure I'm ever going to be the same.

"I'm glad you're proud of yourself." I move my hand up her arm and rest my chin on her shoulder. "You should be."

"I'm going to need a few minutes, but I'll be ready for round two soon." She stretches and yawns. "And maybe a shower."

"We're going to hold off on round two. You're going to be sore, and, after a shower, I'd bet my entire paycheck from Saturday's game you'll be asleep."

"But what if I want more?" Piper shifts in my lap, straddling me. She rolls her hips, grinding against my inner thigh, and I grip her waist.

"I said we're going to hold off on round two, not that I'm not going to take care of you. And we're starting with cleaning you up."

I lift her up and scoot to the end of the bed. I stand, carrying her to the bathroom and flipping on the light. Pico darts out from the nest he's made for himself under the double vanity, and Piper laughs as he skirts by.

"Is that a pile of towels?"

"Yup. He refuses to sleep in the expensive bed I got him and is perfectly content with the towels I bought online. Pain in my ass," I say, setting her down. "Bath or shower?"

"Oh, a bath sounds nice. But only if you join me."

"I'm not sure we'll both fit. You get in. I'll rinse off after you." I turn on the faucet. "Water temperature preference?"

"Scalding hot, please." Piper sits on the ledge of the tub and smiles up at me. "Permission to ask a personal question?"

"Piper." I stick my hand under the water and turn it up a few degrees. "You've had my dick inside you. You can ask whatever the hell you want."

"What do your tattoos mean? They're all so beautiful."

"Wish I had a good story for them, but I don't. Not really. The sparrows match the tattoo Alana has." I tap the birds that span across my ribcage. "We got them when she turned eighteen because she's always been a bit of a free spirit who wants to spread her wings. The fern leaves are for growth and resilience. My first season in the league I rode the bench in Minnesota. Didn't play in a single game. I knew I was good enough to be a starter, but it wasn't my time yet. Then I landed in DC and joined a losing team who set the league record for most defeats in a single season. I needed something to keep me going. It's stupid, but when I look at the ink, it reminds me that I do this because I love the game and things are always going to get better."

"Wow. Look at you being Mr. Positive." She nudges my foot with hers. "And what are you talking about not having a good story for them? That was insightful. Now I feel like I really know you."

"Thoughts?" I ask on a whim, turning off the water and looking at her.

I don't know why I'm desperate to hear her answer. It's like my life hangs in the balance until I know exactly what she thinks of me.

"I like what I see." Piper braces herself on my shoulder and steps into the tub. The water laps over the sides and runs down the porcelain onto the floor, but I don't care. She rests her chin on her knees and grins at me. "Do you like what you see?"

"Yeah." I squat next to her and rub my thumb across her cheek. "Confident, thoroughly fucked, and taken care of looks damn good on you. Think we should keep it that way. Now lie back. Let me wash your hair."

"Liam. You don't need to—"

"And if I want to?"

She reaches out of the tub and takes my hand in hers. She squeezes once and relaxes in the steaming water, golden hair going everywhere.

"Then I'll let you."

"Thank you."

I take my time washing and conditioning her hair. When I finish, I dry her off and bring her to my bed.

I've hooked up with a few women before.

I'm not a playboy who's slept with half the city, but I'm not inexperienced either.

It's never been like this.

Like I simultaneously want time to speed up so I can see her again while also wishing it could slow down so I can savor each and every second with her, stretching them out for as long as I can.

And as she settles against my chest in one of my T-shirts, her head buried in my shoulder and her heartbeat matching mine, I try to figure out why the fuck this time is so different.

THIRTY-FOUR
LIAM

PUCK KINGS

G-MONEY

What's the dress code tonight?

HUDSON

Business causal. What you would wear to the arena on game day.

G-MONEY

So I can't wear the new pair of Crocs I got?

RILEY

Crocs aren't cool, Grant. You're wasting your money on those things.

G-MONEY

I think they're cool. So does Easy E.

HUDSON

Not sure I'd consider it a good thing to have Ethan's vote.

MAVERICK

Coach told me to remind you all we have a game tomorrow. There will be press there tonight, so be on your best behavior.

And you can't leave before he makes his speech.

That was for Goalie Daddy.

ME

And if we sneak out?

MAVERICK

I've got my eye on you.

ME

That wasn't a no.

PIPER

Are you going to the season ticket holder event tonight?

ME

Unfortunately.

I swear we didn't have this many events last season. This is what happens when you give fans a survey and they want the players to be more 'accessible.'

PIPER

Come on! You don't think it's going to be fun?

ME

It's socializing with people who like to tell me how I should do my job.

PIPER

I'll make sure to come up and bother my dear husband.

ME

Can't wait to see you try, wife.

PIPER

Maybe I'll tell you how you should be doing your job better.

ME

Going through a tunnel. Losing service.

PIPER

You're such a shit.

I'LL COMPLAIN for hours about having to socialize with people as a side part of my job, but I won't complain about signing autographs for kids.

I love listening to their favorite stories and how they fell in love with hockey. I like being told I'm their favorite goalie in the league and learning what positions they prefer to play.

The Blackhawks sucked during my childhood. They were the epitome of mediocrity, but that didn't stop me from being a fan. I was obsessed. I listened to the games on the radio with my dad and dissected every single play, explaining what I would do if I were on the ice.

I didn't talk a lot as a kid, but I came alive when I talked about hockey.

When I was eight, I met some of my idols at an event like this one. My parents spent all year saving up, forgoing Christmas presents to put money toward gala tickets, and

Alana was *pissed* she didn't get the Barbie Dreamhouse she wanted.

I still have the signed photos from Kyle Calder and Jocelyn Thibault tucked in a closet at my parents' house for safekeeping. They spent ten minutes with me, letting me chat their ear off about how I wanted to make it to the NHL too.

Their interaction with me taught me how professional athletes should interact with kids. You don't rush them. You don't look bored. You let them lead the conversation, and when they ask for a photo, you smile like you're the happiest fucker in the world.

Because who knows what those kids might amount to. Could be the next Gretzky. Could be the next Maverick Miller. Could be *me*, and that's a humbling thought.

"Thank you, Mr. Sullivan," a small boy says when I hand him back his photograph. "I hope you win the Vezina Trophy."

"I couldn't do it without my teammates." I stick out my hand out my hand and smile when he bumps his knuckles with mine. "Have fun tonight."

He runs away, clutching the photo to his chest, and it still blows my mind people care about me as a player.

"Can I get a signed photo?" a voice says from behind me, and when I look over my shoulder, Piper is smiling at me. "Please?"

"Since you asked so nicely." I rub my lips together to keep from grinning. "Do you have one with you?"

"I do. I carry it around in my pocket since I'm obsessed with you and everything."

"Normal behavior." I pat the stool next to me. "Come on over. I'll personalize it for you too."

"Player of the year right here." She jumps on the barstool. "You look like you're having fun."

"It's for the kids. The next generation of players and people who spend their allowance to come see me play. I'd rather talk to them than the owners with a minority stake in the club."

"Eat the rich, am I right?" Piper puts a photograph on the bar, and I burst out laughing. "Look familiar?"

"Where did you *get* this?" It's an image of me in college, tall and lanky. Before I learned eating protein will help me gain muscle. I look like a totally different person in the goal, and I shake my head at my poor knee positioning. "It's a relic."

"I had to do some *deep* internet sleuthing. The University of Wisconsin has some lovely academic programs, but they don't keep many photos of past hockey teams."

"Because they aren't worth keeping."

"I'd say pictures from winning the Frozen Four are worth keeping. Especially when they feature the great Liam Sullivan." Her fingers drum over the black-and-white image. "A signature, please."

"Anything for a fan." I uncap the Sharpie and look at her. "Any preference on how it's addressed?"

"Nope. Go wild, Sully."

I think for a second and start writing, sliding it her way when I'm finished.

"There you go. Could be worth something one day."

"Could be worth something now." Piper looks at the message and laughs. "This is perfect."

TO PIPSQUEAK:
I TOLERATE YOU
AS A FRIEND.
FROM LIAM SULLIVAN

"Glad you like it. Are you having fun?"

"Yeah." She tucks a strand of hair behind her ear and surveys the room. "Good turnout. Five different people have come up to me and told me how much they appreciate the fresh energy I bring to the broadcast team, so that was an ego boost. The unbelievable part? Three of them were men."

"Look at you. You might be the key to world peace."

"I just might be." She nudges my side with her elbow and stands. "I need to go mingle. There's someone here from the Washington Post, and I want to introduce myself."

"Go be a social butterfly, Sunshine. I'm going to keep hiding in a corner."

"Don't have too much fun." Piper touches my shoulder. Her smile turns soft, and it's the kind of beam I can feel everywhere on my body. "You look great, by the way. You should wear a tux more often."

"Noted." I give her elbow a quick squeeze. "But only for you."

With a parting wave, she heads across the room, and I grab a bottle of water from the bucket of ice to my right so I don't gawk at her ass as she walks away.

"How's Piper?" Maverick asks, sliding up to me.

"What? How would I know how Piper is?"

"Uh." He blinks at me. "Because you were just talking to her?"

"Oh." I pull on my collar and shrug. "She's fine. Off to do an interview or something."

"She's good at her job, isn't she?" He leans against the bar and takes a sip of his water. "Glad you're out with us tonight. I know this isn't usually your thing."

"Didn't really have a choice. Coach told me he was going to bench me if I didn't show."

"He's moved to ultimatums to get you to attend events? Genius. Should've done it years ago. Think of all the fun you've missed out on."

"We have very different definitions of the word fun."

"Come on. There are worse places you could be right now."

"And there are far better places I could be."

"Hey." Maverick squints and lifts his chin. "Isn't that Charlie? The guy who used to do the announcing for our games? Been wondering what happened to him."

I follow his gaze and narrow my eyes when I recognize Charlie Woolworth, Piper's old boss and douche extraordinaire, making a beeline for us.

Before I can try and escape, he takes the spot on my other side, a cocky grin on his smug, punchable face.

"Gentlemen." Charlie sticks out his hand and Maverick gives me a confused look before shaking it. I ignore the invitation and take a long sip of my water. "Are we having a good evening?"

"Can't really complain." Maverick shrugs. "Where've you been, man? I haven't seen you around the arena in ages. Did something happen?"

"What didn't happen is the real question." Charlie scoffs and pulls out a twenty from his wallet. He drops the crisp bill in the tip jar and rolls his eyes. "I lost the job I've had for fucking decades because of a misunderstanding. It's bullshit, if you ask me."

My fingers wrap around the water bottle. The plastic crunches under my tight grip, and I pretend it's his neck. Anger boils in my blood, and I wonder what he'd look like with my fist in his face. I wonder what he'd look like with a black eye and a bruised cheek.

"A misunderstanding? There's a rumor going around you found a new gig somewhere else," Maverick says.

"No new gig, and you can blame Piper Mitchell. That bitch complained about me to HR. She—"

I slam my fist down on the bar so hard, all the drinks rattle. Everyone in the nearby vicinity turns to look at me, but I don't give a shit.

I'm too busy staring Charlie down.

Contemplating his murder and how I'd make it look like an accident.

"I'd be very careful what you say next," I tell him slowly, so there's no room for the dumbass to mishear me. "That's my wife you're talking about."

Maverick drops his water bottle and gasps.

"Your *wife*?" Charlie repeats, venom behind the word. "Maybe you should put her on a leash, Sullivan, so she knows her place. Fucking over someone who has *years* of experience in this industry because she can't take a joke shows me she isn't going to last a goddamn season in the league. They're going to eat her alive. Maybe they'll eat her out, too, and I can watch."

Rage takes over my vision.

I don't see him anymore but Piper instead.

I'm thrown back to that night in Texas when I spotted her crying in the hallway. Shoulders shaking, head in her hands. The way she looked so small and so fucking *defeated*.

She doesn't know I saw her.

She doesn't know I tracked down her other coworker—the nice one—and asked him what happened.

She doesn't know I went with him to HR, sitting by his side while he recanted each and every word this piece of shit said about her.

I've never been so mad in my life.

And seeing him in front of me now? Making it seem like what happened was *her* fault?

I could burn the entire fucking world down.

I act before I can think, setting down my water and grabbing Charlie by the collar. He's easy to lift, and I drag him to a hallway behind the bar before anyone can notice we're gone.

"How about you say that again?" I step close to him so our chests touch. So I can see the fear in his eyes. I stand to my full height, towering over him and making sure he knows *exactly* who he's fucking with. "And this time, look me in the eye when you do."

Charlie swallows. "I-I—"

"Say it." My hand moves to his throat. I've never been in a fight off the ice, but this would be too fucking easy. "Nice and loud, so I can hear you."

"Whoa. Hey. Liam. Easy, buddy," Maverick says from behind me. "Let's take a second here."

"This piece of shit doesn't deserve a second." I look over my shoulder and glare at my captain. "Do you know what he said about Piper? He told his buddy they could bend her over his desk and tag team her. That if she'd just pop open her shirt, he'd give her more airtime. Claimed he was untouchable because of how much power he had. How much fucking power do you have now, dickbag?"

My fingers press harder into Charlie's throat. I could kill him if I wanted to. It wouldn't take much, and I'm so tempted to hurt him the way he hurt her.

"Liam." Maverick tugs on my shoulder. "Put him down. He's not worth it."

She's worth it, though.

I know she wouldn't want me to fight this asshole.

I know she'd want me to walk away.

I know she'd want me to leave him alone and be the bigger person.

Fuck.

I really care what she thinks of me.

"Fucker." I let go of Charlie and take a step back. "If you *ever* talk to her again, I will end you. And I'll smile while I do it."

Charlie looks between us. There's not a second of hesitation before he's taking off down the hallway. He's almost around the corner before Maverick stretches out his hand and gives me a look.

"One second, Charlie," my captain says, jogging toward him. When he gets close, he pulls his fist back. Laughs then decks the guy so hard in the face, he stumbles backward. Blood spurts from his nose, and Charlie groans. "That's for saying shit about my friend. Piper is one of us. Do it again, and I won't be so nice."

"Thought he wasn't worth it," I grumble as the douchebag runs away clutching his nose. "Look at you getting all the fucking glory."

"Wasn't worth if for you to punch him. You're too emotionally invested and would've killed him. To me, he's just a piece of shit. And I really need my goalie tomorrow."

"You didn't have to do that."

"Yes, I did. You had my back when we went in on Emmy's ex during the game we played against him. I have your back now."

"Thanks, man."

"Don't thank me yet. What the *fuck* was that wife comment about?"

I rub the back of my neck. Tension rolls through me, and I don't know what to say. We've kept our drunken wedding a secret since Vegas. You'd have no idea we were married based on how we interacted with each other at the arena.

Unless you asked me where my shitty gift shop ring is.

I keep it in my wallet tucked behind a family photo when I'm not playing.

When I am playing, I loop it through my laces and hide it safely in my skate.

Feels like Piper's been my lucky charm this season, and I want to carry her around with me.

"Vegas. We were drunk. She's using it for my insurance to help with her chronic pain," I explain loosely, and Maverick hums like this isn't the craziest thing he's ever heard.

"Marriage of convenience? Fucking love that trope."

"What the fuck is a trope?"

"You really need to get to book club one of these days so you can learn." He levels me with a serious look. "You have feelings for her, don't you?"

I scoff and shake my head. "We're friends."

"Friends. Yeah. That's why you were ready to crush a guy's skull for talking shit about her."

"I was ready to crush a guy's skull because he treats women like they're the scum of the earth. It's about time someone treats him like that."

"Right. Sure. I don't believe you." Maverick grins and pats my shoulder. "But I'll keep your secret safe, man."

THIRTY-FIVE
LIAM

ME

Come over.

PIPER

Can I hang out with Pico?

ME

I'm offended you want to see my cat more than you want to see me.

PIPER

Can you blame me? He's cute and cuddly.

ME

And what am I?

PIPER

You're tolerable.

ME

Well played, Mitchell.

"HI!" Piper wiggles out of her coat and hangs it on the rack in the foyer. "Sorry it took me so long to get here. I was at dinner with the girls. Traffic was a nightmare, and I had an Uber driver who would *not* stop talking about the stock market."

"Thinking of making some investments?" I lean against the wall and watch her shake off snowflakes from the ends of her hair. "Didn't know you were into finance, Pipsqueak."

"It's only my favorite hobby." She unzips her boots and puts them against the wall, next to my sneakers. Her smile is bright and wide. Her cheeks are a little pink from either the early February wind or the wine she had at dinner. "You look good."

"My sweatpants and T-shirt do it for you?"

"You know what they say about sweatpants." Piper saunters past me in her tights and skirt, heading for the living room. Her soft footsteps pad across the hardwood floor, and Pico peeks his head out of my bedroom. "Especially gray ones."

"I don't know what they say." I sit next to her on the couch, watching Pico jump up and curl into her arms. "Care to enlighten me?"

"Big dicks and all of that," she says, and I burst out laughing. She strokes the cat's fur, her smile turning softer as she relaxes against the cushions. "Are you having a good night?"

"I made a cup of tea after dinner. Had a long shower. And now you're here. I'd say we're moving toward the average stage."

"Did you hear that, Pico?" Piper whispers loud enough for me to hear. "Your dad thinks I'm average. Isn't that sweet?"

"How was dinner with the girls?"

"So fun. Hanging out with them is the highlight of my week, honestly. Trying to coordinate four schedules is almost impossible, but I'd give up time and energy in other parts of my life so I could see them."

"I'm glad." I rest my hand on her calf and yawn. "How much did you have to drink?"

"Only a glass of wine." Her eyes turn a shade darker, and she bites her bottom lip. "It's been a week since you fucked me, and I'm going out of my mind."

"One time and she's addicted," I murmur, wrapping my fingers around her ankle and giving her leg a gentle tug. "Someone's needy."

"I only came here for Pico. And to talk about our trip next week. *Not* you."

"Mhm. Sure you did."

"Are you excited to see your family?" Piper rests her head on my shoulder and brings her legs to her chest. Pico closes his eyes and settles into her embrace. "I can't believe they haven't come to a game this season."

"They normally do, but my dad's branch is understaffed, so getting time off to visit is difficult. I was going to head that way for Christmas until Coach put us through hell with practices during the holidays, and I told my parents I'd make it up to them."

"Please don't think you have to entertain me while we're in Spain. I can handle an afternoon or two by myself while you spend time with them. The last thing I want to do is to get in the way."

"You could never be in the way. They're going to love you."

"Are they going to love *me*, or are they going to love that I'm the person they think you're dating?"

"They'll love you while also feeling sorry you're stuck with my irritable ass."

"You do rank high on the irritability scale. Have you ever introduced them to a girlfriend before?"

"Once. Someone I dated in college. She came home with me for Christmas break."

"Oh *really*?" There's a mischievous glint in Piper's eye. "And why did you two break up?"

"She didn't like the demand of my hockey schedule. Said she needed more attention, which I get, but this is my life. It fizzled out my junior year."

"And no one since."

"A model I was seeing my rookie season. We met on a plane on my way to the NHL draft and my agent set us up. Dated three months and it didn't work out. She's the face of Calvin Klein now, so I don't think she misses me all that much."

"Oh, wow. Okay. Your parents are going to think this is serious." Her laugh is nervous and she clutches Pico tight. "No pressure."

"It's going to be fine. I doubt my mom is going to ask you what I got my degree in."

"What *did* you get your degree in?"

"Spanish and math."

"Hang on." Piper sits up and stares at me. "You majored in *math*?"

"That tone tells me you're surprised, and I'm offended."

"I didn't mean it like *that*. I imagine math is a hard degree on its own, but add in the pressure and time commitment of being a D1 athlete, and that's a heavy workload. You know I think you're smart, obviously, but I didn't know you double majored."

"I did. I wanted something to fall back on if the whole hockey thing didn't work out, but fuck if I had any free time my senior year."

"Will you tell me about Alana? You always light up when you talk about her, so I'm guessing she's very special."

"She is," I say. "I never wanted a sibling. I was pissed when my parents brought her home from the hospital, and my dad tells me I ignored her for months. One day she was learning to walk and fell. She scraped her knee on the rug in our living room, and apparently I ran through the house looking for a first aid kit to take care of her. Guess I cared about her more than I thought."

"Such a sensitive soul." Piper drums her fingers over my heart. "Were you two close growing up?"

"We were inseparable. She followed me everywhere; to the hockey rink, to the skate park the summer I thought I liked skateboarding. You know I don't like many people, but I love Alana."

"Do you like the guy she's marrying?"

"He's not bad. He treats her right and makes her happy. I also threatened to ruin his life if he hurt her."

She laughs. "I've always wanted a brother who looked out for me. I guess I kind of have that now with the team. Sometimes I feel like they'd punch someone if they hurt me."

I want to tell her about what Maverick did. The way he decked Charlie in the face and smiled afterward. But I'm not sure I want Piper to know that I know what the asshole said to her. She's moved past it, and the last thing she needs is bullshit from the past coming up when she's been so successful in her role this season.

"They're good guys, aren't they? I mean, Ethan's infatuation with hot dogs is something else."

"They're the best. Present company excluded, of course," Piper teases.

I smirk. "Fuck you too, Sunshine."

"Can we talk about PDA?"

"In general? I'm not a fan."

"I meant around your family. Our physical relationship applies to the bedroom, not out of it. Are we going to hold hands when we're at the wedding? Kiss? I want to make sure I'm prepared so if I try to give you a hug you don't look at me like I'm an alien with five heads."

I knock her arm with a pillow. Pico glares at me, pissed at being disturbed, and I roll my eyes.

Little shit.

"I wouldn't look at you like you have five heads. Just three. As far as PDA goes, some might help us sell this relationship. Don't make out with me in front of my eighty-year-old grandmother, but you can hold my hand."

"Okay. Hand holding goes on the list. Making out doesn't. Got it. What about kissing?"

"If you want to."

"Do *you* want me to? This is your family, Liam."

This sounds like a test, and I'm not sure how to answer it correctly.

Fuck yes, I want her to kiss me.

Why wouldn't I?

She's soft and warm and a real fucking delight. Maybe I want to show her off. Maybe I want my family to think I'm a lucky bastard who landed an absolute knockout, even if this is all going to end when we get back to DC.

"Sure," I croak. "You can kiss me."

"Got it. Also, I feel like I should tell you I'm not a very good flier. I hate planes. I promise to not make a scene, but I'm definitely going to squeeze your arm during takeoff and landing."

I frown at her. "We fly all the time. I've never seen you panic."

"Watching me, Sully?"

"I'm six feet tall, Pipsqueak. I can see over the seats and could tell if you were up there freaking out."

"I try to focus on what's happening in front of me, not what's happening around me. Distracting myself helps."

"What could help distract you?"

Her eyes darken and she leans forward. She runs her finger down my chest and grins. "I can think of a few things."

"Let's hear them."

"I'm not sure joining the mile high club with two hundred passengers as spectators sounds like my cup of tea, but maybe we could practice tonight." Piper sets Pico down and turns all of her attention to me. "I had an idea, and I wanted to run it by you."

I cup her cheek and run my thumb along the line of her jaw. "You have my attention."

"I thought, well, maybe the best way for me to learn in the bedroom is to critique myself. So to do that, I was thinking, um, we could film ourselves having sex."

"You want to record me fucking you, Piper?" I sit up on my knees and ease her onto her back. Pico darts away, but he's the last thing I'm thinking about. I put my hands on her thighs and push her legs open. "You want to go back and watch how I fill you up when you're home alone and missing my cock?"

"Yes," she whispers, grabbing my shirt and tugging me down until our mouths are inches apart. "But don't pretend like you're not going to watch it too."

I am going to watch it.

On repeat, until I have it committed to memory.

I'll use it when I'm in my hotel room and can't have the real thing, because fuck if I could ever get off to anyone else.

Haven't been able to in four years.

Not since the day I met her.

A video I can play back whenever I wanted to see the way her tits bounce when I bend her over and fuck her into the mattress sounds like the greatest gift in the world.

"If we do that, it could end up anywhere." I pinch her nipple through the wool of her sweater, and her back arches off the couch. "If your phone got stolen, a video of you taking every inch of my cock could end up on the internet. Does that bother you?"

"No." Her eyes flutter closed and her legs wrap around my middle. The skirt she's wearing inches up to her waist and shows off the thigh-highs with little black bows tight on her skin. I rock forward and graze the head of my hard dick against her underwear. She moans and opens her legs wider. "Let them see. They'd know I was yours."

Possessiveness surges through me.

There's an aching need to feel her.

To sink into her.

To consume every fucking inch of her so there isn't a goddamn doubt in her mind she really is mine.

"We'll try out your idea," I murmur, bringing my mouth to her ear. I drag my teeth down her neck and she shivers under me. "But only if you let me film the whole thing. I want you to watch yourself fall apart. I want you to see the way my fingers stretch you out before I fill you up. I want you to hear how you beg and say my name right before you come. I want you to know how much I fucking love being inside your tight cunt. And when we're finished, I want you to look at the camera and say thank you."

THIRTY-SIX
PIPER

"THANK YOU?" I repeat, and Liam nods. "What am I saying thank you for?"

"For giving you the best fuck of your life." His warm palms slip under the front of my sweater and move from my stomach to my chest. Fingers pull down the cups of my bra and pinch my nipples, twisting them in the way I like. My soul leaves my body when he gives me a devastating grin. "I want everybody to know who makes you feel good. Who makes you feel better than *he* ever did."

I know exactly which *he* he's talking about.

Liam doesn't bother to hide his disdain, and something about his vicious tone turns me on. Maybe it's the lilt of possessiveness coating the word or the way he pinches my nipples again, harder this time, like he's trying to tether himself to me.

"You wouldn't be mad if he saw a video of us having sex, would you?"

"Of course I wouldn't. I'd be fucking proud." He pushes my sweater up to my chin, exposing my chest to the cool apartment air. "*Fuck*, Piper. Now I want it even more."

God, I like hearing that.

It makes me feel wanted in a way I never have before. I don't care if it's about revenge or some dick measuring contest: Liam wants to be on camera with *me*.

"Where should we do it? Here?" My words catch in the back of my throat when he dips his head and takes my nipple in his mouth. His tongue circles the pointed peak and I don't bother to stifle my moan. "Your bedroom?"

"My room. Better lighting."

"Oh, this is turning into a whole production. Lights. Camera. Action."

"Nothing about it is going to be fake, though."

Liam pulls his mouth away from my chest and I squirm in frustration. I've been worked up all night, half distracted through dinner at the thought of seeing him.

The anticipation of sleeping with him again has followed me all week, and no matter how many times I've gotten myself off, it's not the same as being with him.

"I've never faked anything with you," I say.

"I know you haven't. You're easy to read, sweetheart." The outline of his cock strains against his sweatpants as he stands, and my mouth waters at the sight of his hard length. "And, after I'm finished with you tonight, you'll be able to see how pretty you are when you come."

I doubt it.

I probably look silly. Like some writhing, desperate mess of a woman who would do anything to be satisfied. I'm nervous to know what I sound like. What facial expressions I make and how my body looks on camera. I'm clueless about angles and poses and the right way to stretch my legs, and I doubt I'm anything more than awkward.

I know Liam is going to make me feel good though, and I want the moment immortalized so I can look at it when our agreement ends. So I can remember what it's like to be on top of the world, even though I can't imagine how the next guy could be any better than the man in front of me.

"My phone is in my coat." I blush and point to the foyer. "Do you want me to get it?"

"I'll grab it and meet you in the bedroom. Ditch your clothes on the way. I want you naked in my bed before I get there," Liam says, voice deep and rough. I feel it all over my body, and I blow out a shaky breath as I prepare myself for what's about to come. "Are you sure you're okay with this, Piper?"

"Yes," I whisper, and I mean it with every fiber of my being. "Are you?"

"If you want a video of us fucking to look back on, that's what I want too." He holds my chin and kisses me. "And what my girl wants, my girl gets."

My girl.

I melt at the endearment and kiss him back. My tongue brushes against his before he pulls away, his hand untangling from my hair and his cock harder than it was a minute ago. He walks out of the living room and I jump into action, heading for his bedroom as fast as I can.

I pull off my clothes along the way. My stockings end up in the hallway. My sweater lands on a doorknob. My skirt gets tossed on his dresser and knocks over a bobblehead of Maverick from a fan appreciation night two seasons ago.

My bra and underwear come off more slowly. I take my time setting them aside then move to the bed, scooting over the covers and relaxing against the pillows. The patterned fabric smells like me, and I smile as I tip my knees open wide, waiting for Liam to appear.

I don't have to wait long.

Seconds later he's in the doorway, his shoulders wide and his hair mussed up around his ears. His eyes meet mine before raking over my body, a slow and purposeful scan that has me clutching the sheets. Curling my toes and sucking in a lungful of air before I combust.

"Find it?" I ask breathlessly, and he holds up my phone. "My password is 9367."

"Any significance behind that?" He palms his hard-on and adjusts himself over the front of his sweatpants. "Or just a bunch of random numbers?"

"Random numbers." I tilt my head to the side, watching him. "Does your password have any significance?"

"Yes." Liam walks toward me and pulls off his shirt. The threadbare cotton joins the pile with my underwear, and I drink in his sharp chest and stomach muscles when his torso is bare. "0807."

"Wonder what that means."

"Maybe one day you'll find out."

He hooks his fingers in the waistband of his pants and holds my phone in his other hand. He wastes no time, shimmying them down his thighs until he's left in a pair of black briefs, his glorious body on display.

Liam is so beautiful. Manly and rugged with his beard and his bruises and battle wounds from the ice, yes. But the softer, more secretive parts are what attract me the most.

Like the way the right side of his mouth always lifts higher than his left when he's smiling. The small scar from his appendix surgery and how his shoulders shake when he laughs. I want to remember them all.

After Spain, there won't be an excuse for me to gawk at him.

I won't be able to thread my fingers in his hair and tug when he brings me close to an orgasm.

I won't be able to admire his ass when he walks from the bed to the bathroom to clean up.

He'll go back to being Liam and I'll go back to being Piper, two people whose paths won't ever cross in this way again.

I'd love to consider a world where we're together.

Boyfriend and girlfriend and a real couple. But we want different things.

I'm becoming more sure of myself. Confident in a way I wasn't six months ago. I know I want to find a partner and I know I want to be loved wholly. Completely. To the point of obsession.

Liam doesn't want a distraction. Until he retires, the only thing he loves wholly is hockey, and it's a shame.

We could've been good, I think. We work well as friends. We work well in the bedroom. We work well doing domestic things like cooking dinner and watching TV, but it's not meant to be.

And *fuck* that makes me want him even more tonight.

"Come here," I say, reaching for him.

Liam closes the distance between us in two long strides. He climbs on the bed, scooping up my phone and straddling me on his hands and knees. I kiss him, savoring the hint of peppermint on his tongue left behind from his nightly tea.

"Gonna hit record," he says against my mouth, and I nod, some feeble show of granting permission.

He moves away from my lips before I can sink into the taste of him. He works his way down my body, kissing and licking every curve of my chest and every valley and plane of my belly. Further down he goes, until he's flat on his stomach on the mattress, his head between my legs and a hungry look in his eyes.

"Fuck," I whisper, every other word in my vocabulary disintegrating to ash when he brings the phone next to his cheek. A thick finger runs through my entrance, and I can tell from his hum of approval I'm already wet. "*Liam.*"

"Look at you saying my name for the camera." His pointer finger pushes inside me without warning and I hiss, the sting brief and fleeting as it turns to exquisite pleasure. "Such a good girl for me, Piper."

It takes all of my energy to hold myself up on my elbows

and watch him record me. The camera is obscenely close to the spot between my legs, and it's the most intimate experience I've had with a man. There are no nerves, though. No hesitations and no worries that I might not be sexy enough.

The only thing that's left is pure, unrelenting bursts of sensation that start at the base of my spine as he adds a second finger and then a third, a gentle *you can take it, baby* followed by *there you go* slipping from his lips as my legs drop open and I lift my hips, making space for him.

I've always thrived on praise.

I've always performed better when I know I'm doing a good job, but admiration from Liam elevates me to a different stratosphere. It has me smiling from ear to ear. Digging my nails into his shoulder and scratching his skin. Desperate to touch him, to make him feel just as good as he's making me feel.

"I've always thought I wasn't able to come during sex. I could never f-find a release from someone else no matter how hard I tried." I gasp when he curls his fingers and kisses the inside of my thigh, sharp teeth gently sinking into the soft part of my flesh. "I can't tell you how happy it makes me to know it's not me. It was him."

Like before, neither of us needs to clarify because we know exactly who I'm referring to.

"You've always had it in you, Piper." Liam licks a hot swipe over my entrance. His tongue moves to my clit, circling as his fingers work in and out of me at the same time, and I groan. "You just needed someone who could help you find it."

I squeeze my eyes shut, the first wave of satisfaction within reach. "How do I—do I look okay?"

"You look absolutely fucking perfect. Now come for the camera, Sunshine, so you can see how well you take my fingers."

It takes another minute or two and then my orgasm grips me. I cry out, swept away by the intense relief. I fall back, my head landing in the cloud of pillows as I grip the sheets and ride the high for as long as I can.

I lift my hips, greedy and desperate, wanting more from him. His laugh is a comfort, bright and bold and proud as he kisses my knee then my hip, slowing his fingers until I have nothing left to give.

"God, you're fucking beautiful," he murmurs, sitting up and reaching his hand my way. "Open your mouth and suck, Piper."

My lips part and he presses two fingers on the tip of my tongue. I close my mouth, tasting myself on his digits, and I notice he's still holding the camera, still filming, and a soft moan works out of me.

I wrap my fingers around his wrist and pull off him with a *pop*. His eyes are hooded, glazed over as he stares at me with so much heat and lust I'm questioning how I'm not scorched to death.

"What now?" I ask, touching his cheek and smiling when he turns his head to kiss the center of my palm.

"You know what now."

Liam climbs off the mattress and shuffles to his bedside table. His muscles flex as he unplugs the lamp and drags the nightstand away from its original spot. He sets the camera up, the lens facing the bed, and I take a deep breath.

"How do you want to do it tonight?" I ask when he turns to face me.

"This is for you, Piper." He steps out of his briefs, cock bobbing free. "What do you want?"

"I want to try being on top." I bite my bottom lip, dropping my hand between my legs. My thighs are slick with my arousal, and I drag my finger through the wetness. "I think I'll like how that feels."

"That sounds good to me." Liam strokes his length then sits on the edge of the bed. He swings his legs over, reaching for me and pulling me into his body. "God. I can't believe I get to do this with you."

"You're telling me." I run my hands over his chest and kiss the scruff of his beard. "Not sure how I bagged a hot NHL goalie, but I'm definitely not complaining."

He grabs a condom from the box on the other nightstand and rips open the foil packet. "You think I'm hot?"

"Nope. I misspoke. I was talking about someone else."

"Thought so."

He rolls the latex over his hard cock and throws the wrapper to the side. Liam lies on his back and holds out his arm, reaching for me. I intertwine our fingers and throw a leg on either side of his hips.

"Hi," I whisper.

"Hi," he answers, palm resting on the back of my neck. "Doing okay?"

"Yeah." I nod. "I'm ready."

"We'll go slow. If you want to stop, you tell me."

"I'm not going to want to stop, Liam." I lower myself down on him until his cock presses inside me. His head drops back and he groans. Confidence radiates through me. I'm fearless. Determined. Sure of exactly what I want. "Not until I take every inch of you."

THIRTY-SEVEN
LIAM

PIPER IS sexy as hell when she's on top of me, but watching her confidence grow is even more of a turn on.

Weeks ago, she wouldn't have said something like that. Now she's looking down at me with wild eyes. Messy hair, swollen lips and so fucking *sure* of what she wants.

It's an honor to have had a role in that.

"Are you going to fuck me, baby?" I ask, moving my hands to her back. My palms run down her spine and settle on her hips, holding her there as she becomes familiar with the stretch. "Make sure you go slow so I can really enjoy your pussy, please, before I die."

Her laugh races out of her, a whoosh of a breath as she sinks down another inch on my length. She holds onto me for stability, sharp nails digging into my biceps as I hold her equally as rough.

"I might be the one to die." Piper gasps when I press my fingers against her pussy the same time she rocks forward. Half of my cock disappears inside her, and I wish I had another phone so I could record her from this angle. "That's a fucking *weapon*."

"So sweet." I circle her clit, momentarily losing my mind

when she rolls her hips in some way I've never felt before. "And so fucking *good*."

I have to will myself to calm down, because from the way she's moving, from the way she's touching her chest and groaning, there's no way in fucking *hell* I'm going to last very long.

"Do you like that Liam?" Piper asks, pinching her nipples. "Am I doing okay?"

"I like it so much. You're incredible."

I can barely remember my own name because I'm lost in the delirious wonder of it all. She's almost fully seated on me, working her way down my length in the most torturous path I've ever experienced.

My vision blurs at the edges and sweat beads on my forehead. It's taking everything in me to keep this slow. To not flip her over and fuck her nice and rough until she comes all over my cock.

"Holy shit," she whispers. "You're so big."

I know the compliment should make me smug, but instead I'm sitting up. Checking to make sure she's doing okay then almost blowing a load when I see how deep I'm buried inside her.

All the way inside her.

She's tight and warm and *so fucking perfect*.

The best I've ever had, and no one else comes close.

I doubt anyone will ever come close again.

"How do you like the position?" I ask, pushing my thumb against her. She's so fucking *wet*, and it's making me lose my mind. "Do you want to try something else?"

"What were you thinking?"

"Hang on."

I lift her off of me and she whines. I kiss her then move her onto her back. Carefully folding her knees to her chest, I grip her thigh with one hand and line up my cock against her entrance with my other.

"*Yes*," she hisses when I tease her. My head rubs against her clit, following the pattern my fingers just used, and she nods. "I liked being on top, but this is so much better. You fuck me so well, Liam."

"How do you want it, Piper? Rough? Slow? Tell me and I'll give it to you."

"I want to try rough. I want you to let go with me. I can take it. I *want* it."

"Okay, wife. I'll fuck you rough." The hand on her thigh moves up her stomach to her neck. My thumb strokes along her windpipe, pressing into her throat as she gasps. "Hold on to the headboard and don't let go."

Her eyes twinkle with excitement and anticipation. I don't bother to go slow, sliding back inside her easily now that she's stretched out and ready for me. I loop my arm under her left thigh, holding her in place, and grin when her mouth pops open in a silent groan.

"More," she begs. "I want more."

"Almost there, baby," I grit out, finally bottoming out in her. "*Fucking Christ.*"

I snap my hips, working in overdrive. I want this to be perfect for her. I want her to walk away tonight sore and satisfied and happy. I want to be the one to do it, and I'll do anything it takes to get her there.

"I'm not sure I'm going to come again if you don't—*oh.*" Piper arches her back when I pluck her nipple between my fingers. "Oh, *god* that's so much."

"Too much?"

"*Fuck*, no. Keep touching me, Liam."

"Where else? Here?" I ask, leaning forward so I can reach between her legs and touch her again. "Do you like that?"

"Yes." Her eyes squeeze shut and she grasps my side, a gasp falling out of her. "I need a little more."

I give her everything I have, thrusting into her like there's no tomorrow. I alternate between touching her chest and her pussy, snapping my hips until her skin turns pink and her breathing turns to ragged gulps of air.

I feel myself clawing toward release, doing everything in my power to not go before her. It's nearly impossible to think straight because I'm so fucking overwhelmed by her.

Piper tightens around me, her orgasm close as her eyes flutter open and she looks right up at me. She's mesmerizing. Absolutely stunning when she palms my ass and urges me deeper into her, increasing my pace.

"You gonna come for me, Sunshine?"

"Yes." She turns her head to the side, her moan low and long when I give her clit a gentle slap. "I'm almost there. *Fuck.* How are you so good at this?"

"Your compliments mean so much." I hike her legs up higher, driving into her until I see stars. "I need to feel you, Piper."

Whatever else she wants to say dies on the tip of her tongue as she falls apart, thighs shaking and chest heaving as I slam into her again and again, on the precipice myself.

"I know you said we have to wear a condom, and I'd never go against your rules," she pants. "But *god* I wish you could come in me, Liam. I've never experienced that before, and I bet you would fill me up."

Jesus Christ.

That's all it takes for me to explode, shattering to a million pieces as I jolt forward, nearly crushing her as I spill inside the latex. I imagine it's her cunt and I almost lose it again, close to shouting her name as she crosses the ledge with me.

I exhale a low breath, bracing my hand on the wall behind the bed to keep from toppling over. I drop my head back, my body and brain slow to catch up and sync together.

Soft, warm hands run up my back. Gentle fingers play with the ends of my hair, and when I crack an eye open and look down, Piper is smiling up at me.

"Thank you," she whispers, moving her hand to my

stomach and tracing the outline of my muscles. "Let's do that again."

"I need a minute." I squeeze her knee and straighten out her legs as I pull out of her with a wince. Collapsing next to her on the bed, I groan. "Maybe twenty. Your pussy killed me, Mitchell."

Her giggle is cute, and I turn to look at her. "I think that's what happens when you're out of the game for so long, Sullivan." She spins on her side and props her head up with her elbow. "You become susceptible to damages. That's exactly why we need to do it again. So your dick doesn't fall off."

I laugh and reach for the dick in question, pulling off the condom and tying it in a knot. "Are you a doctor now?"

"Maybe I should be."

I bring her to my chest and bury my face in her hair. She relaxes into me and I band my arms around her waist, exhausted and happy.

The best fuck of your life will do that to you, I guess.

"Stay the night," I slur, feeling like I'm drunk or high or some combination of the two. "I'll make you breakfast in the morning. And tea."

She makes me want to break all my rules.

"Wow. I don't think I can say no to that." She smiles, and I feel the curve of the grin against my bare skin. It makes me smile too. "Should I stop recording?"

"I forgot that we put all of that on tape." I yawn and sit up, reaching over her so I can grab her phone. I hit the stop button then hand it to her. "There you go."

"Do you, um, think maybe we could watch it?" Her cheeks flush a dark red, and she hides her face behind her fingers. "Or would that be weird?"

"I don't think watching it back would be weird at all."

"You don't?"

"Nope."

"Oh." She peeks at me and laughs, a nervous edge to the sound. "In that case, should we make popcorn?"

I snort. "We can put it on the big screen in the living room if you think you'd like it better?"

"*No*. I'm going to look like an idiot. We don't need that in 4-D."

"You're not going to look like an idiot. Come here." I get comfortable against the pillows and open my arms, extending her an invitation. She's trying not to laugh as she slides up next to me, her body sticky with sweat. "We'll suffer together."

"Fine. But I reserve the right to turn it off at any time."

"Absolutely."

My thumb presses play, and the video begins. Anxiousness rolls off of her, so I rub her arms up and down. Kiss the top of her head and hold her tight.

"Wow," she whispers when she gets an up close shot of her pussy. "I've never—that's the first time..." Piper tilts her head. "I had no idea that's what it looked like."

"Pretty, isn't it? Look how wet and pink and perfect it is."

"Watching it might be hotter than actually doing it." Her hand slips between her legs as her thighs spread. "I kind of want to touch myself again."

"Baby, you get off as many times as you want." I rest my palm on her knee, my thumb pressing into her skin. "But you're making it very difficult to pick where I want to look."

Piper groans and pushes a finger inside herself. It matches the noise coming from her phone and now I'm hard again, the dual sounds scattering my brain.

My eyes bounce between the screen and the easy glide of her fingers, not wanting to miss a single fucking thing from either version of her. When we change positions and she climbs on top of me, real life Piper's breathing hitches.

"*Oh*."

"I know you're two fingers deep in your pussy right now,

and I'm never going to stop you from having a good time, but look at the screen. You see how good we look together?"

"We look perfect." Piper rests her head on my shoulder, her eyes on me as I relive the last ten minutes. "I liked how deep you got when I was on top."

"Yeah?" My cock twitches, aching at her words. At the easy way she's speaking about everything, and even though I like hearing what she thought, I want that mouth around me. Lips on my shaft as she sucks me off. "How about in round two we can see how deep I can get down your throat?"

Her eyes widen and she nods, the red on her skin turning crimson. She's warm to the touch, and I place my hand over hers, wanting to be a part of her next orgasm.

"I want—" Piper huffs and lifts her hips, a line of wrinkles forming on her forehead. "Can you—"

"Tell me what you need and I'll give it to you."

"Bring the screen down a little. I want to come at the same time as you do in the video."

"Dirty girl," I say in her ear, and her moan goes straight to my cock. "Here I was thinking I needed to be gentle with you. I don't though, do I? You want to be bad."

"I've only wanted to be this way with you."

I drag my finger across the screen, fast forwarding until right before we both fall apart. I turn up the volume so she can hear every slap of my hips. Every slick glide of my dick in and out of her. Every one of her groans.

"There you go, Piper. Come on your hand while you watch yourself get fucked. I want to see it."

I don't expect her to come undone so quickly but she does, a beautiful sight as she whispers my name again and again. I ease her down from the high, and when she's thoroughly spent, limbs weak and eyes closing, I lift her in my arms like she's the most precious thing in the world.

She just might be.

I walk her to the bathroom and set her in the tub, running

the water until steam rises from it. I kiss her forehead and smile when she practically pulls me in with her.

It hits me that this has somehow gone from sex lessons to sex to sex with a person I really fucking care about.

I'm not teaching her anymore. She's not learning anything she doesn't already know, but we're still tumbling into bed together.

I can't keep my hands off of her, and she hasn't shown me any signs of wanting to stop, even though she could go sleep with someone else tomorrow.

Maybe that's why it's so good with her: because she cares about me too.

THIRTY-EIGHT
PIPER

"I CAN'T BELIEVE you're going on a trip with *Liam*." Lexi folds one of the shirts I'm packing and tosses it in my suitcase. "I wish I knew what he was like off the ice."

"You've seen him off the ice." I check the weather app on my phone and frown at the temperatures. "I feel like you know him best."

"I stretch his legs, Piper, and he grunts when I ask him a question. That doesn't mean I *know* him."

"I think it's great." Maven watches us from my bed, a hand on her growing stomach and another holding a jar of pickles. "You two are having fun together, right?"

"Yeah," I admit, biting back a smile. "A lot of fun."

"And when was the last time you had fun?"

"A year into my marriage with Steven before he started working ninety-hour weeks. When we hit our second anniversary, I think I went months without smiling."

"I promise I'm not going to go to his house and start shit, but if I *ever* run into him in public, I'm going to give him a piece of my mind." Lexi crosses her arms over her chest and scowls. "I won't hold back."

"Call me so I can help you." Emmy tosses her phone onto

the mattress and stretches her arms above her head. "He's the reason Piper and I drifted apart during college."

"Really?" Maven asks.

"Yeah. He was intimidated by Emmy's career, and he told me she wasn't a good influence." I snort and add a pair of sandals to my bag. "Says the guy who was fucking his secretary."

"Insecure men suck. We need more people who aren't afraid of a woman's success. I mean, look at Maverick. He didn't make the 4 Nations Face-Off team, but Emmy did. Is he crying about it? No. He's making shirts with her face on it to wear to the games."

"He's *what*?" Emmy groans. "God. I don't know if I should be embarrassed or turned on."

"Both, probably." I grin. "How are things going with you two after the wedding?"

"Not much has changed, honestly. I think the reason we work so well is because we have distance between us during the season. It makes the time we're together even more important, you know? Like, I don't want to fight with him when I'm leaving the next night."

"What about when you all retire?"

"I'm so ridiculously in love with that man, it won't matter." She laughs and plays with the diamond she wears when she's not on the ice. "It sounds so silly, but before Maverick, I didn't want to settle down. I didn't want to have kids or this huge family, and I was convinced no man out there would change my mind. Now, kids are all I can think about. Imagining him as a dad makes me emotional, and I know he's going to be the *best* father. Does it suck that I'll have to give up my career to create that life? Yeah, a little bit. Then I think about ten years down the road, and it won't matter. I'll have everything I could want. I've done what I set out to do when I got called up to the NHL: break the glass ceiling for women in this sport. I was the first, but I won't be the last. I can rest now."

"*Jesus*, Hartwell. Miller. Wait—did you change your name?" Lexi asks.

"Not until I retire. I love him so much, but I want my name on the back of a jersey. Not his."

"Oh, he's *so* going to take yours." Maven grins. "That boy wants the world to know you're his."

"I wouldn't be opposed to that." Emmy glances at me. "He keeps asking about you, Piper."

"What? What about me?"

"I don't know. He mentioned something about Liam and a secret and his favorite book trope? He wants to know if you're wearing anything different these days that you weren't wearing two months ago? I have no fucking clue what he's talking about."

"Tell him she's wearing a smile because she is. *Look* at how she's glowing," Lexi says.

"Okay, enough with the flattery. I have no clue what Mav is talking about, Emmy. I'm not wearing anything—" I snap my mouth closed, the chain of my necklace heavy against my skin. I touch the ring hidden under my shirt and turn bright red. "Oh, my god."

All three girls look at me, and I busy myself with zipping up my bag.

Liam and I agreed we wouldn't tell anyone.

I don't know how Maverick found out, but hearing he's kept his mouth closed around Emmy, the woman he tells everything to, surprises me.

"What's wrong?" Maven asks.

"Nothing." I shake my head. I'm not going to violate that trust I have with Liam, no matter how badly I want to tell my friends about what I'm hiding under my clothes. "I panicked about my passport, but I remember where it is."

"I'd pay money to see you pull that prank on Liam when you're at the airport." Lexi grins. "He'd probably freak out."

"Kind of like how I'm freaking out." I groan and climb on the mattress, taking the spot between Emmy and Maven. "I'm nervous about meeting his family. I'm nervous about how we're supposed to act around them. I'm nervous because Liam and I slept together, and I'm nervous because I *definitely* have a crush on him."

"Holy *shit*. You cannot unload all of that on us twenty-four hours before you leave the country." Maven grabs the pillow behind my head and hits me with it. "You slept with him and we're just now hearing about it?"

"I've been busy!"

"Yeah, riding his dick," Lexi chimes in, and I bury my face in my head.

"Yes, we've slept together. Yes, he's amazing in bed. Honestly, the sex I had with Steven doesn't even count. He *never* fucked me like that."

"Details," Emmy demands. "And don't leave out a thing."

I tell them about our first time and our second. I hold back on the video we made, not wanting the gossip to get back to someone who might tease Liam about it. I let them know how good he is. How patient and considerate he is while also having a filthy mouth I dream about.

"And now we're coming up to the end of all of this, and I'm kind of sad." I sit up and bring my legs to my chest. "I know I'll find someone else. I'm not going to be single forever. But then I think about him sleeping with another woman and… I don't know. I don't like it. Which is insane, because he's told me *multiple* times he's not interested in a relationship."

"Neither was Maverick when I first met him. He was the ultimate playboy, but look at him now," Emmy says. "He spends Friday nights sending me articles on what cribs are best for newborns, and I'm not even pregnant."

"Yeah, but Liam's reasoning is his job. He knows how quickly things change in this sport, and he's afraid if he's distracted, if hockey isn't his sole focus, he'll lose everything he's worked so hard for."

Lexi shakes her head and stretches across the foot of the bed. "So show him he can have both."

"How do I do that?"

"I mean, it sounds like you're already doing it. You spend time together. He's playing incredible hockey. And, whatever you're doing in the bedroom is acting like a stretching tool too, because he's in the trainers' room less than he was last season."

"Yeah, because I really make sure to prioritize his hamstrings when we're sleeping together," I draw out, and the girls all laugh. "I respect what he wants and what he doesn't want. I'm not in love with him. It's a crush because he's giving me attention and treating me right. I bet if I went to the bar around the corner and started talking with a guy I met there, I'd feel the same way."

"What if you didn't?" Maven asks.

I don't know.

I haven't let myself think about it too deeply, because we have *such* a good thing going right now.

It's easy and fun.

It's sex, yeah, but I've fallen in love with myself again.

I'm happy. I'm healthy. I'm sleeping with a man who makes me feel like I could be queen of the world, and I've never had this kind of confidence before.

Through learning and exploring and his guidance, I've found my voice in and out of the bedroom. I've been quiet for so many years, but I'm not anymore.

If I had asked any other man to take on this task, they would've failed. I would've given up because of my low self-esteem. Because I felt judged or inadequate.

But not with Liam.

With Liam, I can fly.

"I guess I'll have to experiment and find out," I say, keeping my tone neutral. "Which dresses do you think I should bring? I have four I was trying to pick from."

"The pink one," Emmy says. Maven and Lexi hum in agreement, and I crawl off the mattress. "It's going to look great with your hair."

"That's what I thought too." I add it to my second suitcase and gesture to the other options. "I need one more. We're not going to be there very long, but I don't want to feel like I have nothing to wear."

They help me decide on two more to bring. After we pack my bags and I know where my passport is, we move to my living room with bowls of ice cream. I listen to the things going on in their lives feeling warm, happy, and content.

I'd go through hell and back a thousand times if it meant finding my friends on the other side, and no matter *what* man I end up with, he'll always come second to the three that helped put me back together.

THIRTY-NINE
PIPER

LIAM

Be out front in five minutes.

ME

Okay! I'm ready and looking for you!

LIAM

You're going to be looking for a long time.

I rented a car.

ME

Wow. Goalie Daddy is riding in style.

LIAM

Thought I hated that nickname.

Now I'm not so sure.

ME

It's because you tolerate me.

"WHY AREN'T we going to departures?" I look out the window as we zoom past DCA. "Oh, no. The driver is your kidnapper from before, isn't he? I knew this friendship between us was too good to be true."

"We're flying private," Liam says, not bothering to look up from his phone. He was checking the league standings a few minutes ago, and even though he's on a short hiatus from playing, his attention is still on hockey. "Why would we go to departures?"

"Hang on." I stare at him and tap his screen. He glances at me. "Private? You sent me boarding passes for first-class seats on an American Airlines flight."

"That was before you told me you don't enjoy flying. I thought something with a bed where you could get a few hours of sleep might put you at ease."

"You splurged on an airplane to take us across the Atlantic because I mentioned I don't like to fly? That… that is *obscene*, isn't it?"

"Is it? I figured you'd be more comfortable with space." Liam turns off his phone and slips it in the pocket of his jeans as the driver pulls up to a barbed wire gate. "I've flown private before. It's way more fun than any seat in first class."

"You have? Where the hell are you going, globetrotter?"

"Home to Chicago. I bring Pico with me. He's impossible in a carrier."

"That doesn't surprise me at all." The car turns left on the tarmac, and I spot a plane in the distance. It's not nearly as big as the chartered commercial jet we take on road games, but it's still large. My mouth drops open, and I press my nose against the window. "This is unreal."

We come to a stop, and I climb out. Liam takes my suitcases, walking up the short flight of stairs with the bags like I haven't stuffed every outfit in my closet inside. He dips his head as he steps aboard, and I follow behind him.

The interior is plush leather and cool lights. Big chairs are on either side of the wide aisle, and a couch takes up almost the whole left side of the aircraft. There's a table too, and a minibar in the corner.

It's the most opulent thing I've ever seen, and I lived in one of the nicest penthouses in DC when I was married.

Sleek and modern, everything looks like it's brand new and top of the line. I run my finger across the back of one of the chairs and huff out a laugh.

I know what NHL players make.

I see their nice cars. The jewelry they buy and the outrageous things they purchase because they *can*.

Liam doesn't live like that, though, and this is my first taste at seeing just how rich he is.

A multimillionaire with a huge playing contract. Sponsorship deals and an endorsement with Bauer that pays seven figures a year.

This probably won't put a dent in his bank account, but knowing he spent money on *me* makes me warm. My skin prickles. A fuzzy, fluttery feeling takes up residence in my stomach, and I can't help but smile.

"Thank you for doing this. I really appreciate it," I say.

"Think you'll be less stressed out in here?"

"I sure hope so."

"Good." He cups the back of my neck and squeezes once. "I'm going to grab my bag."

I settle into one of the chairs and relax. The tension about how the next few days are going to go seeps away as I take a deep breath and look out the window, watching Liam clasp hands with our driver and slip some money his way.

He's back a few minutes later, popping into the flight deck to say hello to the pilots before taking the chair across from me.

"Feels like we're about to conduct a board meeting." I fold my hands on the table between us and level him with a look. "What items do you want to discuss today, Sullivan?"

"Dining options. You liked the chicken parm we had at my house, so I requested it ahead of time for lunch today. Oh, and chocolate chip cookies. If you want something else, they have other food."

"You requested one of my favorite meals?"

"Yes?" He blinks at me and frowns. "Is that okay?"

"It's more than okay. I forget how observant you are. I'm not used to it."

"It's my job, remember?" He leans back, eyes never leaving mine. "And you're fun to observe."

"Now I need to do things and see if you're watching. Will you see me flip you off during games?"

"If you're wearing that pink blazer of yours, there's no way in hell you'll be able to hide."

I laugh and pull a book out of my purse. "Don't insult my blazer. It makes me feel like Superwoman."

"I never insulted it."

"I'm going to get you a matching one to wear to the arena. We can be twins."

"Do it, Mitchell. I'll wear the shit out of it." He lifts his chin my way. "What are you reading today?"

"The guys asked the girls to join book club this month, and Riley picked one with a hockey player. Seems a little too close to home, but it's good so far."

"You really like reading that much?"

"Yeah. I love my job, but it's nice to turn off my brain and sink into a world that's not *here*, you know?"

"Not really." He leans forward and plucks the book from my hands. He pats his thighs and grins. "Come on over, Sunshine."

"What?" I try to grab the book back, but he holds it over his head, out of reach. "You don't care about my book."

"I do now." Liam pauses. "Will you read to me?"

My face softens as he watches at me with hopeful eyes. I'm out of my seat without a second thought, rounding the table and climbing into his lap. He wraps his arms around my waist and rests his chin on my shoulder.

"Do you want to see the page?" I ask gently. "Or just hear the words?"

"Hear the words, please. I'm a slow reader, and I don't want to hold you up."

"You wouldn't be holding me up, Liam." I reach up and touch his chin. "What are you most comfortable with?"

"Listening to you. And use your reporter's voice when you read. It's sexy."

"My reporter's voice?" I laugh again. "Do I have one of those?"

"You definitely do. Your tone gets all authoritative. Really pulls you in."

"From the guy who doesn't like interviews, you sure know a lot about how mine go."

"I told you." He hums and closes his eyes. "Observant."

LIAM LINKS his hand through mine as we walk into the hotel hours later.

I know the affection is all for show, the grand finale of this plan of ours, but I like it when he touches me outside the bedroom. A brush of his shoulder in the tunnel. The graze of his glove when he jumps off the ice and heads to the locker room. His pinkie hooking in mine at the end of the night when I'm saying goodbye.

I've always craved physical touch, and a touch from him centers me. Calms me in a way words don't. And when he rubs his thumb against the inside of my wrist in the middle of the lobby, I think we have a real shot at pulling this off.

"Liam!" someone shrieks.

A woman comes charging toward us, and the closer she

gets, the more I can tell she's the spitting image of the man next to me.

Same hook of her nose. Same hair texture and jawline.

She's smiling more than him though, with a twinkle in her eye and a pep in her step I rarely see from him.

"Here we go," he says under his breath, and I squeeze his palm in solidarity.

"I'm so glad you made it." Alana throws her arms around his neck, breaking our contact, and I step back to give them a minute alone. "Don't you ever go six months without seeing me again, you asshole."

"Sorry, Lani." He rubs his hands up and down her arms and kisses her forehead. "I've been a little busy."

"Okay, hotshot with the great hockey season," Alana teases. She elbows his stomach before pulling away and putting distance between them so Liam can't retaliate. Her attention moves from her brother to me, and her grin grows. "You must be the mystery woman he's told me nothing about. Jokes on him. I know exactly who you are."

"Hi." I smile and stick out my hand, surprised when she crushes me with a hug. "Oof. I'm Piper."

"That interview you did with Maverick Miller was fantastic."

"Thank you so much. And thank you for letting me be here to celebrate your special day."

We pull away from our hug and she looks me up and down. "I'm happy you're here and so glad my lug of a brother settled down. For a while there, he wouldn't stop talking about—"

"Where are Mom and Dad?" Liam asks, cutting her off. "We've had a long day. It would be nice to get to our room, shower, and sleep until morning so we're functioning for all your festivities. I feel like a zombie right now."

"Fine." Alana rolls her eyes, but she smiles. "But I'm going to steal Piper away from you at some point. I want to make sure you're treating her right."

"He's actually the worst," I sign, and her mouth pops open. "*But he doesn't know I'm saying that.*"

"*You can sign? Oh, I can't wait to talk shit about him. When did you learn?*"

"*My cousin is Deaf. I've been signing for years. What about you?*"

"*I majored in ASL and communications. I've done some interpreting at large events.*"

"I'm used to her speaking and signing at the same time. This is new." Liam's head bounces between us. "You're both so fast."

"Welcome to how I feel when you start rambling about things in Spanish." Alana flips him off, then turns her attention back to me. "*We'll talk more tomorrow?*"

"*Yes, please. I want you to tell me all about Liam as a grumpy kid. I bet he was insufferable.*"

She laughs and smiles at her brother. "I like her, Li."

He drapes an arm around my shoulder and looks down at me. "So do I. Promise we'll catch up more tomorrow, Lani."

We make our way through the lobby, and I smile. "I adore your sister."

"Doesn't surprise me. Most people do. She's got that air about her, you know?" He points to a couple at the bar. "Those are my parents. We'll say hi then sneak upstairs. How are you feeling?"

"Not bad. The jet lag is starting to hit after that drive from the airport, but I'm doing okay."

We head to the dimly lit space off the lobby. Liam waves, and the man and woman watching us stand with smiles on their faces.

I can see bits and pieces of Liam in them, and my heart warms at the thought of him thirty or forty years down the road. What he might look like with graying hair and weathered hands. He'll have lived a full life then, and I hope he'll still be finding ways to be happy.

"There you are." His mom jumps to her feet and hugs him tight. "We were wondering when you'd get here. How was your flight?"

"Longer than expected because of weather the pilots were working around, but not bad." Liam kisses her cheek then shakes his dad's hand. "This is my girlfriend, Piper. Piper, these are my parents, Cliff and Linda."

"Oh, aren't you beautiful?" Linda hugs me like Alana did. "It's so wonderful to meet you, Piper."

"It's nice to meet you too, Linda. Thank you for letting me join your family these next few days."

"We're so honored to have you. Liam hasn't told us much, only that you work for the Stars, and I can't wait to get to know you."

"I'm an open book. I'll tell you anything you want to know," I say.

"So different from Li." Linda shakes her head, but she follows it up with a smile. "Always so secretive."

"We'd invite you to join us for a drink, but we know you've had a long day. There's a family breakfast downstairs tomorrow morning at eight thirty. We can catch up then," Cliff says.

"Sounds good." Liam holds my hand again and offers his parents a wave. "We'll see you bright and early."

It takes a few minutes for us to escape, a conversation between Liam and his dad about the 4 Nations Face-Off later this week unfolding before we dive into another round of goodbyes.

Thirty minutes later, we find ourselves in our room, and I yawn.

"I'm not sure I've ever been this tired." I unzip my suitcase and pull out my pajama set. "I think I'm going to fall asleep standing up."

"Exactly why I stopped Alana from asking us out. She likes to do things big, and a night with her almost always rolls into the next morning."

"Maybe tomorrow." I smile and walk to the bathroom, too tired to even admire the lavish room and what I'm sure is an ocean view. "I think it went well with your parents, though. I'm pretty sure they believe us."

"They need to believe us for a few more days." Liam pulls off his shirt and folds it neatly before setting it on top of his suitcase. "Alana loves you, by the way."

"She does?" Our eyes meet in the mirror, and my gaze drops to his muscles. I admire the sharp lines of his body and the smattering of hair across his chest and down his stomach. "What makes you say that?"

"The text I got when we were in the elevator." He snorts and unbuttons his jeans. "She asked how much I'm paying you to be here."

"I'll have to tell her I'm doing it for free. She's going to be disappointed."

"Are you done objectifying me, Mitchell? I can see you blushing from here."

"I'm not objectifying you. I'm admiring the view. There's a big difference, Sullivan."

Liam walks toward me. When he gets close, he spins me so my back is against the bathroom counter. He lifts me by the backs of my thighs and sets me on the marble. "Never thought I'd see the day Piper Mitchell talked back."

"What can I say? I'm gaining more and more confidence every day. Pretty soon you'll think I'm a brat."

"This is new. I like it. Can I sleep without my shirt on? Or are you going to have trouble keeping your hands to yourself?"

I tap my fingers on the waistband of his briefs. "Sleep naked for all I care, Sully. I can behave."

His palms rest on my thighs and move up my legs. "Are you sure you want to?"

I'm not sure.

Especially when he's crowding my space. When he's looking at me with heat in his eyes and making me feel important, even in a hotel bathroom.

"No," I whisper, and the corners of his mouth hook up in a smile. "I'm not sure."

"Shower first. Then we'll see if you can resist me." He reaches for the hem of my shirt then pauses, delaying my undressing. His voice dips low and he clears his throat. "I like when you call me Sully. I like when you read to me on the plane. I like that you're patient. I like that you're here with me."

"A lot of people call you Sully."

"They do. But it feels special when you say it."

I trace over his biceps. His muscles flex under my touch, and I still my hand. "I like that I'm here with you too, and I'll read to you whenever you want."

Liam pulls my shirt over my head and freezes when he sees my necklace. "You're wearing your ring?"

I bristle with the silver chain, trying to hide it from view. "Yeah."

"Why?"

"It's silly."

"Tell me anyway."

"It didn't feel right to throw it away. I feel like… like it represents this new part of my life. A part that wouldn't be possible without you. So I keep it close to me."

It's embarrassing to admit this to him, and when he doesn't say another word, I panic that I've crossed a line. He walks away, bending to rifle through his bag, and I have no clue what he's doing.

A minute later, he comes back over with his wallet and hands it to me. Opening it up, I spot his band safely stored behind an old photograph, and I stop breathing.

My heart leaps to my throat. Almost falls out of me when he says, "Me too."

I don't know what it means that we've both kept our rings. Something important, probably.

But I don't have time to think it over, because Liam is taking off the rest of my clothes. Kissing me and carrying me into the shower as warm water wets my hair and runs down my body.

Later, when we're in bed under the stars, I feel his hand wrap around my necklace and hold it there, like he's afraid to let go. The longer I listen to his breathing evening out as he slips into unconsciousness, the more I can't stop thinking about how I'm falling head over heels for him.

FORTY
LIAM

I'M wide awake at four in the morning.

And, after a nine-hour flight that crossed too many time-zones to count, it's goddamn brutal.

I hold back a groan and stretch my arms above my head, knowing there's no chance I'm going back to sleep. I glance down and find Piper sound asleep next to me, dead to the world, and I smile.

Her arms circle my waist. Her head rests on my chest, and she mumbles something about butterflies. I huff out a laugh and carefully slip out of bed so I don't disturb her.

I grab my workout clothes, knowing a trip to the gym is the only thing that will settle me. My teammates are still practicing while I'm away, and I don't want to fall behind. I don't want to get left in the dust, and there's this nervous energy running through me.

When I change and make it downstairs, I hightail it to the coffee shop, needing a vat of caffeine in my system to keep my eyes open. My phone buzzes in my pocket before I can order, and I know who it's going to be without even looking at the screen.

ALANA

How do you feel about a walk on the beach?

ME

With anyone else, I'd hate it.

With you, I can get behind it.

ALANA

Meet you downstairs in five?

ME

Already here.

I add an extra drink to my order and grab the cups, making my way to the lobby. Leaning against a column, I wait for my sister to join me, smiling when I see her exit the elevator in a white sundress and a hat that says BRIDE over the bill in bold letters.

"Christ, Lani. The sun isn't up yet and you're walking around with that thing on your head?" I call out, and Alana flips me off. "I don't think there's going to be any doubt about who's the one getting married."

"Sorry, I don't speak smart-ass." She grins when I hand over her cup and takes a long sip. "Can't sleep?"

"Nope. My body thinks it's ten o'clock back home."

"You're usually asleep at ten."

"I know, and I'm all fucking confused."

"We missed you at cocktail hour last night."

"No, you didn't. I would've irritated the hell out of everyone."

"Yes, you would've. But we still missed you."

"Sounds like you're trying to butter me up. Is there something you want to ask me?"

"No." She rolls her eyes. "Can't I be nice to my big brother?"

"Of course you can." I drape my arm over her shoulder. "It just so rarely happens, I'm not sure how to react."

"Fuck, I've missed you, Li." She throws her whole body into mine and I laugh, hugging her tight. "I wish you could stay longer."

"So do I. The NHL doesn't believe in extended time off though, so my ass has to head back to the cold sooner than I'd like. But fuck it. We'll worry about that in a few days. Ready for some fresh air?"

"Why do you think I picked a destination wedding?" Alana loops her arm through mine and we head for the double doors that lead to a boardwalk. The morning breeze hits my face as we step outside, and I inhale a deep breath of salty air. "It's not warm out here, is it? I should've brought a jacket with me."

"You want to go back and grab one?"

"Nah. I'll warm up as we move. And if I don't, I'm going to force you to carry me back to the hotel. You need to put those muscles to use."

I grin and pull her closer. "How are you feeling about your big day? Do you need to make a run for it before the family breakfast? I can have a plane here in an hour."

"Hush." She smacks my arm and we step onto the sand. "I am not running away from my wedding. Harry and I are very happy together. He's a nice guy who's not intimidated by my success, loves me on my worst days, and makes me laugh. With the parade of shitty men out there, do you really want me to give that up?"

"Never. He's still not good enough for you, but I'm glad you're happy. Feels like yesterday you were a kid who did ballet and wore ribbons in her hair. Now look at you."

"It's weird, isn't it? I'm so grateful for my life, but it scares me how fast everything is moving around me. Mom and Dad are getting older. My friends are having kids. You're nearing forty."

"I haven't hit thirty yet, Lani. Let's slow our roll a little bit."

"Speaking of getting old and having children, how are things going with Piper? Have you told her you're in love with her yet?"

"*What*?" I whip my head to stare at her. "What are you talking about?"

"Oh." She grins. "Are we pretending you don't have feelings for the five-foot blonde you brought with you?"

"What do you know?"

"What do you think I know?"

I narrow my eyes.

Alana's smart, and I've never been able to keep a secret from her. I groan and scrub a hand over my face, knowing today is not the day I start.

"Fine. I have a crush on Piper. It's no big deal. It's not going to be a whole fucking thing, okay? Our relationship isn't real either. It's something we planned so Mom and Dad would get off my ass about settling down because I can't take another second of their badgering. I love them, but *fucking Christ.* Is my personal life all they care about?"

"I *knew* it." She nearly drops her coffee when she claps. "I knew you two weren't actually dating and I knew you had a crush on Piper. You've talked about her *so much* over the years. From anyone else, I wouldn't bat an eye at the mention of a woman they saw at work. But from you? C'mon."

"I've never mentioned her before," I say.

"Bullshit. You told me she works for the Stars. You told me she got promoted. You told me she can't skate, which is information I didn't need to know, but now I do. Oh! You told me about her pink blazer and blonde hair. You've been doing it for years. From the day she first showed up at the arena."

I rub my lips together and stare at the ocean. "It's stupid. She was married when I first met her. I knew she was off-limits, but another part of me knew she wouldn't stay with that sack of shit forever. I've always held out hope that she'd… I don't know. Like me too? It's why I haven't—" I shake my head. "Never mind."

"Come on. You can't leave me hanging like that!"

"It's not important."

"You've never spilled your guts to me about a woman before. That means she's important."

"She is important, which is why I haven't said anything. She went through shit with her ex-husband, and I don't know if I can give her the attention she deserves. I'd never want her to feel like she's in second place because I'm busy giving all my time to my job, but that's how it is. I can't drop everything to be with her."

"Who's asking you to? Dozens of guys in the league are married. They're dads and guardians and able to split themselves between work and personal relationships. Why can't you?"

"Because… I don't fucking know? That's how I am? That's why I limit myself? Because I'm… obsessed? I can't explain it. I wish I could just not give a shit every now and then, but I fucking *can't*."

"Maybe you can find a balance. A world where you can have Piper *and* your job. It would take time, but I bet it's possible."

"Maybe." I sigh. "Doesn't matter, though. She doesn't feel that way about me. In a few weeks, she'll be dating someone else."

"I wouldn't be so sure about that."

"Oh yeah? And what's made you a know-it-all?"

"I saw the way she looked at you last night." Lani's smile turns softer. More reverent as she rests her head on my shoulder. "It's exactly how you look at her. Like she's the only one in the world."

ALANA DOESN'T MENTION Piper again as we watch the sunrise over the water, and neither do I.

We make a detour back to the coffee shop so I can grab a tea for Piper. I leave Lani in the elevator, getting out at the tenth floor instead of riding up to the bridal penthouse with her. It's quiet when I sneak back to our suite. I'm careful as I slip into the bedroom and find Piper in the spot where I left her.

The sheets are bunched at her waist and her hair is all over the pillows. Her left arm is stretched out on my side of the bed, and I smile when she rolls over and runs her hand across the sheets. I sit on the edge of the mattress and watch her for a second, letting myself imagine a world where we do this every fucking day.

I'd make her breakfast. Drive her to the arena and kiss her before getting into my gear. We'd come home together and I'd listen to her while she tells me about her day, nodding along while she mentions broadcasting words I'm not familiar with but want to learn.

It's not much different from what we're doing now.

She sleeps over. We sit on my couch and talk. Sometimes we have sex. Sometimes we don't. She'll read and I'll watch game film, sneaking a look at her every now and then only to find her sneaking a look at me.

It's so fucking *easy*.

Could it be like that if we were dating for real?

Could I give her what she wants? What she fucking deserves?

I put my hand on her back and rub a small circle over her shoulder blades. "Morning," I say, keeping my voice low.

Piper stirs. Her nose scrunches up and her eyes flutter open. She blinks and looks around the room, trying to figure out where she is.

"Liam? What time is it?"

"Time to start getting ready for breakfast. I let you sleep in."

"How long have you been awake?" She yawns and sits up. "You're dressed and drinking coffee, so I'm going to guess a while."

"This is tea for you. I went with hibiscus." I hand her the cup and she takes it eagerly. "Alana and I did a walk on the beach. I tried to get her to skip out on this whole wedding thing, but she's pretty set on marrying the guy."

"Guess you're going to have to live with your younger sister being happy. Such a shame." Piper takes a sip of the tea and lets out a quiet groan. "Oh, I feel revived. I know I slept for hours, but I don't think it was enough."

"You're telling me. I'm going to be dragging all day. Guess it gives me an excuse to be crabby to someone."

"Hey. You're going to have to fake it, buddy."

"I don't want to. I want to go back to sleep." I take the spot next to her and rest a hand on her hip. "You're so warm."

"That's what happens when you stay in bed instead of going outside before the sun comes up." She keeps her cup upright as she curls into me. "Five minutes, then we're getting up."

"Fine. If we have to."

"We do have to. Don't fall asleep, Liam."

"Can't help it. You're so cozy," I mumble, closing my eyes. "Oh. Alana knows we're not actually dating, by the way."

"You told her we're faking it? We've been here twelve hours."

"She figured it out. I've never been able to keep a secret from her, and I caved pretty quickly."

"Now I know your weakness." Piper touches my cheek. "Is it okay she knows?"

"It's fine. This is more for my parents, and I think it'll work out."

"I like when your positive attitude comes out. Tell me, Liam, what else are you optimistic about?"

"Getting you out of your clothes. Ditch your shirt, Mitchell."

"We have to be downstairs in twenty minutes."

I crack an eye open and take her tea from her. Setting it on the table to my right, I roll on top of her and hold my mouth above hers. "Today's lesson is in how to get off quickly, because if you don't finish before we need to head downstairs, you don't get to come the rest of the day."

Piper grins at me, and I feel it everywhere. Behind my ribs. Deep in my heart. The other places no one's reached. Suddenly, Alana's observation comes rushing back to me, and I'm feeling pretty fucking optimistic about that as well.

"Game on, Sullivan."

I SQUEEZE Piper's hand in the elevator. "Ready?"

"The orgasm really helped take the edge off." She plays with her necklace, her wedding band hanging from the thin chain and tucked beneath the neckline of her dress. "I didn't know your fingers could move so fast."

"It's an art. When we get back to the room, I'll teach you how to do that too."

The doors open, and we walk into the lobby. We head for the restaurant, making our way to the private section roped off for the wedding party.

"Finally," my mom says, waving at us with a mimosa in her hand. "We were waiting for you!"

"Sorry, Mom. That was my fault." I kiss her cheek. "Don't blame Piper."

"I was ready to go ten minutes ago," Piper adds. "It really is Liam's fault."

"Where's Lani?" I scan the room, looking for my sister. I

spot her at the end of a buffet table, her arm around her fiancé and a bright smile on her face. "Ah. I don't think that dress is subtle enough."

"Wait until you see her wedding dress. It's gorgeous." My mom's eyes flash over to Piper. "Do you want to get married, dear?"

I groan. "For fuck's sake, Mom. Let her have a pancake first."

"It's okay." Piper smiles and accepts a champagne flute from a passing server. "I do want to get married. Maybe not four thousand miles away from home, but I'd love to have a wedding."

"It's all so lovely, isn't it? Come sit, Piper. Liam's told us *nothing* about you, and I'm hoping you can change that." My mom tosses me a glare as she sits down, and I roll my eyes. "How did you two meet?"

"I'm on the broadcast team for the Stars, and we met in the hallway at the arena." Piper joins her at the table and crosses her legs. "He probably doesn't remember this, but on my first day, I wasn't paying attention to where I was going. I had about eight notebooks in my hands and almost ran straight into him. When I thanked him for keeping me upright, he grunted and went on his way."

It's the real story of how we met, and I want to laugh at all the details she got right. There were about eight notebooks and she did almost run straight into me. I caught her at the last second to stop her from falling, and she thanked me a dozen times before I stalked away, embarrassed and flustered from the pretty girl who smiled at me.

"I'm not sure I grunted," I interject. "I am capable of words, you know."

"Are you?" Piper and my mom ask in unison. They both laugh, and I shake my head.

"This feels like an attack."

"*Anyway*. We've been friends for a while and one day, I

decide to ask him out. It was a big risk because the last thing I wanted to do is ruin our friendship, but I think it paid off in the end," Piper says.

"Oh, that's sweet. We've always harped on about when Liam was going to settle down. He puts so much time and energy into hockey—I'm sure you've seen that. His father and I would never ask him to give up something he loves, but we don't want him to miss out on other parts of his life because he's too busy on the ice."

"I understand. Sometimes I think things are worth waiting for, though. I'm divorced," Piper admits, and I admire how easily she gives up that information.

She doesn't sound embarrassed but proud, like she successfully completed one part of her journey and moved on to the next one.

"You poor thing." My mom gives her a sad smile and touches her hand. "How long ago?"

"A couple years. It was difficult. The worst thing I've ever gone through, but I'm on the other side of it now. I know I got hurt, but if I hadn't jumped into a relationship with the first guy who gave me attention, I'd be in a different place in my life. I might not have landed in DC, and I might not have met Liam. We wouldn't have ended up together, and it makes me sad to think about a life without him in it."

Piper looks at me as she says it, and it doesn't feel like those words are an act. It feels like she means every single one of them, and it makes me sad to think about a life without her in it too.

"I would've always found you," I say hoarsely. "And if I couldn't find you, I would've waited for you. Two years. Three years or four. Doesn't matter."

She gives me that smile again.

The one that makes me feel alive.

Like I've been sleeping for thousands of years and now that I'm finally waking up, she's the only thing I can see.

"You two are going to make me cry and it's too early in the day for tears. You're so strong to overcome that, Piper." My mother grabs a napkin and wipes under her eye. "I hope Liam is gentle with you."

Piper nods. "The most gentle. Who would've thought the big goalie was such a softie? Between me and Pico, I know he likes to pretend he's tough. I see the real him, though."

"Easy there, Sunshine. Don't give away too many of my secrets."

"Oops. Too late."

My mom looks between us and smiles. "Liam, you know I don't care what you do in your personal life. Single, married, dating for fifteen years. It doesn't matter. I just want you to be happy, and it seems like you're both very happy."

I tip my chin in Piper's direction. "Are you happy?"

Her eyes hold mine, and she gives me a slow nod. "Happiest I've ever been. Are you happy, Sully?"

"Very fucking happy," I tell her, and it's the damn truth.

FORTY-ONE
PIPER

"I FEEL bad you're hanging out with me instead of spending time with all the folks who are here for your destination wedding," I tell Alana as we stroll down Avenida Fuerza Armadas. "I'm the most boring person in the world."

"That is *not* true." She sips on her smoothie and pulls her shawl tight around her body. The sun is shining, but the temperature is hovering around sixty degrees. The brisk ocean air makes it feel cooler than it actually is, and I shiver. "Besides, I needed to get out of the hotel. I love my family very much, but all of them in the same space for a prolonged period is not my brightest idea. I got sucked into a twenty-minute conversation this morning with my Aunt Ethel about menopause. I love the lady, but I don't need to hear about what's waiting for me three decades down the road."

I laugh. "So I'm a second choice to menopause? Got it."

"Oh, I really do like you. You should know, Piper, I'm a nosy bitch. Since you're dating my brother, that makes you the most interesting person in the world."

"What do you want to know?"

"Okay, first, I'm a nosy bitch, not a regular bitch. If you don't want to share something, you don't have to. I'm curious about you, obviously, but you don't owe me any explanations about your life."

"I think you'd like my friend, Lexi. You two are very similar." I link my arm through hers and smile. "I'll tell you whatever you need to know, but, seriously. Don't get your hopes up. I don't have an amazing backstory."

"We'll see about that." Alana stops us in front of a bakery and eyes a stack of flaky croissants. "Liam told me you're divorced. I'm sorry to hear that."

"Yeah." I touch my necklace chain, a reflex when I hear his name. A reminder of how different things are this time around, even if it's not based on love. "We met in college and got married young. There were so many signs I missed early on that warned me he wasn't right for me, but I ignored them because I loved him, you know? The divorce was finalized a couple of years ago, and I'm so glad to be past it."

"Is he an athlete?"

"Gosh, no. Steven is in the tech industry. He founded a startup that made a lot of money, worked long hours, never gave me the attention I craved, then slept with his secretary. It sounds so dramatic when I say it back, but I'm okay. Slightly less trusting than I was when I was younger, but okay."

"Good. I love women who overcome a shitty experience in their life and come back even stronger." Alana squeezes me, and I smile. "I've been there. I thought the guy I dated in college was The One. He was older than me, and I thought I could hold his attention. When I turned twenty-one, he dumped me and started dating an eighteen-year-old."

"Ugh. I'm so sorry. It can be hard, can't it? You blame yourself. You wonder what you could've done differently. All the while, it was never your fault."

"Exactly. But we're done talking about the trash that's taken itself out. How do you like working for the Stars? I spent so much time at Liam's games growing up, hockey lost its appeal to me."

"Understandable, honestly. I get burnt out during the season too. I *love* working for the Stars, though. It's fun to be part of an organization that cares about diversity. I know it's a male-dominated sport, but they were the first team with a female on their roster for a regular season game. I'm one of the few female reporters in the league, and Lexi, the friend I mentioned, is the best athletic trainer in the NHL. The job itself is incredible, and sometimes I have to pinch myself to remember this is my life."

"Ugh. That's incredible to hear. We need more women in roles where men don't think we belong. I created a dating app that puts the power in the woman's hands. They're the ones who get to send the first like. They're the ones who initiate conversation. The men on the app can't do anything unless she initiates first, and sometimes, she doesn't want to."

"What do you do for same-sex couples or folks who identify as nonbinary?"

"Your reporter side is coming out, I see," Alana teases. "For anyone who isn't interested in a heterosexual man, there's a random generator to determine which party will start the conversation between two individuals. We have a team who monitors the outcome of the results to make sure users aren't feeling like they're never the ones who get to talk first."

"Wow. That's innovative. I spent a week on dating apps after my divorce and had to delete them because there were *way* too many dick pics. Like, why am I getting a picture of your junk at noon on a Thursday? Yours sounds much more fun. What's the name of it? When I'm ready to dip my toes back in the dating pool, I'll download it."

"Planning on breaking up with my brother?" she teases, and I blush. "Did he tell you I know that you two are faking it?"

"He did, and I feel so bad. That was the whole point of the deal we made, and we messed it up twelve hours in."

"You didn't mess anything up. I know my brother, and I knew he was hiding something."

"You have no idea," I say under my breath, and she gives me a coy look. "Sorry. I'm going to be respectful of his ask and not talk about it."

Alana hums. "The more time I spend with you, the more I like you, Piper. I don't know what exactly you and my brother are doing, but this is the happiest I've seen him in years."

My heart thunders in my chest. I try not to look too eager for more information, so I wait a beat before asking, "Really? How so?"

"You've spent time with him. You know how important hockey is in his life, and that's how it's always been. In high school and college, he was good, but he had to work twice as hard as his teammates. Playing came naturally to them, and Liam was the one trying to catch up to their skill set. That instilled a fear in him, I think. Like, he couldn't take a second off because it would mean he wasn't making the sport a priority. I look at him now and he's smiling. Laughing and laid-back in a way he's never been. He's *present*. I'm not saying you're the direct cause, but you might be."

"We're spending time together." I shrug and adjust my purse strap. "I've slipped into his routine, and he's slipped into mine. I'm not sure either of us realized what was happening, but he's been a constant in my life the last few months. A pillar I've needed as I found myself again. I'm afraid of what could happen between us because I care about him as a person. Because he's my friend, and the thought of losing him terrifies me."

"I've always thought it was silly we put labels on relationships. Why can't two people just spend time together without categorizing it? It doesn't make how you feel about the person any less valid. Am I going to love Harry more when he's my husband? No. If you and Liam are enjoying each other's company, keep enjoying each other's company."

The thought of walking away from Liam makes me sad.

He's patched up all my wounds. Mended me and healed me in a way I used to dream about. I'm sure another man will treat me right, but it's hard to imagine wanting another man when I only want *him*.

My husband.

The irony of being attracted to the man I'm legally bound to when the last time I had a ring on my finger, he wanted nothing to do with me.

A laugh races out of me, and I shake my head at the absurdity of it all. At the path my life has taken this year and how I ended up *here*, in Spain, with the goalie who scowls at everyone but me and happier than I could ever imagine.

"Sorry." I give Alana a sheepish look and dip my chin. "I'm not laughing at you. I love that way of thinking, by the way. I'm having a moment."

"A good moment?"

"Yeah. I'm just really glad to be here. Thank you for getting married."

"Oh, you're very welcome. Did Liam tell you what gifts he got us?"

"Wait. We're supposed to bring gifts to this? Shoot. I totally forgot. I hope my millionaire fake boyfriend remembered."

Alana rests her head on my shoulder. "Yeah. You can stick around, Piper Mitchell."

"You're too kind, Alana Sullivan. Wait. Are you taking Harry's last name?"

She groans. "I wish I didn't have to, but I want to do the traditional thing. Do you know what it is?"

"No, and now I'm afraid to hear it."

"Clutterbuck. I'm going to be Alana fucking Clutterbuck."

I try to hold back my laugher, but it's impossible. I cackle until my sides hurt and tears prick my eyes. When I get myself under control, I look at her unimpressed face and lose it again.

"That is really unfortunate," I wheeze. "You must love him very much."

"I do. I can't wait to go to the DMV and get called Clusterfuck or Flutterfuck."

"Maybe Buttercuck? That's kind of cute."

"I like your optimism." She pats my hand and points up the road. "Want to head back? They're probably going to look for me soon."

"I guess we should. This is your party and all," I say, and we start our walk back to the hotel. "Do you get to DC a lot? If you're ever in town, you'll have to grab dinner with me and my friends."

"We're opening an office on the East Coast later this year, so I planned to make a stop up to see Liam. I'd much rather hang out with you."

"Please. I'd love that. I'll give you my number so you can text me and we can set something up."

"I learned a long time ago to not meddle in my brother's personal life, and I really don't want to piss him off. But I'm going to say this: you're good for him, Piper. As a friend. As a fake girlfriend. As a… whatever else you all are doing. Because I *know* there's something else. Just don't give up on him, okay?"

"I wouldn't dare." I smile at the sunshine on my face and the warmth in my heart. "He's good for me, too."

FORTY-TWO
PIPER

"ALANA REPLACED you as my favorite Sullivan sibling." I lean against the railing of the balcony attached to our room and stare out at the ocean. A hint of salt lingers in the air, and I smile at the scent. "You're in second place now."

"I take it you had a good time together?" Liam rests his back against the ledge and glances at me. "You were gone all morning."

"Did you miss me?"

"Not in the slightest."

"I'm going to pretend like you're lying. We had a great time. She reminds me of Lexi a little bit, with her vivacious energy and not giving a hoot what people might think of her."

"I can see that. I'd be afraid if the two of them were in the same room together."

"You and me both." I smile as a faint breeze picks up pieces of my hair and blows them across my face. "It's a bummer we have to leave the day after tomorrow. I'm having so much fun. Can you tell Coach you've become a citizen and we're staying? Technically, since we're married, I have to go where you go."

"Tempting, but think of Pico. He'd miss you too much if we stayed."

"We could find a way to bring him over. You did rent a private plane to fly us here." I wink at him, and he scoffs. "Who's watching him while we're gone?"

"Hudson. For as much as Pico hates people, he loves dogs. He fits in great at Hud's place."

"It's probably utter chaos, isn't it?"

"I got a voice memo this morning that said everyone was alive, but Hudson needed two stitches above his eyebrow because of a claw incident. I reminded him this was *his* idea, and I got back a nice picture of his middle finger."

"Sounds like the photo I got of your middle finger." I spin so our sides press together and tip my chin up at him. "By the way, I, um, took off my ring for the rehearsal dinner tonight. I thought it would be noticeable with my dress, and I wanted to avoid questions."

I've touched my collarbone no less than ten times in the last hour while getting ready, and a part of me feels naked without the cool band resting on my skin.

It's funny to care about something so small and insignificant—especially when it doesn't represent something real—but I'm incomplete without it.

"Is that your subtle way of telling me you want a divorce, Piper? You get your medicine and go?" Liam smirks. "I knew you had ulterior motives."

"I'm trying to avoid a conversation with your mother about why I'm wearing a wedding band so close to my heart." I lift an eyebrow at him. "Was I supposed to want to stay in this marriage for other reasons?"

"What? My sparkling personality doesn't do it for you?" he asks, and I laugh. "Who needs a wedding band when there's a hickey on your neck that tells the whole story?"

I rub my thumb over the little purple mark I covered with

makeup earlier. The blemish took forever to hide, and I don't know if he's trying to be funny or telling the truth.

"And what's the whole story?" I ask.

"That my wife took my cock so well last night, I had to bite her throat to keep from yelling her name," Liam says, his voice dropping low.

He takes a step away from me, eyes raking down my body and soaking in my outfit.

The pink dress shows off my shoulders. The thin straps are an unwise choice for the night temperatures but far too cute to ruin with a coat. The silk is cool against my skin, hugging my curves and hitting at the top of my thighs.

Months ago, I would've felt self-conscious with his slow and tempting assessment. I would've tried to cover myself up or deflect the attention away, nervous about what he might think.

Not tonight.

Tonight I feel powerful.

Beautiful.

Like a new woman.

"You are..." He trails off and shakes his head, like he's trying to get rid of every thought he's ever had. He glances up at the stars before looking back down at me, his jaw tense and his voice hoarse. "Unbelievable."

"Am I?"

Liam steps back toward me and cups my cheeks with warm hands. "The first day I met you, I thought you were the most beautiful woman in the room. Any room," he tells me, and the world stops moving. "I've seen you bust your ass on the ice. I've seen you naked. I've seen you in blazers that hurt my eyes and sweatpants and team-issued polos. I've seen you in a hundred different outfits, and you've looked good in every single one of them. But this. *This*." He blows out a shaky breath. "This is a dangerous look of yours, Piper. It makes me want things I don't think I'm allowed to have."

There's a lump in my throat I can't swallow around. I'm painstakingly aware of the scent of his cologne. How delicately he holds me, like he's afraid I'm going to break if he lets go, and how still and quiet it is around us.

"What kind of things?" I whisper, and the question gets snatched up by the night air.

He dips his head so our foreheads press together and lets out a sigh. A war rages inside him. I can sense it—a battle of self-control and the desire to share all the secrets of the universe with me, and I wonder which side is going to win.

"You know what kind of things," he murmurs.

It hits me then, with an intensity so strong, so overpowering, I almost fall over because of it.

Here, underneath the stars, in his hold with a touch so grounding, so *safe*, nothing about this feels fake.

It feels real and deep and terrifyingly promising.

There's a future, a life where we grow old together and I never, not for a single second, doubt my worth.

From the way Liam is looking at me, unblinking and soft and like I'm the most important thing in the world, I know he realizes it too.

I want to know all the things he's hiding.

I want to know why he's smiling and what it would take to get him to do that every minute of every day.

I want to be the one to make him happy.

God, I like him so much.

It's a full-circle moment, going from wondering if I'd ever have feelings for someone again after Steven broke me to falling headfirst for a man who couldn't be more his opposite.

He took away my trust while Liam restores it.

He made me feel small while Liam makes me feel like an equal.

He made me feel like I was taking up too much space while Liam keeps making room for me.

My hands shake when I rest them on Liam's chest. I clutch

his shirt, fearful to let him go but needing a minute alone to process all of this. To process the possibilities and the what ifs.

"Would it be okay if I took a second out here by myself?" I ask. My voice trembles with the question, and I sniff. "Before we head downstairs?"

"Of course." Liam touches my cheek, his attention heavy and searching. "Can I help with anything?"

"No. And I'm okay. I just need a minute."

"You take all the time you need." His lips are warm when they press a kiss to my forehead. "Can I tell you a secret?"

"I look like a raccoon with my mascara running?"

"Nope. Not that."

"What is it?"

"There might be a hundred people at dinner tonight, but I'm going to be the luckiest one in the room." He pauses and retreats to the curtains billowing in the February wind, his eyes never leaving mine. "Because I'm there with you."

My heart thumps painfully behind my ribs as he slips back into our room. Everything about the moment is electrified, and I wish I could pause time.

Could it always be like this with him?

Is it just the moment we're in?

Is it real?

Am I overthinking *everything* and seeing what I want to see because I'm treated with a shred of decency?

In four weeks will I feel the same way about Liam as I do right now?

I stare out at the ocean, but the crashing waves don't give me any sort of clarity.

I LEAN BACK in my chair and set my napkin on my empty plate.

My stomach is full. My cheeks are warm from Spanish

wine and laughing so much, and I can't stop smiling at the Sullivan family around me.

"Who picked the menu?" I ask. "It was delicious."

"Me," Alana says proudly. "There was a short time where I wanted to be a chef, but it never quite panned out."

"In your next life, you should go to culinary school. The tapas were such an interesting blend of cuisines."

She grins. "Maybe I will, but for now I'm content with making him a grilled cheese every Wednesday night."

"How did you two meet?" I rest my elbow on the tablecloth and move my empty wineglass out of the way. "Please tell me you have a good meet cute."

"Sort of." Alana looks at Harry and pats his thigh. "You tell it, babe."

"You know about the dating app she created?" Harry asks, and I nod. "I was working at a rival app years ago and was using *her* app to scope out the competition and see what features Steady had that ours didn't."

"And what did you find?" Alana challenges, and Harry grins.

"Less genitalia."

"Kind of takes the fun out of life, doesn't it?" Liam asks. "Who doesn't love seeing a random dude's penis when you're in the middle of Starbucks? If you need a coffee with cream, all you need is a few tugs from him."

"*Liam*," Linda scolds, and I burst out laughing. "This is a five-star resort."

"It's an epidemic, Mom. I would know. I'm on a team with guys who send them."

I cover my ears and groan. "Please stop. I do not need to know which of the boys is out there sending pictures of his junk to the poor women of DC." I wait a beat and look at him. "It's Ethan, isn't it?"

"Obviously it's Ethan. You know what your next update should be, Lani? You should be able to leave star ratings after a certain number of conversations," Liam continues. "It would make sure everyone behaved."

"He's a hotshot goalie *and* a brainiac." Alana blows a kiss to her brother then turns her attention to her husband-to-be. "Anyway. Harry and I matched right before I was heading out on a two-week trip to Japan. I figured he wouldn't be interested when I got home, but when he offered to pick me up from the airport and showed up with a bouquet of roses, I knew it was game over."

"Okay, so you two are soulmates. Got it," I laugh.

Alana tips her chin up. When they kiss, the table applauds their display of affection. "I know some people search for love for years. Some have it and lose it. Some never find it. I'm so lucky to know I won't have to look for it ever again. I have it."

I stiffen.

The moment is supposed to be joyous. A cause for celebration, but there's a whisper of resentment lingering in the shadows.

Disdain for my past and my future creeps up, that fear of being alone, of never finding love again, rearing its ugly head.

Did I use up all the love I had the minute I inked my name on the divorce papers?

Or will the universe grant me another chance?

"You okay?" Liam asks quietly.

"I'm fine."

"Are you sure? I can tell something is bothering you."

"I'm mourning my love life," I say under my breath as the conversation picks up around us. Someone clinks their glass with a fork, and the couple exchange another kiss. "What I had. What I might not ever have again. I'm fine. Really."

"It's okay if you're not fine, given the situation and the memories it might hold."

"I see how deeply Harry loves your sister, and it makes me worry I'll never find someone who can handle me. Who can understand my past and why I'm hesitant about diving into a new relationship. They won't understand how much my career means to me or why I have this soul-crushing desire to work until my body is close to giving out: because I feel like I have to constantly prove myself. I remember sitting at a dinner so similar to this and thinking I found my forever before it all went up in smoke. Who's to say it won't happen again?"

Liam doesn't answer me, and that only reiterates my fear.

It makes me uneasy, like everything that happened on the balcony was make-believe. Something I dreamed up that could never come to light.

It might be a good thing if it didn't happen, though.

We both know how Liam feels about relationships and distractions.

Admitting the feelings I have for him because I've been caught up in a few days of celebration is a major distraction.

He's quiet, lifting his glass of champagne to toast the bride and groom, and the silence is defeating. I plaster on a smile, cheering as the happy couple makes a show of overindulgent displays of affection.

I'm surrounded by love, but I've never felt so unlovable and alone.

FORTY-THREE
LIAM

PUCK KINGS

MAVERICK

How's your sister's wedding, Goalie Daddy?

G-MONEY

We miss you, Sully!

EASY E

Come home soon, Dad!!

HUDSON

I love having Pico here, GK. I think I'm going to rescue a cat.

G-MONEY

Of course you are, animal lover.

HUDSON

Please don't call me that. People are going to get the wrong idea.

MAVERICK

Hey. Whatever you're into, man. This is a safe space.

G-MONEY

Is it? Ethan posted a picture of me with a dick on my cheek in here last night and y'all made fun of me.

EASY E

You did that to yourself, dude. Don't pass out at my place after two beers and I won't draw penises on your face.

You have left the chat
Easy E has added you to the chat

G-MONEY

LOL. It's always funny to see what the tipping point for Goalie Daddy will be. Today it's face dicks.

Wonder what it'll be tomorrow.

SOMETHING IS WRONG WITH PIPER.

She's been acting differently since the rehearsal dinner last night.

All her smiles are strained. Her answers to questions are short. And when I woke up this morning, she was on the other side of the bed.

It's driving me fucking insane trying to figure out what's going through her mind. I missed a dozen texts and forgot to respond to Coach about practice this weekend, too busy racking my brain about what I might have done to piss Piper off.

The lack of response earned me a ten-minute phone call about responsibilities and balancing my priorities. A lecture on how I'm lucky to have a few days away, but that doesn't mean I can blow off everything waiting for me back home.

The chastising made me feel like shit, like I'm neglecting important parts of my life, and I'm still carrying my sour attitude with me as I stand in the hallway outside the hotel ballroom, waiting for my cue to walk Alana down the aisle with my dad.

"Hey." My sister snaps her fingers in my face and I blink. "What's wrong with you?"

"I'm fine."

"Is that why you've been scowling for the last five minutes?"

"I'm not scowling."

"You're staring at the wall like it did something to offend you."

I run a hand through my hair and check over my shoulder. My dad is distracted, busy talking with one of the bridesmaids. Last-minute guests are filing into the chairs arranged in a dozen rows, and I know I have some time before the ceremony starts.

"I'm frustrated," I tell her, dropping my voice low. "I did something to make Piper mad."

"Okay, that's easy. Apologize to her."

"That would be easy if I knew what the fuck I did to make her close up over the last twenty-four hours. And, in the time it's taken me to try to figure it out, Coach has reamed me for not answering my phone, my teammates have told me they like my temporary replacement more than they like me, and I've remembered how much goddamn energy relationships require."

"For fuck's sake." Alana rolls her eyes and checks her reflection in the mirror hanging in the hallway. "You can be so selfish sometimes, Liam. It's obvious your teammates are fucking with you because you don't know how to take a joke. Do you *really* think they want to get rid of the guy who's been with the organization for years and led the team from a losing record to almost being Stanley Cup champions?"

"Maybe they—"

"And you missed a call from your coach. Big deal," she challenges, steamrolling past me. "That's the first time it's probably ever happened, and you're acting like it's the end of the world."

"It's my *job*, Alana, and what I'm paid to do. This isn't some pickup game on the lake up the street from our house. Four days away has me acting like a rookie who doesn't understand time management."

"I see what's happening." Lani grins at me. "You're self-sabotaging."

I rub my jaw. I hate how her attention makes me uneasy. "What the fuck does that mean?"

"It's something my therapist and I talk about."

"You go to a therapist?"

She lifts an eyebrow, daring me to make a comment, but I keep my mouth shut. "You don't?"

Lots of guys on the team go and talk to someone. I'm glad that works for them and I'd never make fun of them for finding an outlet for their stress.

This sport is fucking brutal with the road games and the taunts from fans. Being away from home and spending night after night alone. It can fuck you up if you're not careful, and the league doesn't give a shit about our mental health.

It's all about the money to them.

Fuck if one of their star players has a breakdown.

Maybe I should go talk to someone too.

"Go on. Break it down for me," I say.

"It means you do things that would block your success or prevent you from accomplishing your goals."

"Uh, yeah, I do do that. It's why I don't date. Why I don't

go out and party. Because my goal is to win the Stanley Cup. To be the best goalie in the league."

"I don't mean hockey, you big doof. You're almost thirty. You have a few more playing years left in you before someone younger and better comes along and takes your job. Then what's going to happen? The girl of your dreams will have settled down with someone who didn't make her wait or put hockey above her and where will you be? All alone."

"The girl of my dreams? Piper and I—it's… sex. That's all. I don't *want* a relationship, and I can't be the guy Piper needs. The guy she fucking deserves. She needs stability. Someone calm who comes home to her every night and worships the ground she walks on."

"You're such an idiot and, as disgusting as it is to talk about my brother's sex life, we *both* know it's not just that." The music in the ballroom starts, and Alana tugs me toward Dad. She loops an arm through mine and an arm through his, watching as the line of bridesmaids head down the aisle. "You're going to lose that girl, and you'll have no one to blame but yourself."

The backdrop of the sunset waits for us as we walk toward Harry and the rest of the wedding party. I scan the crowd, looking for a five-foot blonde and not caring about the flower arch in front of me.

She's easy to find.

She always is.

I spot her in the second row of chairs on the left, a bright smile on her face. Her hands are clasped in front of her, fingers intertwined, and even from here, I can see a twinkle of hope in her eyes. I watch her gaze shift from Alana to me, and her smile melts to something different.

Tender, yeah, but hesitant too. Like she doesn't know what she wants from me, and acid bubbles on my tongue.

Would I be okay hearing about the dates she goes on?

Would I be okay watching her fall in love with someone else?

We're friends after all, and I'm supposed to support my friends. I'm supposed to be happy for them and cheer them on.

But I really fucking hate the thought of her with another guy.

Alana's right.

It's not just sex for me.

It hasn't been for a long time.

And I'm going to lose Piper if I don't get my head out of my ass and decide what the fuck I want.

THE RECEPTION IS ROWDY.

Music blares from tall speakers, and I escape outside to take a break from the noise. The patio is quiet and empty, and I smile when I hear footsteps approaching behind me.

"You've never been stealthy." I look over my shoulder and smirk at my mom. "Did you forget all the times we'd drink hot chocolate in the kitchen at midnight after you woke me up with your heavy feet?"

"I have no clue what you're talking about." My mom grins and walks over to join me. "What are you doing out here?"

"Needed a minute to breathe. You know how Lani is."

"The life of every party. It's a shame you have to head home tomorrow. We've hardly gotten to spend time with you."

"I know. And I'm sorry I couldn't make it out at Christmas. I shouldn't go six months without seeing you and Dad, and you shouldn't be the ones always coming out to visit me. I'm going to get better about that. I promise. Feels like I have so much going on lately."

"That's what happens with life. It gets busy, but it slows

down eventually." My mom nudges me with her elbow, and I huff. "Piper's lovely. Is she having a good time?"

"I think so. From the way she's dancing in there, I'd say she's having a blast."

"It's good to see you smiling so much, Li. You work so hard and you don't stop until a job is finished. I know you get worn down by your father and I asking about your personal life, but I want you to know we'd never want you to put yourself in any situation that didn't make you totally happy. If that's hockey. If that's with a woman. If that's with a man or no one at all, I don't care. As long as you're doing what's right for you."

"I don't know what is right for me, to be honest. If I take away hockey, who am I? Some asshole who has a shitty attitude and is easily irritated? I sound horrible."

"No. You're a good man with a kind heart, Li, who's not any less when he's not stopping a puck. Hockey is always going to be there. Important moments and important people won't be. Think of all the memories you and your father missed out on because you were on the road with your travel team."

"Thanks for the pep talk. Haven't done some soul-searching in a while, and you're really helping me with that."

"There's my smart-ass son." She tugs on my ear and I bend down so she can plant a kiss on my cheek. "You should head back inside. I'm sure there's someone in there who wants to see you."

"I don't know about that. I think I might have fucked up somehow."

"So unfuck it up."

"Whoa, Mom. Easy with the language there."

She rolls her eyes and does her best to shove me toward the door. I step back into the ballroom, the music still loud and the party still going strong. I look around until I find Piper standing by the bar, a drink her hand.

I scoot past a group of distant cousins and get tangled up in a conversation with my great aunt that lasts way too long. When I can finally free myself, my social meter is fucking depleted, and I want to go to bed.

"Hey," I say to Piper, and she smiles up at me.

"Hi. I was wondering where you disappeared to. Thought you left for the night."

"Alana would drag me from our hotel room by my ear if I left without saying goodbye." I lift my chin toward her glass. "How's your drink? Do you want another round?"

"I'm okay. It's only seltzer with lime."

"Not in the mood to party hard, Mitchell?"

"Not when we have a transatlantic flight tomorrow." She covers her yawn with a hand and rolls her shoulders back. "But I don't think I have much energy left in me."

"You and me both." The music shifts to a slow song, some love ballad I'm sure Alana took hours to pick. "Kind of feels like the universe is telling us to dance, though."

"Oh, really?" Piper's mouth twitches in amusement and she sets her drink down. "It would be a shame to let the universe down."

I offer her my hand and she threads our fingers together. Her touch is warm and steady as I lead her to the dance floor. I set my palms on her waist and her arms drape around my neck, a natural, easy rhythm to our sway.

"Are you having fun?" I ask in her ear, and she nods.

"Yeah. I didn't think I'd be down for a destination wedding, but it's the way to go. Maybe my next one."

"Tell me how Dickbag McGee proposed to you."

"What?" She bursts out laughing. "Is that what you call Steven?"

"Mhm. I've got a Rolodex of nicknames, Pipsqueak, and the rest aren't as nice."

"You're going to have to tell them to me later." She lets out a sigh before continuing. "He proposed at a work event. There were five hundred people there. I didn't know any of them. He brought me on stage, said a few things about how much he loved me, got on one knee and showed me the ring. I loved him too, but the pressure from being watched by so many people made me sick."

"You hated every second of that proposal, didn't you?"

"I did. It was my nightmare. If I ever get engaged again, I want the proposal to be small. Private. At one of my favorite places like the arena or down by the Potomac on a spring day. I'd like to think the person asking me to marry them knows me."

"Sorry you didn't get that in Vegas. I'm sure I shouted something at you when we were drunk."

"I bet I shouted something back at you because you probably deserved it."

It's my turn to laugh, and I rest my chin on the top of her head. "Are we okay?"

"Is this another one of your existentialist questions?"

"I meant you and me, Piper. Did I do something to piss you off?"

"No. I needed some time to reflect on a couple of things. I'm okay, though."

"Are you sure?"

She smiles into my shirt, and I hold her tighter. "Positive."

I know she didn't go anywhere, but I missed her hugs.

The way she holds me and runs her hands up and down my back.

I missed her laugh and her smile and the way she blushes when I tease her.

God.

I missed *her*.

I don't like a world without Piper Mitchell in it.

The song ends, the music transitioning to a pop hit I don't know any words to. We step away from each other, and I clear my throat.

"Do you want to head upstairs?" I ask. "We can probably head out since they already did the cake cutting and everything."

"Only if we say goodbye to Alana before we leave. Your sister likes me, and I don't want her to get mad at me because you're trying to be sneaky."

"Dammit. I was trying to avoid the goodbyes that are going to take an hour. This is going to be the hard way. Sure you're okay with that?"

"Yes, and you're going to be okay with it too."

Piper takes my hand and leads me across the dance floor. We get stopped multiple times, exchanging pleasantries with members of my family before we finally make it over to the bride and groom.

"Piper," Alana slurs, letting go of Harry's waist so she can hug her. "You're so pretty."

"Wow." Piper laughs and pats my sister's shoulder before pulling away. "Someone's had a lot to drink tonight."

"I'm trying to get her to go to bed, but she said she can't be the first one to leave the party." Harry shakes his head and sighs. "We're going to be here all night."

"I got you covered, man. Lani, Piper and I are heading out. Now you won't be the first one to leave."

"You're going?" Alana pouts and glares at me. "But I never see you."

"I know. We have an early flight in the morning because I need to be back at the arena the day after tomorrow. I'm at fault, but we can really blame the NHL."

"Fuck the NHL," Alana calls out, and Piper buries her giggle in my shirt. "Did you two talk yet?"

"No," I say sharply. "Because everything is okay."

"Aw." She clutches her chest. "You're happy. I'm happy. We're all so happy. Aren't we, Harry? The Clutterbucks are so happy."

"You really drew the short end of the straw with that last name," I tell him.

"Fucking horrible, isn't it? Hey, I hope you have a good rest of your season. Lani and I are going to try to come to a game in April."

"Let me know when. I'll get you all seats." I look at my sister and hold out my arms. "Come here, you drunk idiot."

"I love you, Li," she says. "And don't forget what we talked about. Otherwise I'll kick your ass."

"I won't. But let's stop talking before you say something you shouldn't." I kiss the top of her head and hand her off to her husband. "Your threats always mean so much to me."

After another round of Alana's tears, we finally escape, the lobby quiet as we make our way to elevators.

"Wow. Is that what I was like when I was drunk that night a couple years ago in Canada? When you tucked me in?"

"Yup."

"And I didn't drive you insane?"

"Nope."

"Really?" Piper looks up at me. "I guess you weren't kidding about tolerating me."

"No," I say. Our eyes meet, and it feels like someone stuck their hand in my chest and ripped out my heart. "I haven't been kidding about anything."

FORTY-FOUR
PIPER

ME

Can we go back to Spain?

It's too cold here.

LIAM

I don't have another sister getting married.

Maybe I could find one?

ME

No one could replace Alana, but the sooner the better.

LIAM

I know I said I love my job, but it was really fucking nice to have a few days off.

ME

It was, wasn't it?

Are you getting back into the swing of things?

LIAM

Three days back, and it feels like weeks.

What are you doing tonight?

ME

Hanging with the girls!

LIAM

Girl code. What kind of stuff do you all talk about at these hang outs?

ME

Are you asking if we talk about you?

LIAM

No.

Yes.

ME

Someone is nosy.

LIAM

I prefer curious.

ME

We do talk about you. Nothing bad, though.

It's really just an academic discussion on the validity of glow in the dark condoms.

LIAM

Grant just asked why I'm laughing.

ME

Did you tell him it's because you're ill and losing your mind?

LIAM

I will now.

ME

Can I tell you a secret?

LIAM

Does my mascara make me look like a raccoon?

ME

Close.

LIAM

You hate the glow in the dark condoms?

ME

Closer!

I miss you.

And I'm sorry I got all weird at the rehearsal dinner.

LIAM

Did that happen?

ME

We can pretend like it didn't.

LIAM

Not a fan that we're doing this over text, but fuck it.

I've never been married. I don't know the emotions you might have been feeling, but you never have to apologize for what's going on in your head.

And if I said or did anything that didn't help the situation, I'm sorry.

ME

You didn't. I just have a lot on my mind.

LIAM

Are you going to team dinner the day after tomorrow?

ME

I am. Are you?

LIAM

Yup.

ME

You've been going to more this season. I'm proud of you!

LIAM

I go because you're there, Piper.

Want to talk then like real humans?

If you feel like telling me what's on your mind, I'll listen.

If you want to talk about condoms instead, we can do that too.

ME

I'd like that.

The telling you what's on my mind part.

And I guess the condom part too.

"I CAN'T BELIEVE how far along you are." I smile at Maven's baby bump. "You're freaking glowing, Mae."

"The women who say being pregnant is fun are out of their damn minds." She rests a hand on her stomach and props her legs up on my coffee table. "I'm exhausted all the time. My feet are swollen. I'm hungry, but half the food I want to eat makes me nauseous."

"You're getting there," Emmy says, and Maven glares at her.

"My due date cannot come fast enough. Don't mention childbirth to me, though, because it's terrifying. Someone else pick something to talk about."

"How was the wedding, Piper?" Lexi asks. "I'm still pissed you didn't send us a single photo while you were there."

"The wedding was amazing. Liam's family is wonderful. You all would love his sister, and I'm so glad I got to go." I pause and swirl my wine around in my glass. "I think I did something stupid, though."

"Is this like a tattoo situation? A drunken marriage situation?" Emmy asks, and I choke on my drink.

"Pardon? What makes you say that?"

"I don't know. I'm thinking about things people do that they might regret, and they came to mind." She narrows her eyes and leans forward. "What are you hiding, Piper Mitchell?"

The only way to get their advice about everything that's been on my mind is to tell them the whole story about what's going on between us.

If Maverick can know, my friends can know, too.

"Okay." I set my glass down and rub my hands over my thighs. "I haven't been totally honest with you all. I told you about how I might have feelings for Liam, but I left out the part where I mentioned he's kind of my husband?" It comes out like a question, an embarrassed squeak that makes my cheeks turn bright red. I touch my necklace and follow it up with a disbelieving laugh and a shake of my head. "So, yeah. That's what's been going on."

"Oh, my *fucking* god. You are a sneaky little bitch." Lexi gapes at me. "Are you fucking serious?"

"Since when?" Maven challenges. "I swear to god if you say it's been months, I'm going to be pissed."

"In my defense, I didn't want to upstage Emmy's wedding, but…" I trail off and clear my throat. "New Year's Eve in Vegas?"

"*Vegas*? That was *weeks* ago." Emmy stands and puts her hands on her hips. "You better start talking, Mitchell."

And I do.

I tell them about everything from the insurance to the time Liam came over and helped with my migraine. I mention the moment we had on the balcony in Spain, and when I stop to take a breath, my head is killing me.

"That's what I mean by doing something stupid. At the rehearsal dinner, I said something to Liam about how the last time I was in a relationship, the last time I thought I had found my forever, it went up in smoke. He didn't say anything about those hesitations. He didn't reassure me, and it *terrified* me. I took it as a sign he'd never want that with me, and I closed up after that. I didn't know I wanted that with him, but now I do."

Maven wraps her arm around my shoulder, and I bite my lip to keep from crying. "Oh, sweetie."

"It's all so stupid. It's only supposed to be something physical, and I went and caught feelings. Do I have feelings for Liam? Do I have feelings for any man who treats me better than Steven? We communicate so well about everything else, but I have no clue how to be honest about my emotions."

"Okay. I don't have a lot of experience with relationships, so take what I'm going to say with a grain of salt. But how is a relationship different from what you're doing right now?" Lexi asks. "You spend time together. You sleep together. You're not seeing anyone else. There's no way there's not *some* sort of attachment on his end."

"Maybe there is. I don't know. That would require a conversation about everything, and in the few days that we've been home from our trip, we've both been overloaded with work."

"So make time to talk," Maven says. "Tell each other how you're feeling and decide where it goes from there."

"We're going to get together at team dinner this week. I miss him." I laugh and touch my necklace again, the chain cool against my fingers. "And I don't mean in a romantic sort of way. I miss him as a friend, and I *just* saw him."

"That's good though. Missing people is a normal human emotion, Piper."

"I know it is. I hate to keep bringing Steven up, but it's hard not to compare what I'm going through right now with what I went through then. They can't be more different. Liam's priorities are like his, though, with work coming first. With being dedicated to his career to the point of putting other parts of his life on the back-burner. Would he do that with me? Would he even be able to balance me with everything else?"

"Before you play that game, you need to figure out how Liam feels," Maven says gently. "A conversation will help, and being *honest* in that conversation is important."

"God. This all kind of sucks, doesn't it?"

"It does. But the other side of it is fun." Emmy smiles. "It's nice to be wanted and cared for."

"Do you have a ring?" Lexi looks at my hand. "I haven't seen you wear anything."

"Oh. It's right here." I pull the chain out from under my shirt and hold up the silver band. "I'm pretty sure it's cheap metal because it's already disgusting."

"This is all making so much sense now. After the season ticket holder event you all had, Maverick would not shut up about this guy Liam went after." Emmy sits on the couch and pulls her feet under her. "He said Liam had this dude shoved up against a wall and almost killed him."

"*What*? What guy?"

"Some guy named Charlie? The name sounds vaguely familiar."

My stomach drops to my feet. My tongue is heavy in my mouth and my hands shake. "What else did Maverick say?"

"I don't remember, to be honest. Just that he's never seen Liam so pissed. He threw out a comment about his wife, and all hell broke loose."

"Jesus." Lexi whistles. "Marry that man again."

"Stop." I swat at her, but heat rises on my skin. I love when he calls me that. When he whispers it in my ear right before I'm about to come. It's like our little secret, a taunt to the other man who never treated me like a husband should. "The marriage has *no* impact on my feelings for him."

"Yeah, but you have to admit there's nothing hotter than a man calling you that when he's standing up for you." Maven grins. "Some guy hit on me at a bar once, and Dallas got all possessive. Told him he was standing too close to his wife, and to back up before there was a problem."

"Well, fuck me. Looks like I need a husband now," Lexi says. "Who has a list of available athletes in the DC area?"

"What happened to that minor league baseball player you went on a date with?" I ask, grateful to get the attention off of me for a minute. "Was he cute?"

"Oh, you mean the one who spent half an hour telling me how my job will be obsolete in ten years when robots take over and can patch people up in half the time I can? Yeah. I bolted pretty quickly after that."

"What about one of the guys on the team?"

"Never going to happen. I'm around them too much and I've seen their asses too many times to be attracted to them. I'm not touching a hockey boy with a ten-foot pole." Lexi glances at Emmy. "Unless any of the guys on your team are cute."

"Hard pass."

"Oh! Liam's sister designed a dating app where the women are in control of the conversations. It's called Steady."

"No *way*. I love that one." Lexi pulls out her phone and shows us her profile. "I won't use anything else. Small world."

"Hey." Maven taps my knee. "Everything is going to be okay."

"I know it is." I smile at my friends, encouraged for the first time all day. "Thanks for letting me vent."

We talk about the rest of the season and how the standings are looking for the last two months of games before the playoffs. April is creeping up, and soon we'll be deep in the hunt for the Stanley Cup.

My phone vibrates under the pillow next to me and I grab it, fighting back a smile at Liam's name on the screen.

LIAM

Attachment: 1 Image

Pico misses you.

I didn't say it earlier, but I miss you too.

ME

See you soon, Sully.

LIAM

Can't wait, Pipsqueak.

FORTY-FIVE
LIAM

IT'S BEEN a long goddamn week since we got back from Spain.

I feel like I'm going a hundred miles per hour.

Everything has been busy. Nonstop chaos. With the last part of the season underway, our practices are heating up. Coach is pushing us harder than ever, and I've fallen asleep the second my head hits the pillow every night.

The only reason I'm going to team dinner is because Piper will be there, and I really fucking miss her.

I've barely seen her after touching down on US soil. We pass each other in the arena, but we don't have time to talk. My routine feels fucked up, and I hope a minute or two with her will center me. Get me back on track, because I can't afford to be off my game these next few weeks.

I don't knock on the door to Maverick and Emmy's place. I waltz on in and take off my coat, adding it to the ones on the rack in the foyer.

"GK," Riley calls out, and I lift my head in his direction. "About time you showed up."

"Sorry." I walk into the decimated kitchen and set the

chocolate pie I picked up from the corner bakery on the island. "Had a one-on-one with Coach this afternoon."

"How'd it go?" He hands me a plate and utensils. "Anything going on?"

"Nah. Same old shit." I pile my plate with pasta and salad, adding a slice of bread to the mix too. "You good?"

"Not bad. My shoulder is still fucked up from practice yesterday, so I had to spend this morning in Lexi's torture chamber."

"Sounds horrible."

"Could've been worse."

I don't miss the way Riley smiles when he says Lexi's name. It's fucking hysterical he thinks he's hiding his crush from us, and it's even more hysterical he thinks any of us would actually make a move on her. It's obvious he's into her, and we all know that means she's off-limits.

"There he is," Hudson says when I walk into the crowded living room.

There's a round of hellos and I wave, taking a spot on the edge of the couch on the far side of the room. Settling back, I dig into the Caesar salad, fucking famished.

"Hey." Piper drops next to me on the couch and smiles. "I was beginning to think you fell off the face of the earth."

"Sorry to burst your bubble. I'm alive and well."

"Rats. Guess I can't get rid of you." She leans against the pillows and tucks her feet under her. Her thigh-high stockings taunt me, the hem of her skirt stopping just above the lace. I spy an inch of smooth skin I wish I could run my fingers across, and I turn my attention to the video game Maverick and Grant are playing instead of thinking about the things I want to do with her. "How was your day?"

"Tolerable." I spear a bite of spaghetti and inhale it. "I saw some chicken in the kitchen. Did you make it? Is it edible?"

"No, I didn't make it." She rolls her eyes and sticks out her tongue. "Hudson did. You missed his ten-minute discussion about the spices he used and what kind of marinade he soaked it in for an hour."

"Think the guy might like food more than he likes hockey." I shake my head and shovel another bite into my mouth. "How was your day?"

"Long, but good. I'm trying to coordinate some player spotlights with our social media team, and that took up most of my afternoon. Before you even try to give me shit, I don't have you on the list."

I smirk. "You know me too well. What's the spotlight about?"

"A get to know you, sort of. I ask rapid-fire questions and the guys answer within a few seconds. We want to do a bunch as we head into the playoff push."

"That could be dangerous. Don't ask Ethan anything about hot dogs."

"Thanks for the advice." Piper drops her elbow to her knee and smiles. "Sure you don't want to participate?"

"Nope. I'm all set. You want to go outside and talk when I'm finished with this?"

"How do you eat so fast? You're almost done and it's been three minutes."

"Magic."

"Yes, I want to go outside and talk when you're finished with that. I should probably go ahead and get up, because you're going to be ready to go by the time I put my coat on."

I scoop the last bite of pasta into my mouth and grin. "You're already behind, Pipsqueak."

Ten minutes later, I make my way outside and inhale a deep breath of fresh air. The temperature is tolerable, and I take a seat on one of the chairs on the patio.

"Dammit." Piper closes the door behind her and frowns. "How did you beat me?"

"Probably the height advantage. It helps. I also didn't start talking with Grant about the latest TikTok trend. That's where you went wrong."

"Mind if I join you?"

"Come on over." I pat the spot next to me and she walks my way, dropping on the chair and pulling her jacket tight around her. "Are you warm enough?"

"I think so. Unless you have a fire pit in your pocket, I'll survive."

"Fresh out of those." I glance at her and knock her knee with mine. "What's on your mind?"

"I'm going to come out and say it, and I'd like it if you didn't interrupt me, okay? I've been practicing this in my head all day, and I want to get it right."

"Okay." I nod. "The floor is yours."

"I know when I first came to you about this plan between us, we were going to do our lessons and pretend to date through your sister's wedding. We also agreed this was casual. That it wouldn't go anywhere outside the bedroom, but… I don't want to lie to you, Liam. I… I've started to… well, I like you. Not just sleeping with you, but spending time with you doing normal things, too. And I know that goes against your whole *no distractions* rule, and I'm sorry for breaking it, but I don't want to sleep with you again without you knowing what I'm feeling and how I'm feeling toward you. Which is that I like you. More than a friend. I know it's my fault for falling for the emotional side of sex, but… why are you looking at me like that?"

My lips twitch. "Like what?"

"Like your mouth is broken."

"I think that's called a smile."

"No. You look like a creepy clown."

"Your compliments get better and better."

"It's freaking me out and making me forget what else I want to say."

"What else do you want to say?"

"I… I don't know what else I want to say."

"Can I say something now?"

"Only if you stop with the weird smile thing."

I laugh and rest my hand on her thigh, squeezing once. "I feel like I'm back in middle school saying this, but I like you too, Piper. I have for a while now. Alana gave me a lecture five minutes before she walked down the aisle at the wedding, and I've been thinking about it ever since."

Piper blinks at me. "She did? What did she say?"

"That I need to get my head out of my ass, and I do. Look. We've found ourselves in some weird position where we've slept with each other, we're married to each other, and now we're realizing we like each other. It's all fucking backwards, and I'm having a hard time keeping up."

"Hockey is your priority. You've told me multiple times hockey is the most important thing in your life. Anything besides casual will interfere with that, and I could never do that to you. Not when I know how hard you work to be as good as you are."

I've thought about that a lot since I've been home.

The balances in my life and what's actually important to me.

If I never played another game, would I be disappointed?

Yeah.

I'd be pissed off. I'd hang my head. It would take a while, but I'd get over it. I'd move on and find something else to love.

If I never saw Piper again, I'd be fucking devastated.

This week showed me that.

When I'm not at the rink, I'm thinking about her.

Wondering if she had a good day.

Wondering what she was doing.

Wondering if she's thinking about me, too.

"What we've been doing seems to be working," I say, and Piper blinks at me. "You sleep over. I stop by your place. My game hasn't suffered because of it. Maybe…" I trail off. "Maybe we keep doing that. Hanging out. Spending time together. We're not moving in together or anything like that, but I think you've become part of my routine."

"I have?"

"I got my ass handed me to in our scrimmage yesterday. Haven't played that poorly all year, and the only thing that was different is that I haven't seen you in six fucking days."

"I shut down at the rehearsal dinner because I was looking for some sort of validation from you when I voiced my fears. You don't owe me any of that validation. It's not your job to make me unafraid, and I'm sorry for keeping you out."

"What do you want me to do, Piper?" I cup her cheeks, and there's a hitch in her breathing. "Yell out that I can handle you? I can. Tell you that it doesn't matter if you think you're a mess or too difficult or too quiet or not enough because I think you're everything in the world and more? It doesn't, because I do. I want you in ways I've never wanted anyone else, and it's driving me fucking insane."

"Oh," she whispers. "I-I want you in those ways too, but you're going to have to go slow with me, Liam. I'm terrified. I'm still working on trusting people and feeling like… like I'm allowed to have these things for myself."

"You know how I feel about going slow." I rest my forehead against hers. "Let's try. Let's see how this goes when we don't pretend it's something it's not. It hasn't been lessons or teaching or anything like that for me in a while, Piper. I sleep with you because I want to sleep with you, not because it's part of some sort of agreement or obligation. It's why I'm here tonight. Because I like spending time with you, and because you're my best friend."

"You're my best friend, too." She lets out a watery laugh. "Okay. So we're not fuck buddies. We're not boyfriend and girlfriend. What are we?"

"I don't know. Living in the moment? Which is something

I never fucking do, so you're going to have to be gentle, Pipsqueak. This is new territory for me."

"I told the girls about Vegas," she blurts out.

"I'm surprised you lasted so long without spilling the beans. They better send us a gift."

"When were *you* going to tell *me* about confronting Charlie at the season ticket holder event?"

"I didn't think you wanted to know he was trying to start shit." I shrug. "It got handled, and he won't be messing with you again."

"Are you going to swoop in and take care of all the people who talk shit about me?"

"What if I do? Would that be okay?"

"Yeah." Piper drags her fingers down my jaw, and I savor her touch. I crave it, want more of it. "I think it would be."

I don't know who the fuck I was kidding.

I couldn't stay away from her if I tried.

I'm clueless about how to do this right… whatever the fuck *this* is. I'm not sure.

Only that I want to do it with her.

I leave dinner first and Piper follows behind me. I wait for her downstairs in the garage and we drive back to my place holding hands like it's the easiest fucking thing in the world. We talk about our week. I laugh at a joke that's painfully unfunny, but she's so fucking cute, I don't even care.

FORTY-SIX
PIPER

ME

Hi!

LIAM

There she is.

How was your day?

ME

Good. How was practice?

LIAM

My leg has been cramped for two hours.

ME

Sounds like loads of fun!

LIAM

Want to come over and make it feel better?

ME

That was creepy. Try again.

LIAM

Come over, wife.

ME

Yup. That'll do it.

UNKNOWN NUMBER

Piper, it's Steven.

Did you block my number?

What are you? Five?

Call me back.

LIAM OPENS the door to his apartment before I can finish knocking.

I smile when I see him. He leans against the door frame in a pair of joggers. He's shirtless, and his tattoos almost glow in the hallway light.

"Hey," he draws out. "You look nice. Did you come from the arena?"

"Yeah. My feet are killing me."

"Did you eat dinner?"

"No. I haven't had a second to sit down all day. We finally hired a second announcer, so I was giving her a tour and helping her through the HR stuff."

Liam gestures me inside and I groan in relief when I kick off my heels. I can't make it more than four feet before he's shoving a pile of clothes in my arms.

"Get comfortable," he says.

"Did you have these waiting for me?"

"Yeah. Figured you had a long day and would want to change."

I stand on my toes and kiss his cheek. "Thank you."

"Come find me in the kitchen when you're done." Liam squeezes my ass. "And take your time."

I head for the bathroom in the hall, changing out of my skirt and blouse for an oversized shirt that's loose and soft. It's one of Liam's, well-loved and well-worn, and I smile at the scent of his laundry detergent clinging to the collar.

Pulling the socks on, I pad to the kitchen and find Liam standing over the stove, a dish towel draped over his shoulder.

"What are you making? Can I help?"

"Chicken parm again. You devoured it last time, and I thought I'd whip up some sauce."

"Whip up some sauce," I repeat, sliding next to him. "How casual of you."

"Come on, Piper. I'm not going to *buy* a jar of tomato sauce. That's fucking insanity."

"Of course it is." I smile when he holds out the wooden spoon. My mouth wraps around it, and I moan when I swallow down the small taste. "Holy shit. That's better than the first time you made it."

"I know it is. The first time I tried to get creative, but this is my mom's recipe with a secret ingredient."

"And how many women have you cooked this meal for?" I lean against the edge of the counter and cross my feet at the ankles. "Three dozen?"

"Just you. Only my wife gets to experience the Sullivan Sauce."

"You know, that could have a double meaning if you think about it."

Liam rolls up the dish towel and snaps it at me. My yelp turns to a laugh when he grabs me and holds me to his chest, easily avoiding my flailing and kicking.

"I missed you," he says in my ear.

"I missed you too," I say back, and I mean it.

He sets me down and dishes out a large plate of pasta. We sit next to each other at the island and talk about our days. He smiles when a drop of sauce gets stuck in the corner of my mouth. I nudge his foot with mine and wrap my ankle around his calf.

It's exactly like what we've been doing for so many months, but it feels *different*.

There's not a doubt in my mind he wants to be here with me, and there's a lightness in the air. An easiness that wasn't there before, and I like how natural it all feels. How relaxed Liam is and the way he keeps touching me, as if he's been waiting months to have me like this.

"Your migraine prescription came." He taps the box sitting on the island and pushes it my way. "Make sure you take it when you leave."

"Thanks. Sorry it keeps getting delivered here. They had your address on file, so I went with it."

"No big deal. As long as you take it." Liam levels me with a look. "Are you taking it, Piper?"

"*Yes*, and I'm getting monthly massages. I haven't had any pain in weeks."

"Funny how having access to things can make you feel better."

"That's what we call privilege, buddy." I catch a flash of orange in my periphery and I scoop Pico off the floor, scratching behind his ears. "*Hola, Pico. Tuviste un buen día*?"

"When the fuck did you start speaking Spanish?" Liam drags my barstool over so our knees are touching. "Are you an undercover spy, Mitchell?"

"I downloaded Duolingo last month. Don't get your hopes up. I only know about five phrases, and half of them are asking where the bathroom is."

"Since you're branching out, I guess I'll tell you how I'm branching out."

"Oh?" I kiss Pico's head and look at Liam. "Are you finally interacting with people in full sentences?"

"You're such a little shit."

"It made you do that creepy smile again. Must mean you like it."

"Debatable. I asked the guys if I could join book club this month." He runs a hand through his hair and averts his gaze. "Hudson sent me an audiobook code and told me what book they're doing next month so I can start early."

"Liam. That's incredible. I'm so proud of you."

"Do you think you could read some of it to me when we're together? I like listening to you. It helps me process the words."

"Hey." I stand and touch his jaw. His eyes snap to mine, and I smile. "I'll read you whatever you want. Monster smut. Books about fairies. A thriller that includes graphic details about brutal murders."

"Monster smut? Slow your roll there, Pipsqueak."

I laugh and kiss his forehead. "Sorry. I'll ease you into it."

Liam tilts his head to the side and his lips land on mine. He takes Pico from me, setting the cat down so I can wrap my arms around his neck and step in close.

"Are you staying the night?" He pulls away to move his mouth down my throat, along the line of my neck, and I tip my head back so he can kiss the spot below my ear I secretly love. "Please say yes."

"The only place I'm going is your room."

His stool scrapes across the floor when he stands, a grating sound I block out as he bands his arm around my waist. Tosses me over his shoulder and heads down the hall.

"Is this my new mode of transportation?" I ask.

"Easier access to your ass." Liam rests a hand on the curve of my backside and gives it a light smack. "And that's one of my favorite parts of you."

He kicks the door open and drops me on the bed. I bounce

twice and scramble across the sheets to the pillows. Liam steps toward me, already hard. His hand disappears in his sweatpants as he strokes himself, his wrist moving up and down.

"Should I take this off?" I tug on the hem of my shirt and slowly drag it up my stomach. Liam follows my movements, his strokes turning faster as I drop my legs open and lift my hips. "And these?"

"Please," he begs around a rasp that's delightfully low. "I want to see."

"All this talk about being good. Have *you* been good, Liam?"

"I think I have, but I'll get on my knees and beg if you want me to."

I pull off my underwear first and fling the pair at the wall. My shirt comes next, discarded somewhere else in his room. "How about you get between my legs?"

"*Fuck*, Piper." Liam gapes at me, mouth parted. Cheeks red. A bead of sweat just below his hairline. "My wife is so fucking pretty."

He has to know what that word does to me.

He has to know it turns my brain into a pile of mush.

"If I'm so pretty, get over here and take care of me." I lift my chin and smile. "Please?"

He climbs on the bed and positions himself between my legs. He shoves my knees open wide and runs his finger across my entrance. There's no warning before he pushes inside and I gasp at the stretch, the quick burst of pain subsiding to the bliss he always brings me.

"So wet. And all for me."

"*Obviously* it's for you. Who else would it be for?"

"I don't know, but I like that it's me." Liam presses on my clit with his thumb and I gasp again, sinking into the feeling of unbelievable pleasure. "No one else."

He adds his tongue and another finger, working me up

until there's no doubt in my mind he's the one who takes care of me. He's the one who knows exactly which way to flick his wrist or curl his fingers.

I've tried to imagine other people touching me like this.

Having me like this and talking to me like this.

Would my body react the same way?

Would I like it so much?

When he spreads me open, his tongue diving deep inside me as the shockwave hits, I know the answer is unequivocally *no*.

My legs shake and he soothes me down, his touch turning lighter as the crest of the wave ebbs to an easy ripple. I groan when he pulls away, my nerves electrified and my heart hammering in my chest.

"That was good." I smile at the ceiling. "Give me a second before we go again. I need to catch my breath."

"Take your time, sweetheart." Liam kisses my forehead and moves off the bed. I look over at him and find him tugging off his sweatpants. Stepping out of them and wrapping his fingers around his length. "See something you like?"

"I like the no-underwear look."

"Do you? Think I'll do it again."

"How do you—"

The moment breaks. My phone rings loudly in the kitchen, echoing down the hall, and I jump at the sound.

"Who keeps their ringer on?" Liam asks. "And at that volume?"

"Sorry. I like to keep it on in case there's an emergency. With Maven and the baby and Emmy on airplanes every other day, I want to know if something's happened."

"Want me to get it?"

I gnaw on my bottom lip. Anxiety claws at the pit in my stomach, and I nod. "Could you? I'm sorry. I won't be able to focus on anything unless I know it's nothing serious."

He turns without a second thought, returning a few seconds later. "It says unknown number."

"*Shit.* It must be Steven. I blocked his number a few months ago when he kept texting me. He started messaging me from a new number recently, and I haven't had a chance to block him again. I don't want you to think I'm talking to him or anything like that."

"The only thing I think is that he's a giant fucking asshole." Liam tosses my phone on the mattress. "And that I fucking hate him."

"I do too." I reach for him, wanting to feel him on top of me. Wanting to shake off the old memories and replace them with new, better ones. "I want you, Liam. So badly it hurts."

He plucks a condom from his bedside table and opens the packet, sliding it down his length. "How do you want it tonight, baby?" Liam rocks forward, the first inches of his length pushing inside me. I moan and grip his arm. "Fast? Slow?"

"Fast." My other hand drops to his ass, urging him deeper in me, and it's his turn to groan. "Hard."

"Are you going to let me fuck you like you're mine, Piper?"

"Yes," I plead, closing my eyes. "Because I am yours."

I revel in the manic, possessive way Liam moves. I slip into the stretch and twinge of pain. In feeling so full, so perfect, I fall into a trance.

The trek toward another high is interrupted, my phone ringing again and my restraint growing thin.

"Sorry," I pant, and Liam thrusts into me with menacing intensity. "I should've silenced it."

"And he should've stopped bothering you years ago. Answer the phone, Piper."

My eyes fly open, and I stare at him. "*What*? You're inside me."

"Exactly." He angles his hips torturously, getting deeper than before. Pulling me closer to the edge. I groan and grip the sheets, trying to enjoy the high a little while longer without giving in and free-falling so soon. "If he's going to bother you, let him hear what he's missing out on. Let him hear how I take care of you the way he couldn't. Let him hear how well *my wife* takes my cock."

Fuck.

Those two words almost cause me to combust. The first swell of an orgasm settles low in my stomach. My vision turns blurry. My mouth pops open and I'm gasping for air, burning alive.

Everything around me is hot, the room an inferno, and I've never been so turned on in my life.

I fumble behind me. My fingers wrap around the phone, and I slide my thumb across the screen.

"Hello?" I answer.

"Fucking finally," Steven says. "What the hell are you doing?"

"Nothing," I say breathlessly. Liam doesn't like that answer very much, because he puts a thumb on my clit. Rubs in a slow circle and bends forward, crouching low so he can kiss my neck. "I'm busy right now. What's up?"

"What's up is I've been trying to get a hold of you for weeks. We have things we need to talk about. Money. Finances. Important stuff I've been waiting on you to look over and sign."

"That's not a good idea." I moan as Liam pounds into me, and I slap a hand over my mouth. "You can go through my lawyer."

"Are you—*Christ*, Piper. Are you in bed with someone? Fucking whore."

My face falls and my blood turns ice cold. A look of rage takes over Liam's face, and he gently works my phone out of my hand.

"What did you say to her?" he asks, deathly low.

I don't know what Steven's answer is, only that Liam holds my waist and doesn't let go.

"Liam Sullivan. Oh, I'm on your fantasy team? The next time you see my name, I want you to remember I'm the one who fucks her in the way you never could. She screams my name, and I doubt she even pretended to moan yours. Stay on the line and listen if you want to find out for yourself, but if I hear you call her that word again, you won't like what happens next."

He tosses my phone somewhere in the pillows, not bothering to hang up, and brings my thighs to my chest. A moan laced around a laugh falls out of me, the last few minutes feeling like a fever dream.

"Look at me, Piper," he says, and tenderness replaces the fury in his eyes. "I will never talk to you like that. I will never treat you how he treated you. With me, you're safe. Okay?"

"Okay," I whisper, and a word has never meant more. I reach out and touch his chest, my hand directly over his heart. "I'm yours, you know."

He sinks into me again, and time passes slowly. I don't know how long he fucks me, how long he stays inside me, only that it's the most perfect place in the world.

We fall apart together in a mess of labored breaths as he kisses me then kisses me again, the phone and my past long forgotten.

FORTY-SEVEN
LIAM

"PLAYING WELL TONIGHT, GOALIE DADDY." Maverick knocks my stick with his in the locker room. "Nice save before intermission."

"Thanks." I tug off my gloves and bend over to re-lace my skates, grateful for a few minutes to sit down. "And thanks for keeping the offense on the other end of the ice. This game is a lot more fun when I have a second to breathe."

Maverick laughs and grabs his water bottle. "Just doing my job, man."

I move my attention to the other skate, unknotting the laces and pulling them free. I check to see if my ring is in the spot I've tucked it the last two dozen games, and when I can't find it anywhere, I freeze.

"Shit." I take off the skate and shake it upside down, waiting for the metal to fall onto the locker room floor. Nothing comes. "*Shit.*"

"You okay?" Hudson asks.

"No, I'm not okay." I stand and dive into my locker. I throw my practice jersey out of the way and move my sticks around. "Where the fuck is my ring?"

"Ring? You never wear rings," Riley says.

"My wedding ring," I seethe, crouching down and rifling through my gym bag. "*FUCK*."

"I'm going to need someone to fill me in here, because for a second I thought GK just told us he got married," Grant says. "When the fuck did that happen?"

"I knew. I knew, and I didn't say shit to any of you fuckers," Maverick announces. "I've known for weeks and *holy shit*. It's so nice to have this out in the open and not a huge fucking secret."

"I was the witness," Hudson draws out, and Maverick groans.

"Dammit! Can't I have anything?"

I ignore them, too busy ripping apart all of my belongings to care about who knows what. I don't stop until there's a mess at my feet. Until my chest heaves and I still come up empty-handed.

Squeezing my eyes shut, I will myself to take a deep breath. To calm down and try to think rationally.

I made a diving save in the second period. The ring probably came loose and ended in the back of the goal with a pile of ice chips.

"Piper and I got married in Vegas," I tell my team. Someone gasps. Another drops their stick, and the entire locker room stares at me. "It was an accident. Some drunken thing neither one of us remembers, but we decided to stay married until at least the end of the season. I've worn the ring she gave me at every game, but now I've *lost* the fucking band, and I want it back."

"Whoa," Ethan whispers. "Goalie Daddy is in *love*."

"Boys," Maverick announces, and I lift my chin to look at him. Everyone does. "There comes a time when your personal choices far outweigh the greater good for the team. I had my moment when we played against Emmy's ex and I got to land some punches on him. Hudson had his moment when he left mid-game to be by his mom's side during her last hours.

Seymour had his when he got pulled last season when his wife went to the hospital to give birth. We're paid to be professional athletes, but we're humans first. And humans have emotions. Goddamn feelings we're allowed to express, no matter what the media says." He scans the men in the room, stopping at me to make sure I heard those last few words. "So. Here's what's going to happen. We're going to go out there. We're going to sacrifice our warm-up, and we're going to find Liam's ring even if it means crawling on our hands and knees."

"Miller," I start to say. "You don't have to—"

Maverick holds up a hand, stopping me. "You have my back. I have yours. End of discussion. Captain's orders are to find that damn ring."

Our eyes lock. I give him a single nod, and I hope I can convey the gratitude I have for him. "Winner gets a thousand bucks," I add. "And a night at the bar with me."

"Oh, shit." Grant practically runs out of the locker room with Ethan hot on his heels. "This is a once in a lifetime opportunity," he yells as he disappears.

The room clears out until it's only Maverick, Hudson and me. I put my skates back on and look at my teammates.

"That was a hell of a speech you gave," I say to Maverick.

"Liked it?" He grins. "I've turned all soft now that I'm married. Guess I can say the same about you."

I shove his shoulder and he laughs. "Fuck you."

"Ah. There he is. My grumpy guy."

"Word of advice, Sully," Hudson says, and I glance his way. "Take it from someone who always wished he had more time. Telling someone how you feel about them is the most important thing in the world. Because one day you won't be able to tell them anymore, and you'll regret all the times you kept your mouth shut."

I put my hand on Hudson's shoulders. "Your mom would be proud of you, man."

"Yeah." He smiles, ever the optimist even when he's in the depths of hell. "She would be."

"WHY COULDN'T you have gotten a yellow band?" Riley calls out as he circles the crease for the fourth time. "Would be a lot easier to spot than a piece of fucking silver metal."

"I'll make sure to tell the gift shop where I bought it to stock up on different colors. They'll be happy for the feedback," I draw out. "Goddammit. Where the fuck did it go?"

"Any luck?" Hudson asks.

"I'm not finding a damn thing."

"Don't lose faith, GK," Riley says, moving his stick over the ice. "You have to have hope."

"It's the hope that kills you," I grumble under my breath.

I get up and skate to the corner of the rink, the bend right against the boards. Fans bang on the glass and yell my name, but I keep my head down. I keep my eyes trained firmly on the ice, and my hope slowly wanes.

"*Hey*," Maverick yells, and I jerk my head up. I look over my shoulder and see him waving at me from the opposite end of the ice. I take off, whizzing past our opponents who look at me like I'm out of my fucking mind. I probably am. "Is this it?"

He holds up a metal band. Relief sinks into me and I laugh, reaching for it and curling my hand to my chest when it's safely in my hold.

"That's it," I say, and my teammates huddle around me.

You'd think we just won the Cup with how enthusiastic they are, and I blow out a breath that releases what feels like a thousand pounds sitting on my chest.

"I believe in miracles," Grant yells, hugging me around my middle. "Let's fucking gooooo!"

"See?" Riley jabs my knees with his stick. "Look what having hope does."

"You might be onto something." I squat down and loop the aglet through the ring, double and triple knotting the laces and tucking the jewelry deep in my sock for extra measure. "Thanks, you fuckers. Let's win this fucking game."

"No one else I'd get on my hands and knees for." Maverick kisses my helmet. "Well, except for Emmy."

"God, shut up, Miller." I shove him off me, but I'm smiling from ear to ear. "No one wants to hear that shit."

"Don't lose that thing again," he says to me pointedly, and I nod.

"Don't plan on it. I'm keeping it safe this time."

WE WIN BY ONE GOAL.

A wrist shot from Hudson just over the red line seals the deal and descends the arena into chaos. The victory cements us at the top spot in the East and the best record in the league, a far cry from our losing season four years ago.

I go down the line, shaking our opponents' hands and pulling off my goalie mask. I give Hudson a high five before he's called to do an interview with ESPN, the national broadcast wanting to hear his thoughts on his game-winning shot.

I take my time leaving the ice, letting myself celebrate this change in luck we've had. Winning feels *good*, and it's nice to enjoy it with the fans instead of hearing boos after another loss.

At the other end of the rink, I watch Piper get set up for her postgame interview. Her cameraman holds up two fingers and she nods, adjusting her earpiece into her ear so she can hear over the noise of the crowd. She looks left then right, a frown settling on her mouth when she realizes she doesn't have a player lined up.

There's always someone waiting to jump in and chat her ear off, but tonight, there's no one.

Hudson is still talking to ESPN. Maverick is signing autographs, his back turned toward her. Grant and Ethan are posing for photos with a group of kids in the stands, and Riley is gingerly moving toward the locker room with Lexi, an ice pack on the back of his neck after a rough fall in the final seconds of the game.

Her frown shifts to panic when her cameraman holds up one finger and gestures around her. She says something with her hands, and the microphone that's usually glued to her palm almost falls to the ice.

I grind my teeth together and make a split-second decision, skating over to her just as she's given a thirty second warning.

"What are you doing here?" she asks, and I *hear* the anxiousness in her tone. The way she's rushing her words. "I'm going live in—"

"Thirty seconds. You need someone to talk to?"

"Yes, but not you."

"Wow." I laugh. "I'm a little offended."

"You know what I mean. You don't do interviews. You never talk to the media."

"Think I might like them if you're on the other side."

Piper blinks, and relief floods her face. She bites her bottom lip and her gaze snags on mine. "Are you sure?"

"Come on, wife," I murmur, dropping my voice low. "Ask me a question."

Her cheeks turn bright red. She takes a step back and almost topples over, but I grab her by the arm before she can fall. She swallows and I track the bob of her throat when the red light turns on the camera and she plasters on a megawatt smile.

"Thanks, Bradley. I'm here with Liam Sullivan who recorded

twenty-eight saves tonight in front of the hometown crowd. Liam, this victory puts you as the number one seed not only in the East, but the entire league. It's number eight in a winning streak, which is the longest winning streak any team has amassed this season. What do you attest the Stars' recent success to?"

"Chemistry," I say, leaning on my stick and looking down at her. "We're in a groove where everything is meshing well. We've spent so much time playing together, we know each other's strengths and weaknesses. We're able to compensate if someone is slightly off their game, and we all just really want to fucking win."

"A, uh, quick reminder we're on *live* television," Piper says, arching her brow at me.

"Sorry. Didn't mean to get you in trouble, Pipsqueak. I'll pay the fine, don't worry. What else do you have for me?"

Her cheeks go from red to crimson. I like riling her up. If all interviews were this fun, I'd do them after every game.

"You had another fantastic performance tonight, which brings you up to twelve shutouts for the year." I stand up a little straighter. A smile twitches on my mouth and I stare at her, impressed. No one's ever been so kind to me in a line of questioning before—not even back when I was a college player—and I warm at her attention to detail. "You're also the league leader in save percentage. What goes through your mind when you're out there, night after night, giving it your all? Does it eventually wear you down?"

"There's physical and mental fatigue. That's part of the game. How you react to that fatigue is what is most important," I say when she lifts her microphone my way and nods in agreement. "Do I get worn out? Every night. Do I know I have a team I can rely on when I'm not at my sharpest? Yeah, I sure as shit—sorry, heck—do. I know I didn't miss a save tonight, but it also doesn't register in my head I had a shutout, you know? I'm out there grinding until the buzzer sounds, and at the end of the night, I want my team to have the most points."

"Final question for you, Liam, and we'll let you get back to celebrating with your teammates."

"That eager to get rid of me?"

Piper rolls her eyes, but she's grinning. "I am, actually. Before the third period, the team came out and had an unusual warmup. There was a lack of stretching and a lot more… crawling. Do you have any comment on this new pregame ritual?"

I bark out a laugh. "The internet is going to have a field day with that, aren't they?"

"You all are already trending on social media."

"Great. As for the crawling, we were looking for something."

"And did you find it?"

"We did."

"Must've been pretty important."

"Yeah." My eyes lock on hers and I smile. "Most important thing in the world to me."

"I'm going to send it back to Bradley and Clarissa who will break down all of tonight's highlights for you. Thanks for sticking around with us. Stay safe, be kind, and we'll see you back here the day after tomorrow for the Stars' showdown against the Cleveland Vipers."

The cameraman gives us the all clear and Piper rolls back her shoulders.

"You're good at your job," I say.

"Did you think I wouldn't be?"

"I knew you would be, but you're *very* good at your job."

"And you're going to get me in trouble with my boss with your colorful language." She sticks out her tongue. "Cursing twice on national television, Sullivan?"

"Sorry. It slipped out. I'd say it's not going to happen again, but there won't be another interview, so I'm safe."

"You wouldn't consider doing another one? I wasn't too invasive, was I?"

"You were perfect. It's just not my thing."

"Thank you for jumping in. I really appreciate it. You saved me from having to talk to myself for five minutes."

"Happy to help."

"Are you going to tell me what you lost now? Instead of being vague in front of thousands of people?"

"Nah." I grin at her. "It's much more fun this way."

FORTY-EIGHT
PIPER

I DIDN'T EXPECT to slip into Liam's life so easily, but I have.

February turns to March.

The snow melts, and we keep seeing each other. Some nights after a loss, he wants to be alone. Other times he drives me back to his apartment, silent but affectionate with his hand on my thigh and the weight of a defeat on his shoulders.

We go to team dinner together. I'll walk in a few minutes after him. He slips out a few minutes before me. I'm pretty sure the team is catching on, but no one says anything.

Like tonight. Grant winked at me when I slipped on my jacket, and earlier I saw him slip Ethan twenty bucks when I sat next to Liam on the couch.

"You're deep in thought," Liam says as we walk down the sidewalk to his place. "What are you stewing over, Pipsqueak?"

"Oh, my mind is a treacherous place." I rest my head on his chest when he drapes an arm around me. "I think the guys have a bet going on us."

"What makes you say that?"

"There was an exchange of cash based on our seating arrangement."

"Really? Now we have to fuck with them." His fingers

brush through the ends of my hair and tug on the long strands. "Next week you'll sit next to Hudson."

"I like when you're scheming."

We ride up to his apartment and he lets us inside. I smile at the pair of shoes I have by the door and the cardigan I left on the foyer table.

Last night, I noticed Liam cleaned out a drawer in his dresser for me, and it shows me he's trying. Trying to fit me in with practice and games and messages from his parents about the trip they're planning to DC. Trying to balance the things he cares about without neglecting the other parts of himself, and it means so much.

And I'm trying too.

Trying to be trusting. Trying not to compare him to my past. Trying to not anticipate the other shoe dropping and just being *here*.

"Want some dessert?" Liam asks, and I follow him to the kitchen.

"Depends." I jump on the counter and swing my legs back and forth. "What do you have?"

"Carrot cake. And, listen, before you try to turn nose up at it, it doesn't have raisins. I fucking hate raisins."

"I hate raisins too!"

"Look at us. We're an old married couple with similar interests. We're going to take over the world." He sets a plate between us and slices off a bite. "Open up, please."

I smile and open my mouth. The bite is sweet, and I hum around the cream cheese frosting. "I think I like that better than I like sex."

"I should be offended, but I think I agree." Liam cuts off a bite for himself and swallows it down. "Delicious, isn't it?"

"Don't feed me anything else the rest of the night. This is all I want."

He grips my chin and tilts my head back. His kiss is soft, savory, and I taste walnuts on his tongue. A hand works in my hair, pulling my ponytail free before settling on the back of my neck. I sigh, relaxing into him as he nudges his way between my legs and takes up the space where I love him to be the most.

"Bedroom?" Liam asks against my mouth and I nod, needing him. *Wanting* him.

I wrap my legs around his waist, smiling when he lifts me off the counter and walks us down the hall. He sets me on his bed and I fumble with the button of his jeans, my actions hurried, my heart racing.

Pulling the zipper down, I tug on the denim, my intentions clear when Liam steps out of the jeans and kicks them away. His briefs do little to hide his body and I pull those off next while he takes off his shirt, the two of us working in tandem until he's naked in front of me.

"I want you in my mouth, Liam." I run my finger up his length. My thumb drags over the pre-cum on the head of his cock, my touch more assured, more confident than it was weeks ago. I know how to do this. I know how to make him fall apart, and *fuck* do I want it. "Would that be okay?"

"Do you trust me?" he asks, and I nod. I trust him more than I trust anyone in the world. "Get on your back and let your head hang off the bed."

I listen to him, getting into position as I scramble across the comforter. "Like this?"

"Perfect." He grips his shaft and gives himself a few strokes. His other hand touches my chin and pulls down on my bottom lip, opening my mouth. "Breathe through your nose."

I inhale, waiting as he towers over me, and he moves his fingers to the back of my head. He slowly works the first half of his cock in my mouth and tears prick my eyes. I relax my jaw, giving him more room in my mouth to fill, and he hums his approval.

"So fucking sexy," he murmurs, reaching down the front

of my shirt and pulling the cup of my bra down. "I love watching you suck my cock, Piper."

The position doesn't give me much room to move, and I rely on him to do the work. I moan around him when he pinches my nipple, my legs spreading and my fingers dropping to the hem of my skirt.

"Going to get a little deeper, baby. Want you to choke on it." I gag when he thrusts his hips, his length almost too much. "Perfect."

His words might be filthy, but his actions are considerate. Like in how he wipes my eyes. How he gently pulls out of my mouth, my saliva covering his length.

"Sit up," he tells me.

"I need to take my clothes off."

"Can't wait that long."

I sit up and spin, my legs dangling over the edge and heat rising on my skin. Liam tugs on my calf, laughing when I almost fall off the mattress and kissing me when I finally get settled.

He shoves my skirt up to my waist and I smile, teasing him as I lift my hips and take off my underwear. I'm bold, ambitious when I touch my clit, his name a whispered gasp that falls from my mouth.

His touch runs up my thigh, the bump of his hand against mine reminding me this is wicked. A sin, but not one I'd care to repent for. I don't give a shit about damnation or hell or anywhere else I might end up, because when he bats my hand away and shoves three fingers inside me, I've never wanted to be angelic a day in my life.

"Piper." His voice is thick. Maybe it's lust. Maybe he's tipsy from the one beer he had at dinner. Whatever is aiding him, I love it. I want more of it. "Can I—"

"Please," I whisper, wanting him to know how badly I want him too.

This is different from what we've done when we've been intimate before.

This is a need. A desire. Agony in the most blissfully wonderful way, and I think I might die without him.

I prop up on an elbow, wanting to commit tonight to memory because I know it's monumental in the grand scheme of *us*. Something special, something cherished, and I'm surprised by the look of admiration in his eyes. The way his hands trace up my sides then back down, squeezing my hips.

I never seen Liam like this with his ragged breathing. Falling apart at the seams. Losing his self-control in the name of something deeper than sex. He can't pick a spot on my body he wants to focus on, so I help him. I spread myself open, letting him see all of me.

"You are…" He trails off and shakes his head. "I've never been with someone as magnificent as you."

There are so many things I want to say to him.

Silly things like *thank you*.

Thank you for bringing me out of the dark.

Thank you for making me feel beautiful.

"Show me," I whisper. "Touch me, Liam."

There's a tremble to his touch, like the room is shaking. Like this is *real*, a living and breathing thing outside these walls we both know the name of. His thumb presses against my clit. His mouth is on my neck, a warm swipe of his tongue against my throat nearly catapulting me into space.

"Fuck," he says, but it's not a curse. It's beautiful and pleading. The mattress dips so he can ease me back. So he can take up more space and move into my orbit. "I could fuck you all night. Could touch you all night. Could just… *fuck*. Be with you all night. And the next and the next."

"So be with me," I say, and his eyes blaze with fire.

Liam pulls his fingers out of me and reaches for a condom. I touch his wrist, stopping him, and he looks at me.

"You okay?" he asks, and I'm not sure I am.

"Would it be okay if—" I take a deep breath. "Can we try without a condom?"

His gaze is piercing, a lightning bolt to my heart. He drops his head back and blows out a breath, staring at the ceiling instead of me. I might've said the wrong thing, but before I can worry about it, he's kissing me. Brushing his nose against mine and laughing into the crook of my neck.

"You want that?"

"I want it with you," I say. "I've never had sex that way, and I want you to be my first."

"I haven't either," he says, and the room is a blur of colors. Of shapes and sounds and sensations. "And I've wanted to with you from the first time I fucked you. But if I fuck you without a condom, Piper, you should know it's going to be difficult to ever give you up. It's going to be hard to walk away from you, because once I sink into you without anything between us, I'm not going to want anything else for the rest of my life. I'm going to want to fuck you every minute of every goddamn day."

"I'm on birth control," I tell him, running my fingers down his chest because that sounds magical. Magnificent and exactly what I want.

"That's good." He nods and pulls away. "That means I can come inside you, doesn't it?"

Liam lies on his back and motions for me to straddle him. I throw a leg over his hips and look down at him. "I know being exclusive was part of this, but I haven't been with anyone else, Liam. Just you. And I want you to know that."

"It's only been you from the beginning. No one else, Piper."

Sinking onto him without the feeling of latex is dizzying. I transcend time, floating above my body as I work the head of his cock inside me first then relax enough to take the rest of him.

I let go, my body knowing his and the things he likes best.

I realize as he cups my cheek, his touch heavy on my skin, this isn't fucking. This is something so much more substantial, something far more important than anything we've ever done.

When he's close, he looks at me, a question in his eyes.

"Can I—"

"Yes," I whisper. "I told you I'm yours, Liam."

"You are. And I want everyone to know it."

I revel in his release and the mess it makes and the way it finally feels like I've seen every part of him.

After, he cleans me up and hugs me tight. Pico settles between us, our breaths turning soft as we drift off to the world where this exists forever.

FORTY-NINE
LIAM

I WAKE UP AND YAWN.

When I turn over, I see Piper's phone on her side of the bed, and I wonder if she's on the balcony again because she can't sleep.

I smile and kick off the sheets, making my way through the apartment to the noises coming from the kitchen. It might be the middle of the night, but it's bright as hell out here. I round the corner and find her in one of my big T-shirts. Socks that come halfway up her calves and a messy bun that makes her blonde hair look like ribbons of sunlight. She turns on the stove and sets a kettle on the burner, a mug sitting on the counter and Pico rubbing against her ankles.

I like the look of her in my space. Slotting into my life and revolving around me like we've been doing this for years. She's not a distraction. Not a chore or a burden, and in the weeks we've been spending together, not once have I felt like I've had to make a sacrifice between hockey and her.

I clear my throat, wanting to make my presence known, and Piper jumps a foot in the air. She yelps and Pico darts away, taking off for the hallway.

"*Jesus*, Liam." She turns and scowls at me, and I can't help but smile at the dangerous look in her eye. "What the hell is wrong with you?"

"Did I do something?" I walk toward her and grab a mug for myself. "Or are you just skittish?'

"Asshole." Piper huffs and checks the burner. "Did I wake you up?"

"Nope. Woke up on my own. Missed you and wanted to come find you."

"Well, here I am. Helping myself to your tea. You have a very fancy setup here, Sullivan."

"I stocked up when you started staying over." I shrug and tap the box of tea bags. "Wanted you to be comfortable."

Her face softens, and she tugs on the waistband of my pajama bottoms. "You're too nice to me."

It pisses me off she considers stuff like this *nice*, when it should be the bare minimum. I don't want to know all the details about how her ex treated her—I've heard enough—because it's going to make me want to buy her everything in the world she could want. I already want to spoil the shit out of her, and knowing I'm making up for lost time only fuels the fire.

"I have something for you," I say.

"Is it a friend for Pico?"

"Slow down there, Pipsqueak." I reach for the junk drawer to the left of the stove and pull it open. "Hold out your arm and close your eyes."

"You're going to cut off my hand, aren't you?"

"Severed limbs aren't really my jam, but close." I grab a paper towel and run it under the faucet. When it's wet, I wrap my fingers around her wrist and turn her arm. I peel back the plastic film from the small temporary tattoo I bought at the drugstore the other day and drag my fingers over her pulse point. "You told me something when we were in Edmonton."

"I told you a lot of things in Edmonton." She huffs at the memory, then quiets when I press the tattoo on her skin.

"Which was your favorite? When I propositioned you for sex?"

"I mean, have you seen me complaining?" I cover the tattoo with the cloth and hold it there. "Open your eyes."

Piper watches me move the paper towel away and laughs, holding up her wrist. "A tattoo? What is it?"

"A lotus flower. It represents strength and resilience."

"And why are you giving me a tattoo?"

"Because it's one of the things you said you wanted, and I want them too. With you. Slow dancing in the kitchen. Kissing in the rain. Getting matching tattoos and being an absolute idiot with the next person you fall for. Be an idiot with me, Piper. I'm begging you, because I'm head over heels for you."

Her fingers shake as she traces the outline of the flower. "I've never wanted to be an idiot before, but you make me want to be stupid. You make me want to get married in Vegas and laugh until my sides hurt. I thought I knew what being happy was, but then I met you, and everything changed. That wasn't me being happy. *This* is me happy, and it's because of you."

There's so much else I want to say to her.

The important words.

The stupid words.

The three words that have been echoing in my head this last week. I hear them when she smiles at me across the ice. When she waves at me and blushes. Right now, as she looks at me like I'm someone who can keep her safe. Like I'm someone she wants to keep around, and this, *this*, suddenly means more to me than anything I've ever done in my playing career.

Fuck the accolades.

Fuck the wins.

Fuck a losing record or the Stanley Cup or making the All-Star team.

They don't mean shit if I don't have her around.

"I think…" I trail off and dance my fingers down her jaw. Tuck a piece of hair behind her ear and smile. "I think I've been waiting for you my whole life, Piper Mitchell."

"I think I've been waiting my whole life for you too, Liam Sullivan." She beams at me then looks at the junk drawer. "Did you get a tattoo for me to give you?"

"Yeah, but it's nothing special."

"Okay, now you have to show me."

I pull out the four leaf clover and shrug. "They had a deal for buy one, get one free."

"Look at you being thrifty." Piper plucks the tattoo from my possession and motions for me to hold out my wrist. "My turn to mark you, Sullivan."

She goes through the steps, taking her time to read each direction carefully. I laugh when she has trouble peeling back the plastic film, and the glare she shoots me is the cutest thing I've ever seen.

I didn't expect to be putting on temporary tattoos with someone in my kitchen at three in the morning.

I didn't expect to have *anyone* in my kitchen at three in the morning, but I like that I'm here. I like that she's wearing my T-shirt and blowing on my skin, her eyelashes fluttering up at me while her mouth curves into a smile, pleased with the results.

"There." She drags her thumb across the tattoo, slow to pull away. I'm close to begging her to keep touching me. To give me a hundred other tattoos wherever she wants if it means she gets to put her hands on me. "Now you're lucky."

"How do I look?"

"Not nearly as cool as me, but it's not bad. I like the real ones better."

"Guess I need to get another real one. Ready for the next thing I have for you?"

"Is it your dick?"

I burst out laughing and shake my head, proud of her sass.

Proud of her confidence. Proud of the journey she's going through to get to here.

"No. It's not my dick, unfortunately."

"Anything else is going to be very disappointing."

I take her hand in mine and rest the other on the small of her back. Her breath hitches when she realizes what we're doing, and hope flickers in her eyes. I hum a tune I heard on the radio, swaying back and forth with her until the kettle whistles and we both forget about everything except each other.

FIFTY
PIPER

LIAM

Are you busy tonight?

ME

Depends who's asking.

LIAM

I'm asking.

ME

Oh? I'm free as a bird. What's on the agenda?

A loud club?

Somewhere with a lot of people?

A loud club with a lot of people?

LIAM

Very funny.

I'm taking you on a date.

A real date outside the house.

ME

You are?

LIAM

Yup.

Be ready at seven. Jeans are fine.

ME

Are you going to tell me about where we're going?

LIAM

Nope. It's a secret.

GIRLS JUST WANT TO HAVE FUN(DAMENTAL) RIGHTS AND GOOD SEX

ME

EMERGENCY. Liam is taking me on a date tonight and said jeans are okay. What else do I wear?

LEXI

A sweater will be perfect!

EMMY

And socks. Don't forget your socks.

ME

What do you all know?

LEXI

Nothing.

MAVEN

Nothing.

EMMY

Something. But that's because I'm married to the guy who can't keep a secret to save his life.

ME

Not true. He kept the secret about Liam and me being married. I'm impressed with that, by the way.

EMMY

You and me both.

MAVEN

Casual is good, Piper!

ME

I'm nervous. Why am I nervous? I've seen the man naked dozens of times, but the minute he says he's taking me on a date, I get butterflies?

LEXI

Because you loveeee him!

ME

Stop it. That's a big word.

LEXI

Almost as big as his dick?

ME

I'm done with you.

"IS THE BLINDFOLD REALLY NECESSARY?" I cross my arms over my chest in the front seat of Liam's Range Rover and turn my chin in his direction. "Feels a bit dramatic, if you ask me."

"Sorry. My kidnapper insisted," he says, and I bite back a laugh at his joke. "I didn't want to argue with him."

"Fine. But I if I meet this kidnapper, I'm going to have some words for him." I relax against the cool leather interior and huff. "I'm not really a fan of surprises."

"You're not?"

"No. I think walking into my ex-husband's office and seeing his head between his secretary's legs was enough of a jump scare to last a lifetime."

"I'm taking you to the rink," Liam says immediately.

"You are? Is there an event tonight? I didn't think there was anything on the schedule with the playoffs only a few weeks away."

"Nope. Nothing on the schedule It'll just be us."

"And what are we doing at the rink?"

"You'll see," he tells me, and I hear the smile behind his words. "But I promise you won't see my head between anyone's legs."

"Very reassuring." I reach over, searching for his arm or his hand or something so I can touch him. So I can feel his warmth. "How was practice today?"

"Fine. We were sloppy in the game last night, and Coach took it out on us this morning. We went through shootout drills, and my legs are shot."

"Is that why we're going to the rink? Because you can't stay away?"

"Kind of."

Liam cuts off the engine and unbuckles his seatbelt. I hear him open his door then open mine, helping me to the asphalt. His arm drapes over my shoulder as he guides me down the familiar path I've walked hundreds of times.

There's the beep of his credentials, then cool air greets me. I smile when he leads me down a long stretch of hallway, his hand in mine and his thumb rubbing against the inside of my wrist.

It's colder wherever we are, and I figure we're probably near the ice. At the end of the tunnel where I usually stand during games. I don't hear any other sounds, though. No music. No noise. No conversations.

I'm in the arena every day, but there are always dozens of other people around. I'm used to the whistles and plays being called out, not utter silence.

"Okay." Liam pulls the blindfold over my head and I blink under the house lights. There's a carpet rolled out to center ice, and I spot a table sitting right over the logo. "We're here."

"What is going on?" I laugh when I see plates and glasses set up, and he tugs on my hand. "Are we trying out a game the fans are going to play at intermission?"

"We're having dinner. You told me the arena is one of your favorite places. Why would I take you anywhere you don't love as much?"

I look at him and find him watching me, waiting for validation, and I don't know what to say.

How do I tell him how thoughtful this is?

How do I tell him I'm not used to being listened to?

How do I tell him dinner at the rink is going to make me cry because it means I'm here with him, near the spot where we first met, wondering how my life has turned out this way?

How do I tell him it's the most perfect thing in the world?

"Liam," I whisper, his name coming out like two reverent syllables. "You did this for me?"

"I'd do anything for you."

It's simple. Short and sweet and five words I've never heard before, but they stick to my heart. They sweep out the cobwebs and air out the last remaining fears I have about starting something new. About starting over with someone I care about very much.

"This is..." I trail off, emotions threatening to grip me. Threatening to suffocate me, because this man is the epitome of kind and wonderful and perfect. "Thank you."

"Come on." He holds my hand as we walk across the carpet and scoots my chair in for me. "I hope you're hungry."

A noise from my left is magnified in the empty arena, and I turn, watching Maverick skate leisurely across the ice holding a server's tray.

"Evening, folks," he says, stopping in front of our table. "Thank you for joining us for dinner tonight. You'll see a menu on your plate. Would we like to start with a glass of wine? I recommend the house red, but the Sauvignon Blanc is also a good choice."

I gape at Maverick and the tuxedo he's wearing. He's rolled the pant legs up on top of his skates, and he looks absolutely ridiculous.

"What do you think?" Liam asks me, and I shake my head.

"I'm sorry. I'm still processing Maverick's outfit. You're in a *tux*."

"You *think* I'm in a tux. It's actually a Halloween costume from the thrift store."

"Wow." I laugh and glance at Liam. "Red sounds good."

"Red it is," Maverick says, skating away.

"Are we having any other visitors?" I ask, and Liam shrugs.

"Guess you'll have to wait and see."

Hudson comes out next, setting down bread and mozzarella sticks as an appetizer. He talks for ten minutes about the Italian breadcrumbs covering the cheese, only leaving when Liam shoots him a look that has me trying not to burst out laughing.

Grant comes next, handing us both a salad before tossing

me a wink. Ethan brings out a plate of hot dogs and cups of condiments, letting us know he called in a favor with Dave to have the food delivered.

Riley is there too, passing off our entrees and helping Maverick refill our wine glasses. When I've eaten every bite of the pasta dish in front of me, I lean back in my chair and grin.

"Wow. You got everyone to help. How'd you pull that off?"

"I told them I was nervous as shit about taking you on a date, and they jumped in. They know you're my favorite person, and they know I wanted to do this right. I would've done the same for any of them."

"You would've?"

"Yeah. Would've complained for hours, but I would've done it." Liam stares at me across the table and tips his head to the side. "Ready for the next part of the date?"

"What else do you have up your sleeve, Sully?"

He bends forward and pulls a pair of ice skates. "Want to be an idiot with me, Pipsqueak?"

"Oh, god. What's that saying about returning to the scene of the crime?"

"The first time was a tragedy, wasn't it?"

"Are you sure this is a good idea? You have a *very* important stretch of games coming up, and I don't want to be on the end of Brody Saunders's wrath if you hurt yourself in your off time."

Liam scoots his chair back and stands. "I want you to learn."

"Is knowing how to skate a prerequisite for spending time with you?"

"No. I want you to learn for you. I've taught you a lot of things over the last couple of months, Piper, and it pisses me off I didn't get to teach you how to skate the first time. Consider this a door closing on your past. After tonight, everything you want to learn, I'm going to be by your side while you do it. Encouraging you. Motivating and supporting you. You won't be embarrassed or afraid of anything ever again."

I want to weep.

I want to laugh and scream and hug him tight.

I want to tell him all the ways he'll never be the person from my past, starting with the gentle way he cares about me.

The way he *loves* me, and the way I love him.

I think.

The word terrifies me. Scares the absolute shit out of me, because I can see what happens when you abuse it. When you turn it into something wretched and broken and messy.

I've seen the worst side of love, but here I am, staring at Liam and knowing deep within every fractured piece of my soul, I am completely and irrevocably in love with him.

"Hey." He moves around the table and squats in front of me. "What's wrong?"

"*Nothing*. This is the most thoughtful thing anyone's ever done for me, and I'm having a hard time processing it."

Liam's mouth hooks up in a smile. His eyes twinkle and happiness almost radiates off of him. "Wanna do a lap, Sunshine?"

I nod, afraid to say anything else. I might blurt out how I feel about him. I might ask him to stay with me forever because I'm terrified of a world without him in it.

He helps me switch my sneakers for the skates, lacing them up and tapping the toe when I'm ready to go. I wait for him to put his own skates on, watching the easiness of his movements and how natural he looks being near the ice.

"All right." He holds out his hand and I stand, our fingers locking together. "Remember: it can't be worse than last time."

"That's debatable. Tonight you could hit your head."

"Might knock some sense in him," Ethan hollers from the stands, and Liam flips him off.

"I didn't know we had an audience," I say, and he sighs.

"That was part of the agreement. They would help but only if they could watch us act all, and I quote, 'cute and shit.'"

"Look at you." I reach up and pinch his cheek. "You're like a walking romcom. Guess we better give them a show."

We take the first lap slow. By the third lap, I'm more comfortable. My posture is straight, my eyes are straight ahead instead of down at my feet, and I loosen my death grip on Liam's hand.

"I can finally feel my fingers," he says when I pull away. I shove him, knowing it won't do much damage, and he grabs my wrist. "Bad move, Pipsqueak."

Before I can prepare for his retaliation, Liam lifts me above his head like I'm a figure skater. I squeak when I see how high I am and feebly swat at his back.

"Oh, my god. Put me down, you big ogre."

"No can do. I overheard the guys say they have a bet going for tonight, and I kind of want Hudson to win."

"He deserves a win, doesn't he?" I close my eyes, not wanting to look at the ground. "Fine. But don't make me stay up here very long. My life is flashing before my eyes."

His laugh is loud and bold, and it melts into me. "You win. I'm putting you down."

I expect him to set me down quickly, but Liam is slow. He drags me down the front of his body, holding me there, and I wrap my legs around his waist.

"What else is included in this bet?"

"I heard something about ice angels and disgusting displays of affection."

"I thought you hated PDA."

"Wouldn't mind it with you. Especially if it means Ethan loses a hundred bucks."

I smile and touch his cheek, his skin warm and soft. "Seems like you don't mind a lot of things with me. Interviews. PDA. Sleepovers. Hanging out with each other every single day. You're the one doodling my name in *your* journal, aren't you?"

"Guilty," he says, and his nose brushes against mine. "You gonna give me an exit survey for our first date, Pipsqueak? The areas where I can improve?"

"Yeah. You lose a point for not kissing me."

"Better fix that." Liam brings his lips to mine. He kisses the corner of my mouth and grins. "We both know how I feel about being the best."

FIFTY-ONE
LIAM

PIPER

Happy end of the regular season!

How are we celebrating the best record in the league?

ME

With you.

Come over, baby.

PIPER

I'm already on my way.

"IF YOU DO something horrible like tear your ACL next season and can't play, I think you have a future in culinary." Piper polishes off her dinner and scoots her plate away. "How are you *this* good at so many things?"

"I'm also not good at so many things, like listening to directions. Maverick yelled at me because I read ahead for book club, but I'm not going to slow down."

"Are you a fan of monster smut now?"

"I think I'm converted." I stand and grab her dirty dish, dropping it in the sink with mine. "What other weird shit can you throw at me, Mitchell?"

"I'll give you a list." She crosses her legs and takes a sip of her wine. "Want some help cleaning up?"

"Nah. I saw the heels you wore to the arena today. I bet your feet are swollen as hell."

"They're bigger than Maven's and she's growing a damn human inside her. Come on, let me help. I know you had a long day with playoff prep. You shouldn't have to clean up alone."

"Fine. Come on down, Pipsqueak. You can wash and I'll dry."

Piper jumps off the stool and makes her way next to me. "I like doing these things with you. Washing dishes. Watching shitty television. Complaining about the curtains you need to fix in your bedroom."

"Are we at the stage in our marriage where this is nagging?" I laugh when she grabs the sink nozzle and sprays me, warm water soaking my hair and shirt. "That was not a smart move, wife."

"Whoops." She gives me an innocent smile. "Better take those clothes off and get dry, husband."

"If you wanted me naked, Piper…" I wipe my eyes with the back of my hand and touch the hem of my shirt. "You could've just asked."

"It's way more fun this way. You don't get to—"

I move before she can react, grabbing the nozzle out of her hand and spraying her in retaliation. She screeches and runs to the other side of the island, shielding her face with the plate we used for our salads.

"Two can play that game," I say.

"How are you so *fast*? You're like a freaking ninja." She looks down at the wet shirt clinging to her torso. I can see the outline of her nipples through the sheer material and I turn the water off, a new plan in mind. "This is a different side of Liam Sullivan, and I like it."

"Goalie, remember?" I scoop her up and walk her down the hall to my room. "This is who I am now. Life is a hoot, and I'm goddamn fun."

"Who knew all it took to lighten you up was getting laid by your perfect wife?"

"Someone's cocky. You're right, but you're also cocky."

"It's a shame you didn't have sex for years. Think of all the fun you missed out on by not banging your choice of women."

When we get to my room, I set her on my bed. I take a step back and stare at her, all the humor leaving the room.

"I've never had a choice of women," I say.

Piper frowns. "What do you mean?"

"Ask me why I haven't slept with anyone in four years, Piper," I say, and it comes out like a plea. Like I'm fucking *desperate* for her to hear this.

"W-why haven't you slept with anyone in four years, Liam?" she whispers.

"The same reason I haven't looked at a woman in four years. Why it wouldn't have mattered who won me at the charity auction or tried to get my attention. Ask me why I keep my wedding ring tied to my skates," I blurt out. Her eyes widen and she inhales a sharp breath. "Ask why I haven't washed off the temporary tattoo you gave me *days* ago. Ask me, Piper," I beg. "Please."

"Why?" she whispers, but I know she knows the answer. I can tell by the way she reaches for me. In the softness of her fingers as they touch the back of my neck and how quickly she scoots to the edge of the bed. "Why, Liam?"

"I can say it's hockey. I can say it's because I didn't want to be distracted. I can say it's because I care about my position, but that's all bullshit. The day you walked into the United

Airlines Arena was the best day of my life. It was a Wednesday. Partly cloudy. Eight-five in the first week of August. August seventh, actually," I croak, and her eyes blur with tears as her attention bounces to my phone on the bedside table. "You ran into me. After, you introduced yourself. Stuck your hand out like you were the most important person in the room. I saw the ring on your finger and knew I couldn't get close to you. Couldn't get to know you. Not in the way I wanted. That fucking diamond taunted me for months until one day, you showed up and it wasn't there anymore. And for the first time since I laid eyes on you, I felt a sliver of hope." I laugh, still not convinced this is all happening. Still not sure she's really here with me. "I've never been an optimistic guy, baby, but the day I found out you were single was the day I started believing. We talked here and there. Had that night in Canada where I was so nervous, so fucking careful with you, I wanted to scream. And then you asked me to fuck you, and I did. But I fucked it all up, because I fell in love with the way you laugh. With the way you smile. With the way you're brave and bold and so fucking beautiful."

I pause for a breath. I wipe the tears from her cheeks and tip her chin back, wanting her to look at me so she doesn't miss a single word before I start again.

"I fell in love with your determination and your drive. With the way you speak into a microphone and how *hard* you work. I fell in love with your kind heart and the way sometimes, when I'm feeling really fucking positive, I let myself believe you might one day love me back. When you're ready. But you take all the time you need, sweetheart, because I'm not going anywhere."

"Liam," she says, and I want to keep going. I want her to hear everything before she makes up her mind, so I put my hand gently over her mouth.

"You know I'm not a man of many words, but with you, I have a lot to say. I'm not finished," I tell her, and her eyes crinkle in the corners. "I know you've been hurt. I know it's hard for you to trust. I know it's difficult for you to believe what happened to you once won't happen again. And, look. I'll sit here and promise you everything in the world. Money. Safety. Anything you could ever want. But they won't mean shit if I don't tell you this: I will love you, Piper Mitchell, until my dying days. When it's stormy. When it's sunny. You will always have my full attention. You've had it for years and you weren't even mine. I wasn't kidding when I said you're my favorite person in the world. No one else could ever come close."

She mumbles something against my palm, and there's a moment of panic. A world where she doesn't feel the same and I'll have to deal with the sucker punch to the gut as I watch her live her life with someone else.

"You are my favorite person," Piper starts. She touches my cheek, and *fuck*. I ache for her. One graze of her fingers and I'm on top of the world. Feeling like I can fucking *fly*. "The patience you've shown me. The respect you've shown me. The kindness you've shown me these last couple of months..." She shakes her head and laughs. "Thank you isn't good enough. You've changed me. I wouldn't be the woman I am today without you."

"That's not true. You would've gotten there on your own. You're strong. Capable. You didn't need a man. You just needed someone who believed in you."

"And you do believe in me. I told you I'm scared, and I am, but I know you'll never, ever hurt me. I think I've known that for a while now, which is why I went to you in the first place. Why I feel safe and secure whenever you're around. I love you too, Liam. So unbelievably much. What I feel for you is... I'm not sure there's a word to describe it. To define just how... you..." Piper trails off. Fresh tears stain her cheeks and I hold her tight in my arms. "You fixed me, Liam."

"You were never broken, Piper."

"I love you," she says again, the three words muffled against my chest. Cemented in my soul and close to piercing my heart. "You're the best thing to ever come out of my heartbreak, and even though it hurt like *hell*, I'd do it again if it meant finding you."

There are a thousand things I want to say to her. A thousand things I want to do, but for now I ease her onto the bed. I lie beside her and kiss her—soft at first, then hungrier, like she's going to slip out of my grasp at any second.

I know she's not. She's mine and I'm hers for as long as she'll have me. A day. A week. A month. I don't care, and I'm not going to take a goddamn second of her time for granted.

I show her how I feel with my hands. Then my tongue and my teeth and my mouth. With the careful way I strip her naked and kiss every inch of her body I've come to adore. I fuck her gently, *lovingly*, and know there's no rush.

A million lifetimes with her won't be enough.

It'll never be enough.

But *fuck* if I'm going to work until my body gives out to make sure every day is the best fucking day of her life.

FIFTY-TWO
PIPER

"WHY AM I so nervous to see your parents and sister?" I check my reflection in the foyer mirror and fix my hair. "I've met them before."

"Maybe because tonight we're telling them we're actually dating?" Liam walks up behind me and wraps his arms around my middle. He drops a kiss to the top of my head and smiles at me. "And the whole marriage thing."

"Do we have to? Can we pretend we're not legally bound to each other? I like thinking your mother likes me. I don't want her to assume I'm trying to steal your money or something like that."

"Why would she ever assume that?"

"I don't know. I just want tonight to go well. Steven's parents never liked me."

"Because they're assholes. Guess the apple doesn't fall far from the tree." Liam moves his lips to my forehead, dropping a kiss there too. "It's going to be fine, Piper. Really. We're going to dinner. They're heading back to their hotel. Watching the game tomorrow, then they'll be on their way back to Chicago until I visit them this summer. Be yourself. They already like that version of you."

"Fine." I sigh and untangle myself from him, spinning in his hold so I can stand on my toes and kiss his jaw. "Are you going to keep your beard forever?"

"Haven't really thought about it. Why?"

"I like it." I drag my fingers across the stubble and smile. "It looks good."

"So I don't look good without it?"

"Nope."

"I'm never shaving again. Thanks for deciding that for me, Pipsqueak."

I laugh and pick up my shoes, slipping my feet into the heels. "Where are we going to eat tonight?"

"A steakhouse downtown that Alana wanted to try. They're meeting us there, by the way. Figured you'd probably freak out on the drive over and want to be alone."

"You know me so well." I sling my purse over my shoulder and put my hands on my hips, looking at him. "Ready to go?"

"Yeah." Liam's eyes roam down my body. They take in my dress, the slit that comes up to my knee, and leave a scorching path of warmth when they get to my hips. "*Fuck*, baby. You look so good."

I bristle at the attention as if it's something new, but he's been showering me with compliments for weeks. Telling me how much he loves my hair. The nail polish I wear. The new pantsuit I bought for game nights and the underwear I put on when I got out of the shower tonight.

There's never a doubt in my mind how he's feeling about me, and every time Liam looks at me like this—with heat behind his gaze, a starved look on his face—I feel like the luckiest girl in the world.

"Thank you." I spin so he can see the back of the dress and he walks toward me, fingers bunching the material near my waist. "Careful. Don't wrinkle it."

"Sorry," he murmurs, his mouth at my neck. "I don't want to ruin the look. I only want to touch."

"Then we need to go before you do something like rip the thing in half. You have no self-control."

"Don't give me ideas, Pipsqueak." With one more kiss he pulls away, grabbing his keys off the wall and spinning them in his hold. "Ready?"

"If we have to."

"We do, and you're going to be just fine."

We take the elevator down hand in hand, his thumb rubbing against my wrist and my heart racing in my chest.

I don't know why I'm panicking.

Alana and I text every week. We were on a FaceTime call together last night while she held up different dresses, sifting through a pile of clothes so I could help her pick one for tonight.

I think it's because this time, I love him.

I love him so much, and I want them to see that. I want them to understand he's *it* for me, and I'm going to do everything in my power to protect him. To guard his heart and treat him right. I don't want anything in exchange except to be loved in return, and he's doing that *so* well.

Liam opens the door to his Range Rover for me, his hand giving my ass a squeeze as I climb into the car. A laugh spills out of me, wild and free, and I glance at the grin on his face with immense pride and joy.

I do that.

I make him happy, and *god*, does he make me happy too.

"What are we listening to tonight?" I ask when Liam drives us out of the garage. "Want to try that gong track I sent you yesterday?"

"That's a big fuck no, Mitchell. And same with the country tracks you tried to slip onto my pregame playlist. It was a big surprise going from Beethoven to hearing a song about tractors."

"I did *not* put anything on there about tractors." I roll my eyes and reach across the car to swat at his arm. He wraps his fingers around my wrist and kisses my knuckles. "You're being dramatic."

"It's fun to rile you up." He smirks and sets my hand on my thigh. "We'll be there soon."

The drive to the restaurant takes fifteen minutes with the evening traffic, and when we pull up out front, Liam hands over the keys to a wide-eyed valet driver alongside a wad of cash. He drapes his arm around my shoulders as we walk in, and I relax into him. Into the familiarity of his embrace and how content and happy I feel being in his arms.

"Piper!" Alana calls out, and I give her a big wave, approaching the table.

"Hi!" I squeal and hug her, laughing when she spends three minutes admiring my dress. "Hi, Linda and Cliff."

"We're so glad you all could make it." Linda hugs me too, and she squeezes me extra tight. "I know Liam's schedule has been busy with the playoffs starting, so sneaking us in is much appreciated."

"I'll always make time for you." Liam kisses his mom then moves to his dad, giving him a firm handshake. "No drinking for me tonight, though. Don't even try me, Lani."

"Do you ever have fun?" Alana rolls her eyes and sticks out her tongue, but I hear the teasing tone behind her question. "Sit, sit!"

Liam holds out my chair for me, waiting for me to get comfortable before he scoots me close to the table. I'm transported back to our date, the fun we had and the way his laughs echoed around the rink as we skated for a full hour.

We've gone out a few other times since—a night at the movies and a cruise down the Potomac—but as we enter the postseason, his free time has diminished. Practices are longer. He's sleeping more, and the last thing I want to do is disrupt his perfectly curated schedule.

I'm so happy to be here with him tonight, especially because we're surrounded by the people he loves.

"How are you feeling about the game tomorrow, son?" Cliff asks, and Liam sets his napkin in his lap with a shrug.

"Fine. Atlanta is good. Can't believe they dropped so low in the standings the last few weeks of the season, and they're going to be sneaky."

"You're ready." I pat his thigh and he laces our fingers together. "I can't wait to see how hard you all play."

"I haven't been to a game in years," Alana admits. "I'm *stoked* to be there."

"If any of my teammates hit on you, you tell me," Liam warns her. "And I'll kick their ass."

"Nah. I'm going to like the attention." She laughs and takes a sip of her wine, her eyes bouncing over to me. "What about you, Piper? Anything exciting happening in your life?"

I know she's teasing, but Liam and I exchange a look. I desperately wish I had a glass of wine, and I clear my throat. "Yeah, actually. Liam and I wanted to talk to you all about a few things."

"Piper and I got married in Vegas a couple months ago," Liam interjects, taking the lead, and his mom's mouth pops open. "It was a drunken accident we decided to stick with because her health insurance sucks. When we came to Spain, we weren't actually dating, either, but we are now."

"It's my fault," I blurt out. "I asked for Liam's help with something, and I'm to blame for pretending to be in a relationship. I hope you all can forgive me for not being honest with you."

Cliff and Linda exchange a look, and they burst out laughing. I tense, my spine straight and my foot tapping on the floor. Liam runs his hand down my arm and back up, trying to keep me calm, but I have no clue what's going on.

"Oh, honey. We knew you two weren't dating at the wedding. We knew you two had feelings for each other, but we know you were only playing the role of his girlfriend," Linda tells us.

"*What?*" Liam thunders. "How the fuck did you figure it out?"

"We've been married a long time, son. We can tell these things. Just glad you two figured it out," Cliff says, and I bury my face in my hands.

"This is embarrassing." I groan and shake my head. "And here I was freaking out for no reason."

"The wedding comes as a shock," Linda says. "What's the story there?"

"Tequila," Liam and I say in unison, and he snorts.

"I told her we should get married, so we did. We kept it going because of her insurance, but now…" he trails off and tugs on my hair. I open my eyes and look up at him. "Now I think we might enjoy it for a while."

"I'm a little disappointed you didn't have a *real* wedding so I could see you drunk at your reception." Alana smirks. "But thinking about you intoxicated enough to get *married* to someone is going to hold me over."

"I wonder if there are any pictures from that night," I say, and Liam fumbles in his pocket. He pulls out his phone and shows me his screen, a photo of me trying to lift him off the ground as his background. "Oh, my god. We look so stupid, don't we?"

"Should've known it then." Liam kisses my forehead and nudges my side. "That I liked being stupid with you."

His words warm me from the inside out. They take up every crevice, every broken part of my heart, and I lean into him, savoring how much I've healed because of him.

"We do. We also look happy," I say, and his grin is soothing. Grounding in a way I've been searching for for years, and I wish I could remember every detail of our time in Vegas. Maybe there's a video out there of us laughing our heads off, arms wrapped around each other and not a care in the world. "I'd do it again."

"Me too," he says, and I know he means every word.

"I'm so glad to have you as part of the family, Piper," Linda says, and my feet come back to the ground. "You make Liam so incredibly happy, and I love to see him live a little bit. We want him to win tomorrow and the rest of the season, obviously. We know how much winning the Stanley Cup would mean to him, but I like seeing him like this even more."

"That's because of you," he murmurs in my ear, low and soft, so only I can hear. "No one else could make me act like this."

"Stupidly in love with me, Sullivan?" I ask, tapping his cheek.

His beam stretches wider, and I give him a matching one in return. "You have no idea, Mitchell."

FIFTY-THREE
LIAM

THE FINAL SECONDS of game five of the Eastern Conference Finals tick down, and fury rolls through me.

We played like absolute shit tonight.

You wouldn't know we had the best regular season record in the league based on our performance. I gave up three fucking goals and we couldn't score on the other end to save our lives.

It should've been the night to put Boston away for good with our three-one series lead, but now we have to head back to the Garden for game six in front of a rowdy, ruthless fanbase.

The buzzer sounds, signifying the end of regulations, and I'm goddamn grateful to escape from the boos and taunts from our hometown crowd. It was a sellout tonight, and I can hear the passion in their yelling. The anger when someone throws a cup of beer on the ice and gets escorted out by security.

They want the Cup in DC *so fucking bad*, just like we do, and to watch us crumble under pressure at the highest stage when they should've been celebrating another trip to the Finals is disappointing as shit.

"Hey." Hudson hits my stick with his. "Chin up, GK."

"Don't deserve to keep my chin up," I grumble, I yank off my helmet and scrub a hand over my face, irritated. Mad. Fucking exhausted and drained of energy. "This loss is on me."

"Bullshit. The five of us didn't do what we were supposed to do either," he challenges, and I pull back, surprised. It's rare for there to be such ferocity in his tone, for him to be so riled up, and I don't know what to make of it. "I missed two wide-open looks in the second period. Maverick couldn't get close to the fucking crease, and Ethan lost that last face-off that could've given us some momentum. We win as a team, and we lose as a team. Nothing about this is on you."

"Could've played better. Could've done my job better." I trudge to the locker room with him skating by my side, ignoring the fans who are sticking around to still boo us. "Three fucking goals. That's fucking abysmal."

"So you had an off night? Big deal. We'll bounce back the day after tomorrow and lock this shit up on the road. It's more fun that way. Fuck Boston."

I huff at his optimism and scan the tunnel, looking for Piper.

I'm always looking for her and her bright blazers and flowy pants.

I spot her standing with Lexi, her arms crossed over her chest and her microphone tucked in her back pocket. She's not going to ask any of us for an interview, and that's probably for the best. I'm afraid of what someone would say if they got put on live television after such a shitty night.

Her eyes meet mine as I pass, and a small smile curves on her lips. I feel it in my chest, my heart skipping a beat under her attention. Some of the frustration I'm carrying melts away when she subtly touches my glove before pulling her hand away.

I didn't know how much I needed to see her until right

now, and I don't know if I want to be alone or if I want her to hug me. I don't know if I want to go on a long walk and clear my head or hurry home so I can curl up in bed with her.

Instinct would tell me to keep my distance. To stay in my head and not let any outside noises in. I have a job to focus on. A shitty performance to clean up and damage control to take care of, but none of them mean *shit* because I want her by my side.

It's going to have to wait, though, because when I take a seat in front of my locker, Coach enters the room, and I know he means business.

"Not our night tonight," he says gruffly. He rakes a hand through his hair then wraps it into a fist at his side. "We have two more chances to close this out. I'm your coach on the ice, not in life, but I'm going to give you all one piece of advice: don't wallow in this shit. Live it. Face it. But after tonight, it's gone. Nothing we can do about it now. We've got work to do, and we're not going to accomplish anything if we're dragging our asses in Boston because we feel sorry for ourselves. We know what we need to fix: aggression. Defense. Having each other's back."

"Sorry," I tell the guys, and they all glance at me. I hate the attention, but it needs to be said. "I was off tonight. Let three past me that I usually stop. It won't happen again. Be mad at me, not yourselves."

"Fuck that," Maverick says, standing in the center of the room. "I'm mad at all of us. I'm mad at myself. I'm mad at Hudson. I'm mad at Ethan. I'm mad at Finn. *Fuck*. I'm mad at the equipment manager for fucking up my blades and not making sure they were sharp enough, and I'm mad at myself *again* for not noticing during warmups. It's not going to do us any good to sit around here and be pissed about this loss, though." He yanks off his gloves and throws them at his locker, knocking over a water bottle. "We know we're better than this. Everyone do what they need to do tonight, and let's come back tomorrow ready to close this out in Boston."

The team mumbles in agreement. Everyone turns their focus to different things; Hudson calls his dad. Maverick puts his head in his hands and mumbles something under his breath. Grant excuses himself, slipping into the hallway to say hello to his younger sister.

I grab my phone from my duffle bag, surprised to see a message from Piper waiting for me.

PIPER

Lexi is going to take me home. I'm sure you want to be alone tonight. Call me tomorrow?

ME

Come over. Please. Use the spare key. I'm going to take a drive, but I'll be there soon.

PIPER

Are you sure?

ME

I want you there. You're the only good thing about today.

PIPER

Then that's where I'll be. Take your time <3.

A year ago, I would've laughed at my teammates if they told me they were running home to a woman. I would've asked if they cared about the loss. If they even wanted to show up to game six, or if they preferred to stay home.

I used to want to be alone. I used to want nothing to do with anyone after a loss—especially someone else—but not anymore. Now I want her. I *need* her. She's the only one who's going to be able to calm me down, and I'm counting down the seconds until she's in my arms.

I rub my hand over my chest, an ache there when I think

about how fucking lucky I am to have her. How glad I am to have her in my life and how she's the solace I need at a time like this. How much I love her and how I'm going to do my best to not shut her out, to not shut down, because I want her to know she has a place, even when I'm pissed as hell.

"You good, GK?" Riley asks from beside me and I hum, giving him a curt nod.

"Fine." I ditch my gear for my suit and tie so I can get the fuck out of here. "I'll see you tomorrow."

I take the long way home, driving down by the river and letting the May air whip through my hair as I take deep breaths. The usual thoughts that come with defeat run through my head: *I'm not good enough. I suck. I'm too slow. I'm getting too fucking old.*

I linger in them for a while, soaking them in and gritting my teeth as my fingers curl around the steering wheel. My anger turns to disappointment. Self-defeat and self-loathing. I give myself an hour before I take a deep breath, shove the thoughts aside, and start the trek home.

The closer I get to my apartment, the more settled I feel. Like my anger is seeping away, bit by bit. It's almost like a magnet is tugging me, calling my name and drawing me nearer and nearer.

Her.

I park and take the elevator up, slipping inside the foyer and shutting the door behind me.

"Piper?" I call out, and I don't get an answer.

Maybe she left. I'm later than I said I'd be, and sitting around waiting for my grumpy ass doesn't sound like it would be a lot of fun.

"Living room," she yells back a beat later, and I frown at her muffled voice.

I shrug off my suit jacket and toss it on the table, making my way down the hall. Panic rises in me when I don't hear any other noise, and almost face plant on the rug. When I round the corner to the living room, I stop in my tracks at the sight in front of me.

Piper is there, in all my gear.

My helmet. My pads. My jersey and skates.

Looking tiny and small and like the clothes are swimming on her.

She's holding Pico, and a miniature helmet sits on his head too.

I blink at her, and she lifts the goalie mask up.

"What the hell are you doing?" I ask.

"I know you're probably pissed about tonight, and I thought I'd do something to cheer you up." She shrugs, barely able to lift her shoulder under the weight, and kicks the blade into the rug. "It's stupid, but I wanted you to laugh."

I stare at her, watching as she sways on her feet and nearly topples to the ground. Pico looks terrified, his eyes wide and claws sinking into her chest, and that's when I lose it.

I burst out laughing.

Tears stream down my face, and I cackle so loudly, I'm afraid the people fifteen stories down can hear me.

"What the fuck is this?" I gasp for a lungful of air. "What is Pico wearing?"

"I got him a little helmet!" Piper holds up the cat and he glares at me, pissed off with all of his life choices, and I cackle again.

"How long did this take you?" I wheeze, putting a hand on the wall so I can stay upright. My legs are killing me, and I think I'm hallucinating. Losing my mind because she looks so fucking cute and so fucking funny at the same time. "And how long have you been standing like this?"

"I only got up when I heard you at the door. It took me forty-five minutes to put all this on." She lifts an arm in the air. "I can't believe you wear this every night. No wonder you're built like a Greek god."

"Your flattery really does things to me, Pipsqueak." I stalk toward her, watching her set Pico down. I tip her chin back, careful to take off the helmet so it's not heavy on her head, and smile down at her. "God, I fucking love you."

"Did it work?" she whispers, eyes wide and gloves grabbing at my shirt. She can't get a good grip, and a fresh wave of laughter rolls through me. "Or do you want to kick me out?"

"This is the best thing I've ever seen. Please don't ever take it off. Wear my jersey for the rest of your life. The skates too. *Baby*. You didn't have to do this. You must be so uncomfortable."

"So uncomfortable," Piper repeats, but her mouth breaks out into a wide grin. "I just wanted to make you happy because I love you, too."

"I *am* happy."

"I meant after the game. I know you're probably beating yourself up, and I thought maybe if I took the attention away from the loss, you'd be in a better mood."

"Well, you certainly did that. Did I even play a game today? I can't tell because you look so fucking sexy."

"Oh, so female hockey players do it for you?"

"Nah. You do it for me, Pipsqueak. Hockey player. Reporter. Don't care."

Her smile softens, and she touches my cheek. "I'm sorry about the loss," she says. "Please don't get in your head. You're a magnificent player who didn't have his best night. You'll be right back where you're supposed to be in a few days."

"I know," I tell her, but somehow, the affirmations mean so much more coming from her. "I'm so fucking lucky to have you."

"I can go. If you want some space. I know you prefer the quiet after a loss, and I—"

"No." I shake my head and pull her tight to my chest. I hold the back of her head, relaxing for the first time all night at the feel of her pressed against me. "I prefer you. Come sit with me. Come be with me."

And she does.

I need to shower. I need to stretch. I need to down a Gatorade and get some sleep, but I put my head in her lap instead. I look up at her, recanting the game in excruciating detail until I can give it up, until I can let it go, and then I close my eyes. I settle when she puts a hand over my heart, her touch warm, steadying, and the only thing I need.

FIFTY-FOUR
PIPER

"HUDSON. We're heading into the final period of game seven of the Stanley Cup Finals. All season, your team has worked for this moment. What are you feeling right now?" I ask, holding out my microphone to the defenseman.

"I'm not going to lie, I'm nervous as hell." He laughs. "There's pressure on us, obviously, especially because we had the best record in the league this season. Being at home helps; I can feel the fans behind us, you know? That's going to give us the push we need for these last twenty minutes."

"What are you going to focus on as we head into the third period?"

"Consistency. We let our focus slip when we get excited with a breakaway and come up short on converting a good possession to a goal. We have to follow through."

"Thanks, Hudson. Enjoy the rest of the game."

THIS IS the most stressful night of my life.

After a thrilling series with the San Diego Bearcats, we're back in DC for game seven, just like everyone thought we would be. The teams have exchanged victories up to this point, and if history is anything to go off of, the Stars *should* win tonight.

That's the agony of sports, though.

Nothing about them is guaranteed, especially in game seven.

The tension in the arena is palpable. The hometown fans have been on their feet for the entirety of the game, and the noise is deafening. I'm afraid to breathe too hard, fearful a forceful exhale will bring the puck too close to Liam and sneak by him.

I glance at him now, poised in the goal, mumbling under his breath and moving side to side to stay loose. He's been unreal tonight, only giving up one goal while stopping nearly twenty-five.

He tracks every player, every stick movement, every slice of a skate with excruciating precision. I'm not sure I've seen him blink, and when the guys came out after the last intermission, a focus I haven't seen from him this season graced his face.

My attention moves to the clock, the two minutes left in regulation moving too slow. Both teams have a single goal, and a tie would mean overtime. With how fatigued the guys are looking, the last thing we need is free hockey, no matter how thrilling the sudden death gameplay might be.

Everyone—from the players, to the fans, to Bernie behind the camera—knows this isn't going to be a back-and-forth shootout; both defenses are too good.

The next team to score will be the winner.

The referee blows his whistle, signaling the end of the timeout, and adrenaline echoes in my ears.

"Goddammit." Emmy bangs her fist on the glass. "Let's fucking *go* Miller."

Maverick tears past us in a blaze of white jersey and a

cocky grin, blowing her a kiss before taking off after the puck. I laugh and drape an arm around my best friend.

"He is the *only* guy in the league who would purposely move away from game play so he could flirt with his woman," I say. "You're a lucky lady, Emerson Hartwell."

"I want him to win more than I'd want myself to win. Maybe that makes me a terrible player, I don't know, but I don't give a shit. He sacrifices so much of himself for this game. I want him to have something tangible to show for it."

I said the same thing to Liam earlier this afternoon in his living room when he was packing his game day bag. We were quiet while he slipped into his routine—a late lunch. A candy bar. Classical music blaring in his headphones as he stretched before putting on his suit and tie.

He reached for me, though. Intertwined our hands and stroked his thumb over my knuckles when I kissed his palm. I whispered to him how proud of him I was. How honored I was to watch his performance this season and that no matter what happened tonight, I'd be on the other side waiting for him.

I want him to win *so badly* though, and I know *he* wants to win so badly too. I saw the determination, the grit and the desperation in his eyes during warmups, and even from all the way over here, I can see it now.

"If there's anything the guys can do well, it's play under pressure. I think—"

A burst of excitement at the other end of the rink cuts me off. I crane my neck and stand on my toes. A shot gets fired off toward the Bearcats' goal. I gasp when it comes up inches short and the Bearcats collect the rebound.

"Shit," Emmy hisses as the Bearcats offense takes off. Their destination is obvious, and the air leaves the building as they head straight for Liam.

"Come on." My fingers curl around my microphone. My hands won't stop shaking. "Come on, honey. You can do it."

Liam crouches down. Points his toes forward and holds his left hand out in front of him, ready for whatever shot they might fire his way. He moves an inch to his left then an inch to his right, squatting even lower as number forty-seven winds up.

The defender pulls back like he's going to fire between Liam's knees but changes direction at the last second. He aims higher, for the upper left corner of the goal, and Liam's body goes flying as he dives, stretches back, and reaches his hand behind him.

Liam lifts the puck in his glove. The building erupts, and before I have a second to catch my breath and celebrate his stop, he's passing the puck to Maverick, who takes off in the other direction and covers the ice in eight long glides.

I glance up at the clock and there are ten seconds left. Nine, eight—

"Fucking shoot it, Miller," Emmy yells, and I swear to god he turns his head our way. Grins at her. Pulls back with the slap shot of all slap shots that goes soaring into the net as the final horn and goal horn sound sound simultaneously.

Everyone around me screams. Emmy jumps up and down, and I grab my small notebook out of my back pocket, ready to grab someone for an interview. Confetti drops from the ceiling and covers the ice and the crowd. Music blares, and I can't hear myself think.

I watch Liam skate over the red line. His teammates surround him and Maverick, but he shoves past them. Throws off his gloves and drops his stick on the ice. He bolts toward me, blades slicing across the Stars logo, eyes locked on mine. I don't have a second to breathe before he's yanking me out of the tunnel. Sweeping me off my feet and hugging me to his chest.

"Holy shit," he yells into my neck. "Holy *shit*."

"Oh my god." I start to cry. A sob escapes me and I hug him tight, afraid to let him go. "You did it. You did it baby."

"Did you see that?"

I wrap my legs around his waist and pull back to look at him. I unbuckle his helmet and yank it off his head, throwing it to the side. I touch his sweat-soaked cheeks and brush his hair out of his eyes.

"Every single second. I've never seen anyone play so hard. That save was phenomenal. Something they'll be talking about for years."

Behind us, the rest of the team is celebrating. Maverick is on Hudson's back, his arms in the air. Grant is lying on his back and making snow angels in the confetti. Ethan skates a lap around the rink, the trophy over his head, and Riley is putting a Stanley Cup Champions hat on his head.

"You should be over there," I say. "With them. Your brothers. Not with me."

"No." He shakes his head and cups my cheeks. "The only person I want to celebrate with is you."

His skate slips out from under him and we go tumbling to the ice. All I can hear is his laughter. All I can feel are his strong arms around me. All I can see is his bright and smiling face, and it's all *perfect*.

"I am so proud of you," I whisper, a moment I want just for us. "You do unbelievable things."

"I couldn't have done it without you."

"*Me*?" I laugh. "I haven't done anything!"

"Bullshit. You encouraged me. Supported me. Believed in me. You make life so fucking fun. You're the thing that's keeping me afloat. I always got by on being happy enough, but I didn't know what happiness was until I met you. Not really. Now every day is the best day of my fucking life. Because of you."

My shoulders shake and tears stream down my face. I know my makeup is running. I know I have snot in my nose, but I can't bring myself to care. Not when he's looking at me like I'm the most important thing—like I'm the *only* thing in the whole goddamn world.

"I love you," I whisper. "I love you so much, and—" Another sob rattles my chest. "I'm so proud to be a chapter in your book, Liam."

"A chapter in my book?" Liam pushes up on his elbows, his mouth inches away from mine. I see a scrape on his cheek. The flecks of gold in his dark brown eyes and the salt on his forehead from dried sweat. "You're the whole damn story, Piper. There's some hazy version of myself that existed before I met you, and then everything after. I've never loved anything like I love you, and I'll never love anything else like I love you."

My insides twist tight. I don't know if I want to laugh or cry harder. Maybe a little bit of both. How can I not when he just accomplished the most important thing in his career and he's spending time with *me*? When he's saying things that make me believe in a forever where I'm not going to get hurt? A life that's full of joy instead of sadness. That's full of laughter instead of feeling like I'm not good enough.

I could shatter into a million pieces.

"Hey, you two lovebirds." Ethan loops his arms under my shoulders, hoisting me off Liam. "Keep the PDA down. There are *children* around."

Grant takes my spot, jumping on Liam's chest as Maverick and Hudson follow suit. I laugh when Ethan skates us across the ice and stretches out my arms.

"Tell me you'll never let go, Little P," he jokes.

"I'll never let go, Easy E."

"Even when that goalie pisses you off?"

"Nope."

"Okay, fine. How about when you accidentally get married in Vegas again? I can't believe you kept that from us, by the way. You're sneaky."

"Not even then." I smile and close my eyes. "You're stuck with me for the long haul, Richardson. You all are."

"Good. You keep things fun around here."

We make a full lap of the arena, and I take in the celebrations. The fans still in their seats, clapping and high-fiving. The arena operations crew rolling out a carpet for the commissioner to make his way onto the ice. Bernie waves at me frantically, and I know I need to get my microphone and get in front of the camera.

"You have to put me down, Ethan. I need to finish my job like you all finished yours," I say, and he sets me down next to the group of guys clustered near center ice. "Thanks for the ride."

"Anytime you want to have some real fun, you know my number." Ethan winks and takes off after Riley, chasing down the trophy.

"If he lays another finger on you, I'm going to murder him," Liam draws out. He hands me my microphone and scowls in Ethan's direction. "Someone needs to put him on a leash."

"That'll be the day. Maverick," I call out, looking for the captain. "Come talk to me, please."

"He's on ESPN," Hudson says, gesturing to the large headset Maverick is wearing. "Who do you want instead?"

"Back off, Hayes." Liam nudges him out of the way. "I want to talk to my wife on camera."

"You want me to interview *you*?"

"Why not? The last time went well. I can pretend to have a good time for two minutes."

"Are you sure? I bet Hudson is more than willing."

"I'll be in the wings on backup in case he starts acting like he's going to get in trouble with the FCC," Hudson teases, and Bernie gives me the one-minute warning.

"No cursing," I tell Liam sternly, and he rolls his eyes.

"It was one time, and it slipped out," he says. "How much longer am I going to have to pay for my crimes, Pipsqueak?"

"For a very long time." I tug on his collar and bring his mouth to mine. "Forever, maybe."

"Sounds like I need to do it again. Just to make sure I can keep you around."

"I swear to god if you—"

"Five seconds," Bernie says, and I smile at the camera.

"We're back at United Airlines Arena and I'm here with Liam Sullivan, who might have had the play of the year in the final seconds tonight with a game-winning save. Liam, what went through your mind during that sequence?"

"Couldn't let Miller show me up," he says, bending down to talk into the microphone. His arm loops around my waist and pulls me close. "Gibbons had a heck of a shot, and I was in the right place at the right time."

"What's the first thing you're going to do to celebrate?"

"I don't know. What do you think?" He looks down at me. "Should we get some burgers and fries? Take a trip to Europe for the rest of the summer? Go to Disney World like the NBA and NFL guys do? Maybe we can have a night with Pico on the couch. Pretty sure my hamstrings are going to hurt for a fu—very long time after that."

I blush at his inclusion of me. Our friends might know about our relationship, but the outside world doesn't.

I guess they do now.

"I think Pico would like that very much," I manage to get out. "Any comments on Maverick's game-winning goal?"

"Dude's a fu—dang showoff." Liam grins and I narrow my eyes at him. "But he deserved for that to be his. It's about time the trophy came home to DC."

"Thank you, Liam, and congratulations on the win." I turn to the camera, but I can feel him staring at me. "We're going to send it back to Bradley who will break down all the stats from tonight's game. Stick around."

Bernie gives me the all clear, and I tuck my microphone in my back pocket.

"Almost had you there, didn't I?" Liam says, kissing the top of my head. "Wanted to keep you on your toes."

"You're never allowed to be in front of a camera again."

"Well, shucks. How will I survive?"

I shove his arm and he picks me up, skating me toward the bench.

"Put me down." I laugh. "What are you doing with me?"

"Giving you time in the sin bin for that rough hit. Means I get a power play, Pipsqueak."

"And what the hell are you going to do with that?"

"Dunno. Might ask you to marry me for real. Might move you into my apartment so I can see you every morning. Might love you until you're so sick of me, you'll be fucking begging for me to leave you alone. And you know I like it when you beg." He opens the penalty box and sets me on the bench. He crouches in front of me and grins. "Want to stick around to find out?"

"Yeah," I whisper, the pressure in my chest expanding when my eyes meet his. When he takes my hand and kisses my palm, resting it against his cheek. "I think I'd like that a lot."

"Good." He taps my knee. "I'm just getting started with you, Sunshine."

EPILOGUE

ONE YEAR LATER
Piper

"MORNING, PIPER!" CJ, the security guard stationed at the entrance to the arena, calls out.

I wave at him and head for the media room, behind schedule but not wanting to be rude. "Morning, CJ. How are the grandkids?"

"They won't stop talking about the tour you gave them last week. Sarah wants to be a hockey player now. Watching from the stands isn't going to cut it anymore."

"As she should. We need more female hockey players, and Emmy will be thrilled. Tell them they're welcome at the arena anytime."

I hum as I make my way down the familiar tunnel, in a good mood that seems to follow me everywhere these days.

It's been a wild year since the Stars won the Stanley Cup.

I secured a contract extension, got promoted to lead play-by-play commentator—becoming the first woman in NHL history to hold the position—and dove headfirst into working my ass off.

After an aggressive free agency period last summer that had dozens of teams vying for our guys with signing incentives and massive paychecks, our core group of players came back in an attempt to repeat their championship run.

So far, it's going exactly like we hoped. They're deep in the Eastern Conference finals, up three games to one against New York, and hoping to close out the series tonight at home.

They *really* want to keep the Cup in DC.

My friends are as happy as ever, with Maverick and Emmy settling in nicely out in the suburbs and Maven and Dallas welcoming a healthy baby boy who is as cute as can be. He's pulling himself up to stand already, and I think they have a future football player on their hands.

My sweet Lexi is still a proud single woman who would rather not do a project than ask a man for help. Stubborn and sharp, I admire her ability to not give a fuck.

"Little P! There's my favorite reporter!" Ethan calls out, grinning at me.

I can spot his black eye from over here. The mark and bruise on his cheek are left over from a motorcycle crash that landed him in the hospital for two weeks and earned him a string of expletive-laced text messages calling him out for his daredevil ways from the team once they knew he was okay.

"I'm one of the only reporters, Ethan." I laugh when he scoops me up in a hug and spins me around. "Gosh, I'm glad to see you. You look so much better than you did in the hospital."

"That's because those gowns don't bring out all my pretty features."

"Glad to see your humility didn't take a beating in your collision with the guardrail."

"I'm invincible, P, and I feel fan-fucking-tastic. It was a little touch and go there for a while, but I'm on the mend. Bummed I can't play if we make it to the finals next week, but I'll be back stronger next season and ready to kick ass."

"You must not be very good if the boys are doing fine without you."

"You've gotten snarkier since you started rendezvousing with Sullivan. I like it." He sets me back on two feet and flashes me another grin. "What are you doing here so early?"

"We have one of the most important games of the season tonight, and I can't sit at home. I'm too jittery there." I fix my skirt and give his shoulder a gentle nudge. "And stop doing strenuous activities. Lifting me could hurt your stitches."

"Rude of you to assume I'm so weak I can't lift you. You're light as shit." He turns for the locker room. "I'm going to terrorize Maverick and Hudson for a bit. Don't work too hard. You need to have some fun in your life too."

"Says the guy dealing with a concussion." I laugh, heading the opposite direction before another player can catch me off guard.

"Going somewhere?" a deep voice says from behind me, and I can't help but smile at the familiar tone.

It's the same one that whispered *good morning* in my ear just before the sun came up earlier today. The one that asked if I wanted it *gentle or rough* last night when his hand was buried in my jeans and his mouth was on my neck. The one that said *I love you* a million different ways over the last year, my favorite being the heart he holds up when he skates on the ice, finding me in the crowd right away.

"Yes, actually. Away from all you boys." I glance over my shoulder. Liam is leaning against the wall in jeans and a T-shirt, watching me. His eyes roam down my body greedily, taking in my outfit, and a flash of heat blazes behind his gaze. "You're annoying."

"At least we're consistent." He walks my way. A smile draws at the corners of his lips and the pink mark I left on his throat two days ago sneaks out from under his collar. When he gets close enough to reach me, he tugs on my skirt and pulls me into his hold, arms settling around my waist. "Hey, Sunshine."

"Hey, Sully."

His warm fingers curl around my chin and lift my head so he can press a kiss to my mouth. I melt into him, sinking into the feeling of being home, of being loved, of being so unbelievably happy, sometimes I think I'm dreaming all this up.

I laugh every day. I smile every day. I hear how incredible I am, how wonderful I am, how proud he is of me *every single day*. I could burst from the wonderfulness of it all, but I've learned to sink into it. To recognize this is what I deserve. What I've waited for, and I've welcomed it with open arms.

Liam and I did things backward with the whole getting-drunk-and-married-in-Vegas thing, so we've spent the last year backpedaling. Dating each other. Getting to know each other on a level where I can tell you his goals, his biggest dreams, and his scariest fears.

Neither one of us offered up the idea of a divorce, and the further removed we got from the inebriated ceremony, the more I fall in love with him.

Which is wild, considering I'm obsessed with the man. Wearing his jersey to the arena. Getting a little *L* tattooed on the back of my right forearm.

He has a matching one on his left arm, so he must be obsessed with me too.

"Are you busy?" Liam moves his mouth to the spot below my ear, kissing me there and brushing his nose against my cheek. "Or can I steal you for a while?"

"Depends. Is it to make out in a supply closet?"

"Something far more serious than that. We're at work, Mitchell. Have some decorum."

I untangle our limbs and look up at him. I revel in the grin on his face and the wrinkles around his eyes. The scrunch of his nose and the laugh lines that have gotten deeper in the last twelve months because he's learned not to take life so seriously.

"Is it your hamstring? Are you hurt? I *knew* we shouldn't have played paintball with the guys last weekend. If Coach finds out you—"

Liam cuts me off with another kiss. Hungrier this time, like he's been starving for years and finally getting the chance to eat.

"It involves you, actually."

"What did I do?"

"It's what you're going to do. The team is putting together a women-in-sports montage to feature on social media next month, and they want to feature you."

"What's so special about little old me?"

"Must be the whole first-female-broadcaster accolade. Oh, or the Broadcasting Hall of Fame nomination after only one year in the field. Maybe the nonprofit you and Emmy started that hands out scholarships to women in athletic-centered careers caught their attention?"

"That is a lot of attention. It's not just me, is it?"

"Nope. Women from different divisions will be featured. You'll be in it for two minutes tops."

"Okay." I nod, grateful for a platform to shout out my love for female athletes. My adoration for women in sports and all the roles those jobs encompass. "I'll do it."

Liam holds out his hand. I lace our fingers together and he tugs me to the media room. I'm expecting a whole production team. Big lights and half a dozen cameras that capture all the angles of this interview, but when we walk inside, there are only two stools set up in front of a single camera.

"Pick a seat," he says.

"This is weird," I answer, choosing the one on the left. "A little bit like an interrogation."

"You've interviewed dozens of people over the years." Liam sits next to me. He barely fits on the stool with his long legs and wide shoulders. When he's as settled as he can be, he grabs the edge of my chair and drags me over to him, our knees knocking against each other. "Now it's your turn to be in the hot seat."

"Oh and *you're* doing the interviewing? I thought you hated being in front of the camera. The Christmas cards we sent out last year featured ugly sweaters and your scowl."

"Piper Mitchell. When did you first realize you liked sports?" he asks, ignoring me.

"I was a coxswain on my high school crew team, and that was my first real exposure to athletics. In college, I worked at the arena box office selling tickets. I was there for basketball, volleyball, and hockey. I loved the energy the students and fans brought, so on one of my days off, I decided to go watch a hockey game. I've been hooked ever since."

"Did you always want to work in sports?"

"No, not really. I've always liked talking to people. Learning their stories and getting to the root of why they operate the way they do. When I was younger, I wanted to be a teacher. My early teenage years, I wanted to do something with psychology. When I got to college, I discovered I could have a career that merged both sports and talking people's ears off. I started in the sports broadcasting department and never looked back."

"You can only pick one favorite Stars memory. What is it?"

"You need to step up your interview questions, Sullivan. That one is easy: watching you win the Stanley Cup. That save at the end of regulation was unbelievable."

"Everything else I do in my career is going to be shit," Liam agrees, and I laugh. "Speaking of goals: where do you see yourself in five years?"

"Wow. That was a nice pivot." I cross my legs and tap my cheek. "I'd like to still be with the Stars. I love our broadcasting team, and I think we're doing good work. I'd love for our nonprofit to expand throughout the country and not just be confined to the DC and Maryland area. I hope I can keep inspiring young women out there who are afraid there isn't space for them in a world dominated by men. We have to make our own room, and we're getting there."

"Let's talk about your personal life. I hear you got married."

"Yeah, to this guy I got drunk with in Vegas. He wouldn't let me get a divorce, though. I'm kind of stuck with him."

"He sounds horrible."

"The worst, honestly."

"Let me know if he ever gives you any issues. I'll put him in his place."

"Sounds a little bit like you're flirting with me." I lean forward, invading his space. "I'm not sure my husband would like that very much."

"I can probably take him." Liam kisses my forehead, and I smile. "Who decided getting drunk then married was a good idea?"

"Tequila, apparently."

"That son of a bitch." He lifts my hand and examines my fingers. "I see you're wearing a ring."

"It's nothing special, but I like it."

"Tell me about the proposal. Was it nice?"

"Did you miss the part about tequila?" I laugh again. "I'm pretty sure the handle of alcohol was proposing to me."

"Huh. Doesn't sound very romantic."

"It might not have been at the time, but I like what we have now: a life together. A friend for Pico. Driving to the arena and hanging out with all the people we love so much. You know I don't need all that fancy stuff."

"Hang on a second."

Liam stands and pulls a wrinkled piece of paper from his pocket. It's weathered and worn and had to have been read a hundred times.

"What's that?"

"This?" He unfolds the corners delicately. "A list of all your favorite things. A list of all the things you hate. Important dates and the proposal you wished you had."

My heart hammers in my chest. "You wrote all of that down?"

"Every word. I started it when this was casual between us, but then I kept it. Added things to it here and there over the weeks that passed. Some are more important than others, but all of them are important."

I squint at the paper and try to make out his messy handwriting. I see *dogs* circled and underlined three times under things I like. *Spinach* under things I hate. A note scribbled in the top left corner that says I prefer the right side of the bed and have to sleep with socks on. It's detailed. Thorough. The entire page—front and back—is covered, and I nearly stop breathing.

"You don't need all that stuff now. There's nothing to study or learn."

"You think I didn't have a plan, Piper?"

"You always have a plan," I whisper.

Liam steps close to me. I can smell his cologne; woody with a hint of spice. Can see the flecks of gold in his eyes and the tan on his neck from when we spent too long outside on the balcony two weekends ago, curled up on a chair and enjoying the fresh summer air.

"I wanted to make sure when I got to this part, I wouldn't fuck it up. I wouldn't give you roses when you so clearly like —" He reaches past my shoulder and grabs a bouquet wrapped in brown paper. The stems are tied with a neat bow around them, and I smile at the burst of color. "Peonies."

"These are beautiful. But why are you—"

"I wanted to make sure if I ever got the chance to do this for real, I'd do it right. You told me you wanted small. Intimate. In a place you love surrounded by the people you love. Nothing fancy or over the top. A restaurant was certainly out of the question and on the big screen during a game was a death wish waiting to happen."

He takes the flowers from me and sets them on his stool. He helps me stand, rubbing his palms up and down my arms. There's a slight shake to his hands, a nervousness I've rarely seen from him in the twitch of his palms.

Liam Sullivan is the epitome of calm, cool, and collected. The master of operating under pressure, but right now, he looks *terrified*.

"Piper Mitchell. I love you very much. It hurts when you're not around. I miss you when you're gone and I count down the minutes until you come home. I've never cared about someone the way I care about you. I've never felt like I can be myself around anyone the way I can be myself around you. And, the craziest fucking thing is, you love me too. You love me when I'm grouchy. When I'm mad at the world. You hold me close when I don't want to talk to another person." Liam shakes his head like he doesn't believe the things he's saying, even though they're all true. "Your first wedding sucked. Your second wasn't much better. I think the third time will be the charm, and you'll make me the luckiest fucking guy in the world if you marry me again. For real."

"Oh my god." I throw my arms around his neck. Tears prick my eyes and my vision goes blurry. It feels like I'm short of breath. Crossing the finish line of a race I've been running for *years*. "Yes. *Yes*. Of course, Liam. Of course I'll marry you again."

"No tequila this time. Just you and me, and a hundred of our closest friends."

"That might be the most romantic thing you've ever said to me." He smiles then digs into his pocket, pulling out a velvet box. He opens it and a diamond blinks back at me, bright and twinkling and entirely too big. "I can't wear that. I'm going to get robbed."

"At least you can cut their cheek if they try." Liam slips the ring on my finger and kisses my knuckles. "I know you like the old band, and I do too. I don't need a new one, but I'll get you a new one if you want to match the set."

"No." I shake my head and cup his cheeks, the new piece of jewelry heavy on my hand. "I want the shitty gift shop silver for the rest of my life. I don't care if they don't match. You can't spoil me too much."

"Going to spoil the shit out of you from now until eternity."

"Can we come in now?" someone yells from behind the door, and I bury my face in Liam's shirt. "We're fucking dying out here, man."

"Come in, you fuckers," Liam answers, and the door flies open.

There's so much noise my ears hurt. The boys clap a hand on Liam's shoulder, congratulating him. They take turns kissing the top of my head and putting me on their back, celebrating. Maven, Emmy and Lexi are here too, jumping up and down when I show them the ring.

It's loud and warm and perfect. Exactly what I missed out on with my first two proposals and exactly what I've always wanted. I don't know how I ended up here, with a man who looks at me like I hung the moon and a group of friends I couldn't dream up if I tried, but it was worth wading through the shit for.

It was worth the nights I spent crying and the days I felt alone, because right now, surrounded by the most important people in my life and in my favorite spot, I know there will never be another moment when I'm alone.

"Sorry for all the chaos." Liam presses his lips to my cheek and plays with my sleeve. "I thought it would be a little more organized than this shitshow, and this isn't exactly intimate."

I wipe my eyes. "It's perfect. I wouldn't have it any other way."

"You mentioned a while ago that you wouldn't take

another man's name again." His hand moves up to my hair, cupping the back of my head. "And I want you to know I'd never force you to take mine. In fact, I've been thinking about taking yours."

"Oh?" I lift an eyebrow. "What kind of power play is that?"

"Only that you're a badass woman, Piper Mitchell, and it would be a goddamn honor to share a name with you."

"We might be able to make that happen." I nudge his stomach with my elbow and he lifts me up, tossing me over his shoulder. "*Hey*. What are you doing?"

"Taking my wife away from all these goddamn hooligans. I'm a selfish man, Piper, and I want you all for myself."

"Say *my wife* again."

"I'll say it as many times as you want." Liam waves to his teammates and ignores their catcalls. He marches us to the locker room and a thrill runs up my spine. "So much you're going to be sick of me."

"I could never be sick of you."

"We'll see about that." His palm cups my ass and he squeezes the curve of my backside. "Ready for your next lesson, wife?"

"What are you going to teach me today, Goalie Daddy?"

"It's a math project. We're going to measure the distance between your ass on the locker room bench to my mouth between your legs when I'm kneeling on the floor."

"Wow. I hope I can handle that. Will you go slow with me? It's my first time, and I really want to do well."

Liam's touch turns gentle, and I feel it behind my ribs. In the spot carved out of my chest where his love for me resides and all the way down to my toes.

"I'll wait the rest of my life for you, Sunshine," he says, and I can hear the smile infused in his words. "You take as long as you need."

COMING SOON

The DC Stars will be back with more stories soon! Here's who else you can expect to get a book… and a little about each one (in no particular order)!

Hudson (single mom, chef, ASL rep, roommates)
Riley (injury rehabilitation, boy obsessed, forced proximity)
Grant (off-limits woman, age gap where she's older, secret relationship)
Coach Saunders (one night stand, player's sister, age gap where he's older)
Ethan (accidental pregnancy, forced proximity, it's always been you)

ACKNOWLEDGMENTS

This was the hardest book I've ever written.

Coming off the success of Face Off, I was terrified to put another book out in the world. There's the fear that it won't be good enough. That everyone will hate it. That it'll never measure up to how book one did.

I hope I did Piper and Liam's story justice.

Thank you so much for reading! I hope you enjoyed Power Play! If you did, I'd be grateful if you left a review on Amazon or Goodreads. Positive reviews do wonders for indie authors like myself!

Thank you to my beta readers who gave honest and important feedback and helped make this book what it is today.

Thank you Britt and Hannah for your editing wizardry. You all are incredible at what you do.

Thank you, Kim, for another beautiful cover! I can't wait to keep the series going!

Thank you, Ellie (@lovenotespr) for handling ARC signups/cover reveals/everything! You are superwoman!

To Mikey and Riley: I love you very much.

Lastly, to the book community. To every BookToker, Bookstagrammer, reader, reviewer, enthusiastic friend who has screamed about my work. None of this would be possible with you. Thank you for shouting about our stories. Thank you for your support. You're out here changing lives, and I'm grateful for all of you <3.

ABOUT THE AUTHOR

Chelsea is a flight attendant and romance author who writes fun, fresh, and flirty love stories with plenty of spice. When she's not making fictional characters banter for twenty chapters before they finally kiss or serving chicken or pasta on an airplane, you can find her trying to pet as many dogs as she can.

ALSO BY CHELSEA CURTO

D.C. Stars series

Face Off

Power Play

Love Through a Lens series

Camera Chemistry

Caught on Camera

Behind the Camera

Off Camera

Boston series

An Unexpected Paradise

The Companion Project

Road Trip to Forever

Park Cove series

Booked for the Holidays